Never Coming Back

TIM WEAVER

Never Coming Back

VIKING

VIKING
Published by the Penguin Group
Penguin Group (USA) LLC
375 Hudson Street, New York, New York 10014

USA | Canada | UK | Ireland | Australia | New Zealand | India | South Africa | China
penguin.com
A Penguin Random House Company

Published by Viking Penguin, a member of Penguin Group (USA) LLC, 2014

First published in Great Britain by Penguin Books Ltd.

LIBRARY OF CONGRESS CATALOGING-IN-PUBLICATION DATA
Weaver, Tim, 1977-
Never coming back / Tim Weaver.
pages cm
ISBN 978-0-525-42686-8 (hardback)
1. Missing persons--Investigations--Fiction. 2. Private investigators--Fiction. I. Title.
PR6123.E2245N48 2014   823'.92--dc23   2013048534

Printed in the United States of America
10 9 8 7 6 5 4 3 2 1

Set in Garamond MT Std and Gotham
Designed by Amy Hill

For Erin

PART ONE December 2007

1

When the night came, it came fast. The sky yellowed, like a week-old bruise, and then the sun began its descent into the desert floor, dropping out of the clouds as if it were falling. The further it fell, the quicker the sky changed, until the sun was gone from view and all that remained was a smear of red cloud, like a bloodstain above the Mojave.

The city limits emerged from the darkness about twenty minutes later: to start with just small, single-story satellite towns, street lights flickering in the shadows either side of the Interstate; then, as the 15 carved its way through the Southern Highlands, a brighter, more persistent glow. Housing estates, strip malls and vast tracts of undeveloped land, illuminated by billboards and the orange tang of sodium lights; and then the neon: casinos, motels and diners, unfurling beyond the freeway. Finally, as I came off the Interstate at Exit 36, I saw the Strip for the first time, its dazzling, monolithic structures rising out of the flatness of the desert, like a star going supernova.

Even a quarter of a mile short of its parking garage, I knew the Mandalay Bay would be a step up from the last time I'd stayed in Las Vegas. On my first trip to the city five years before, the newspaper had taken care of the booking and left me to rot in a downtown grind joint called The George. "George," I later found out, was casino lingo for a good tipper. Except the only people doing the gambling at The George were the homeless, placing 25c minimum bets on the blackjack tables out front so they could scrape together enough for a bottle of something strong. This time, as I nosed the hired Dodge Stratus into a space on a huge rooftop parking lot, I passed eight-story signs advertising a televised UFC fight at the hotel in January, and I knew I'd made the right decision to book it myself: last time out, the only fighting I'd seen anywhere close to The George was of the fully drunk kind.

I turned off the ignition and as the engine and radio died, the sound of the Las Vegas Freeway filled the car; a low, unbroken hum, like the rumble of an approaching storm. Further off, disguised against the sky except for the metronomic wink of its taillight, was a plane making its final approach into McCarran. As I sat there, a feeling of familiarity washed over me, of being in this city, of hearing these same sounds, five years before. I remembered a lot from that trip, but mostly I just remembered the noise and the lights.

I opened the door of the Dodge and got out.

The night was cool, but not unpleasant. Popping the trunk, I grabbed my overnight bag and headed across the lot. Inside, the hotel was just as loud, the cars and planes and video screens replaced by the incessant *ding, ding, ding* of slot machines. I waited in line for the front desk, watching as a young couple in their twenties started arguing with one another. By the time I was handed my room card, I was ready for silence—or as close as I could get.

I showered, changed, and raided the minibar, then called Derryn to let her know I'd arrived okay. We chatted for a while. She'd found it hard to adapt to our new life on the West Coast initially: we had no friends here, she had no job, and in our Santa Monica apartment block our neighbors operated a hermetically sealed clique. Gradually, though, things were changing. Back home, she'd been an A&E nurse for twelve years before giving it up to come out to the States with me, and that experience had landed her a short-term contract at a surgery a block from where we lived. She was only taking blood and helping doctors patch up wounds—much more sedate than the work she'd been doing back in London—but she loved it. It got her out meeting people, and it brought in a little money, plus she got weekends off too, which meant she could go to the beach.

"You going to spend all our money, Raker?" she asked after a while.

"Not tonight. Maybe tomorrow."

"Do you even know how to play cards?"

"I know how to play Snap."

I could tell she was smiling. "I'd love to be a fly on the wall when you sidle up to the blackjack table pretending you know what you're doing."

"I *do* know what I'm doing."

"You can't even play Monopoly."

"My biggest fan talks me up again."

She laughed. "You'll have to take me with you next time."

"I will."

"I'd love to see Vegas."

I turned on the bed and looked out through the window. Millions of lights winked back through the glass. "I know. I'll bring you here one day, I promise."

. . .

At one-thirty, I was still awake, even if I didn't understand why. I'd been up until four the previous night filing a story, was fried after the five-hour drive down from LA—but I just couldn't drop off. Eventually, I gave up trying, got dressed and headed downstairs.

When the elevator doors opened, it was like time had stood still: the foyer, the sounds of the slots, the music being piped through speakers, it was all exactly the same as I'd left it. The only thing missing was the couple screaming at one another. This was the reason casinos didn't put clocks up: day, night, it was all the same, like being in stasis. You came in and your body clock disengaged. I looked at my watch again and saw it was closing in on two—but it may as well have been midmorning. Men and women were wandering around in tracksuits and shorts like they'd just come from the tennis courts.

I headed to a bar next to the hotel lobby. Even at one-fifty in the morning I had plenty of company: a couple in their sixties, a woman talking on her phone in a booth, a guy leaning over a laptop, and a group of five men sitting at one of the tables, laughing raucously at something one of them had said. Sliding in at the stools, I ordered a beer, picked at a bowl of nuts and flicked through a copy of the *Las Vegas Sun* that had been left behind. The front-page story neatly echoed the one I'd been sent down to follow up: Las Vegas, the bulletproof city. While some analysts were predicting a recession inside the next twelve months, America's gaming capital was set to make a record eight billion dollars.

About ten minutes later, as I got to the sports pages, a guy sat down beside me at the bar and ordered another round of drinks. I looked up, he looked back at me, and then he returned to his table with a tray full of shots. A couple of seconds later, a faint memory surfaced, and—as I tried to grasp at it—a feeling of recognition washed over me: I knew him. I turned on my stool and glanced back over my shoulder. The man placed the tray down on the table—and then looked back at me. *He knows me too.* There was a moment of hesitation for both of us, paused at each end of the room—but then it seemed to click for him, a smile broke out on his face and he returned to me.

"David?"

As soon as he spoke, the memory became fully formed: Lee Wilkins. We'd grown up together, lived in the same village, gone to the same school—and we'd left the same sixth-form college and never spoken since. Now, almost twenty years later, here he was: different from how I remembered, but not that different. More weight around his face and middle, hair shaved, dark stubble lining his jaw, but otherwise the same guy: five-ten, stocky, a scar to the left of his nose where he'd fallen out of a tree we'd been climbing.

"Lee?"

"Yes!" An even bigger smile spread across his face and we shook hands. "Bloody hell," he said. "I thought when I saw you, 'He looks familiar,' but I just never figured . . ."

"Are you on holiday here?"

"No," he said, perching himself on the stool next to me. "I live here now. Been in Vegas for two years; been in the States for seven."

"Doing what?"

"You remember I wanted to be an actor?"

"I remember that, yeah."

He stopped; smiled. "Well, it didn't work out."

"Oh."

"No, I mean it didn't work out in the way I thought it would. I spent my first five years in LA trying to catch a break, waiting tables and turning up at auditions. Got some minor roles here and there but nothing anyone would have seen me in. Then I started compering at this comedy club in West Hollywood, and things got a little crazy. Ended up going down so well, I *became* the act. That went on for a year, then I was offered a job down here in Vegas, as the main compere at this big comedy club just off the Strip. A few months back, I was offered an even *better* job by the guy who runs the entertainment in the MGM hotels, so now I travel between here, the Luxor, New York, the Mirage, the Grand, all of them. It's been pretty amazing."

"Wow. That's incredible, Lee. Congratulations."

"Right place, right time, I guess."

"Or you're just really good at it."

He shrugged. "I can't believe it's you. *Here.*"

"I know."

"So what are *you* doing in Vegas?"

"You remember I wanted to be a journalist?"

"Yeah."

"Well, that *did* work out."

"Fantastic. Are you working now?"

"Yeah." I looked around me. "Well, I'm working tomorrow."

"You live here?"

"No. I'm just down from LA for the night."

"Doing what?"

I tapped the front page of the *Sun*. "Writing about money."

"Are you a correspondent or something?"

"Just until the elections are over next year, and then I head back to London. The paper's pretty excited about the idea of Obama, which is why I'm out here so early."

"Anyone's better than Bush, right?"

"I guess we'll see next year."

"How come you're based on the West Coast?"

"I was based in DC last time I was out, but this time I'm here for much longer. So, I'm spending six months in LA to cover the buildup from California, and then I move to DC to cover the last six months from Capitol Hill." I nodded at the *Sun* again. "Thing is, at the moment, it's still early days, so there's nothing to talk about. Which is why I'm down here trying to justify my existence."

"Not a bad place to come for a night."

"Noisy."

He laughed. "Yeah, I guess it is."

We ordered more beers and sat at the bar and talked, covering the nineteen years since we'd left home. I'd grown up on a farm, in the hills surrounding our village, but when I headed to London and it dawned on my parents that I wasn't going to be taking over the running of it anytime soon, they started winding it down and paying into a cottage.

"And then Mum died."

Lee gave a solemn nod of the head.

I shrugged. "It was pretty much all downhill from there: I helped Dad get the farm sold and moved him into the village, but he could never really handle it on his own."

"Is he still around?"

"No. He died almost two years ago."

I hadn't been back home since.

The conversation moved on and got brighter, Lee telling me how his mum had remarried and now lived in Torquay, how his sister was a teacher, how he was still single and loving it, even if his mum wanted him to settle down. "They flew out earlier in the year, and Mum basically asked me when I was going to get married, once a day for three weeks." He rolled his eyes, and then asked, "So how long have you been married to Diane?" He was busy polishing off his fifth bottle of beer, so I forgave him the slip-up. We were both a little worse for wear: him—two bottles ahead of me—on alcohol, me on a lack of sleep.

"Derryn."

"Shit." He laughed. "Sorry. Derryn."

The bar was quieter now, all the men he'd been drinking with earlier off in the casino somewhere. "It'll be thirteen years this year."

"Wow."

"Yeah, it's been good."

He nodded. "I admire you, man. Envy you too." He nodded a second time and then sank the rest of his beer. "And now I've got to use the can."

He rocked from side to side slightly as he shifted away from the bar, and patted me gently on the shoulder as he passed. Then he headed to the toilets.

And I never saw him again.

A couple of minutes later, after picking up where I'd left off with the *Las Vegas Sun*, I looked up in the direction Lee had gone and saw a man standing next to me. I hadn't seen him approach. His body was facing the bar but his head was turned toward the paper, reading one of the stories on the front page. A second later, he glanced at me and realized he'd been caught out. "Oh," he said. "Sorry. That's incredibly rude of me."

He was English.

I looked over his shoulder, in the direction of the toilets. No sign of Lee. When my eyes fell on the man again, his head had tilted—like a bird—as if he was studying me.

I pushed the paper toward him. "Here."

"That's really good of you," he said. "Thanks."

"No problem."

He smiled. "You're English."

"Yeah. Looks like we both are."

He was in his late forties, thin and wiry, with a tan and a smooth, hairless face. As he smiled, I could see he'd had his teeth done. They had an unnatural sheen to them that you could only get away with on the West Coast. He perched himself on the edge of one of the stools, still smiling. "Are you out here with work or something?"

"Just for a couple of days."

"Ah, I didn't think you looked like a whale."

"Whale" was what casinos termed the world's biggest gamblers. He was dressed smartly: pale blue open-necked shirt, black jacket, denims, black leather shoes polished to a shine. His dark hair was slicked back from his forehead and glistened under the lights.

"You wouldn't be sitting here for a start," he said.

"If I was a whale?"

"Right. You'd be living off your complimentaries—your free flight and free suite and free food from the restaurant—not drinking alone in the bar at the foyer." He seemed to realize what he'd just said. "Wait, I didn't mean that how it sounded. Sorry."

"Don't worry about it."

"I mean, I'm one to talk, right? I'm here too." He laughed briefly, then flipped the newspaper closed. "Do you know how much casinos pay in comps to the high rollers?"

He leaned in toward me.

"Any idea?"

"Wouldn't have a clue," I said.

"Anywhere between three thousand and five thousand dollars. But do you know how much the high rollers will lose at the tables?" He lowered his voice, like he was imparting some ancient secret. *Twice that much.* No one beats the house. High rollers come in here with their credit lines, and their casino-paid hotel rooms and five-star meals, thinking they're going to defy the odds, that the casino's losing out. But every game here—*every* game in *every* single casino in the city—is designed to give the house a mathematical advantage."

The man shifted from side to side, one hand pressed against the stool between us, the other flat to the marble of the bar. He was missing nails on the first two fingers of one hand, like they'd been torn off. "You know what they call that?" he asked quietly.

"Call what?"

"The mathematical advantage?"

I glanced over the man's shoulder. Still no sign of Lee. It must have been five or six minutes since he'd left. The man moved in closer when he didn't get a response, his fingers inches from mine. I glanced down at his missing nails, then back up at him.

"It's called 'the edge,'" he said.

He finally moved his other hand off the stool and on to the marble, as if waiting for service. At the other end of the bar, the barman started to come over but then the man made eye contact with him—a tiny, fractional swivel of the head—and the barman stopped immediately, as if he'd been hit by a truck. When I looked back at the man, something had changed in him—something subtle—and a flutter of alarm took flight in my chest.

We stayed like that for a moment, the *ding, ding, ding* of the slots ringing around us, then I slid off the stool, pulled a couple of ten-dollar bills out and left them on the counter for the barman. I turned back to the man. He was about five inches shorter than me, but it didn't make me feel any easier around him.

"You off to bed?" he said.

"Something like that."

I went to step around him—but then he grabbed me by the arm and pulled me into him. His grip was like a vice. I stumbled, completely knocked off balance. Then instinct kicked in: I pushed back at him and ripped my arm free.

"What the hell is the matter with you?"

He realigned himself: both hands flat to the counter. "Let me give you a piece of advice."

"Let me give *you* one: don't *ever* touch me."

I went to leave.

"Someone will always have the edge over you, David."

I stopped. Turned back to him. "What did you say?"

"You're just flesh and bones like everyone else."

"How do you know my name?"

There was a threat in him now, as if he'd completely changed his appearance somehow. His eyes seemed darker. His face was twisted up like an animal about to strike. "Go back home to your wife," he said, looking me up and down. Then he leaned in and dropped his voice to a whisper: "And do both of you a favor: stay out of our business."

"*What?* I don't even know you."

"No," he said. "But you know Lee Wilkins."

He nodded once, eyes fixed on mine, then pushed past me and headed out into the casino. Inside a couple of seconds, he was disappearing into the crowds.

Inside ten, he was gone.

PART TWO   November 2012

2

The boy trudged across the shingle beach, six feet from where the waves were breaking on the shore. Their noise was immense: a roar, like an animal, and then a deep, visceral boom which passed right through him. When the tide began its retreat again, sucked back into the sea, the pebbles became caught in the wash and he could hear a soft, chattering sound, as if thousands of voices were calling from beyond the sea wall. On the other side of the eight-foot wall was the village: old fishermen's cottages, a pub, a few shops and businesses. This side of it were boats, lined up on the beach, masts chiming in the wind.

He adjusted the straps of the backpack and heard the equipment clatter around inside: the line, a new net he'd bought with the money from his paper round, and some old bacon his mum had given him that morning. He was carrying the bucket in his hand. It was early November, freezing cold, but this was always the best time to go crabbing. At this time of year there were no tourists—which meant he didn't have to share the crabs.

The village was set in a bowl, with coves cut into the faces of the hills on either side. In order to get to the coves, you had to climb over a series of rocks that rose up out of the shingle at both ends of the beach. To the boy, the rocks—hewed and polished by the relentless power of the sea—looked like the tail of a dragon, the bulk of the creature still submerged somewhere beneath. On the other side of the tail, in the coves beyond, hundreds of rock pools had formed in the grooves and chasms of the beach. That's where the crabs would be, washed up and spat out by the tide.

The boy started the climb.

Carrying the bucket at the same time made it harder. Normally his dad hauled all the equipment for him, but he was away with work and had told the boy he was big enough now—at almost thirteen—to go by himself. "As long as you're careful," his dad kept saying. The sea spray and the rain could make climbing more difficult but he was doing okay: after five minutes he'd got up on to the top of the tail and was looking down at the first of the coves. It dropped down about sixty feet from where he was, a thin sliver of shingle running from the shoreline to where the hills at the back started their steep ascent. The rest was just rock pools, sea washing over them, foam bubbling in the clefts and rifts.

He started down, bucket—gripped in his hand still—clattering against the rock, his eyes fixed on where he was placing his feet. Wind roared in, once, twice, pulling him around like it had reached out and grabbed him—but then he jumped the last few feet, on to the shingle, and the wind died instantly as he stepped into the protection of the cove. All he could hear now was the sea breaking on the beach behind him.

Placing the bucket down on the shingle, he removed his backpack, unzipped it and started taking out the equipment. Crab line. Short-handled net. Bait. He attached the bait to the line, grabbed the net and the bucket, and made his way across the cove to the rocks at the back. *As long as you're careful.* He placed his feet down just as deliberately as before, not wanting to have to explain to his dad how he had managed to snap the line, or cut himself, or both. Halfway across, he heard the sea crash again behind him, an even louder and longer roar than before, and when he looked back he saw a wave rolling in toward him. He wasn't worried about getting wet, but he *was* worried about getting knocked over, so he reached forward and grabbed hold of a thin column of stone. The sea washed in, almost knee high, soaking his trousers and boots, and flattening out in the space ahead of him. Once it started drawing out again, he looked to the backpack and saw it was safe, perched in a high groove where he'd placed it after getting the equipment out. He headed to the rock pools right at the back of the cove where it would be too far for the sea to reach him. There, he could drop the line into the pools without fear of being soaked a second time. High tide had been an hour ago. The waves may have been loud, may have been fierce, but they were slowly retreating. In another hour, they'd be weakened. An hour after that, they'd hardly make it to him at all.

He placed the bucket down next to him, made sure the bait was secure and sat next to the deepest rock pool in the cove. It was about five feet down. The boy dropped the line in, feeding it out of a box his dad had made for him. It was like a fishing reel, with a small handle on the side that he could use to draw the line back in. He held the box with his left hand, and let the line run over the first two fingers of his right hand so he could feel any movement, however slight, if a crab went for the bait.

Then he noticed something.

Twenty feet away from him, right at the back of the cove, between the last of the rock pools and the sharp incline of the hill, it looked like someone had left some bait behind. He shifted on the rock, trying to get a better view from where he was sitting, but all he could see was a white slab of meat. Chicken maybe, or pork. His dad always said bacon was best, but the boy had caught loads of crabs with pieces of old chicken. Oily fish was good too, but not as good as meat. Generally, crabs weren't fussy eaters.

As his eyes moved around the cove, he realized there was even more of the bait, a foot to the left of the other lot, just below his eye line. He placed the line box down—securing it in a crevice it couldn't escape from—and got to his feet. The surface down to the bait was slick with seawater. He took a couple of careful steps, then dropped down on to his backside and slid the rest of the way. Up close, he realized the bait was wrapped in plastic—like the type he kept his bacon in—and was longer than he'd first thought: it dropped away into a gully, the rest of it half-disguised by shadows. Beneath the plastic, he could see evenly cut strips of meat, identical seashells—bizarrely—attached to each one.

He reached forward.

Then stopped.

He glanced between his hand—still hovering over the plastic covering—and the meat inside; back and forth, as if his mind had made some sort of connection but he hadn't quite caught up.

Then, a second later, it hit him.

A whimper sounded in his throat as he scuffled back on his hands, reversing as far from the bait as he could. He tried to gain purchase on the rocks but his feet kept slipping, the heels of his boots sliding off the surface. "Dad!" he yelled, an automatic reaction, even though his dad was at work, miles away, and the boy was out here on his own. *"Dad!"* he screamed again, tears forming in his eyes as he desperately tried to claw his way back up to where he'd left his line.

Thirty seconds later, he got there—but he didn't even stop for the line. He didn't stop for his bait, or his bucket, or his backpack either. He just clambered across the rocks, back over the dragon's tail, and ran as fast as he could along the shingle to his house at the end of the sea wall. His mum was in the kitchen, organizing cakes for his sister's birthday, and when she looked at the boy, at his tears, at the wide-eyed terror in his eyes, she grabbed him, brought him in close and made him recount what he'd seen.

And he told her how the seashells had been fingernails.

How the strips of meat had been fingers.

And how the bait had been a hand.

3

Half a mile away, as the boy was telling his mother what he'd found, Colm Healy pulled his Vauxhall up alongside a cottage he'd been staying at for the last four months. On the passenger seat were two shopping bags. He grabbed them, got out and headed inside.

After putting the food away and making himself a coffee, he sat at the window and smoked a cigarette. The view, even in late autumn, was beautiful: the gentle curve of the shingle beach; a long line of pastel-colored fishermen's cottages; the high sea wall and the masts rising up from behind it. Sea spray dotted the glass and wind cut in from the water, swirling and buffeting the cottage—yet, to Healy, after twenty-six years in the Met, and even longer in the city, this was as close to silence as he had ever known.

A minute later, the silence broke.

On the table in front of him, his phone started buzzing, quietly turning circles. He didn't have a ring tone these days, which he preferred because it meant he missed a lot of calls. His ex-wife. The people he'd worked with. Men and women from his old life he'd happily never see again. But there was always a risk he might miss the one call he cared about: the call from his boys. So he brought the phone toward him and turned it over.

Liz Feeny.

He thought about letting it go to voice mail. Any conversation with Feeny was a conversation without a conclusion. She'd been phoning him constantly for the past couple of months, looking for any kind of closure, any kind of answer. But there wasn't one.

There was no happy ending.

He pushed Answer and flicked to speakerphone. "Liz."

"Colm."

Her voice was soft. It sounded like she'd already been crying. "This isn't really a good time," he said, lying. He looked around the kitchen. Dishes stacked up in the sink. Cereal boxes left on the counters. "I'm right in the middle of something here."

"Why do you still answer my calls?"

"What do you mean?"

"When David described you, he always said you were difficult to break down. Angry. Aloof. When I first started calling you, that was the man I expected to find."

Healy didn't say anything.

"But I've never *found* that man." She paused. "You've never been like that. I know you hate talking to me, but you still answer my calls." Another pause, this time for longer. She sniffed, stopped, sniffed again. "Why do you answer my calls, Colm?"

"I don't know," he said.

"Do you feel sorry for me—is that it?"

There was nothing in the question, no malice, but there was no right answer: yes, and she would cling on to it and use it as some kind of excuse to call him more often; no, and he would be telling her never to call again. *So? If you hate her calling so much, just tell her.* Except he couldn't do that. Because, deep down, he wasn't sure he *did* hate her calling.

Reaching across the table, he lit another cigarette and opened the window. Smoke drifted out through the gap, vanishing into the rain. For a moment his thoughts turned to David Raker. Everything Raker had told Liz was right. And maybe when the pressure was turned up, Healy would become that man again. But here, in this place, miles away from the life he'd once known, Healy felt like a different man. She may only have been using him, may only have been calling him because he was a vessel for something else—some sort of connection to Raker—but, in her own way, she needed him. And that was the first time anyone had needed Healy, for whatever reason, for a very long time.

"Colm?"

"It's hard to understand," he said.

"What is?"

"Why what happened, happened."

"Is it hard for *you* to understand?"

He looked out through the window. "Yes."

"You mean that?"

"Yes."

She didn't sound like she believed him.

"Listen, Liz, I know this is tough to hear, but—"

"I know what you're going to say," she cut in, her voice quiet. "I know what you're going to tell me to do. Accept it. Move on. Try to forget about what happened to him."

He didn't respond. She'd second-guessed him.

"*Right?*"

"Right."

"Well, it's not so easy for me," she said. "I'm still here in London with all the memories, living next door to his empty house. I haven't got myself a nice little holiday cottage in Devon to disappear to and forget about everything that happened."

"I haven't forgotten about what happened."

"Haven't you?"

"No."

Outside, the wind came again—harder and more forceful than before. The house seemed to wheeze, like the foundations had shifted.

"He was so similar to you," she said.

"Yeah, you said that before."

"He was chasing after ghosts, just like you."

"Look," Healy said, trying to maintain the composure in his voice, "I know what it's like to lose someone. Remember that. I've been where you are—I've been through *worse* than you—so I know how it is."

She cleared her throat, but didn't say anything.

"You can't forget about it. I understand that. But you need to try. You need to start processing what happened. Sooner or later, you need to start facing it down."

Silence on the line.

"Because Raker's gone, Liz. And he's never coming back."

4

An hour later, Healy was sitting in the corner of the pub, a small, dark, two-room building with pebbledash walls and a thatched roof. A fire was going in the corner and locals were lining the bar, perched on stools. They all had their backs to him, which he liked, and there was no music being played or TV on—just the murmur of conversation—which he liked even more. Nothing made him more depressed than being forced to listen to some landlord's CD collection. When he looked up from the paper he was reading, he could see the regulars were all in; a mix of old sea dogs, their skin etched and weathered like the rocks on the beach, and younger couples in their thirties, part of the new money that the affluent surrounding areas had brought in. Healy was neither, but he had fitted in pretty well here by keeping himself to himself and only speaking when he was forced to.

About ten minutes later, as he sank the last of his beer, a man in his fifties entered the bar. Healy recognized him, just from having been in and around the village for the last four months, but he didn't know him. Didn't know his name, or what he did. The man was wearing a green waxed jacket—soaked through from the rain—and had wild, grubby hair, and a beard like coils of twine. As he came in, his Wellingtons slapped against the stone floor, puddles of water and mud following in his wake as he moved first to the bar, eyes scanning the locals, and then out into the middle of the room. A couple of the regulars greeted him, but the man didn't respond in any way; instead he continued looking around the bar, into the barely lit coves, where other regulars—alone, like Healy—were hunched over their drinks, either reading or just staring into space.

Then the man locked eyes with Healy.

He came over, stopping in front of the table Healy was sitting at, and stood there, rain dripping off him. The locals had all turned on their stools. There was no gentle hum of conversation anymore. Just silence.

Healy closed his newspaper. "You all right, pal?"

"You the copper?" the man said.

"Not anymore."

"You used to be, though, right?"

Healy looked out beyond the man. All eyes were on him.

"I used to be."

"You need to come and see this."

"See what?"

For the first time, the man seemed to realize everyone inside the bar was listening to their conversation. He turned back to Healy. "It's better if you see it yourself."

Three of them climbed up over the rocks and down toward the cove. The boy followed behind, reticence in every step, as if he were returning to a place he'd vowed never to go again. Healy followed the man who'd come to get him, and behind them both was the boy's father, still suited and booted, having just returned home from work. He'd wanted to come out here to prevent his son having to see anything more than he already had. Healy knew less than anyone. He hadn't got much out of any of the locals—many of whom he could see behind them, watching from the other side of the sea wall—but he doubted anything he was about to find was good. He'd worked murders at the Met long enough to see the connections, however small, between crimes; he knew that people handled death differently, but once you'd discovered a body—bereft of life; hollow and empty—it always left something of itself in the person who'd found it. Some held it together, some broke down, but everyone had that same look; a memory, deep and resonant, that would never fade.

When he'd left the pub, he'd told the landlord to call the police, but he and the villagers seemed reluctant, as if inviting the police in would shatter the equilibrium. Healy could understand it on some level: one of the reasons he'd come here in the first place was because he'd had enough of the city; its darkness and corruption. The people in the village had stayed here their whole lives because they'd wanted to avoid the same thing.

Healy watched as the man from the pub stepped down on to the sand of the cove, feet sinking into the shingle, the dad following in his wake. "Don't go any further!" Healy shouted to them, trying to prevent them contaminating any evidence that was down there. The rain and the wind would have damaged the scene already, but they had to preserve what they could. Healy shouted again for them to stop. This time they listened, but didn't look back, as if unwilling to cede control to Healy. Finally, alongside Healy came the boy—maybe only twelve or thirteen—his face ghostly white, his hands rolled into fists at his side, eyes fixed off to his right, at the highest point of the cove, where something was sitting. Healy tried to get a better view of what it was, then dropped down a couple of feet to a platform gouged out of the rock. All the time, rain jagged in, almost horizontal, swirled around by the wind rolling off the sea.

Dread slithered through his stomach as he made the last jump down into the cove, and his boots started disappearing into the fine shingle. He looked at the man from the pub, then at the dad, then at the boy—cowed and frightened—waiting in the space behind them all. Waves crashed on the beach. "Stay here," Healy said to them all, including the boy. "Don't follow me. We need to preserve whatever's here."

He waited for a moment, watching to see whether they were paying attention, and then he started making his way toward the back of the cove. Sea spray stalked him as he moved. He climbed toward a raised platform of rock at the far end of the cove and, as he did, he got a better view of what the boy had found.

It wasn't crab bait.

He doubted the boy had even seen the whole thing: it required a level of elevation, a physical height, the boy simply wouldn't have. Healy took another step forward. The wind and the rain masked the stench of decay, but it was there, in the background; accumulating, getting worse.

I thought it was a piece of sliced meat at first, the kid had told Healy, chewing his bottom lip as they left the pub. *I thought it had shells stuck to it.* But it wasn't shells and it wasn't sliced meat. Healy looked back to where the men and the boy were waiting. Clouds sloped over the hills either side of the beach, dark and twisted and pregnant with even heavier rain. Then the smell came again and he turned back to it, wrapped loosely in plastic, most of it—apart from an arm—washed up into the shadows of a gully.

Pale and skinny.

Bloodless.

5

Soon after, the police descended on the village. Healy had made the call himself, from inside the cove, and then waited for them on the main beach. He'd sent the locals back to the other side of the sea wall. The first responders found him—two uniforms with about five years' experience between them—and as he explained who he was and what he'd discovered, he saw the color drain from their faces. In this part of the world, most cops would go their whole lives without seeing a major crime scene; but for these two it had taken less than three years. He took one of them back over the rocks and down the other side to see the body while the other one stayed and called in CID and forensics. Healy pointed to where the arm snaked out from the shadows. Perched on top of the rocks, the uniform eyed it nervously for a second before nodding and retreating to the safety of the beach.

Healy followed.

Scene of crime turned up forty minutes later, forensics in tow. Inside an hour they had a tent erected as close to the cove as possible, and the SOCO—a weatherbeaten guy in his early sixties—had set up an incident room in the village hall. Techs did their best to preserve evidence, to scour the cove for what had been left behind with the body, but the whole time the wind and rain carved in across the bay. Healy watched from the sea wall with the others, until eventually a plainclothes detective came up the beach toward him, flanked by a second. Both were dressed in gray suits and police-issue raincoats.

"Can I have a word, Mr. Healy?" the older one said, a guy in his forties with prematurely silver hair and a salt and pepper beard. It was the type of question that wasn't really a question. The other one, skinny and tall and in his thirties, said nothing, just followed behind.

The inside of the village hall was small and cramped, wet footprints crisscrossing at the entrance. A trail of rubber mats had been laid out, branching off in one direction to a forensics setup, where techs had placed evidence bags under the watchful eye of a uniform; and in the other direction to a room beyond a serving hatch that had a table and four chairs in it. Everything smelled musty, of disrepair and age, and beyond the serving hatch it was worse: boiled food and furniture polish.

Healy sat down at the table and the younger detective—without even being asked—disappeared back into the hall to get them all a cup of tea.

"You've got him well trained," Healy said.

The detective looked up, a wry smile on his face, and leaned back in his seat. "DCI Colin Rocastle," he said, placing a hand on his chest. "That's DC Stuart McInnes."

"Colm Healy."

"I'm told you used to work for the Met."

"Twenty-six years."

"That's a long time."

"The Met would probably say too long."

Rocastle smiled. "You don't look retirement age."

But Healy understood: *So, why did you leave?*

"I'd just had enough."

Rocastle nodded and looked down at his pad, dotted with rain, ink running, notes smudged. He didn't seem convinced, but he didn't say anything else. In the silence that followed, Healy almost started talking again, almost started weaving a supplementary lie, but then stopped: these were tactics he knew so well, had used every day of his life for a quarter of a century, but which—five months after he'd been fired from the police force—he'd almost become entrapped by. The long pause. The uncomfortable silence. The need of the witness, or the suspect, to fill gaps in conversation. It was Interviewing 101, part of every manual ever written on police interrogation. What bothered him wasn't the quiet between them. What bothered him was that he'd been so close to walking into the trap.

This place is making you soft.

Rocastle looked up at him, as if sensing he was turning something over, but Healy just stared him out. The lies, the half-truths, they weren't coming as easily anymore. He was out of shape and he was losing his edge.

". . . cross the body?"

Rocastle was talking. Healy looked at him. "What?"

"How did you come across the body?"

Healy started to recount, in detail, how he'd been approached by the man in the pub, then led down to the cove, along with the boy and his father.

"The guy in the pub's a fisherman, right?" Rocastle said.

"I don't know what he does. But he had been down to the cove once already, before he came to get me. He said the boy's mother had come into the village, and he'd happened to be the first person she found."

"You don't believe him?"

Healy shrugged. "He wasn't surprised by what we found there, as if he'd already had the time to process it. How quickly does a person go from shock to acceptance?"

"What do you mean?"

"I mean, his face didn't show anything when he got down there a second time. How do you think someone would react the second time they saw a corpse?"

"People process things differently."

"It was a dead body."

"So what are you suggesting?"

"Maybe it wasn't the second time he'd been down there," Healy said. "Maybe it was the third, or the fourth, or—"

"Thanks, Mr. Healy."

Rocastle didn't write anything down.

Healy eyed him. "You spoken to him?"

"Yes."

"And what did he say?"

Rocastle placed his pen down, initially at an angle to the pad, before readjusting it so it was perfectly adjacent. Small things built a picture of someone at the start, and that one tiny movement told Healy that Rocastle liked precision, liked everything to fit together.

"I can't discuss that, Colm," he said.

Colm. Trying to soften the blow, one cop to another. Except Healy didn't think it was that. It was nothing more than a hunch, but he got the sense Rocastle thought the fisherman might have some other story to tell too; perhaps some other reason for having gone to the cove first. Healy, curiosity aroused, made a mental note of it.

"How long have you lived here?" Rocastle asked.

"Four months."

"You like it?"

Healy leaned back in the old, wooden chair. It creaked under his weight, and as he moved, the dead air in the kitchen shifted and he could smell boiled food again. "Yeah," he said. "It's nice. No one ordering me around. No one trying to stick a knife in my back."

"Metaphorically or literally?"

"Both."

"You fall out with someone at the Met?"

"I can't really discuss that, Colin," Healy said, and Rocastle nodded his reply. *Touché.*

Moments later, McInnes returned with three Styrofoam cups, tea sloshing over the edges and on to his hands. He placed them down on the table. Rocastle took one and sipped from it, but his eyes never left Healy. "So why'd you choose Devon?"

"Why not?"

"You didn't have any reason?" Rocastle picked up the pen again, its nib hovering over a fresh page of the pad.

Healy shrugged. "Someone I knew has a place down here."

"A friend?"

"I don't have many friends."

"An acquaintance, then?"

"What's the relevance of this?"

Rocastle glanced at McInnes as the younger man sat down next to him, tea in one hand, cell phone in the other. "You know how it works," Rocastle said. "We'll obviously need to have a chat with everyone in the village, so we can see who knows what."

Healy took one of the Styrofoam cups.

"Colm?"

He looked at Rocastle. "David Raker."

"Sorry?"

"That's whose house it is."

6

Five months ago, my heart stopped for seven minutes. I can't articulate what happened in the time I was gone, maybe because there aren't the words, but I remember it being more light than dark, like sunlight refracted through glass. When my heart started up again, the first sensation was of weight: of skin, and bone, and blood; of tendons and nerve-endings. Then came the sounds, fading in like music: the voices from the medical team, the ECG, cars passing on the street outside and, further out, doors closing and people talking.

When I opened my eyes for the first time, there was no one in the room with me. I turned on the pillow one way, then the other. A white room, green floors, blinds twisted shut at the window. Still drowsy, I drifted off to sleep again. When I woke for the second time, Healy was there, sitting next to my bed, checking his phone. He was unshaven and unkempt, tie loose, shirt tails spilling out over his trousers. He didn't notice me shift in bed, but he heard me grimace and suck in air, pain blooming in my stomach from the knife wound. As he put down his phone and leaned toward me, memories started going off like fireworks, one after the other. My parents, Derryn, the people I'd found and tracked down in the months after she'd died, and then the last of them: the man who'd tried to take my life on June 19. The one who'd left me to die.

I woke with a jolt. For a second I was confused, hands slick with sweat, heart thumping. But then, out of the shadows of the living room came objects and furniture I recognized, and, as I looked through the window, reality set in and I remembered where I was.

Automatically, my fingers were drawn to my stomach. The bandages had been off for a month, but through the thin cotton of the T-shirt I could feel the scar: a thick knot of hard flesh, like a barnacle clinging to a rock. Some days, deep inside my gut, it felt like I could still feel the point of the blade; a cool ache, like a memory, right in the center of my stomach. More often, though, I felt nothing; or, at least, nothing physical. The only pain that resonated was inside my head. I'd dream of crawling across the ground toward my phone; of dialing the first number I could find, anyone, any help at all; and then somewhere faintly, right on the periphery of my memories, I remembered a couple appearing, seconds after I thought they'd walked right past me, and the woman giving me CPR. After that, it became a blur of indistinct images, flickering like a strobe, until Healy arrived. That was remarkably clear: him running toward me, flanked by paramedics.

The man who had tried to kill me had been caught a couple of weeks later. He'd left behind a trail of bodies, of which me and a cop—a man called Bartholomew, the man leading the hunt for him—were the last two. Bartholomew hadn't been as lucky as me. They'd found him just as I'd reached the hospital in the back of an ambulance, tubes coming out of me, wires connected to every muscle in my chest. While I was being operated on, he was lying dead in his home.

I'd talked countless times—to Derryn in the weeks before she finally succumbed to cancer, and to Liz who came after her—about the debt I felt for the missing; about the responsibility I put on myself to bring them back into the light. It was something I only became more certain of in the years after, when sitting down with the families was like sitting in front of a mirror. The grief they felt for the people they'd lost, the sadness, the need to dig in and cling on, I recognized all of it. And when I came back after those seven minutes, that debt and responsibility hardened and formed, and I realized that, despite everything that had happened, this was who I was.

The missing were still my life.

7

The beach was lit by orange street lamps, clamped to the sea wall at fifty-yard intervals, and the pale glow of the pub, its light spilling across the shingle like an overturned pot of paint. On top of a blistered red pole out front, its sign swung in the wind, making the same rusty squeak every time it returned to the center. Everything had been blanched by sea salt: walls, doors, frames, patio slabs. In the twenty-four years since I'd left, only the name had changed. When I was growing up, it had always been called The Pike—as in the fish. Now it was called The Seven Seas, presumably because the owners thought that would play better with the tourists. But in truth what would play better with the tourists was a ground-up refurbishment. From the outside it looked almost derelict, and inside it wasn't much better. Cramped and dark, it was a two-room celebration of 1970s decor, with awful, threadbare patterned carpets, faded paintwork, and countless nick-nacks stuffed into every available space as if they all needed to be filled. It was busy too. Most of the time, Tuesday evenings were one-man-and-his-dog nights, but not tonight. Tonight the whole village was out, and they were talking about the body.

I scanned the room and saw Healy seated at the back, in his usual spot, facing the room so he could see what was going on. He had two drinks in front of him, one almost finished, the other untouched. I squeezed my way through the crowd, sat down and brought the beer toward me. "Cheers," I said, and he just nodded, his eyes fixed on someone over my shoulder. I turned and followed his gaze. He was watching a guy from the village—a trawler fisherman called Prouse—talking to a small group of men.

"Where were you?" he asked. His eyes didn't leave the man.

"When?"

"I called you earlier and told you to come down to the village hall."

"I was in the middle of something."

His eyes flicked back to me. "Really?"

"If that cop needs to talk to me, you told him where I live."

"You *were* listening to what I said, right?"

"You're not a cop anymore, Healy."

He frowned. "What's that supposed to mean?"

"It means you don't owe them anything. It's not your job to round up the suspects and throw them into the back of the van. Not for this Rocastle guy, not for anyone."

"I know that."

"Do you?"

He eyed me but didn't respond. He'd become more controlled in the months since I'd known him, but it was still hard for him to bite his tongue. He was used to hitting out, used to lying and misleading when he needed to, and this new life—miles away from the city, miles from his ex-wife and two boys—was new and probably, in its own way, quite daunting. This wasn't his playground. He wasn't operating from a position of strength. He'd needed to get out of London because it was suffocating him; he'd been fired, he was still mourning the loss of his daughter, and he was on the verge of doing something rash in the days before I was attacked. After I was finally released from hospital, I needed to get away too, and I owed Healy my life, at least in part. So I offered him a room in the cottage my parents had left behind for me. I never put a time frame on it—I guess because I saw us driving each other insane inside a couple of weeks—but somehow we were four months down the line and he was still here.

"Your woman called for you again," he said, fiddling with the lid on his cigarette packet as wind pressed again at the walls of the pub. "You ever gonna call her back?"

"You seem to be handling it pretty well."

He smirked. "That's cold."

"It's not cold."

"What, you saying this is you all warm and fuzzy?"

"Why are you even taking her calls?"

"Because you're not."

I looked at him.

"She started calling me when you stopped answering your phone." He studied me, got no answer, and finished his pint. "She's desperate. What am I supposed to do?"

"Stop taking her calls."

"What's wrong with speaking to her?"

"This is *my* life."

"I doubt she'll call again, anyway," he said after a while, shrugging. He pushed the pint glass away from him. "I told her you were gone and you weren't coming back."

"Why did you tell her that?"

"Well, that's pretty much what's happened, isn't it?"

Again, I remained silent. I'd never talked to him about the reasons Liz and I had separated, and the reasons I could never go back to her, but sometimes it felt like he'd guessed. In the days before I got stabbed, I'd started to realize she didn't understand why I did what I did, the debt I had to the missing, and I realized I couldn't face a future where all I did was fight with her about it. Healy got that part—because he was driven by the same kind of ghosts as me—but while sometimes I felt the two of us were getting somewhere, able to understand each other, at other times he'd say something to me or look at me in a certain way, and I'd see that he was still the same man I'd never fully got to grips with: full of anger and resentment and bitterness. We had an attachment, most of it unsaid, in the loss we'd suffered and the way we'd been drawn together in our working lives; and we had an emotional tie to one another too, however slight: I'd saved his life once, and he'd repaid the favor. But, mostly, Healy was a wall I couldn't break down. Part of me wondered if he thought he was helping by taking Liz's calls; the other part, perhaps the part of me that had grown to know him over the past year, thought he was doing it so he had something over me. As long as I couldn't be sure, I couldn't discuss it with him, and whatever it was we had—our connection; our friendship, if it was even that—carried on undefined.

"They reckon it's a man," he said.

"The body?"

"Yeah." He nodded, using his thumb and forefinger to remove a sliver of tobacco from his lips. "No decomposition, that's the thing. Or, at least, none that I could see."

"So it's fresh."

"Or frozen."

"By the air temperature?"

"By a refrigerator." He shrugged. "They didn't tell me anything. I'm just going on what I saw. No sign of decomp anywhere. It was in good condition too—seriously good—so if you want my guess I'd say someone put him on ice before he gassed up."

If you froze a body before putrefaction kicked in, you could keep it indefinitely with few, if any, signs of decay. As long as it wasn't allowed to thaw, bacteria couldn't feed on it, and the body wouldn't break down. No gases. No acids. I watched Healy turn his empty pint glass, deep in thought, and I could see what was going on in his head: he'd got a taste of his old life, had felt—however briefly—the buzz of a case, and now he was struggling to rein his curiosity back in. I doubted he'd be willing to watch from afar, and as that thought came to me I turned and looked back at the man he'd been studying.

"What do you want with him?" I asked.

He flicked a look at me. "Eh?"

"The one you've been watching."

"Any idea what he does for a job?"

"He's the skipper on a fishing trawler. What's your interest in him?"

"He was the one who found the body."

"So?"

But he didn't respond. Instead he grabbed his coat, scooped up his cigarettes and stood. He didn't like the fact that I'd second-guessed him, so now came the blank. He just remained there, stock-still, any response or emotion wiped from his face. Except I knew that look. I'd seen it many times—and it was a look that couldn't lead anywhere good.

"Back away, Healy."

"Don't talk to me like I'm a child."

"You know what happened last time."

He glared at me, but he knew I was right. The reason he was down here in the first place was because he didn't know where to draw the line. "Maybe *you* should take a bit more interest in the case, then," he said to me, removing a cigarette from its packet. "Keep your mind occupied; help the healing process." He was being facetions now, so I didn't bother rising to the bait. He nodded in the direction of the bar. "I heard a couple of the locals talking about this village being cursed—so who knows what it could lead to?"

"Cursed?"

"Some woman and her family who used to live here."

"What are you talking about?"

He buttoned up his coat. "I'm going for a smoke."

8

The wind was dying down by the time I left the pub, but rain still swept in off the water. Fifteen minutes had passed since Healy had gone for a cigarette, and he hadn't returned. I looked along the front of the building, to where a group of smokers had gathered in the same place, underneath an overhang of thatch: three men, all of whom I recognized but didn't really know. They nodded. I nodded back. Then I looked across the beach.

On the other side of it, next to the cove, were two huge lights: one faced up the beach, lighting the way to the village hall; the other was partially obscured in the cove itself, facing the direction the body had been found. Although he'd done his share of stupid things in the past, if the police were still there Healy wasn't going to be sniffing around the crime scene. But something had got to him, which meant he probably had some sort of plan in place.

Something reckless.

"David?"

I turned. A woman emerged from the pub—gray-haired and slightly stooped, in her late sixties or early seventies—a silhouette for a moment against the brightness of the interior. Then, as she came further out into the drizzle, I remembered seeing her at the bar: she'd been sitting on one of the stools, talking to the guy who ran the butchery in the village. I hadn't paid much attention to her then, but now, as the light from the pub cast a glow across her face, something about her struck a chord with me.

"David?" she said again.

I stepped toward her. Nodded.

"Don't you remember me?"

I smiled as though I did, but the truth was, I couldn't recall where I'd seen her; whether it had been in and around the village over the past few months, or before that, when I'd been here as a boy. I'd maintained a pretty low profile since moving down from London, rarely going out, healing in isolation, so it was more likely the second.

She saved me from embarrassment: "It's me. Vera Kane."

It came flooding back: she was the aunt of a girl I'd dated when I was in my mid-to-late teens. Emily. We'd gone out for almost eighteen months, and then tearfully ended it when I'd got a university place in London. I took a step toward the old woman, and we moved all the way back under the thatched overhang. "Mrs. Kane. How are you?"

"I'm doing okay—for an old woman. How are you?"

"I'm well. You look good."

"You liar," she said, winking.

"I'm surprised I haven't seen you around."

"Oooh, I don't live here," she said. "I'm down in Kingsbridge. I don't come back very often because my bloody hips are agony and I've got no family here anymore. But when I heard what was going on . . ." She stopped; nodded to the beach. "Well, I've still got friends in the village and I was worried one of them might be the person that they . . ."

I followed her gaze. "Right."

"How long have you been back?"

"Four months."

"In your parents' old place?"

"That's right."

She nodded. "So, I wonder who it can be?"

I glanced down at the beach again. "I don't know."

"I thought your policeman friend might have said."

She meant Healy. "No. Unfortunately, he didn't."

A flicker of disappointment in her face. I understood then: she was after some fuel to take back into the pub, something fresh she could use. I didn't blame her. Knowledge was power in a village where everybody knew everything about everybody else. There was no way she could have known Healy's history, the fact that he was an ex-cop with a life as patched up as mine. She would have just seen him being led to the body by Prouse the fisherman—and then into the village hall by the investigating team for a cozy chat.

"How's Emily?" I asked.

She took a second to tune back in. "Oh, she's good, love."

"She still local?"

"Totnes, yeah. I'm seeing her tomorrow."

"Well, say hello to her from me."

"I will."

The conversation was fizzling out. "Nice to see you, Mrs. Kane."

"Yeah," she said. "Nice to see you too, love."

. . .

The cottage had been bought by my parents when they'd started to fall out of love with the farm. When I was growing up, my dad and I used to go out shooting in a belt of woodland at the back of the property, where he'd set up targets for me to hit. I made it clear early on I wasn't interested in taking over the farm, so he started to cling to the idea of me being a marksman in the army, just like his brother had been. I didn't want to be that either, but I loved my dad and wanted to see him happy, so we compromised: whenever I was down from London, we'd go out shooting, hitting targets just like the old days.

Then, in March 2005, Mum died.

We got back from the woods, rifles under our arms, and found her slumped on a bench at the front of the farmhouse. She'd had a stroke. Dad fell apart after that. I sold the farmhouse for him, moved him into the cottage, and for a while he started to seem a little brighter. Then, in January 2006, I got a call from one of his neighbors, who'd been around to see him. He'd died quietly in the living room, looking out at the sea.

On the approach, up a narrow, winding road that took you out of the heart of the village and into the folds of the surrounding hills, I could see that same window, sitting in shadow under a sliver of slate-gray roof. Unusually for the village, which was dense, its buildings knotted together in a clump at the edge of the beach, the cottage sat alone, hemmed in by trees about seventy feet above sea level. It was why Vera Kane and the rest of the village had rarely seen me: I'd spent the first two months trying to live again.

And the following two wondering where I went next.

9

The next morning, Healy was gone before I got up, so I put some coffee on and sat at the kitchen window, looking out at the beach. Even this early, as the sun clawed its way up behind a wall of cloud, uniforms stood along the sea wall, black marks against the gray of the concrete. Rain started to fall as a bunch of techs in white forensic suits emerged from the village hall, ducked under the cordon and headed down to the cove. I tried to spot Healy among it all but couldn't see him, and then felt bad for assuming the worst.

After I'd showered and had some breakfast, I went back to repairing an old chair that my dad had bought a few years before his death. He'd been an amateur collector of antiques, though not a very successful one, but it had kept his mind occupied in the weeks and months after Mum had gone. The chair was worth nothing, but I was slowly working my way around the house trying to give everything, even the junk, an upgrade.

A couple of hours later, just after eleven, I was washing my hands in the kitchen sink—trying to remove grease from my skin—when I heard a car pull into the driveway. I assumed it was Healy, but when I didn't hear him approach I dried my hands and went to the back door. It was a Suzuki Vitara, parked with its rear toward me.

The rain was heavy now, drawing the light from the day, and as I stepped further on to the porch, the security lamp sparked into life and I saw movement in the car.

"Can I help you?" I said above the rain.

More movement, and then the driver's door opened and a woman got out, shoes crunching on the gravel, her back to me. Then she turned—and I realized who it was.

Emily Kane.

"David?"

The moment she spoke, memories came alive. It wasn't just her voice, it was the way she carried herself, the slight reticence in her. Suddenly it was so familiar, as if no time at all had passed since we'd last met. In reality, it had been twenty-four years.

"Emily."

A full smile bloomed. "Yes!" She seemed delighted I'd recognized her, but apart from the wear and tear of time—the lines, the creases—she looked remarkably similar: five-three, slim, dark hair scraped back into a ponytail, a face full of tiny, delicate angles. She'd always been slight—build, height, the way she spoke, the way she stood—and, as I gradually recalled each little part of her, more memories came flooding back: sitting on the sea wall watching the boats rock on the waves, the late-night walks to the coves, and then everything that came after when you were teenagers and in love for the first time.

I walked over to her and immediately dwarfed her, and we stood there facing each other in a moment of awkwardness. Did we kiss? Shake hands? How did you greet a girlfriend you hadn't seen for almost a quarter of a century? In the end I leaned in and politely kissed her on the cheek and, to prevent any more discomfort, immediately asked her inside. She thanked me and followed me through the rain to the front door. I turned back to her and smiled. "Let me apologize up front for the mess you're about to witness."

"I'm sure it's fine," she said.

"I'm normally pretty good at washing dishes."

She laughed, maybe politely—I didn't know her well enough to tell the difference anymore—but, if it was put on, that was okay. She was trying to figure out how similar I was to the boy she remembered.

Inside, I put the kettle on and offered her a seat at the table overlooking the beach. Under granite skies, the lights from the crime scene were on, casting a long, bleached glow across the shingle, turning it pale and oddly beautiful. Emily sat there, bag perched in her lap, a half-smile on her face. But for the first time there was something else: a hint of sadness. It was a look I'd come to recognize easily and often in the families of people who went missing, and I knew instantly she wasn't here to catch up on old times.

"Wow," she said. "David Raker."

"It's great to see you, Emily."

"And you."

"Did your aunt tell you we bumped into each other last night?"

She colored a little. "Yes. She mentioned that. That's why I thought I'd pop by." But we both understood this wasn't a social call, and as she realized I'd figured her out, her fingers started drumming nervously on her bag. I glanced at her hands. No wedding ring. No indent to suggest one had been there recently. "I hope you don't mind me . . ."

"Not at all. You're living up in Totnes?"

"Yes. I don't come here much. Just pass through sometimes. Mum and Dad are both gone now, and the only time I'm down this way is when I see Vera in Kingsbridge."

I told her I was sorry to hear about her parents, and she talked for a while about her house in Totnes, a town about thirty minutes inland. She had an apartment, five minutes' walk from the quay. "I have a studio at home," she said. "I work as a graphic designer."

"I remember you used to love to draw."

"Yes." She smiled. "Times are really tough—but I get by okay."

"That's great to hear. And what's Carrie up to these days?"

Carrie was her sister. She was eight years older than Emily, yet—growing up—the two of them had been uncannily similar, despite the big age difference. But as I waited for her reply, I felt the change coming, and remembered what Healy had said in the pub the night before: *I heard a couple of the locals talking about this village being cursed . . . Some woman and her family who used to live here.*

"Carrie?" she said. "Oh, she's, uh . . . that's why . . ." She trailed off.

In my line of work everyone was hiding something, but the road to the truth often played out the same way on their faces: a tremor of emotion followed by a composed blank. It was their need to offload, their need to get to the bottom of what had happened to the person they loved, followed by the fear that the truth might end up being worse than not knowing. It was a confession and a denial all at the same time, and it seemed obvious that, whatever she was about to tell me, it was going to be about her sister.

"What happened to Carrie?" I said.

She didn't react to the question, accepting that she'd already given herself away. Her fingers played with the strap on her bag and, slowly, her eyes shimmered. When she looked up, she seemed even paler, even smaller, even more beaten down.

"She and her family," she said quietly. "They all disappeared."

10

"I went to see Vera this morning and she mentioned seeing you last night," Emily began, both of us sitting at the table with coffees. "She said you were just like she remembered."

She paused, looking at me. I wasn't the person they remembered—certainly not now, and not even before I'd been attacked—but I smiled, putting her at ease, and let her continue.

"This sounds like I'm stalking you, but after I left her place this morning I thought I'd google you, see if I could find you on Facebook or Twitter. I thought I could maybe drop you an e-mail, see how you were. But instead I found all these news stories about you, about what you'd done. The families you'd helped. The men you'd tried . . ." She glanced at my stomach. "I read about what that guy did to you. How your heart . . ."

Stopped.

I nodded but didn't say anything, watching her in the half-light of the kitchen. She stared back. Composed. Still. Then, gradually, there was a movement in her lips.

She dabbed a finger to her eye. "I'm sorry."

"Don't be."

She smiled, and then brought her coffee toward her. "I'm sure you moved down here to start again. To get away from people like me. I just . . ." Steam passed her face as she looked down into her mug. "I just don't know where else to go. She's my sister."

"You said the whole family disappeared?"

"Yes."

"When?"

"January 7."

"So, that's Carrie and who else?"

"Carrie, her husband Paul, Belle and Liv—their two girls."

Five months after dying, I should have ended the conversation there. Deep down, I knew I wasn't ready for this; not physically, maybe not mentally either.

But I didn't.

I let her carry on.

"They live an hour from here, just west of Buckfastleigh," she continued, tone flat and barely audible, as if the story had been told countless times. I didn't read anything into it. They all became like this sooner or later, wading across old ground, looking for the same answers in the same places. "I'd driven up there from Totnes, because Carrie and I were supposed to be going out in Torquay with some friends. But when I got to the house, no one answered. Their cars were still on the drive, the lights were on in the house, so I rang the doorbell, five, six, seven times." A pause. "Nothing."

She stopped altogether then and seemed to waver, her upper body swaying like a boat listing on ocean swells. "The front door was unlocked, so I let myself in and went along the hallway. They always had a nice house. I know this sounds weird, but it always *smelled* nice. Flowers and coffee and candles. But it didn't smell nice when I went inside that night. I walked through to the kitchen and the dinner was still cooking."

"It had just been left like that?"

"Yes," she said, nodding. "I remember it vividly. The potatoes were still cooking even though there was no water left in the pan. The pork steaks were burned to a crisp. Vegetables were half prepared, just left there on the chopping board. It was like the four of them had downed tools and walked out of the house. There was nothing out of place." She turned her coffee mug, lost in thought for a moment. "In fact, the opposite, really. Everything was *in* place. Even the table was set: cutlery laid out, drinks prepared."

"Did it look like they'd left in a hurry?"

She shook her head, but in her eyes I saw a flicker of hesitation: as if she'd remembered something but wasn't sure whether it was even worth bringing up.

"Emily?"

"The milk," she said.

"Milk?"

"The fridge had been left ajar. This big four-pinter was lying on the floor, and all the milk had poured out of it, across the linoleum. But that was it. That was the only thing. Even the dog was still wandering around the house."

"Did you check upstairs?"

"I checked the whole house."

"Anything stolen?"

"No."

"Money, bank cards, wallets, phones, TVs, DVDs, computers—you know the kind of thing. None of that had been taken?"

"No."

"Would you know if it had?"

"The TV was on in the living room, Paul's computer was on in his study, Liv's toys were scattered all over the floor of her room. But not like the place had been turned over. Not like that at all. It was like Liv—like all of them—had *just* been there."

"Moments before?"

"Right. It was like a museum."

She meant it was a snapshot of time; nothing but the milk out of place. The food was still cooking, the lights were still on, the TV, the computer, the cars, the dog.

"You presumably tried calling them?"

"Yes."

"No answer?"

"Their phones were still in the house."

I reached across the table and grabbed a piece of paper with a shopping list on it. It was everything I needed to repair the fence panels out back. For now, it would have to do as a makeshift pad. I'd left the real one back in London, I suppose as some sort of symbolic gesture. Except here I was, four months after leaving the city, doing everything I shouldn't have. Part of me knew this was already a mistake: my feelings about taking on work from people I knew had hardened and crystallized over the past two years, mainly because I'd done it once—for a woman Derryn had worked with—and, in trying to find her son, I'd been left with scars on my body that would never heal, and memories that would never fade. And yet, as Emily recounted the disappearance of her sister and her family, I felt a buzz of electricity in my stomach. For the first time in months, I felt normal.

"What's Carrie's surname now?"

"Ling."

I started making some notes. "Her husband's Paul?"

"Yes."

"And the full names of the girls?"

"Annabel and Olivia."

"Did you file a missing persons report?"

She nodded. "I called them right away. They told me to come to Totnes station. The PC there asked me a few questions, filled in some paperwork, then said a team would be by the next day to take DNA samples and look around the house."

"They didn't find anything?"

"No," she said, eyes on me, hands flat to the table either side of her mug. "They took lots of things away for analysis, but it all got returned eventually."

"Do you remember exactly what they took?"

"Paul's computer, their phones."

"Whose phones?"

"Carrie's, Paul's and Belle's."

"Annabel had her own phone?"

"She's almost twenty-five."

I put down the pen. "So, how old is Liv then?"

"Eight." But she didn't need me to fill in the blanks. "Both Paul and Carrie wanted kids pretty much from the moment they got married, so they started trying straight away, but both of the girls were . . ." She shrugged. "Both of them were a struggle. Belle less so, I guess, but Olivia definitely. Both times they ended up having to get . . . you know . . ."

"Help?"

She nodded. "Yeah, help."

"IVF?"

"Right."

"So the age gap between Annabel and Olivia is seventeen years?"

"Yes."

I wrote that down. "Annabel was still living at home?"

No reply. I looked up from my notes and Emily was staring across my shoulder, set adrift in thought.

"Emily?"

She flinched. "Sorry."

"Are you okay?"

"Yeah, fine. What was it you asked?"

"Was Annabel still living at home?"

"Yes. She'd been at university up in Bristol for four years; she'd done an MA in English Literature. But she couldn't get a job anywhere. You know what it's like at the moment."

I nodded. "So she moved back home?"

"Yes. She got some part-time work in Newton Abbot, teaching

drama to students, but she was applying for jobs all over the country. She had plenty of interviews, but never seemed to quite make the cut. So she kept going with the teaching gig right up until . . ."

"They all disappeared."

"Right."

I'd filled one side of the paper, and as I turned it over I saw something change in her face. An expectation. A glimmer of hope.

"Were Paul and Carrie having any problems?"

She frowned. "Problems?"

"Were they fighting?"

"No. No way."

"They didn't fight?"

"They fought, but never seriously. Carrie and I were always close—you probably remember that—and she never talked about arguments. Paul was very even-tempered."

"What did he do?"

"He was a doctor."

"Did he work here in the village?"

"No. In Torquay. He was a pediatrician."

"And Carrie?"

"She was a stay-at-home mum."

"But they were doing okay?"

"Nice house, nice cars, nice holidays—I'd say so."

"Carrie never complained of financial worries?"

"No."

"What about Paul?"

"I didn't really have that kind of relationship with him."

"You got on all right with him, though?"

She glanced at me, and I could read her thoughts like they were written across her face: *Was that a loaded question?* "You mean, did he leave because of me? No."

"Don't be offended," I said to her. "I'm trying to close off dead ends. You're the person who knew them. You're basically the best hope of finding out where they went. I'm sure this isn't anything that you haven't heard already from the police."

She shrugged. "I haven't spoken to the police for months."

"When was the last time?"

"July, August—whenever they returned Paul's wallet."

"That was the last thing they gave back to you?"

"Yes."

"Why did they hold on to it for so long?"

She paused, uncertain. Maybe she'd never thought of it like that. The police would have held on to a lot of the Lings' property and gradually fed it back over time as it became obvious it wasn't going to lead anywhere. She probably stopped noticing.

"I don't know," she said eventually.

"Okay. But, clearly, Paul left his wallet behind too?"

"On the kitchen table," she said, and started to drift away again. Her eyes dulled as the memories rolled back to her. I waited it out, finishing my notes. Then, after a while, she said quietly, "Who leaves like that without their wallet?"

Two hundred and fifty thousand people went missing every year in the UK, so lots of people left for lots of different reasons. But the truth was, most missing persons cases were pretty mundane: teenage runaways, depressed middle-aged men, people in their twenties and thirties drowning under the weight of mortgages or unemployment, terrified of not being able to feed their kids. Often, the missing left without anything. They got up and walked away: wallets weren't taken, bank cards weren't touched, e-mails weren't sent. It wasn't the wallet that interested me, it was the way the house had been left.

All the signs of being a family home.

But none of the family.

11

Healy arrived back a couple of minutes later, at twelve-thirty, rain running off his jacket, hair matted to his scalp. When he saw Emily he paused at the doorway, as if he wasn't sure whether he was intruding on something. Then he seemed to realize it would now look even stranger if he backed out and closed the door, so he came in, shrugged off his coat and hung it up. He stank of booze and cigarettes, which meant he'd been at the pub since it opened. As far as first impressions went, it wasn't going to win any awards.

"Colm, this is Emily."

He came over, his eyes switching between us.

"Colm's a homeless Irishman I found wandering the streets."

"Ha ha," he replied, and shook hands with her. "Lovely to meet you, Emily." There was warmth in his voice, and it was probably fake, but she wouldn't have been able to tell. That was the thing with Healy: he could play the game with the best of them.

"Are you visiting?" she asked him.

"David's been kind enough to rent me a room for a while." He gave me a fleeting look. He'd offered to pay me rent countless times, but I'd always refused. Part of him, I'm sure, hated being a charity case, but he was realistic: he had no job, no savings, and he needed somewhere to stay. And, ultimately, if it wasn't for Healy, I'd already be in the ground. "How do you two know each other?" he asked.

I glanced at Emily.

"We were friends growing up," she said.

But he must have read something in her face—must have seen the real answer—because he made an *oh* with his mouth and started patting himself down, searching for his cigarettes. "Well, I'm going to leave you both to it," he said, and when he looked at me I could see a trace of guilt in his eyes; some hint that he'd been doing something he shouldn't have. I wondered what it was, wondered where he'd been since I'd got up, but let it go. I'd find out soon enough. Healy was a good liar, could evade and avoid, but I could read him better than anyone. I'd get to the truth.

He shook Emily's hand a second time and disappeared upstairs.

"He seems nice," she said.

Nice wasn't a word that got used much around Healy, but I agreed with her and moved the conversation on. "So, did the police have any leads?"

"None they talked to me about."

"No sightings of the four of them?"

"They said there were lots, but none that led anywhere."

"Who was your point of contact?"

She paused, opened up her bag and started searching around inside, taking out a small, brown leather diary. "To start with, it was . . ." She found it. "Colin Rocastle."

I went to write it down and then stopped, pen hovering above the piece of paper. *Rocastle.* He was the detective leading the investigation into the body on the beach. I remembered Healy mentioning him the day before, when he'd called to say the cops wanted to speak to everyone in the village. Rocastle probably worked out of Totnes—there was no CID department in Dartmouth anymore—which explained why he was at both scenes. Then a second thought emerged: what if they sent Rocastle because they needed someone experienced at the Lings' house, because there was something that required his nous? A family going missing was unusual, worrying, but until it became a kidnapping or a murder—and this disappearance never had—it wouldn't require a DCI.

I set the pen down. "You said the family lived in Buckfastleigh?"

"Just west of it, yes. A development called Harbourne Lake."

She gave me their address. I didn't know the area all that well, but I knew it was about twenty miles away, along some slow, narrow roads. Maybe not quite an hour, but close to it.

"Okay." I paused for a moment, staring down at the notes I'd made. Five months ago I was lying dead on a trolley. Now I was on the brink of returning to my old life, to the world of the lost. Somehow I expected to feel conflicted about it; instead all I felt was a subtle, magnetic pull. "Okay," I said again. "I'll take a look at the house tomorrow."

A smile broke on her face. "*Thank you*, David."

I held up a hand and the smile immediately dissolved again. "I'm not in the kind of condition you need someone to be in when they're finding the person you love. It's only been four weeks since my bandages came off." I paused, looked at her: she'd bowed her head slightly, perhaps because she thought this was all about to end in rejection. "I'll do some asking around," I said, and she looked up at me again, hope sparking in her eyes. "I'll find out as much as I can about what happened to Carrie,

Paul and the girls. But five months ago, doctors were busy reviving me. I'm still recovering. And if things go . . ."

I stopped.

If things go bad.

Emily was frowning at me, trying to figure out what it was I'd been about to say, and for a second I realized how much I'd changed in the four years I'd been doing this, how much I'd come to learn about the darkness in men. In her weakest moments she probably saw her sister's family dead in a ditch somewhere, inside a car that had never been found. Victims of an accident. Victims of fate, destiny, or whatever she believed in.

But I didn't see any of that.

I saw devils and executioners, men who felt nothing for the people they took, and even less for the families left behind. And the thing that frightened me the most was that I didn't even have to try hard to remember them.

I just had to close my eyes.

Roots

The taxi came up the road, sun glinting in its windshield, a silver crucifix dangling from its rearview mirror. The doctor sat on the porch and watched its approach. At first he couldn't see the women inside, both of them hidden behind the gray tint of the windows. But then, as the cab bumped on to the sidewalk at the bottom of the driveway, he spotted them, side by side in the backseat, and recalled again how different they both were.

Getting to his feet, he walked down to meet them, sun pressing against his back, beads of sweat instantly forming along his hairline. The day was hot—as hot as it had been all year—without even a hint of a breeze. Somewhere further out, in another part of the city, he could hear the distant wail of police sirens, but otherwise the only sound was the unending buzz of insects coming from the folds of the mountains behind the house.

As he got to the car, the rear doors opened on both sides and the women got out. On the side closest to him, Carrie Ling emerged from the cab, smiling at him. "Good morning," she said brightly and, as he greeted her back, the doctor moved around and opened the door for her daughter. Annabel Ling, crutches already in her hands, slid out of the car, smiling at him. He smiled back, held an arm out for her, and she used it to hoist herself up and out of the car, readying her crutches for the journey up the drive.

"And how are you ladies today?"

"We're good," Carrie said. "How are you, Eric?"

Eric Schiltz, temporarily distracted, watched Annabel move around the car: she barely needed her crutches to walk now. Her gait was a little stiff still, but she had good basic movement and her weight was being transferred evenly between legs. "I'm fine, thank you," he eventually said to Carrie, and then his eyes fell on Annabel again. "Even better seeing your daughter like this." When Annabel stopped at the bottom of the drive and looked back at them both, he said, "Why did I give you those crutches again, Belle?"

Annabel laughed. "It feels almost normal now."

"It looks almost normal too."

"Thank you, Eric," Carrie said to him, touching a hand to his arm.

He nodded. "Come. Let's get into the cool."

They headed inside, into a marble-floored foyer, where an air-conditioning unit, high up on one of the walls, hummed gently. Ahead of them, in the middle of the room, the stairs wound up and around to the second floor in a spiral; on the ground floor beyond, doorways led into a living room, kitchen and bedroom, then left into Dr. Schiltz's study.

"Wow," Carrie said. "What a beautiful home you have."

"Oh, that's very nice of you."

"How long have you lived here?"

"Here, in this house? About ten years. But I've been in the city for almost twenty-five. A lot of people don't like it here, especially in the summer—it can get up to one hundred and ten, one hundred and fifteen degrees in July and August." Schiltz gestured toward the air-conditioning unit. "But that's what they invented that thing for, right?"

He closed the front door.

"Okay. Let me give you the guided tour."

He led them around the house, first into the living room, which—via a set of wall-to-ceiling folding doors—opened out on to a deck and a swimming pool, and then into the adjoining kitchen, open plan, finished in marble and oak. All four bedrooms— one on the ground, three upstairs—were variations on the same color scheme, subtle pastels, with striped accessories, and then finally they all ended up back in the ground-floor foyer.

"And this is my study," he said.

Inside, a desk sat in front of a huge window, looking out over the foothills of the mountains. Like every other room, it was beautifully finished, although it felt less like it had been torn from the pages of a magazine, the walls lined with medical certificates and photographs, the desk home to an untidy in-tray, and a series of trophies earned out on the city's golf courses. "Sorry about the mess," he said to them, scooping up some papers and dumping them in the top tray. He pulled a couple of chairs out from the wall. "Let me go and get you something to drink."

While the women settled in, he went through to the kitchen and poured them both some lemonade, and when he got back, Annabel was standing, using the back of the chair as an anchor and slowly rolling her hips. He'd given her some exercises to do in order to build up her core strength, but she'd recovered even faster than he'd hoped.

"How's it feeling?" Schiltz asked.

Annabel smiled. "It feels really good."

He sat down at his desk, and both he and Carrie watched Annabel finish up her routine. When she was done, Carrie turned to him. "I can't even begin to thank you."

"Honestly, it's not me you have to thank."

She nodded. "I know. But . . ."

"It was my pleasure, Carrie."

Annabel sat down. *"Thank you, Dr. Schiltz."*

"If you call me Dr. Schiltz again, I'll have to put you back on the operating table and unfix you," Schiltz joked, searching his in-tray for a checklist he'd printed out that morning. *"I hope you'll both keep me up to date with how it's going once you get back."*

"We definitely will," Carrie said.

"When do you go?"

"Thursday."

"Two more days to get a killer suntan, then."

The women laughed.

"Sorry about this," Schiltz said, pulling the in-tray toward him. *"I printed out some things I need to go through before I can give you the final sign-off, and now it's gone missing."* He moved from tier to tier, unable to find it. *"Old age never comes gracefully."*

"Can we help?" Carrie asked.

"No, it's fine. I obviously went and left it somewhere this morning." He got up. *"You two make yourselves at home. If I don't return in five minutes, send a search party."*

He headed out into the living room, looking for the paperwork, checking drawers and cabinets, before moving to the kitchen. There was nothing in either room. He circled the decking area, even though he knew he hadn't been out to the pool that morning, then came back inside and headed upstairs. He didn't remember taking the checklist up to his room, but inside a couple of seconds he found it there, perched on his bedside cabinet.

"Old age really doesn't come gracefully," he said quietly.

Scooping up the form, he returned to the study.

As he entered, Annabel was in a standing position again, hands gripping the back of the chair, gently lifting her legs, one after the other, like a ballet dancer. Carrie had moved too: she was behind her daughter, standing at a cabinet in the corner, where eight photographs—all in frames, each frame different—were lined up on top. She had her back to Schiltz and was leaning toward one of the photos, phone in her hand at her side.

"I think I'm getting the hang of this," Annabel said.

He smiled. *"You'll be a ballerina before you know it."*

Carrie turned, surprise in her face, as if she hadn't realized Schiltz was back. But there was something else too. Something he couldn't put his finger on. Was it guilt? His eyes drifted to the photos. There was nothing worth seeing: just pictures of *friends and family, taken over the course of Schiltz's sixty-six years. He dropped the form on to the desk and moved across to where she was standing. She slipped her phone into her pocket and smiled warmly at him, and he started to wonder if he had read too much into her look.*

He took in the nearest photo: the eightieth anniversary of the golf club, him at the front with the runners-up trophy he'd won that day. He liked that photo. He looked good in it: slim and lean, not too gray, tailored suit jacket and a blue open-neck shirt.

"Are you jealous of my runners-up trophy?" he joked.

Carrie looked embarrassed now. "Sorry. I was being nosy."

"It's fine. Be as nosy as you like."

She nodded, her eyes returning to the photos. He watched her for a moment and saw her attention fall on a picture right at the back. "When was this taken?" she asked.

He reached for the photograph she was referring to and brought it toward them. The picture must have been over forty years old. Schiltz couldn't remember the last time he'd looked at it.

"Goodness," he said. "I'd forgotten this was even here."

"I like your fashion."

He smiled. "Pretty dashing, eh? I guess this must be the early 1970s."

"You were all friends?"

Schiltz looked at the three men in the picture, their arms linked around each other's shoulders. Schiltz was one of them, standing to the left. The picture had faded over time, become a little discolored and frayed at the edges, but the frame—and the photo's position away from the window—had helped to disguise the damage. "Yes," he said, finally. "Best friends."

"Are you still friends?"

"Definitely. They're like brothers to me." He studied the photograph for a long time, Carrie watching him, Annabel continuing her leg exercises. "I bought a scanner a few months back, so I could get all my old pictures on to computer before they started to get beyond repair. I've got so many, though, I've . . . well, kind of been putting it off."

"That's a good idea."

"To put it off?"

She smiled. "No, to scan them in."

He shrugged. "I don't want to lose these memories."

"Well, maybe you can start with this one."

"Yes," he said, his eyes moving between him and his friends. Finally, he returned her smile and placed the photograph back on top of the cabinet. "Maybe I can."

12

After Emily had gone, I walked through to the living room and sat down in a chair by the window. Like most of the furniture in the cottage, it had belonged to my parents, its arms marked by years of wear, the material worn thin, the pattern bleached by age. Outside, I could see Start Point lighthouse further along the coast, like a bone-white finger breaking out of the earth. Mostly, though, on this side of the house, all I could see was the garden.

I booted up my laptop, pulled a stool toward me, then googled the Ling family's disappearance. Nationally, it hadn't got much coverage. One single-column story in the *Daily Mail*; a short in the *Guardian* and *The Times*. Both were light on details and included the same soundbite from Rocastle, probably issued through a catch-all press release. There was nothing juicy about the story a day in, just a very basic framework of events, which was probably why coverage died out pretty much as soon as it had begun. If the police had given the press the house—everything untouched, TV still on, toys on the floor, spilled bottle of milk—they'd have generated some buzz, but it was a catch-22: they didn't want to release too much information too soon, as with any case, and the surface detail didn't intrigue the media enough for them to start digging deeper.

Local press coverage lasted longer, but hard information was thin on the ground, which meant either the police had kept the details locked down or—more likely—the case had quickly fizzled out. Ten and a half months down the line, with no sign of the family and no further updates for Emily, certainly suggested as much. Even so, there were a couple of things that nagged at me. The first was Rocastle, and his involvement in the case. The second was Paul Ling's wallet, and the amount of time it had taken for it to be returned. It could have been nothing. Extra caution on the part of the police, or maybe an administrative error. But seven months seemed a long time to hold on to it.

I turned back to the laptop.

On-screen was a front-page story from one of the local newspapers, the family's photo on the right, their faces clear even if the colors were washed out. Emily had given me their basic personal details, but it was good to put names to faces. At the back of the group was Paul Ling. Fifty-three. Balding. Mustache. Five or six inches taller than his wife, who was to his right, his arm around her. Carrie looked just like Emily: slim, small, dark hair, dark eyes, exactly the same smile. The only difference was that, at fifty, she was eight years older. To Paul Ling's left, also smiling, was Annabel. *Belle.* She was definitely more like her mother than her father; her frame a little bigger maybe, her hair a little lighter, but neither by much. Height-wise, she was midway between Carrie and Paul—probably five-eight—and had her hair up in a ponytail, revealing a beautiful face, full of gentle sweeps. In front of her—Annabel's hands on her shoulders—was Olivia, seventeen years younger than her sister at just eight, but much more like Paul.

"Your girlfriend gone?"

Healy stood in the doorway closest to me, which led out of the living room to the stairs. He'd showered and changed, but still smelled of booze. I didn't bother responding.

He came further in and collapsed on to the sofa opposite me.

"Is she why you won't speak to Liz?"

I looked at him. "You don't know what you're talking about."

"She was an ex, though, right?"

I didn't reply.

"Emily, I mean."

"I know who you meant, Healy."

"So was she?"

"Was she what?"

"An ex?"

"Why do you care?"

His gaze lingered on me. "You need to tell Liz."

I closed the laptop. Said nothing.

"You owe her," he said.

"Owe her what?"

"An explanation."

"Is that her talking—or you?"

"I don't know," he said, leaning back. "I just know I chat with her, and whatever you think's happened between you, she needs to hear it." He stopped. Looked at me. Slowly, something changed in his face; something softer, less severe. "It reminds me of . . ."

"Of what?"

"Of a place I've been before."

He meant his marriage. He meant the terrible mistakes he'd made. And he meant the aftermath, when the case he was on was falling apart, when his wife and kids told him they hated him, and when the last conversation he ever had with Leanne, his daughter, was a screaming match that ended with her storming out. Ten months later, he found her dead in a room full of so much suffering I sometimes wondered how he slept at night.

I nodded that I understood and then watched him for a moment, half formed in the dull light of the living room. This version of Healy—this quiet rendering of him—was the one I was always trying to get at because it was the part of him I liked. He didn't show it often but, when he did, it felt like a call for help; as if, subliminally, he wanted this part of himself to be pulled to the surface.

"I'll try and call her tomorrow," I said.

He nodded. "I think she'd appreciate that."

"And you?"

"What about me?"

"You know what I mean, Healy."

He shrugged. "She's your girlfriend, not mine."

And yet, even as he said it, even as he raised his defenses again and began to look more familiar, something of the other Healy remained. Somewhere in his face there was a bleakness, as if the thought of me sorting things out with Liz—or, more likely, me telling her it was definitely over—had shifted things into focus. The calls would stop. She wouldn't need Healy anymore. And whatever she'd brought to his life would be gone.

"I'm going out," he said.

I watched him disappear into the kitchen, listened to him open and close the front door, and then opened the laptop again. The photograph of the Lings popped back into view. Close in on the four faces. Carrie. Paul. Annabel. Olivia. My eyes moved between them, one after the other, back and forth.

Father. Mother. Daughters.

Something seemed more obvious this time.

Paul was Asian. As I'd been walking her back to her car, Emily had mentioned that his parents were from Hong Kong and had moved here two years before he was born. Carrie was Caucasian. Olivia was a good mix of the two: Asian in and around the eyes, the cheeks, in the soft triangle of the chin; Caucasian in the center of her face and her bone structure. But Annabel wasn't like that at all. She looked exactly like her mum: one hundred percent Caucasian, with no hint of her father.

Nothing in the cheeks. Nothing in the eyes.

Nothing of Paul Ling at all.

13

Early the next day, I got up and found Healy was already awake, sitting next to the open window in a vest, smoking. Cold air escaped into the house, but the wind and rain were gone and, in the skies above the sea, narrow slivers of blue broke between clouds.

As soon as I entered the kitchen, he nodded in the direction of the kettle. "Water's just boiled," he said. "We've run out of coffee. I'll go and get some later."

After making myself a mug of tea, I sat down opposite him.

"Emily's family went missing."

He looked at me, nodded, but didn't say anything.

"Her sister, brother-in-law, their two daughters."

"Where did they go missing from?"

"From their home. She reckoned their place was like a time capsule: the TV was still on, he'd left his computer running, the younger girl's toys were all over the floor, food still in the oven, dog still wandering around the house. Like they'd just stepped out."

He finished his cigarette and pulled the window shut.

"You working for her?"

"I said I'd do some asking around."

A hint of a smile on his face, one whose meaning we both got: *You say that now but wait until this starts to go deeper. Before long, it'll be just like all the other cases. And you won't be able to let go.*

"Do you want to come along today?" I asked him.

"Where are you going?"

"Buckfastleigh. To see the house."

He looked at me, left hand—wedding band still on—flat to the table; right hand clamped around a mug of tea. "Yeah, all right," he said, finally. "Let me get changed."

We took Healy's car so I could make a couple of calls on the way. The first was to Spike, an old contact from my days as a journalist. Originally from Russia, Spike had come here on a student visa, but when that ran out he'd stayed on illegally. That wasn't the only law he'd broken. Spike was like a skeleton key: as a hacker, he accessed names, addresses, e-mails and phone numbers for me, never leaving a footprint. I'd used his talent, such as it was, more than ever since my change of career, especially in the early stages of a case when I was trying to build a picture of the missing, and the life they'd left behind.

"Pawn shop," he said when he answered.

"Is that with an *a-w* or an *o-r*?"

A moment of confusion. "*David?*"

"How you doing, Spike?"

"*Man*, how are you?"

Spike's accent always made me smile. It was barely recognizable as Russian now, completely Americanized except for a soft European lilt.

"I'm good," I said. "It's been a while."

"I read about you online. You okay now?"

"I'm fine."

"That's good, man, that's good."

"Listen, I need your help on something."

"Anything."

We were a couple of miles from the Lings' house, negotiating our way through the western fringes of Buckfastleigh. I had the phone on speaker so Healy was looped in. Working with someone wasn't exactly a new experience for him, yet it had been a long time since anyone at the Met had trusted him enough to partner up. But if he was rusty, I was rustier. I'd spent my life, as a journalist and then an investigator, working alone. On the two occasions I'd tethered myself to someone, it had been Healy, and both times it had gone bad. I'd asked him to get involved here because, when he was good, he was seriously good; he offered a feel for a case you couldn't teach. But there was a flipside, an inherent risk: that, sooner or later, he'd lose control and everything would go south. If he was involved in something else, trying to dig deeper into the body on the beach, this was a good way to keep him close and to lessen any damage.

"Spike, I need a full background on someone. Two people, actually. A couple." I gave him as much as Emily had passed across on Paul and Carrie. "Absolutely everything you can dig up, stick it in the file. Work, credit histories, repayments, bank accounts . . ."

"You got it."

"I'll need their cell phone records, and their landline—the last six months of 2011 and January this year for both financials and phones. Actually, you can throw a third name into the mix as well. Annabel

Ling." I thought for a moment about including Olivia. But she was eight. She didn't have a phone, a bank account, wouldn't own or pay into anything. It seemed pointless. "One other thing: when you source the phone records, if you can also get street addresses for the incoming and outgoing calls, that'd be great."

"Consider it done."

"Actually, I lied: that wasn't the last thing."

"What else?"

"I need access to their e-mails too." Unsurprisingly, Emily didn't have the login details for any of the Lings' e-mail accounts—Paul, Carrie and Annabel all had their own—but she *was* able to give me the addresses, which would be more than enough for Spike. I read them out to him. "Passwords for those accounts would be useful."

"You got it."

"Thanks, Spike."

"By the way, I've shifted my bank account."

Spike's bank account was a locker at the local sports center. He gave me the pin number for it and, when we were done, I'd leave the cash there for him to collect. For obvious reasons he wanted to stay out of the banks and off the taxman's radar.

"Fine," I said. "I'm not in London at the moment, but give me the details and, once I'm back, I'll deposit whatever it is I owe you. You know I'll be good for it."

"I do. It's great to have you back, David."

"Thanks, Spike."

I hung up just as Healy pulled off the A38 into a narrow lane with signposts for Harbourne Lake. Two minutes further on, we found a cluster of five houses, obscured by trees, all of them old fishermen's cottages but renovated beautifully in the same style: thatched roofs, gleaming whitewashed walls, colored doors and matching window shutters, immaculate gardens with driveways leading up to recently added extensions, all of it finished in a patchwork of sandy brick. The lake itself was about a mile long by about half a mile wide, unfurling beyond the houses, and the views were stunning, even as autumn slowly gave way to winter: reedbeds and marshes; red berries dotted like perfect drops of blood along the banks; gulls, terns and warblers drifting across the surface of the water, which, with no wind, was like glass.

The houses were roughly laid out in a triangle, the Lings' house furthest back from the road, at the apex. Both cars—a blue BMW X3 and a black Golf GTI—were still on the drive, presumably where they'd been since the family went missing on January 7. Emily hadn't arrived yet, so Healy bumped on to the pavement and I made the second call.

This one was to another old contact.

Ewan Tasker was a semiretired former police officer who'd gone on to work for the National Criminal Intelligence Agency, its successor SOCA, and then as an adviser at SOCA's replacement, the National Crime Agency. Our relationship had originally been built on mutual understanding: he fed me stories on organized crime that he wanted out in the open, and I was always the one that got to break them first. But, over time, we began to become more friendly and, after I left journalism to nurse Derryn through her last year, it had solidified into friendship. These days I had no way to repay him for his help, other than money, which he would never accept. So my penance was a charity golf day once a year at his club. It was double the fun for him: he raised money and got to laugh at me.

"Raker!" he said, as he answered the phone.

"Task—how's things?"

"Good. I can still go to the toilet by myself, so obviously that's a massive bonus." He laughed, but—even at sixty-three—he was in great condition. "How's the stomach?"

He'd come to visit me in the days after I'd been stabbed.

"It's getting there."

"It takes time."

"Yeah. I need some of whatever you're taking."

He laughed again. "So, you back on the job?"

"Kind of."

"Sounds mysterious."

"Not really. I'm just helping out a friend, said I'd do a bit of hunting around for her. I was wondering whether you might be able to get hold of a couple of things for me."

"As long as you don't forget your debts."

"December 18, right?"

"Right. Injuries or not, you're playing."

It was the date of the next charity golf day. I was paired with Tasker's wife, who—like him—played off a single-figure handicap. I was going to get annihilated.

"I'll be there," I said to him.

"Good. So how can I help?"

I gave him some background on the disappearance of the Lings, and then cut to the chase: "First off, I'd like to take a look at the original missing persons report."

"That's easy enough."

"I was also hoping you could run their names, their home address and their car registrations through the PNC, the PND and HOLMES. To be honest, I'm pretty sure all you'll find is that original missing persons report, but it's an avenue I want to close off."

All three were databases: PNC held convictions, cautions and arrests, individuals who were wanted or missing, vehicles registered in the UK, and stolen property; PND allowed regional police forces to access each other's data immediately, rather than having to wait for the information request to filter through weeks later; while HOLMES was the system forces used to cross-check major crimes. The family's prints—and any other prints found at the house—would also be in NAFIS, the national fingerprint database. But, as it synced up with PNC, if the police had lifted anything from the house that led to anyone or anything, we'd probably already know.

"Leave it with me," he said.

"I appreciate it, old man."

I killed the call just as Emily's Suzuki emerged from the lane. Healy looked out to where the vehicle was approaching, and then back to me. "I could have got you that."

"Got me what?"

"That information."

"The missing persons file?"

He nodded. "I've got guys right there."

"You don't work for the police anymore, Healy."

The mood changed instantly. "What?"

"I didn't mean it like that," I said, trying to head him off. If I looked at him sometimes and caught a glimpse of another man, the one I liked, the one who had saved my life, I looked at him just as often and saw this version: angry and unwilling to cede any kind of control to anyone. "Number one rule is to insulate yourself. You know that. You don't need me to *tell* you that. Task can get us the information we need on the Lings—but the most important thing is he can get it without raising any flags."

"Don't patronize me."

I rolled my eyes. "I'm not patronizing you."

"These are people I've known for *years*."

"You know we'd still be taking a risk."

"How?"

"Involving them is a *risk*, Healy."

He turned to me. "How's it risk? Because this *Task* you speak to used to work for SOCA and my guys are just regular cops? That makes him *better* somehow? Give me a fucking break. My guys are there at the coalface, they've got the computers *right there*. They're not sitting in semiretirement with the cigars out and their feet up on the desk."

"Task still advises three days a week at—"

"Whatever."

"Look, Healy—"

"No, *you* look, you self-important little prick. I've been doing this for twenty-six years. I was a cop while you were still getting a hard-on for your English teacher."

Silence settled between us.

As Emily got out of her car, Healy started to do the same. But then I grabbed his arm and pulled him back in. "Listen to me," I said, ignoring the look on his face, and leaned in. "You'd better not screw this up for me."

"Let go of my fucking arm."

He tried to wrestle free of my grip but I held on. "Listen. You got fired from the police. Those people there you call friends, colleagues, whatever they were to you—they aren't going to go out to bat for you, because they don't want to end up like you. I know, one hundred percent, I can rely on Tasker. No mistakes. No trails. Can you say that about the men you know? Can you say it with absolute certainty?" I paused. He just looked at me. "I asked you along because I thought you could help. But if this is how it's going to be, if this is what I'm going to have to deal with, you can pack your bags and go home."

We stayed like that for a moment.

And then I let go, got out of the car, and went and met Emily.

14

Immediately inside the front door, the house opened up into an entrance hall. High ceilings angled in toward a glass dome, light pouring through from above. Off to the left was the staircase. Ahead of us, expensive oak floors ran the length of the property, branching out into a kitchen and a living room. To our right was a door through to a study, which, as I moved further in, I could see connected with the living room through an open archway.

The house had been cleaned and cleared up, and looked immaculate. But it wouldn't have looked like this the day the family went missing. It would have been a mess then. Food on the stove. TV and computer on. Toys on the floor. I headed for the kitchen, a big, airy room with portholes running across one wall that looked out over the lake, and a black high gloss and brushed steel finish. Marble counters. Expensive wall mosaics. Built-in fridge, freezer, dishwasher and washer-dryer.

Behind me, I felt Emily move in, Healy drifting off into the study.

I stood at the sink and looked out over the garden. Compared to the size of the house, it was relatively understated. A square of lawn, a terraced area, a series of patio slabs with pot plants on them and then, right at the bottom, a black and red kennel.

"What happened to the dog?"

She fell in beside me. "I'm looking after her."

"And she was just wandering around the house when you got here?"

"I opened the front door," she said, nodding along the hallway, "and she came out of the kitchen toward me. Her bowl was full, so they must've only just fed her."

As I tried to imagine what the kitchen might have looked like the night Emily turned up, my eyes drifted to the fridge. It was pushed in under a marble counter, next to the freezer. Somewhere on the floor in front of it had been a bottle of spilled milk.

There were two possibilities: it had fallen out accidentally when Carrie or Paul or one of the girls had opened the fridge door; or one of them had been holding it and then dropped it—maybe out of surprise. Ultimately, they both led in the same direction: why was the bottle just left there, on the floor, untouched? The only logical explanation was that, moments after the milk spilled all over the kitchen, the family had left the house.

Either by choice.

Or by force.

A second door led out of the kitchen and into the living room, which then looped back around to the study. Healy was in the living room, on his haunches in front of a bookshelf full of DVDs and ornaments. I wandered through, casting a glance over the room, then moved on to the study. It was compact and nicely furnished: oak desk, top-of-the-line PC sitting in the center surrounded by a wireless printer, external hard drive and CD tower. Cut into alcoves in the wall behind it were bookshelves. I stepped in closer. Most of the contents seemed to be related to Paul's work—medical encyclopedias, journals, countless books on pediatrics—but on the top shelf was a small selection of Chinese books in plain black covers, symbols running the length of the spines.

Emily was standing in the doorway through to the living room.

"You said Paul's parents were from Hong Kong?"

She nodded at me.

"So, did he speak Cantonese?"

"A little."

"But not much?"

She wandered through and followed my eyes to the books. "He was born here, but he was always interested in where his family came from. He took Carrie and the girls back to Hong Kong a couple of times, to see some of his parents' family. He always said his Cantonese was bad." She smiled. "But it sounded pretty good to me."

My eyes drifted back to a picture of the family on the shelf in front of the books. The four of them seemed happy enough, appeared to be pretty close-knit, and normally I wouldn't have read into it anything more than that. Pictures were just doors that returned me to certain points in time—to how the missing had looked, physically, before they left. Beyond that, more often than not they were lies: smiles that only lasted the blink of a shutter; a frown as someone was caught off guard; the blank, emotionless gaze of the unaware. Yet this photograph was, in its own way, quite revealing: Annabel was standing to the side of her father, arm around his waist, and the difference between them was starker than ever; more even than in the picture I'd seen of them the previous day. There was nothing, not even a tiny hint of him, in her. No physical traits. No sign of his heritage.

"Mind if I ask you something?"

Emily shook her head. "Of course not."

"Why was it Paul and Carrie had to go the IVF route?"

She frowned as if she didn't understand the relevance.

"In this photo"—I held it up to her—"in pretty much every photo I've looked at of the four of them, I'm not seeing a lot of Paul in Annabel."

She got it then. "Oh."

"Did they use a sperm donor?"

Her eyes moved across the room to where Healy had wandered in. He'd finished his run-through of the living room. He looked between us, saw that we were in the middle of something, and backed out of the study. A couple of seconds later, he was opening and closing kitchen drawers.

"Yes," she said finally.

"They used a sperm donor?"

"Yes."

"Both times?"

She understood where this was going: *I'm not seeing a lot of Paul in Annabel, but Olivia* . . . "The two of them wanted kids, pretty much from the start, but they found out inside six months that Paul had a low sperm count. Carrie was never that . . . ambitious. She never wanted a career, she was never concerned with money, particularly. What she wanted, above all else, was to start a family. He came from a big family—two brothers, who are back in Hong Kong now, and a ton of cousins—so I suppose it felt pretty natural for him too. He was twenty-eight, she was only twenty-five, but they were ready by then."

"So, after he got the news—"

"They were referred to an IVF clinic down in Plymouth. The specialist there said their best—probably only—option was a donor. They didn't think about it for very long."

"Why didn't they try to find an Asian donor?"

"They did, but . . ." She looked around the study and then out of a square of window in the corner of the room. "In the eighties, Devon wasn't what you would call 'multicultural.'"

"They didn't think about going elsewhere?"

"To another clinic?"

"Right. Somewhere with more options."

"I'm not sure. I guess they probably talked about it, but after the disappointment of finding out about Paul, and then all the consultations and the paperwork, I think they just wanted to get on with it. Plus, I'm not sure it bothered Paul, really. It wasn't like Asian culture was massively ingrained in him; his background was important to him, but he was born here, he'd lived here all his life, this was his home. I don't think he saw himself as English, or British, or Chinese. He just saw himself as Paul Ling. This was the country he was in; Carrie was the woman he married. In the end, all that mattered to him—to both of them—was to have a baby, to have a family, and to start something special." There was a tremor in her voice toward the end, but there were no tears. Maybe, almost a year down the line, she'd cried herself out. "In any case," she went on, "I don't imagine any parent loves their child for the way it looks. None of that matters once they're born."

"So, what changed the second time around?"

She looked at me. "What do you mean?"

"Did it suddenly matter to Paul that his child looked like him?"

"No," she said. "I don't think so. But there was a seventeen-year gap between Belle and Liv, and in seventeen years the clinic had managed to attract a wider range of donors. So, this time, the option was there for them and they decided to go for it."

I nodded, got out a new notebook I'd bought that morning, and took down some of what she'd said. "Why wait seventeen years?"

"To have Olivia?"

"Carrie would have been—what?—forty-two?"

"Right."

"Why wait until her forties?"

"Why not?"

I shrugged. "Higher risks, lower success rate. Plus, you said she wasn't career-orientated, so it wasn't like she was invested in whatever job it was she was doing."

Her eyes were fixed on the photograph, caught in a memory somewhere. Maybe something Carrie had said to her. Maybe some reason for waiting seventeen years.

"Emily?"

She started slightly and looked at me. "They were happy with just one, and then, when she hit her forties, Carrie started to feel a pull for a second. It happens."

I studied her, but if she was hiding something else, it was well disguised. I let it go for the moment, finished my notes and told her I was going upstairs to look around.

Paul and Carrie's bedroom was done out in a warm cream, with built-in wardrobes and a huge oak bed. I went through their bedside cabinets, pulled a couple of storage boxes out from under the bed and sifted through their closets. Everything was neat and tidy: shoes lined up in the wardrobes, clothes folded into piles on shelves, expensive, name-brand clothes on hangers. It was obvious someone—almost certainly Emily—had been through the house in the months after the family disappeared, tidying all the rooms up.

The bedroom had a connecting, again spotlessly clean, which included a black-and-white-tiled wet room. Matching towels were stacked in an alcove, like a set of dominos. Next to that was a bathroom cabinet. I opened it up and looked inside. Deodorants. Hand creams. Sometimes prescription medication could give you an in, but there was nothing like that. The closest the Lings had was a bottle of Calpol and some cough mixture.

I moved to the next bedroom.

Annabel's.

Like her parents, it was pretty understated. Cream walls, no posters now she was in her twenties, no toys, no games. This was, as expected, a room belonging to an adult. On one wall were three bookshelves, a mix of paperbacks and research tomes. I stepped in closer. Brecht. Stanislavski. Books with names like *Directing a Stage Play* and *Set Design*. I remembered Emily saying Annabel was teaching drama between applying for other jobs. There was no way to gauge for sure because I didn't know any of the family, and only really knew Carrie as a memory, but I started to wonder whether part of the reason Annabel might not have been able to get a full-time job was because she didn't really want one. Maybe she didn't try as hard as she could have. Maybe because teaching kids drama was all she really wanted to do.

There were three big wardrobes full of clothes. As in Paul and Carrie's, everything was neat and tidy. When I closed the doors on the last of them, I felt a pang of frustration. It was easy to understand Emily's mind-set. I completely got her reasons for going over everything, for putting the family's things back in place as if readying it for some kind of homecoming. It was an emotional response, a practical one too. But there was no sense now of how the house had been left. Anything that had been even slightly out of place in the days after the four of them went missing had been put right. The previous night, Emily had said the house was like a museum when she'd got there on the day they vanished. But she'd got it the wrong way around: *this* was the museum, everything arranged and composed as if it were some kind of show home. Now there was no going back to the way it had been left on January 7.

Before I headed across to Olivia's room, I booted up Annabel's Mac-Book, which was sitting on a corner table with a printer to the side. I had a quick search around but then decided to take a closer look when I got it home, so shut it down again and took it with me.

Olivia's room seemed the most incongruous: posters of boy bands on the walls, a Disney Princess clock, a *High School Musical* duvet and curtain set in a cabin bed with stickers dotted all over it—but no mess. It was the bedroom of an eight-year-old if the eight-year-old never played in it. Toys had been put into giant boxes, or into a two-door fitted wardrobe. When I went through the wardrobe, there were clothes on one side and even more toys, also in boxes, on the other. Like her sister she had a laptop, except this one was another toy: chunky red plastic, yellow keyboard, small ten-inch screen and a camera—molded to look like a caterpillar—sprouting from the right-hand side. It sat on a desk that pulled out from under the cabin bed, alongside pencil tins and safety scissors.

When I got back downstairs, Healy was busy disconnecting the computer in Paul Ling's study. As he started coiling the leads, I told him not to bother. My parents had an old PC at the cottage, along with all the connections. We could use that, and plug the tower into their CRT. Wobbling slightly as he hoisted it up off the desk, he took the tower to the car, and I placed Annabel's laptop alongside it. Then I headed back into the house and did another sweep, making sure I hadn't missed anything.

As I came back around to the front door, a feeling nagged at me. *This is the place they disappeared from.* Most of the time, in the cases I took on, the victims' houses were part of the journey; a stop-off in which I familiarized myself with them. But with the Lings it was different. This wasn't a stop-off.

This was the entire case.

15

After telling Emily I'd call her as soon as I had any updates, we drove home in silence. Healy had never been big on apologies, even when he knew he was wrong, so I let local radio fill the gap in conversation. The DJ was talking about the body on the beach.

Heading up the narrow lane toward the cottage, I caught a brief glimpse of a figure on my driveway—the bob of a head, the flash of a vehicle—before they were gone from view again. But ten seconds later, I found out who it was. "Rocastle," Healy said, nodding toward a gray-haired man standing at the front door. He turned as he heard us pull in through the gates, eyes narrowing, frown forming. "Plainclothes officer" had to be the biggest misnomer going: even in civvies, cops rarely looked like anything other than cops. The way they dressed, their facial expressions, their body language, it was all a dead giveaway, and Rocastle was the dictionary definition of police. He watched the car come all the way in, eyes never leaving me, then started a slow, cautious approach.

I got out.

He looked from me to Healy and then back again, and started fiddling around in his jacket pocket for his warrant card. I saved him a job. "That's fine, DCI Rocastle."

He halfheartedly smiled his thanks.

"I was hoping I could chat with you about the recent events on the beach, Mr. Raker. Nothing sinister. As I said to Mr. Healy yesterday, we're canvassing the whole village."

I told him that was fine and, after he and Healy had greeted each other, we headed inside, leaving the computers in the car. He might not have thought anything of it if we'd popped the trunk and got them out. But he might. Often, the early stages of my cases were about dancing around the police, about getting a feel for their involvement in the lives of the people I was trying to find—and only then approaching them. Rocastle had been at the Lings' house in the hours after they'd gone missing, so I wanted to talk to him just as much as he wanted to talk to me. But he was an experienced cop, and they were always the most controlled; less prone to slip-ups. They had a feel for the flow of conversation and where it was headed, and if he saw it going somewhere he didn't like he'd shut it down. I doubted Rocastle would tell me anything about

January 7 purely out of choice. So the computers stayed where they were because they would give him pause for thought, and how you got at men like Rocastle was basically how you got at anyone.

You cornered them.

Rocastle and Healy talked in general terms about the body on the beach, but, as I'd expected, Rocastle sidestepped anything important. In a weird reverse of how he'd been the previous day, Healy hardly seemed interested in the answers he got and I remembered again how he'd disappeared for hours at a time the day before. Whether this was all an act for Rocastle or not, I didn't know, but I wanted the truth. Without it, I risked him contaminating the search for the Lings with the fallout from whatever he was doing.

I made us all coffee, and then Rocastle and I sat at the kitchen table. He got out a pen and a pad and sat them perfectly parallel to one another, while Healy remained at the front door, which was slightly ajar, leaning against the frame while he smoked. Rocastle started off by talking blandly about what they'd found on the beach, but most of it was what had already been reported in the media, probably because he was the one who'd signed off the press release. But then, about a minute in, as he danced around a potential revelation about the condition of the body, a thought came to me: *Why send Rocastle up here?* He was a DCI, probably ten years past door-to-doors. I quickly considered the reasons: a lack of manpower, or at least a lack of *available* manpower, but that seemed doubtful given the gravity of the crime; perhaps he was the kind of SIO that liked a firm hand on the tiller, one who didn't fully trust anyone's instinct but his own; but much more likely was that he'd picked and chosen which people he wanted to interview in the village.

And, for whatever reason, I'd made the cut.

"So, I'm asking everyone this," he began, flipping open the front page of his pad. It had no notes in it at all, although slivers of paper remained in the spiral binding where he'd recently torn them out. Sometimes the clearest picture of a person came from the smallest things: the way he'd set his pen and paper down parallel to one another pointed toward a meticulous mind; the way he'd torn out the last notes in the pad—as if to keep them away from prying eyes—suggested a suspicious one too. He looked at me. "Could you tell me what you were doing on or around Monday afternoon this week?"

It was Thursday now. Healy had found the body on Tuesday. So police obviously believed, probably on the advice of the pathologist, that it had either washed up or been dumped twenty-four hours before that. He'd have had a hard job narrowing down time of death if the body parts had been in water for long; "immersion" meant skin started to wrinkle and loosen during the first week, and by the second week it started to detach completely. The fact he'd been able to be so accurate meant Healy's theory could have been right.

The body had been frozen.

"I was here," I said.

"At home?"

"All day. Healy can back me up on that."

Rocastle looked over his shoulder. Healy nodded.

"Why did you move down here?"

"I like it down here."

"You didn't have any particular reason?"

"My parents lived in the village. This was their house."

He nodded, making more notes. I flicked a glance at what he was writing, but it looked like it was some sort of shorthand—except I knew shorthand and I couldn't decipher it. *A system only he can translate: a way to disguise his thoughts.*

"So you weren't down in the village at all?"

"No."

"And you didn't see anything?"

"As in?"

"As in, anything worth reporting."

I frowned. "Like I just said, I was here all day."

"So that's a no?"

"Obviously it's a no."

He nodded, made some notes. "You don't look bedridden."

"What do you mean by that?"

"I'm just wondering why you stayed inside all day on Monday."

I studied him. I was tempted to say *Because I wanted to*, but it was best I kept him onside for the moment. "Some days I still feel tired."

"How do you mean?"

I lifted up my T-shirt, and for a moment Rocastle looked surprised. Then he saw the pink scarring on my stomach. "It's been five months. Sometimes it's still painful."

"I see." He glanced at his pad. "So you're sure?"

"About what?"

"That you didn't see anything?"

He wrote something else down, on a fresh line and in a fresh jumble of words. I glanced at Healy for a moment, and in his face I saw the same expression I must have had. *He's trying to lead me somewhere.* Finally, when Rocastle looked up, there was nothing in his face. An unreadable blank.

"Mr. Raker?"

"What?"

"You're absolutely positive you didn't see anything?"

But now he'd tilted the question in a different direction. No longer an attempt to bait me, or even really an accusation. Just an innocent point of clarification. I studied him for a second time, trying to decide exactly what his play was—and then it came to me.

"Mr. Raker?"

"You already knew I'd been stabbed."

"I'm sorry?"

"You already knew all about me."

A flash of something in his face—just a split second of reaction—but there long enough for me to see that I'd been right. He'd done background checks on all the people in the village—and I'd been the one with a file. The missing people I'd found, the killers I'd ended up hunting, the detectives I'd had to cross. All my statements, all the lies I'd weaved and managed to convince them of, there in black and white. I wasn't sure if he'd come here because he saw something in my past that suggested I might be capable of killing a person and dumping them out to sea, or whether he'd come as some kind of warning. *We know who you are. We know what you do. Stay the hell away.*

He leaned forward. "I'm going to level with you, Mr. Raker. I *do* know about you. I'm not sure if what's in the database is everything. I guess only you and"—he glanced back over his shoulder—"perhaps Mr. Healy know whether you were one hundred percent honest with the Met."

He waited for an answer that didn't come.

"You have a habit of getting involved in cases that don't seem to have a hell of a lot to do with you." A pause. A shrug of the shoulders. He glanced at Healy again, as if giving him the chance to answer on my behalf. "Maybe you have a strong opinion on that, or maybe you don't—but ultimately I don't really care. For your opinion, *or* for those cases. Because those cases weren't here. I don't want to sound uncaring for my fellow boys in blue up north and in the Met, but I frankly couldn't give a rat's arse about their crime scenes. But I give a rat's arse about mine. Are we both clear on that, David?"

David now. Trying to make himself seem like a good guy, someone reasonable. But it was clumsy psychology, the first amateurish thing he'd done since he'd arrived.

"Mind if I ask you something?" I said.

The response took him by surprise, but he did a good job of disguising it. His eyes narrowed slightly and then he set his pen down next to his pad. Adjusted it. Looked up.

"Does the name Carrie Ling ring any bells with you?"

"Who?"

"Carrie Ling. She and her family disappeared on January 7."

A look on his face like he genuinely had no idea who I was talking about.

"She used to live here in the village."

He shook his head.

"Her sister arrives to find the front door unlocked and everything still on: TV, computer, food cooking on the stove, the whole thing. Except the family is missing."

A flash of recognition.

"You remember them now?"

He nodded. "Yeah. I remember them. What about them?"

Apart from a momentary lapse, he'd conducted this whole thing perfectly. Given nothing away. Made his point. Now he'd turned the conversation around again: no longer on the defensive, but forcing me to reveal my hand. "Do you think there's any link?"

"Between what?"

I smiled. *He's playing dumb.* "Between the Lings and the body."

He stared at me, shrugged. "Why would there be a link?"

"I don't know. I'm just thinking aloud."

"Anything's possible. But we're talking about a family that lived twenty miles from here. Does every case within a twenty-mile radius have to be linked to this one?"

"She used to live here, in the village."

"A long time ago, as I recall."

"True."

"Are you telling me you're working for them—is that it?"

"No one's working for them—they've never been found."

His eyes narrowed. "That sounds like a sly dig, David."

"It was just interesting that you were involved in both cases."

A smirk passed briefly across his face, and he leaned in toward me. "Look, you're a clever guy. That's probably why everyone at the Met hates you. But you're barking up the wrong tree. There's no link and there's no grand conspiracy. I don't care if you're looking into that family's disappearance. I really don't. What I care about is closing my case, and if you're getting in my way—and given your history, you can't blame me for coming up here to make sure you're not—you're making life complicated for me, and *that's* when we have a problem."

We sat facing each other in silence for a moment, and then he got to his feet, pushed his chair under the table and started buttoning up his coat.

"Would you be willing to share anything on the Lings—"

"Thanks for your time." He pushed a business card across the table. "If you think of anything that might be useful, do let me know. Otherwise, let us do our jobs."

After he left and we'd heard his car leave the driveway, Healy came over and sat at the table, fingers opening and closing the lid of his cigarette packet.

"So what do you make of him?"

I watched Rocastle's car—a dark blue Volvo—weave its way down through the lanes toward the beach, where, just marks against the shingle, the same uniforms were positioned at equal intervals, preventing people from getting close to the rocks.

"Raker?"

"I think he's smart."

"Cocky, you mean."

"Not cocky. Just smart."

"You in love?"

"We've had our fight for today, so you can suffer this next bit in silence because I don't want another." I paused, saw anger flare in his eyes, but pushed on. "Whatever it is you're getting involved in, whether you're trying to prove something to yourself or you think they've missed something you picked up, tread carefully. Rocastle won't get near you when you're on your game, Colm—but if you're off it, he'll nail you to the wall."

"You can't speak to me like that."

"Just think about it, okay?"

"I've thought about it."

And then he got up, grabbed his coat and headed out.

16

I set up Paul Ling's PC and Annabel's MacBook in the living room, put some coffee on and started going through them. Paul's desktop pointed toward a tidy mind: a series of applications on the left, then a line of folders with names like "Photos," "Receipts," "MA" and "Research papers." I went through them methodically. The folder of photos turned out to be shots from a conference he'd done the October before the family disappeared. The folder marked "Research papers" was a mixture of papers he'd submitted as part of his ongoing studies, and articles he'd written for the *Lancet* and the *British Medical Journal.* The "MA" folder was just a page of notes, most of which seemed to be about the Soviet Union in the late 1940s and early 1950s. It was just a list of historical events, detailing how the country had seized its opportunity after the Second World War. I didn't know what it related to, but there was a section headed "Medical care" toward the bottom of the page, so I figured Paul must have been in the middle of constructing something.

Next, I fired up the browser and went through his history. Two weeks before the family disappeared it had been Christmas, so the trail back to the beginning of December was full of online retailers. When I clicked on the links it clearly pointed in the direction of gifts Paul and Carrie Ling had got for their girls. One of them was the chunky red plastic laptop, with the caterpillar camera, I'd seen in Olivia's room. The MacBook that was now sitting in front of me had been bought for Annabel for Christmas: there were a series of links in Paul Ling's history to the exact same model, and when I checked Safari on the MacBook I saw Annabel's history only went back as far as Christmas Day.

Clearly, the Lings weren't struggling for money.

In just two weeks Annabel had visited almost as many sites as her father had in two months, but there weren't many surprises. Facebook and Twitter, Reddit, Tumblr, Pinterest. The MacBook had remembered her username and password for both Facebook and Twitter, so I went in and looked around. On Facebook she'd had 1,123 friends, and scores of them had posted to her wall pleading for her, and her family, to come home. Her last status update had been on the morning of January 7, before she'd headed off to work: *Looking forward to teaching my fab 11yo's today!* Previous updates were just the same: work, nights out, funny things she'd found. Nothing to suggest any problems.

I went through Twitter doing the same checks, looking for tiny inconsistencies, for posts that didn't sit right, for anything that struck me as odd—but after ten minutes I moved on. I went through her folders, through her hard drive, applications, cookies, cache. Nothing. As I leaned back in Dad's old chair, the leather wheezing beneath my weight, I flicked a look between the two machines.

Father. Daughter.

Police would have been through both computers in the weeks after the family vanished: in the history there was activity after January 7, but only revisiting sites Paul and Annabel had already been to. That pointed to the investigators doing the same thing I'd just done: clicking on links, following the same paths through the Web that the Lings would have traveled. So far, all roads headed toward a dead end: nothing on the computers, nothing on a first search of the house, and Emily hadn't been updated for months. I was starting to see why the police investigation had stalled.

Taking a break, I padded through to the kitchen.

As the kettle boiled, rain spat against the kitchen window, and when the wind came it was hard and aggressive, pressing and grabbing at the house until every wall seemed to sigh and every pane of glass rattled. I saw my phone sitting on the table, pulled it toward me and thumbed through my address book.

Eventually I got to Liz's number.

My finger hovered over the Dial button, Healy's words still swimming through my head. *Whatever you think's happened between you, she needs to hear it.* He was right, even if it felt disconcerting taking relationship advice from a man like him. The silence of unanswered calls wasn't what she deserved, even if—ultimately—all I would be doing by calling her was confirming what she already knew.

We'd come to the end.

And now it was over.

17

Healy looked out through the glass of the old red phone booth, rain spattering against the windows, wind whistling as it passed through rusted-out gaps at ankle level. He'd walked the entire length of the sea wall, from one end of the village to the other, in order to get here, in order to make this call, and now he was drenched. Rain matted his hair to his scalp, darkening it like it had been dyed, and he was damp all the way through to his skin.

He removed the handset from the cradle, wedged it between the side of his head and his shoulder, and fed a couple of coins into the slot. Then he removed his phone from his pocket, placed it on top of the dial box and scrolled through to the number he wanted to call. He could have waited for Raker to head out, or he could have gone somewhere private, like the lane outside the house—but this was a call he didn't want Raker to see him making. He didn't want it showing up in his Call History, or on any itemized bill. Which was why he was making it from a phone booth almost a mile away from the house.

He found the number he wanted, punched it into the dial box and waited for it to connect. As it started to ring, he looked left and right, back along the sea wall toward the village, and the other way, out of the village, along the Ley. The Ley was an oval-shaped expanse of fresh water further along, separated from the shingle beach by a narrow stretch of road. At the other end of it, in among the folds of those same hills, surrounded by oak and ash forests, was where Raker had said his parents' farm had been. Healy didn't care about that now, though. He didn't care about anything but making sure he was alone.

"John Sampson speaking."

Healy cleared his throat. "John."

"Uh, yeah. Who's that?"

"It's . . ."

Maybe this is a mistake.

Maybe I shouldn't have called.

No.

No, screw Raker. I don't take my orders from him.

"It's Colm Healy."

A pause. "How are you?" came the reply, but it sounded strained. Put on. Healy could hear Sampson moving, passing people. Then a creak. Then there was total silence.

"John?"

"What are you calling me for, Colm?"

Healy looked out at the beach. "I just wanted to—"

"I'm at work."

"I know. I just wanted to find out how you were."

"I'm fine."

"Good. That's good. How's the family?"

"They're *fine*. What do you want, Colm?"

"I was just . . . I was thinking maybe . . ."

"What?"

"I've got this thing I'm working on and—"

"You want help?"

"I just need a—"

"Bryan Strydom said you called him this morning."

"Yeah. I called Bryan. So? I worked with him for years."

"He said you wanted him to see what he could find out about a mur-der down in Devon—and you wanted a background check on some fisherman. Are you *insane*?"

"What's that supposed to mean?"

"What do you think it means? Not only were you asking Strydom to break the law and do a database search for a member of the public, but you were asking him for details about an *active case*." Sampson paused. "Does any of that sound remotely okay to you?"

"Like I say, I've known Bryan for year—"

"It doesn't *matter*, Healy. You don't work for the Met anymore."

Healy stopped. "I just thought—"

"You thought wrong."

"Samp, listen—"

"No, *you* listen, Healy. I knew you a long time. You were a good cop-per once. But if you call me or any of my team again, I will put you down, and I will make sure—"

"Fuck you, Samp."

Healy hung up.

He stayed like that for a moment—fingers around the handset, eyes on the beach. The sea suddenly seemed to roar as it crashed on the shore, and then the crackling sound of shingle followed as it was dragged back into the wash. Healy thought of Raker. *You got fired from the police. Those people there you call friends, colleagues, whatever they were to you—they aren't going to go out to bat for you, because they don't want to end up like you.* The waves came again and again, massaged by the wind, climbing their way up the shingle in a relentless assault. *I know, one hundred percent, I can rely on Tasker. No mistakes. No trails. Can you say that about the men you know? Can you say it with absolute certainty?* Finally, there was the smell of salt, a reminder of where he was.

"Raker was right," he muttered.

The words were so big, such a stark realization, that for a fraction of a second there seemed an odd kind of silence in the phone booth: no rain, no wind, no waves from the beach. And then, the next second, all the noise seemed to come at once, like water breaking through a bough.

Healy squeezed the handset tight, knuckles blanched, teeth clenched—and then he smashed it against the windows of the phone booth, over and over.

Thirty seconds later, there was no glass left in it.

And all he could feel was the rain.

Let the Cards Fall

Saturday, August 13, 2011 | Fifteen Months Ago

There were five of them in the courtyard. They sat at the edge of the pool, all in shirt sleeves, empty beer bottles stacked in the center of their table. From inside the villa they could hear music and laughter, could see men wandering around, some still dressed in the sharp, tailored suits they'd landed in; some already on their way to undressing as they led attractive, paid-for women half their age into the villa's secluded side rooms.

Outside, though, things were different.

The night was utterly still, no movement on the surface of the pool, no breeze passing through the palm fronds, just the gentle hum of traffic from Las Vegas Boulevard. The game of blackjack had quickly descended into silence as a sixth man—a shipping magnate called Stuppuco, acting as dealer—slowly went around the table, watching the hand signals from the men as they decided whether to hit or stand. The last of them, more chips in front of him than anyone else, was Eric Schiltz. He'd had a good night so far, and it was about to get a whole lot better. He maintained his composure as Stuppuco got to him, and then swept the flat of his hand across his cards. He was going to stand.

"Okay," Stuppuco said. "Let's see 'em, boys."

They all flipped their cards over and, inside a second, the other men zeroed in on Schiltz's hand. An Ace and a Jack: twenty-one. Groans of disappointment went up in unison.

"Are you cheating, Schiltzy?" one of the men joked.

Schiltz winked at him. "Only with your wife."

Laughter erupted among the group, and as Schiltz pulled a whole new set of chips toward him, whatever tension had built up in the last game instantly fell away. More jokes got passed around the table, mostly at Schiltz's expense, before they all broke into smaller clusters, talking about the NFL preseason, the recession, Obama, and then their plans for the rest of the night. Finally, one of the men, a Hollywood exec with a belly as big as his drug habit, peeled himself out of his chair and offered to go and get another round of beers. As he left, Schiltz's cellphone started ringing.

He pulled it out and looked at the display. Caller unknown. "Listen," he said to the others, "if I come back and find these chips missing, I'll operate on all of you."

More laughter.

Schiltz wandered across to a quieter part of the courtyard, where a second door, leading through to one of the bedrooms, was closed, its curtains pulled. Beside him the wall that ran the circumference of the courtyard dipped slightly and he could see over it, across the Bellagio's lake, to where the Eiffel Tower at Paris—on the other side of the Boulevard—erupted out of a bed of light and reached into the black desert sky.

"Hello?"

A buzz on the line.

"Hello?"

Nothing. Schiltz waited another five seconds, then when there was no response he hung up. Just as he did, the doors to the bedroom opened, almost on to him, and as he stepped back to see who it was, he realized it was Cornell, immaculately dressed in a gray shirt, black trousers and black brogues, his hair slicked down, not a strand out of place along his arrow-straight parting. Cornell didn't notice Schiltz at first, but as he moved further into the courtyard, Schiltz came out from behind the door. Inside the room a woman, naked from the waist up, was hoisting a tight pink dress up over her thighs.

"Eric," Cornell said. "I didn't see you there."

"This looks bad," Schiltz said, smiling.

Cornell glanced at the woman, fully in her dress now, and then seemed to realize what Schiltz meant. "Oh, her. Don't worry. I know you're not the Peeping Tom type."

"Then my cover remains intact."

Schiltz smiled again but got no response from Cornell. He nodded to the table where his chips were still stacked up in piles. "I was the Blackjack Butcher tonight."

Cornell nodded.

He didn't talk much, didn't smile much either, which always struck Schiltz as strange given how much he must have spent on his teeth. But Schiltz had known Cornell long before he'd paid out for a Californian grin, and he'd been exactly the same then.

"Do you want one of your own?" Cornell asked.

"Huh?"

"I can arrange it for you." He glanced back at the woman, who was applying some lipstick and running a brush through her hair. "Someone like that."

"I'm fine, thanks, Jeremy."

"You have someone else in mind?"

"No."

"Are you sure?"

Schiltz frowned. "I'm sure."

"Only, I saw you in the hotel bar earlier, talking to someone."

"Oh, her. Talking was all it was."

"You seemed to be getting on pretty well."

Schiltz shook his head. "She was a fifty-dollar-an-hour hooker."

"So?"

"So, that's not really my scene." Suddenly, Schiltz's phone started buzzing again. Another unknown number. "Excuse me," he said to Cornell. "I need to take this."

Cornell nodded.

Schiltz stepped away and pushed Answer. "Hello?"

"Eric?"

"Yes."

"It's Carrie Ling."

"Carrie. How are you?"

"I'm good. I just tried calling you a minute ago, but I don't know what happened—I could hear you but you couldn't hear me." A brief pause on the line. "Wait, I've just realized how late it is there."

He looked at his watch. "One in the morning."

"Oh, Eric, I'm so sorry. I didn't even think. Did I wake you up?"

"It's fine. Honestly. I'm up in Las Vegas for the weekend, so the likelihood of me getting to bed early was always going to be slim."

Carrie chuckled. "Well, I'm sorry all the same."

"Really," he said. "Don't worry."

Out of the corner of his eye, Schiltz saw Cornell take a couple of steps away from him and look over at the blackjack table. This is what he liked to do: watch other people.

"How's Annabel?" Schiltz asked.

"Oh, she's doing great."

"She's a tough cookie, your daughter."

"She is. But you were a miracle worker."

That made him smile. "You should do my PR."

They talked for a while about Annabel's recovery, about making some slight adjustments to her exercise routine, and then Carrie began talking more generally about settling into life back home. "Do you ever miss Devon?" she asked him eventually.

"It's where I grew up. Sometimes I miss it a lot."

"I guess you've got all your photos."

"I guess so."

"How's the scanning going?"

"It's going well," Schiltz replied, looking across the courtyard. Cornell had moved again, perching himself on the steps leading out of the bedroom. He was about six feet away, arms resting on either knee, fingers locked together, half obscured by shadows.

"Did you start with that one of the three of you?"

"Which one was that?"

"The one in your study, of you and your two friends."

"Oh, that one. I can't remember if I started with that one or not."

"But you scanned it in?"

"Yes, it definitely made the cut. Why do you ask?"

"I was just wondering. I thought it was a nice photo."

"Yeah," Schiltz said. "I like it too. It's the only one I've got from that period of the three of us. Funnily enough, I e-mailed a copy of it to both of the guys yesterday."

"Did they like it?"

"One of them's back in your part of the world, and he's terrible at checking his e-mail, so I don't expect to hear for a while. But the other is here tonight. I'll go and ask him later. I'm sure he'll get a kick out of it. We all look devilishly handsome, after all."

Schiltz smiled and turned around, facing off along the edge of the pool toward the makeshift blackjack table. His eyes fell on Cornell. He was standing again, staring into space as if deep in thought. Or listening to Schiltz's conversation.

"Listen, Carrie, I'd better go."

"Yes, of course. I just wanted to ask you about those exercises."

"Well, it's lovely to hear from you."

"Thank you again, Eric."

"Say hello to Annabel, Paul and Olivia."

"I will. Bye, Eric."

Schiltz hung up.

Immediately, Cornell picked a hair from his shirt sleeve and took a couple of steps toward Schiltz. "Couldn't help overhearing your conversation."

"That was private."

He shrugged. "You said you e-mailed some kind of picture?"

"Jeremy, I don't want to be rude, but it was—"

"Neither do I," Cornell said. "I didn't mean to pry, Eric. Honestly, I didn't." He held up both hands. "I apologize if I offended you. That was never my intention."

"I appreciate—"

But then Cornell took another step toward him, stopping a foot from Schiltz, an emotionless, clinical expression on his face; an expression betraying every word of the apology he'd just made. Schiltz had seen this side of Cornell before, rarely and only in fleeting glimpses, but always directed at other people. Now it was directed at him.

"It's my job to protect this group," Cornell said.

Schiltz held up a hand. "It's just a photograph."

"I want to see it."

"It's just a photograph, Jeremy."

"Then I'm sure there's nothing to worry about."

Schiltz had a room on the thirty-second floor. They left the villa, walked through to the main hotel and rode the elevator up in silence. As they passed the tenth floor, Cornell finally turned to Schiltz. "I'm sorry about this, Eric. I just want to set my mind at rest."

Schiltz shrugged.

"You have to understand where I'm coming from: that group downstairs in the villa, it's full of some of the world's most successful businessmen. Discretion is key."

"I'm familiar with the rules, Jeremy."

"I know you are."

"Then why the need for this bullshit?"

"I just like to keep on top of things."

There was no hint of the person Schiltz had glimpsed earlier; Cornell was back to who he was most of the time: smart, serious, quiet, watchful. If he hadn't known him since Cornell was a boy, Schiltz would have probably added sincere and apologetic to the list. But the truth was, deep down, Jeremy Cornell wasn't either of those things. He was something else.

Schiltz just wasn't sure what.

The doors pinged open, and Cornell gestured for Schiltz to lead the way. Schiltz turned right, down a long, kinked corridor to his room. As he approached, he removed his keycard from the breast pocket of his shirt.

"Weird," he said quietly.

"What?"

He shook his head. "I just thought I brought both keycards out with me."

He slid the card he had into the reader and popped the door open. Inside it was dark. He used the card to activate the lights, and headed straight to the table, on the other side of the bed, where he'd left his laptop on to charge.

He stopped; looked at Cornell.

Immediately, like an animal picking up a scent, Cornell knew something was up. He took a step closer to Schiltz, head tilting to one side. "Is there a problem, Eric?"

Schiltz looked around the room.

Cornell watched him. "Where's the picture?"

"On the laptop."

"So where's the laptop?"

Schiltz gazed at the empty table. "It's gone."

"Gone where?"

"Where do you think?"

Cornell took a step closer. "Someone stole it?"

"I don't know how—"

"Someone stole it?"

"Yes," Schiltz said, his voice raised. "Of course someone stole it!"

"Who would steal it?"

"I don't know."

"Who else has got a key to your room?"

Schiltz looked at Cornell: the missing keycard. "No one."

But both of them were thinking the same thing: the prostitute Schiltz had been talking to in the hotel bar earlier in the evening. He'd never had any intention of paying for her, but she was friendly and for thirty minutes he'd enjoyed her company.

And while he was distracted, she'd stolen his room key.

"What was her name?" Cornell asked.

"I never asked her."

Cornell glanced at the empty table. "What was the picture of?"

Schiltz looked at Cornell, incredulous. "Seriously?"

"Yes."

"Who cares about a bloody picture?"

"I care."

"Are you listening to what I'm saying? My laptop has been stolen!"

"I heard you."

"It's got private information on it."

"Who were you on the phone to, Eric?"

"Are you kidding me?"

"Just tell me and then I'll help you find—"

"It's totally irrelevant."

"I'll decide whether it's relevant or not," Cornell said, and took another step closer. There was a sudden twist to Cornell's voice, a subtle, menacing shift in tone, and when Schiltz faced him, Cornell had changed. Still, rigid, not even a flicker of a muscle.

"It's just a picture of the three of us."

"You three men?"

Schiltz nodded, contrite, cowed, aware instantly that he was allowing himself to be muzzled, but incapable of doing anything about it. The whole atmosphere had changed—Cornell had somehow turned the conversation on its head with a single look.

"So who was asking about it?"

"Just a woman I know."

"Her name?"

He studied Cornell; one last futile attempt to fight back.

"Her name, Eric?"

Schiltz swallowed; felt a little nauseated.

"You're going to give me her name, Eric."

Then, finally, Schiltz relented. "Carrie," he said. "Carrie Ling."

18

In the hours before it got dark, I put up the fence paneling in the back garden that had blown down during gales the week before. Dad had never been a big believer in power tools; anything that plugged directly into an electrical socket he viewed with a deep and pervading suspicion. However, he did buy himself a nailgun to help put up fences, back when he'd been managing fields of livestock on the farm, and as rain continued to lash in, it made my task easier, even if—by the time I was finished—I was soaked to the bone.

As the last of the light disappeared, I heard my phone going inside the house. I left the nailgun outside and headed through to the kitchen, where my cell was buzzing on the table. It was Ewan Tasker. I'd asked him to source the Lings' missing persons file.

"I'm not going to lie to you," he said after we'd chatted for a while, "I seriously doubt you're going to be putting this case to bed based on what's in the official file."

"It doesn't amount to much?"

"Most of it you probably already know."

"I'll take the official version, anyway—just to be sure."

I could hear him tabbing through pages on his computer. "Okay. So, your friend Emily Kane calls police on January 7 and tells them her sister, brother-in-law and nieces are missing. Next day, she files an official report at Totnes. Any of this news to you?"

"It's confirming what I already know."

"For some reason, after taking Kane's statement, the uniform at Totnes decided to fire it up the line." He anticipated my next question: "Why? Can't say for sure. There's nothing in the statement that would set alarm bells off, and scene of crime came up with a whole lot of nothing at the house. No sign of a struggle, nothing stolen, no blood. My guess is the PC thought it was weird that a whole family just disappeared like that."

"You would have done the same?"

"Punted it up the tree? Yeah, I probably would have. I mean, I've never heard of that before. Families vanish all the time, but usually they turn up pretty quickly. It's hard for a family of four to disappear, plus the way the house was left—that's pretty unique."

"So what happened when CID got involved?"

"January 9, forty-eight hours after the family go missing, two detectives take a forensic team to the house. Detectives . . ." He paused, trying to find their names—but I already knew one of them was Rocastle. "Detectives Rocastle and McInnes. First one's a DCI, second's a DC." I heard him clicking through more pages. "Forensic team dusts the place down, fingerprint lifts, DNA samples, all the usual stuff—nothing. Nothing on the databases then and nothing now. I rechecked everything for you. The only things on there are the things you'd expect: their legally registered cars, their house, et cetera, et cetera. There're no cautions, no arrests—all the adults have got a clean bill of health."

"So no mention of anything being stolen from the house?"

"No."

"Nothing being withdrawn from their bank accounts?"

"No. There *is* a pretty extensive evidence inventory here, which I haven't looked at too closely. You'll probably want to pick that apart when I send these printouts over."

"Thanks, Task. Anything else?"

"Did you know they called in the MPB?"

The Missing Persons Bureau. Seventy-two hours after someone went missing, the police could call on the assistance of the MPB. They were the UK's only dedicated missing persons team, logging about a thousand searches a year, working in conjunction with police forces to identify missing people, and put names to bodies and remains.

"No," I said. "I didn't know that. Did they find anything?"

"No. Reading between the lines, it looks like the case went south pretty quickly, even with the MPB involved. Rocastle jacked it in after a few days, so McInnes was—"

"Hold on. Rocastle only spent a couple of days on the case?"

"Three days. Total."

"Does it say why?"

"Yeah: the case was going nowhere. I'm paraphrasing, but you can see it all over the file. I've had my fair share of these, believe me." He stopped. A couple of taps. "Last recorded activity was July 23, when they called Emily Kane to update her on the progress of the case—or lack of it, I guess. It's an unusual case, but the police work here seems pretty solid." A couple of clicks. "Oh, and all their computers came up clean too."

I processed everything I'd heard. If the computers had come up clean, that almost certainly meant their e-mails had too, though I'd still double-check once Spike got me the login details. The involvement of Rocastle was interesting, though. The three days he'd spent on the case suggested he didn't see anything worth pursuing in it—but it didn't explain why he'd been involved in the first place. It wasn't unusual for senior officers to lead missing persons cases—far from it—but it was unusual for someone with Rocastle's level of experience to be dropped in as SIO on a case where there was no body, and no evidence to suggest the family was in any immediate danger.

"What about sightings?" I asked him.

"Well, this is where it'll get fun for you. Fifty-two possible sightings in the weeks after the family went missing, and none of them are up to much."

"Not a single one of the fifty-two?"

"They elevated three to 'Maybe if we're desperate,' but—reading between the lines—they're the best of a bad bunch. You know how it works: you field a shitload of calls, some will be useful, most will either be cases of mistaken identity, morons trying to get in your way, or old-fashioned crazies. It's unusual to get nothing—but it happens. I've only skimmed these, but you can see why police weren't getting too excited."

"So what are we looking at?"

"This Emily woman didn't tell you about these already?"

She hadn't mentioned them specifically, although she'd said that the police had told her the sightings didn't amount to much. "I'm not sure she knew about them."

"Probably because the police decided against telling her. Personally, I always like to communicate everything—good or bad—but I can understand their reticence on these. False hope can create bigger problems." He stopped, reading from something. "Okay, so one was down your way, at some country estate in Dartmouth. The second was here in London, near the ExCeL. Plus, they were looking at some kind of anonymous call too."

"Can you talk me through them?"

"Sure. The Dartmouth sighting was at a place called Farnmoor House, the day after the family went missing. House and land are owned by a guy called Carter Graham. He's some kind of mega-businessman; spends a lot of his year out of the country, so he wasn't at home. Gardener there—a guy called Ray Muire—reckons he spotted Paul and Carrie Ling and 'a third party' crossing fields about a quarter of a mile from the house."

"A third party?"

"Yet to be identified."

"Only Paul and Carrie? What about the girls?"

"This Muire guy reckons just Paul and Carrie."

"So, what, the police didn't take him seriously?"

"I'm giving you the edited highlights here, but I think, in the end, they doubted his abilities to spot anyone from further than a distance of about six feet. He had some kind of a degenerative eye problem, diagnosed by a doctor Rocastle spoke to. This quack said Muire was a year out from full blindness. Rocastle did the interview himself before he left the ship, and asked Muire about his eyesight. In the transcript, Muire agrees his eyes are on the wane, but he seems to be pretty accurate with some of his descriptive detail."

"Such as?"

"Just the way he sets the scene, the way he describes the house and what he saw of the Lings. It's an odd interview. I've only given it a cursory glance, but it starts off very accurate, very clear, then slowly becomes more rambling—and eventually incoherent."

"Sounds like it could be nerves."

"I don't think so. It doesn't feel that way to me. It feels more like he forgot what his own story was. But that first ten minutes or so, when he's recalling things with a real sense of clarity, that's probably why police zeroed in on him. That, and his location: they paid special attention to any sightings close to where the family lived and worked."

"What about the second sighting?"

"At a set of temporary roadworks on Victoria Dock Road. You know it?"

I did. It ran parallel to the ExCeL convention center in east London. It was a weird place for the Lings to have been spotted. "Yeah. I know it. Who was the wit?"

"Guy who worked for the council digging up roads. He said he read about the family's disappearance online and reckons he saw two of them—the girls this time—two days after the sighting at Farnmoor. That's January 10. They were in a car: a red Ford."

"With who?"

"A male. White. That's about it."

"No other description?"

"No. Police never tracked down the Ford either. McInnes traveled up to London and did an interview with him, but this guy wasn't able to provide much of a description of anything, other than the girls looked a bit like the ones he'd read about. To be honest, I'd trust the blind guy at the house before I trusted this guy Barry Rew."

"That's his name?"

"Yeah. Rew's a recovering addict, been done for drug possession, receiving stolen goods, laying hands on an ex. The cherry on top was getting banged up for five months off the back of the riots last year when he walked out of PC World carrying ten iPads."

"So what made this sighting stick?"

"One tiny detail in his interview: he said Olivia was holding a Mickey Mouse soft toy while she was sitting in the back of the car. Police found photos of her at home with the same toy, but that detail never got made public. Rew couldn't have known before."

"Did they ever think he might be involved?"

"That was the other reason Rew's sighting made the grade."

"They wanted to keep an eye on him?"

"Correct. You would too if all you had to go on was the word of a thieving, woman-beating ex-smackhead."

I wheeled back. "Did anyone speak to the guy who owned the country house?"

"McInnes spoke to Carter Graham on January 12. He had to do the interview via video link, as Graham was in his New York office. Again, they seemed pretty happy with the answers. Graham has a ton of land in and around Farnmoor, and a lot of it is public right of way, so there's just no way he can account for who uses it and who doesn't."

Most missing persons cases led to sightings and most sightings amounted to nothing. I trusted Task's initial take, and trusted him to spot anything that didn't feel right in either sighting, but it would need closer attention once he sent the file through.

"You said there was an anonymous call too?"

"Yeah." He paused as he searched for the page. "Someone called the police and said they saw Paul and Carrie the day after they were allegedly seen on the grounds of Farnmoor. This time they were at a place called . . . uh . . . Miln Cross. You know it?"

"Yeah," I said. "I know it."

But it seemed unlikely they would have been there. Miln Cross was nothing but a ghost now: a tiny fishing village, right on the edge of the sea, that had been wiped out in a freak storm. I hadn't been born at the time, but locals had talked about it for years afterward, their voices hushed as if its sudden destruction had frightened them somehow. In just two hours, fifty-foot waves and a devastating landslide had reduced fourteen houses, a shop, an inn, a chapel and the forty-two people inside them to nothing but bones and memories. It was only five miles along the coast, two shy of Farnmoor, so it worked in terms of the locality of the first sighting, but even before I'd left home to go to London in 1988 it had been closed to the public, and was now just a dangerous graveyard of broken buildings and yawning chasms ripped from the earth by the power of the storm.

"What did the caller say?" I asked.

"Direct quote: 'I'm calling about that family that went missing—the Lings. I saw the husband and wife at Miln Cross today. You should go down and take a look.'"

"That's it?"

"That's it."

"Man or a woman?"

"Man."

The obvious question was why keep the call anonymous? The only reason I could think of, given the supposed location of the sighting, was because the caller was trying to throw police off the scent—or that there might have been consequences to making the call.

"Did the team head down to Miln Cross?"

"Yep. Nothing doing. I think the reason they liked this one more than all the other calls was because it mentioned *just* Paul and Carrie— same as Ray Muire had done."

Finding nothing at Miln Cross didn't surprise me. Which just left the motivations of the caller.

"Is there an audio file of the phone call?"

"Yeah. I'll send it over."

"So, January 8, Paul and Carrie are seen with an unidentified third person, at Farnmoor; January 9, they're seen at Miln Cross; January 10, the girls are spotted in a red Ford near the ExCeL in London with an unidentified white male."

"That about sums it up."

My mind was already racing ahead: if I placed any sort of faith in the sightings, it meant I had to work from the possibility that Paul and Carrie, and Annabel and Olivia, were taken to different places. The question was why.

And whether any of the witnesses could be believed.

19

By the time Healy got back to the village he was numb from the cold, soaked through to the bone and burning with anger. He'd destroyed the phone booth, left glass in glittering mounds at its base, the phone swinging by its cord, the casing chipped and broken from being smashed against the dial box—but the rage hadn't died down. Sampson's words still pricked at him; the snide insinuation that Healy couldn't cut it as a cop anymore. *I can cut it*, he thought. *I'm still a better copper than you'll ever be, you patronizing prick.*

An icy blast of wind carved in off the water, bringing him out of his thoughts. Late afternoon light was beginning to dwindle, and further along the beach he could see spotlights being readied for another night. A man and a woman, both in forensic suits, were standing on either side of the first light, making minute adjustments to its position. The body would have long since been shipped off to the morgue, so this was the endgame, a final search for anything they'd missed. As he moved adjacent to the sea wall, Healy watched both the techs. If he could have got the inside track on who they'd found in the cove and what the coroner had discovered, he knew he'd have Sampson choking on his words. He'd have them all choking. What got to him more than their refusal to help was the thought of what they were saying about him: the talk in the office after Sampson put the phone down, the laughter, everyone joining in to paint him as some kind of a flake.

You're not a cop anymore.

That's what Raker had told him a couple of days before. Maybe it hadn't hit home then, but it was hitting home now. The Met, the people he'd worked with and trusted, every case he'd ever put to bed, any family he'd ever been able to bring any kind of peace to, it was all ancient history now.

None of it meant anything.

On his right, the thatched roof and whitewashed walls of The Seven Seas came into view. The day was foul, a mix of rain and wind and bitter cold, but at the side, in one of the alleyways that ran between the buildings at the sea wall, he spotted a solitary figure huddled under the overhang of the roof, smoking. For a while, all Healy could see was the person's outline and the slow, rhythmic glow of a cigarette, but as he got closer the figure shifted slightly and some of the light from the pub washed out across him.

It was the fisherman.

The one who'd found the body.

Healy looked up into the hills beyond the pub, toward Raker's house. There were no lights on, but he was up there somewhere, looking at pictures of the family, trying to figure out where they'd gone. *You're not a cop anymore.* Healy's eyes flicked back to the fisherman. He was still dressed in his blue bib and brace trousers, unzipped yellow jacket over the top and matching boots, and his sou'wester hung from his neck by the chin strap. He must have come straight from the boat. He eyed Healy for a moment, then nodded.

"How's it going, pal?" Healy said.

The fisherman shrugged. "Can't complain."

"Mind if I join you?"

The fisherman shrugged a second time. "Free country."

Healy stepped in, under the overhang, propped a cigarette between his lips and went hunting around in his pockets for a light. "Good day out on the boat, then?"

The fisherman took a drag. "Decent enough."

"Where's the trawler moored?"

"Brixham."

Despite Healy not being able to locate his lighter, the fisherman just watched, not offering the use of his. "What's your name, pal?"

"Why?"

"I'm just interested," Healy said casually. "Been here a while and I feel like I don't know enough about people. I'm Colm Healy." He offered his hand.

Eventually, the fisherman took it. "Prouse."

"That your first name or your last?"

"Last."

Healy finally found his lighter, cupped one of his hands around the cigarette and lit up. He took a long, deep drag. "How's it going with this beach thing?"

Prouse's eyes fixed on him. "What do you mean?"

"The body you found."

He studied the fisherman in the shadows of the overhang, watching for anything in his face. This was as close as he'd got to Prouse since the fisherman had come up to him in the pub. In the silence, Healy's mind spooled back to a conversation he'd had with Rocastle, a couple of hours after finding the body. *He wasn't surprised by what we found there, as if he'd already had the time to process it. Maybe it wasn't the second time he'd been down there. Maybe it was the third, or the fourth, or the . . .* Rocastle had cut him off, not interested in hearing the rest of the theory, but the theory had legs, Healy felt sure of that: even some detectives would balk at the sight of a victim left like that.

And yet the fisherman's face had shown nothing.

"So what's the verdict?"

Prouse looked at him. "About what?"

"About the body. You heard anything?"

"Look, I did my interview, I told them what I found down there, and that's all I've heard from them." Prouse took a last drag on his roll-up. "If that's the *last* I hear of it, that suits me just fine. I feel sorry for the poor bastard who they found down there, but I ain't interested in finding out anything more than I have to." He flicked his cigarette out into the night and they both watched it burn out and die in the rain. "I don't know if you're working with the police or what. If you want me to talk on record, I will do that—but I ain't doing some impromptu interview, here in the pissing rain. That all right with you?"

"I was just interested."

"Yeah, well, I ain't." The fisherman pulled up his sou'wester. "Now if you'll excuse me, I'd better get home."

Healy nodded.

Prouse nodded back, zipped up his jacket and headed out into the night, following the sea wall past the pub, toward the cottages at the far end of the village. As he watched him go, Healy wondered if he'd called it wrong. The fisherman was quiet and stoic, but that didn't make him guilty. People tended to be like that down here, enduring and reserved, hewn from a tradition of speaking their minds only when they needed to.

You're not a cop anymore.

Taking a last drag on his cigarette, Healy stubbed it out on the wall of The Seven Seas and headed inside the pub.

20

Healy arrived back at the cottage just after nine. I knew he'd been drinking even before he stumbled into the living room and collapsed on to the sofa. He looked between me and the two computers—Paul and Annabel's—still sitting on the table in the corner, and then to the laptop perched on my knees. As his eyes moved around the room, they shifted in stages, like they were dragging on something. He was finding it hard to even focus.

"Fun night?"

He shrugged. "Same old."

I went back to what I was doing. After getting off the phone to Task, I'd googled Carter Graham. Sixty-seven. Divorced. Born in south Devon—hence him having a home at Farnmoor, about seven miles east, along the coast—but in pieces I'd read in *Forbes* and *Business Week*, and a profile in the *Financial Times*, it sounded like he spent most of his time eating plane food. His company, Empyrean, provided what they called "investment opportunity analysis," and had offices in London, Frankfurt, New York, LA, Sydney and Tokyo. According to the *FT*, Graham toured them almost constantly for ten months of the year, looking for gaps in the market—start-ups, small businesses with big growth potential, and up-coming industries. Staff in his regional offices were scouring the local markets the entire time; when they found something, some business or technology they thought represented a potential money-maker, Graham flew in, listened to the pitch and decided whether to get his checkbook out or not. "He's seen as something of a white knight," the *FT* added, and it was hard to argue with the business model: the company goes stratospheric, he creams off a chunk of the profits, everybody makes lots of cash.

In the *Forbes* piece, it said Graham had started Empyrean in Dartmouth in 1967 at the age of just twenty-two, before shifting the whole operation to London shortly after—then things *really* started taking off. In 1971 he opened his first international office in Los Angeles. He didn't talk much to the media, *Forbes* describing him as "a very private man," and he was particularly protective of his personal life, which meant the same basic information got trotted out time and time again: divorced once, but "still on good terms with" his ex-wife, and no children. There was almost nothing else, bar a small mention of when his parents had passed on: his mother in 1962, and his father in 1968. If he'd vowed to keep his private life out of the media, he'd done a pretty decent job.

"I'm going back to London."

I looked up at Healy. He'd wriggled his jacket off and was sitting—legs spread, hands resting on his belly—in the middle of the sofa. "What are you talking about?"

"I've had enough of it down here," he said.

"You'd had enough of it in London."

He shrugged.

"What's brought this on?"

He shrugged again. "I don't belong here."

"And you belong in London?"

"What, you cut up I'm leaving?"

His defenses were up, which normally meant he was reacting to something. Either something he'd done, or was about to. "You do whatever you want to do," I said to him.

"There's nothing left for me here."

I went back over all the conversations we'd had over the past seven days, trying to pinpoint the origin of this moment.

"Where are you going to stay?" I asked.

"I've got a few mates up there."

I nodded. *Not too many anymore.*

Then I remembered what I'd said to him outside the Lings': *You got fired from the police. Those people there you call friends, colleagues, whatever they were to you—they aren't going to go out to bat for you, because they don't want to end up like you.*

"Is this about earlier?"

He flicked a look at me and then away again, and I had my answer.

"I just like to run my cases a certain way," I said.

"I don't know what you're talking about."

"We're trying to have a conversation here, Healy." He shifted on the sofa, slow and lethargic, and I suddenly remembered he was drunk. "Let's talk about it tomorrow."

"Talk about what?"

"We'll talk in the morning," I said again.

He eyed me, like he suddenly realized I'd worked him out, and then he got up, stumbling slightly, and headed upstairs without saying another word.

After he was gone, I returned to the sightings of the Ling family, booting up both Paul and Annabel's computers for a second time. I went through them, folder by folder, program by program, looking for any connection to Carter Graham, to Farnmoor, to Miln Cross or to London ExCeL. There was nothing. By eleven, as the wind started to gather momentum outside, nearby branches scratching at the windows, I shut both computers down and headed up to bed.

Two hours later, I was still awake.

The next morning, Healy emerged just before eight. I was sitting at the kitchen table, cup of coffee in front of me, looking down toward the beach as the tide rolled in. He shuffled in, dressing gown on, half squinting as if bright sunlight were arrowing in toward him. In reality, the sky was a perfect ceiling of granite-gray cloud and it was drizzling.

I watched him pour himself a coffee and then, when he was done, he stood at the counter and looked across the room at me. Immediately on the defensive. He might have been hungover, but he obviously remembered enough of what we'd talked about the night before. I didn't play up to it. On the table in front of me was the local paper—the body on the beach still the hot ticket, even though the crime scene was now just a distant memory—and, as he remained standing, I started flicking through it again.

A couple of minutes passed, both of us silent, and then he disappeared back into the living room. I carried on reading the sports pages. Twenty minutes later, shaved and showered, Healy returned to the kitchen, pulled out a chair and sat at the table with me.

"You were right—is that what you want to hear?"

I flipped the paper shut. He was eyeing me like he was waiting for a comeback, some sort of put-down. "It was never about that, Healy."

"You think I haven't got anything left in the tank." That last part seemed to hang in the air, as if he were processing it for the first time too. "Everyone thinks I'm done."

"I don't think you're done."

He shrugged. "Maybe you're all right."

"Who's 'all' of us?"

"It doesn't matter." His fingers rubbed together, like he wanted a cigarette. "I need to get back to London, get some normality back in my life. This isn't a real existence."

"What have you got back in London?"

He looked out through the window, and for a second it was like he was thinking out loud. He was watching the beach, the sweeping arc of the hills, the crashing waves. He was wondering if he really *did* want to leave all this behind for a city that had rejected him, for work colleagues who placed no trust in him, for the memories of a daughter he no longer had. But then he probably realized that if he had little left in London beyond his two boys, he had even less here. I had physical and emotional ties to the village, ties to this house, to the place where I'd grown up. Basically, the only attachment Healy had was me.

"I need to get back into work," he said. "Some shitty security job signing people into a building." He paused, the faintest hint of a smile on his face. "Something to forget about what I used to do. Something to help . . ." He stopped a second time, but I got what he meant: *Something to help me forget I was once a cop.* There was a sadness in his face as that dawned on him, and it felt like I glimpsed the origin of this moment: maybe a phone call to the people he'd worked with, trying to prove to me and to himself that he was still important; maybe nothing in return but a wall of silence.

"You're a good cop, Healy."

He looked at me.

"No one can take that away from you."

"If I was so good, why did I get fired?"

"You did the wrong things for the right reasons."

He shrugged again. "You ever coming back to London?"

On the table, beside the newspaper, were my notes. I pulled them toward me. "I want to take care of this first."

"Then I guess I'll see you on the other side."

I nodded. "I guess you will."

Two hours later, his car was packed. He hadn't come with much in the first place. We'd both escaped London for different reasons, but we'd both escaped fast.

We shook hands in the rain, and I told him to call me once he was settled in, and then I watched his red Vauxhall take off down the hill, chugging along the lane that snaked toward the beach. At the bottom, a bright red speck against the concrete of the sea wall, the car seemed to pause, as if Healy was unsure whether to commit to this.

And then, a second later, he pulled away and was gone.

PART THREE

21

Farnmoor was a huge, seventeenth-century manor house buried in a crinkle of coastline two miles south of Dartmouth. The single-lane approach was beautiful. Framed by high trees, it gradually opened out on to a patchwork of rolling hills and sweeping sea views. The house itself remained hidden virtually the entire way down until, about a quarter of a mile short of the front gates, it emerged from a curve in the earth, its manicured front lawn flowing into a bank of craggy coastal rock and finally dropping away to the sea.

Beyond the gates, two hundred yards along an arrow-straight driveway, eleven cars were parked in a line, as well as a van with DART GARDEN SERVICES on the side. I pulled the car up outside the gates, buzzed down my window and pushed the intercom. A short, sharp squeal, then silence. As I waited for an answer, I listened to the sea crashing on to the shore somewhere below.

Bzzt. "Yes?"

I turned back to the intercom. "Hi. My name's David Raker. I'm doing some work on the Ling family disappearance. I was hoping I could speak to someone about it."

I left it at that. Carter Graham wasn't home—I'd already called his London office and talked the receptionist into revealing he was out of the country—but, judging by the number of cars parked out front, someone other than the gardener had to have been working here on at least a semi-regular basis. Graham might have been rich, but no one had eleven cars unless they were collecting them; and if he was a collector, he wasn't going to be buying beige Vauxhall Vectras.

A pause. "What did you say your name was?"

"David Raker."

"Okay. Hold on a second, please."

The intercom went dead again. About ten seconds later, the same woman came back on: "I'll buzz you in and meet you out front."

I thanked her and waited for the gates to open. They fanned out slowly, wheezing on their hinges, and I took off up the drive, gravel spitting out from beneath the tires. Halfway along, the front door opened, a huge slab of oak with a small half-oval pane of glass cut into it, and a woman in her early forties emerged from the house, pausing at the top of a set of sandstone steps. She watched me all the way up the drive and into a space next to the Vectra, and didn't break her gaze as I got out of the car and grabbed my notebook from the back. I headed over to meet her.

"Mr. Raker?"

"Morning."

She smiled. "Katie Francis. I'm Mr. Graham's PA here at Farnmoor."

Slim and attractive, her hair scraped back into a ponytail and dressed in a green skirt-suit, she looked every inch the harassed assistant: cordless telephone in one hand, a desk diary in the other. Through the door behind her I could see people moving around: a female in a cleaning tabard, and a chef carrying empty silver platters.

I stopped short of her on the front steps. She nodded. "You'll have to bear with us, I'm afraid—we're throwing a charity gala dinner here tomorrow, so it's a little manic."

She nodded again and I realized it was a habit of hers, like the bridge between one conversation and the next. I followed her into the house. It was beautiful: original oak paneling everywhere, without the musty stench of a stately home. Every room had been furnished with a modern twist: light, airy colors, all creams and browns and reds, contemporary art, twenty-first-century furniture. I only caught brief glimpses of each, but I was immediately impressed by Graham's tastes. From one room came the whine of a vacuum cleaner; from another the conversation of workmen. One corridor branched off and headed toward a kitchen. Another headed in the opposite direction to a locked door. Ahead of us was a wide corkscrew staircase that gracefully wound up to the first floor, carpeted in cream and lined with photographs of Graham at various social functions. "This way," Francis said, and as we headed up I glanced at a few of the pictures. Him with a former prime minister. Him at another charity gala, surrounded by four members of the England football team. Him shaking hands with a renowned media mogul.

At the top of the stairs the landing unfurled, leading down to further rooms. Francis took me in through the first door. In front of two huge bay windows was a desk, perched alone with a Mac on top, a small steel bin at its feet, and a leather office chair so comically huge it looked like it belonged to a Bond villain. Apart from a smaller, less impressive chair for visitors to sit on, the rest of the room was empty: literally no other furniture, just plain magnolia walls and a carpet in the same color.

"Please, take a seat." I sat and retrieved my notebook while she walked around the desk and sank into the chair. "So, you're some kind of . . . detective?"

I smiled. "Some kind of one."

"You're *not* a detective?"

"I'm a missing persons investigator. I find people." I got out a business card and slid it across the desk to her. "At the moment I'm doing some work for the Ling family."

She nodded again.

"Does that name ring any bells with you?"

"Yes, of course."

"You remember the family?"

"Well, I never knew them personally, but I obviously knew about their disappearance. The police came up here after they went missing because one of our staff claimed to have seen them near the house. I managed to put the investigating team in touch with Mr. Graham—he was in New York at the time—and I think everyone came to the conclusion that it was a case of mistaken identity. Why, has something changed?"

"No. Nothing's changed."

She seemed confused. "Okay."

I held up a hand. "There's no mystery, I promise. This is kind of a favor to the family. I just need to check all this sort of stuff off the list to make sure I'm up to speed on what the police did after the Lings vanished. Then I can do the opposite." I smiled again, and this time she responded, smiling herself and gesturing for me to continue. "So, maybe you can start by just giving me a brief overview of the setup here?"

"The setup?"

"You run the house for Mr. Graham while he's away?"

"The house, the grounds, his interests in the local community. He still has great affection for the area, as you can probably imagine, and likes to get involved in local issues when he returns to Farnmoor. He has PAs in each of his offices who deal directly with regional issues; I deal with the *really* regional issues." She smiled. "I enjoy it."

"How many people are employed at the house on a full-time basis?"

"Full time? Just me. I'm here five days a week, Monday through Friday, 9 a.m. to 6 p.m. Those are my official hours anyway. Sometimes Mr. Graham needs me in earlier, or needs me to stay later; it'll depend on what his diary is looking like, and what his plans are when he's back in the country. I do late nights and weekends on an ad hoc basis too, if we've got something like this charity gala going on."

"So, some days you're here on your own?"

"No. Never on my own. Mondays, Wednesdays and Fridays we have a cleaning team in. Tuesdays and Thursdays it's the gardeners. Other people come and go too." She realized I wanted to know who. "Oh, you know: delivery men, that sort of thing."

"So, what can you tell me about Mr. Graham's gardener, Ray Muire?"

"Ray." A softer expression filled her face, as if Ray was someone she liked a lot. "Ray was an old family friend of Mr. Graham. They went to school together. When Mr. Graham started Empyrean in 1967—right here in Dartmouth—Ray made the furniture for his office. Mr. Graham reckons Ray was one of the cleverest guys he'd ever met, in any line of work—you should see the furniture he made. There's a set of book-shelves downstairs that Mr. Graham commissioned for his sixtieth birthday. They're exquisite. Anyway, Ray was never the type to slow down, so even after he'd officially retired he used to come back and mow Mr. Graham's lawns once a week. That's why the police referred to him as a 'gardener,' I think. But he was never a gardener. Not really."

"So is he around today?"

"No." A flicker of sadness told me what was coming next. "Ray died in February. He was only sixty-seven. The same age as Mr. Graham."

"How did he die?"

"He'd been out for a drink in Totnes, and on his way home . . . well, he lost his footing and fell into the river. He was washed away. Police found him the next day."

"He was drunk?"

She seemed a little embarrassed to admit it, as if she were betraying Ray Muire's memory. "Yes," she said finally. "Police said he was three times over the legal limit."

"Was he a big drinker normally?"

Another pause. "Yes. I suppose he was."

"How did Mr. Graham take Ray's death?"

"Not well, as you can probably imagine. He paid for the funeral, made sure Ray's wife didn't have to contribute, and then took two days off to fly back from Tokyo to attend. If you know Mr. Graham, you'll know that's pretty unusual." She shifted forward in her seat and dropped her voice to a whisper. "But he made it back for Ray Muire."

"Ray was partially sighted, right?"

"Right. That was another reason police reckoned he'd strayed too close to the water's edge—and, to be honest, one of the reasons why he had to scale back some of his responsibilities here. We couldn't in all good conscience have him rewiring plugs or fixing our plumbing when he was losing his eyesight. But mowing the lawn was fine—he just pushed it across the grass and then left one of the younger men to do all the edging."

She smiled again.

This was all getting a bit cozy and contemplative so I backed out and pushed on. "How did you first find out about what Ray supposedly saw here—did he tell you he thought he saw Paul and Carrie Ling himself, or did he go directly to the police?"

"The first we heard about it was when the police turned up here."

"I wonder why Ray didn't speak to you himself?"

She frowned. "What do you mean?"

"He seems to have been well liked here, felt at home here, was good friends with Mr. Graham—I'm just wondering why he didn't go to you directly."

"Mr. Graham was out of the country at the time."

"But you were here, right?"

She paused, looking like I'd accused her of something terrible, but the question seemed like a pretty obvious place to go: Graham wasn't around, she was the only full-time member of staff here, and presumably everyone at Farnmoor knew that. She was, for all intents and purposes, the only point of contact while the boss was out.

"I don't know," she said.

"You don't know why he went to the police first?"

"No."

"He hadn't fallen out with Mr. Graham?"

She frowned. "No. Absolutely not."

I retraced my steps back through the conversation, to when I'd first mentioned Muire to her. I could tell immediately that she'd liked him, so I had to assume the feeling was mutual. "Do you think he might have been embarrassed about saying something to you? As if, by doing so, he was accusing you—and, indirectly, Mr. Graham—of being involved in something you shouldn't have?"

She seemed to give it some thought, her eyes off in a space across my shoulder, nails of her right hand drumming out a rhythm on the desk. Finally, her lips flattened and she started shaking her head. "I don't know. Maybe. I think the only person who would be able to answer that is Ray. I'm guessing the police still have his statement to hand?"

"Yeah, I'm guessing they will."

The printouts from the case file were in the process of being sent to me, so without looking at Muire's witness statement myself, I could only really go on Task's impressions. Rambling and incoherent was how he'd described Muire's interview, at least toward the end, and—based on how Katie Francis had painted him, as a lovable, infirm drunk—it wasn't hard to see why.

"Where was it Ray Muire claimed to have seen Paul and Carrie Ling?"

She got up from her desk, went to the window and gestured for me to join her. Through the glass there were a series of fields, one after the other, like a patchwork quilt; each was fenced and gradually dropped down toward a sheer cliff face. "The tenth field along is where Mr. Graham's land stops," she said. "See the barn?" She was referring to a big, empty corrugated steel outbuilding in the third field. "Ray said he saw them—with someone else, if I remember correctly—just in front of that."

"That's, what, a quarter of a mile away?"

"Probably a touch more." She pointed to something else: a narrow path running along the bottom of the fields, parallel to the cliff edge. "That's the public right of way," she said. Wire mesh fencing protected walkers from going over the side. "It goes way beyond the Farnmoor boundaries, but anyone can pick up the path just outside the main gates and follow it down. They can't get *inside* here without coming through the gates first, but anyone can come around the boundary and follow the path."

I nodded. "What would be the chances of speaking to Mr. Graham directly?"

Given his relatively low profile, I wasn't expecting the response to be positive. Instead, she nodded. "I can certainly see what I can do."

"I'm happy to chat with him over video conference."

"Ah, well, that's just the thing," she said, leaning toward the computer and clicking on something. "He's back in the country tomorrow for this charity gala. If I ask him nicely, he might be prepared to set aside some time before the guests arrive."

"That would be great."

"The only thing is, as you can imagine, Mr. Graham is in demand— so if I give you a call late tomorrow afternoon telling you he's got a gap in his diary, you're going to have to drop everything and drive like a maniac to get here."

I smiled. "I'm pretty certain I can do both of those things."

After I left Katie Francis, I walked out into the fields a little way. The wind was icy coming in off the water, and the waves made an immense roar as they crashed on to rocks somewhere over the edge of the cliff. I stopped in the middle of the first field and looked ahead to where the barn stood—disused and open now, its basic structure still intact, but only a few of its panels in place. *I think police doubted his abilities to spot anyone from further than about six feet*, Ewan Tasker said. *He had some kind of a degenerative eye problem. This quack said he was a year out from full blindness.* It was hard to make out detail on it, even with good eyesight like mine. I didn't see how it was possible for Ray Muire.

I turned around and headed back to the car.

The Teeth of the Trap

Friday, August 19, 2011 | Fifteen Months Ago

The diner was at the north end of Paradise Road, squeezed between a run-down motel and an adult bookstore. On the opposite side of the street was a square of undeveloped land, scorched brown by the desert sun and fenced off from passersby. A FOR LEASE *sign stood in the middle, burned and weathered by age. Beyond that, looming over Las Vegas Boulevard, was the Stratosphere hotel, its tower reaching up into a cloudless sky. Apart from the occasional cab ride to the neon lights of Fremont Street, taking the elevator to the top of the 1,149-foot observation deck was about as far north as most tourists came, and none made the journey east to Paradise; certainly not since the Sahara had closed.*

That's probably why Cornell had wanted to meet here.

Carlos Soto nosed the black Lincoln into the corner of the parking lot and killed the engine. It was lonely, litter blowing across the tarmac, no one else here this early. Beyond the gentle tick of the engine cooling, he could hear the hum of an air-conditioning unit on the outside wall and the faint sound of people's voices through a side door, left ajar, about twenty feet further back. He adjusted the rearview mirror so that he could see when Cornell pulled into the lot, then buzzed open his sunroof.

Warm air drifted in. Early mornings in the desert could be cool late in the year, but this was August and there was nothing cool about August. It was already sixty-eight, even though the sun was still a pale molten disc shimmering above the horizon.

The sun was the only thing that closed in Vegas.

His old man used to tell him that all the time growing up. They'd lived in a house near Hartke Park, just him, his pa and his mom, and often Soto and his dad used to sit on the back stoop and watch the sun bleed out along the ridges of the Spring Mountains. They'd never had any money, never went on vacation, never even saw his mom's family, even though they only lived down in Henderson. His childhood wasn't bad exactly, it was just small and unremarkable. All he'd done growing up was ride with his pa down to the Strip where Carlos Sr. had worked as a cage manager. The abiding memory of his youth was hanging around in the foyer at the Desert Inn for two hours every day, waiting for his mom to come and collect him after she'd finished her cleaning shift at The Dunes.

His mom had gone on to higher service when he was eighteen and, after that, he and his pa got closer, leaning on each other; basically, two men completely out of their depth. His mom had been the glue that had held the house together, and without her it felt like every minute of every day they were waiting for things to fall apart. So, four months later, he lied his way into an entrance exam for the Las Vegas Metropolitan Police Department, and a month after, he started as a cadet. He'd made his dad proud that day, so proud Pa had taken him out for a steak. It was the first time Soto ever remembered that happening, and the last: the old man went downhill after that, and two years later Soto was burying him in Woodlawn Cemetery.

A minute passed.

Then two.

He glanced in the rearview mirror, checked his watch, then checked his phone to see whether he'd missed any messages. After fifteen years on the force, he'd been offered the job of Director of Security at the Bellagio, the equivalent of a city police chief, by an old friend who was now the HR Director there. He'd taken it in a heartbeat. He'd been looking for a way out, and knew, if he failed to do anything about it, the Department would eventually destroy him. So he made the move, leaving behind a life that had been his entire existence for a decade and a half, for neon and noise and camera feeds.

He cycled through his messages. They were all from the keno manager: there'd been an incident the night before in the keno lounge, where a couple of men had started throwing punches. Soto didn't give much of a shit about it—drunk people tended to fight; there was no mystery in that—but there was paperwork to fill out and a report to file with LVMPD. All that was secondary, though, at least for now: he wasn't looking for texts or missed calls from the keno manager, any other manager or any department head. He was looking for messages or calls from the guy he was supposed to be meeting.

Soto didn't know much about Jeremy Cornell. All he could say for sure was that Cornell was English and he organized a get-together every three months for a bunch of international high rollers in the Lakeview villa. Neither Soto, the casino manager or the Director of Operations asked much more than that: the villa cost six grand a night, which the casino waived because the whales spent their evenings playing six-figure hands in the baccarat bar, before running up drinks tabs into the tens of thousands of dollars at their villa. They came to Vegas for anonymity, and—for better or for worse—that's what the casino gave them. No one was about to ask questions that didn't need asking, and no one was going to say no if Cornell wanted something done.

Soto glanced at the clock again.

Checked the rearview mirror.

He started to remember the Saturday before—the last time they'd been in—and then all the times before that. Most of the men were pretty normal: rich guys letting off steam, pissing money away like it was water, and screwing anything that moved. But Cornell was different. He was pleasant enough on the surface, but, underneath, he had this way about him; this stillness. The times Soto had spoken to him face to face, Cornell would talk blandly, refusing to commit to any point of view unless it directly affected him or the group, but while he could keep up a conversation, it was always obvious that he wasn't engaged in it. The times Soto had watched him from afar, he'd seen a man who liked to stand there in the shadows, barely communicating, watching the rest of the high rollers, like he was waiting for someone to make a mistake—say something or do something they shouldn't. Soto assumed Cornell was a firefighter: the minute one of the whales screwed up, he stepped in to put the flames out, to maintain the sanctity of the group, to brush whatever had been done under the carpet. Whatever Cornell was, Soto didn't like him.

He checked the rearview mirror again.

Still no sign of him.

"Where are you, asshole?"

Then there was a tap at his window.

Soto turned in his seat, in the direction of the motel next door—and then recoiled. "Shit!" Cornell was standing right outside the driver's door, one hand already on the roof, the other at his side. For a brief second the early morning sun cut across his face, across his smooth, tanned skin, and all Soto could see was his eyes, dark, as if even the sun couldn't light them.

Cornell leaned right into the glass. "Morning," he mouthed.

Soto buzzed down the window, glancing in the rearview mirror again. No car, which meant he'd walked from somewhere. So, how the hell did Soto manage to miss him?

When the window was all the way down, Cornell's eyes moved quickly around the interior of the Lincoln and then pinged back to Soto. "How are you today?" he asked.

"I'm good. I didn't see you come in."

Cornell said nothing in response, just tilted his head slightly to the left.

Soto scanned the parking lot again and turned back. "You said on the phone you had a problem when you were in on the weekend?"

"Yes," Cornell said, mouth peeling back to reveal two lines of perfectly white teeth. That was another thing Soto didn't like: Cornell dressed smartly, had a desert tan and teeth that cost money. He looked completely normal when you saw him at a distance. But then you got up close, and things started to change, subtly, slowly, as if his appearance was a deliberate reverse of the person he actually was. Some kind of trap.

"So, what's the problem?" Soto asked.

"It's a delicate issue."

"When is it not?"

Cornell nodded, as if he agreed. "When we were at the hotel on Saturday, one of our group . . ." He paused; tilted his head a little further. "How shall I put this? Eric, unfortunately, had something taken from his room."

Soto frowned. "Taken?"

"His laptop was stolen."

"Why didn't you report it?"

"We didn't feel it was necessary."

"You need to report all break-ins otherwi—"

"It wasn't a break-in."

Soto paused. "I'm not sure I follow."

Cornell blinked a couple of times and then the point of his tongue emerged from between his lips. "He met someone in the bar. This is all very embarrassing."

"She was a prostitute?"

"Correct."

Carlos looked away. He'd come all the way up here for this crap.

"I need to find that laptop," Cornell said.

"Okay."

"It contains some . . . sensitive material."

"Such as?"

No response. Cornell blinked again, almost in slow motion.

"Such as?"

"I don't think we need to get into that, Carlos."

Soto shrugged. "Fine. I'll go back and see—"

"No."

"No what?"

"We'd like to handle this internally."

"Who's 'we'?"

Cornell didn't react. "I'd like to keep this quiet."

"Who am I likely to tell?"

"I know the room keys at the hotel keep a record of the time, date and whether they've been issued to a guest or a hotel employee," Cornell continued, as if he hadn't heard the sarcasm in Soto's reply. "I know each lock keeps track of the last two hundred times the key has been used to open the door. I know there's a camera forty feet to the left of the room. Given that level of technology, I feel confident we can handle this ourselves, internally, so you don't have to worry yourself about it."

"You're asking me to distribute guest information and CCTV footage." Soto shook his head. "There's absolutely no way I can sign off on that."

Cornell said nothing.

"Look, we value your—"

"I'd like that information."

"I can't give it to you."

"I'd like you to give it to me."

"Look, I cannot give you that information. We'll always try to accommodate any and all requests you have, because we value your custom, but I ca—"

"You live down at Southern Highlands, right?"

Soto felt a flutter of disquiet. "What?"

Cornell nodded. "San Sevino. You bought a little two-story place down there after your father died. Very nice. All gated and safe, mountain views, three-car garage."

"How do you know where I live?"

Cornell just stared at him.

"Are you threatening me now—is that it?"

Again, no reply. Cornell stepped away from the Lincoln for the first time but kept his hand on the roof. "Carlos, people like you don't need to be threatened, because you can see the bigger picture. You can see this isn't worth you losing your job over."

"Fuck you."

Suddenly—a flash of movement—Cornell leaned right into the Lincoln. Soto jolted, shifting back automatically, his knee banging against the steering column.

"You listen to me, you fucking wetback," Cornell spat, his diction immediately changing. "One click of my fingers and you're gone. You get that, right? The people in that group, they've got more money in their wallets than you've got in your whole fucking life. So you're going to do this for me, because you want to know what happens if you don't? I make one call, and inside an hour you lose everything."

Soto stared at him.

Cornell must have seen something in Soto's eyes—some kind of acquiescence—and straightened, adjusting his jacket. "In three days we'll meet back here," he said, playing on his Englishness again, pronouncing every word. This was the image he'd built: the quiet, thoughtful, articulate expat. "Same time. You'll bring all the relevant CCTV footage for the night of August 13: foyer, reception, casinos, bars, restaurants and, most importantly, the thirty-second floor. You'll bring all relevant information from every card used on that floor to help me narrow down the search."

"And if I don't?"

He sighed. "Do we need to go over this again?"

"Maybe I don't care if I lose my job."

"Maybe it's not your job I'm talking about."

A smile pierced Cornell's face—like a crack in a pane of glass—and then, slowly, all the light seemed to leave him: his expression, his eyes, the way he spoke. For the first time, Soto really saw the man beneath the disguise: not the regular guy in the regular clothes, but the person he'd only glimpsed in flashes.

The teeth of the trap.

"Are we clear, Carlos?"

Soto nodded once.

Cornell nodded in return.

Then, a second later, he was walking off, across the parking lot, and—as quickly and silently as he'd arrived—he was gone again.

22

As I got to the main road, about half a mile from the front gates of Farnmoor House, my phone started buzzing on the passenger seat. I scooped
it up and put it in the hands-free.

"David Raker."

"David, it's Spike."

He was calling back with the information on the Lings I'd requested:
financial history, phone calls, passwords for the e-mail addresses. "Spike.
Good to hear from you."

"Sorry it's taken me a day to get this over."

"No apology needed. What have you got for me?"

I could hear the gentle tap of a keyboard. "Everything you asked
for I've managed to pull together. Incoming and outgoing phone calls
for dad, mum and daughter. Addresses for each of the callers. Passwords for their e-mails. And a full financial history. That's what took the
time. These days, it's a pain in the ass trying to extract those things."

"I appreciate it."

"Hey, it's my job."

"Anything leap out at you?"

"Not really," he said. "It's all pretty standard stuff as far as I can tell,
although I haven't gone deep into anything. You're the detective, I'm the
criminal, remember."

"I remember. You going to send it to me?"

"Already done. Separate PDF files for both the financial history and
the phone calls, and then the passwords for the e-mail addresses in the
actual body of the mail."

I thanked him and killed the call, then pulled out on to the main
road. A couple of miles further on, as the snaking coastal road narrowed,
rising and falling above a series of beautiful crescent-shaped beaches, I
stopped at a pub called The Church. It was a pokey one-room inn, with
white walls and slate-gray roof tiles, perched on a mound of land—as
the name suggested—behind an old Saxon church. I liked it a lot. It had
character, log fires and cold beer, and—best of all, given south Devon's
flaky 3G connection—it had free Wi-Fi. I flipped the trunk, grabbed my
laptop and notebook, and went inside.

It was quiet. I headed over to the fire, placed my laptop down on the nearest table, and ordered a beer and some food. After chatting politely with the landlord for a while, I connected to the Wi-Fi and logged on to my e-mail. Spike's message was waiting for me.

I dragged the two attachments on to the desktop—one labeled "Financials," one "Phone Records"—but read through his e-mail first of all. He was basically just going over what he'd told me on the phone. At the bottom were the login details for each of the Lings' personal e-mail accounts. Paul had a work account too, and if I felt like I needed to go down that route, I'd have Spike hunt around in the hospital system for his details. But for now I concentrated on the three addresses I had.

There wasn't much to find in Paul Ling's account. Two pages of messages, forty-seven in total, suggested he got pretty aggressive with the Delete button. I went through the other folders—Sent, Drafts, Spam, Trash—and found nothing of interest. Going through each of the messages, one at a time, was like an echo of the life I'd seen on his PC desktop: discussions with other doctors, the submissions to medical journals, lighter conversations with friends and family.

I moved on to Carrie's account. There were about three times as many messages as I'd found in her husband's inbox, but as she'd been a stay-at-home wife and mum, most were conversations with friends and family. She was on Olivia's school committee, and looked to have taken part in a volunteer program on Mondays, where she went into the school and read to the kids. But otherwise, the same names came up time and time again: friends, fellow school committee members, extended family, a reading group she was involved in in Kingsbridge. There was one surprise, though: an e-mail thread entitled "Dissertation," in which I discovered Carrie had been sixteen months into a two-year part-time MA in History at Exeter University. When I followed the thread back, I discovered that she already had a BA in History from Exeter, which I vaguely remembered once I'd read it, although she'd graduated years before I started dating her sister. Something else came back to me as well: the folder on Paul's PC marked "MA." It hadn't been Paul's, it had been hers. She'd been the one interested in the Soviet Union after the Second World War.

Finally I moved on to Annabel's e-mail account. Somehow this felt more intrusive, wading through the messages a 24-year-old had been sending friends, potential suitors, and the teenagers she'd had in her drama class. But nothing stood out.

I closed the e-mail account, and moved to Paul and Carrie's financial history. Like everything else so far, it was black and white. Plenty of money in savings, none of it withdrawn in the time since they'd been missing. Manageable mortgage, insurance policies that had remained unchanged for three years, an ordinary list of direct debits—council tax, phone bills, satellite TV—no loans, no money on their credit cards. If they'd left of their own accord, they hadn't left under any kind of financial pressure.

Next were the phone records.

This was a mammoth job. Three phones and one landline, itemized bills for each one, with names and addresses for each of the incoming and outgoing calls in the last six months of 2011 and January of this year. Immediately I could see that no calls had been made from any of the phones after the family disappeared on January 7, which gave me a definitive full stop, but would ultimately make it harder to find them. Zero calls meant there was a clean break: either they'd done their homework, created a foolproof back-up and made their escape, knowing everything was in place; or it meant they'd been pulled out of their lives against their will, and whoever had done it had covered their tracks. I scrolled quickly through the July-to-December data, seeing if any names leaped out, but as I returned to the top of the first page—to the landline—my food arrived.

After I was done, I ordered a coffee and started over again, edging through the list of calls to their landline. They didn't use it much. That wasn't unusual: with so many free minutes in cell phone packages, fewer people used landlines these days. I was through the itemized bill inside twenty minutes, with little or nothing to stop me along the way.

Carrie Ling's cell was next. I cross-checked the names Spike had got me with the names in her e-mail account and noticed that, generally, the people who were calling her were the same people e-mailing. I doubted I'd find much at the school committee or in her reading group, but three-quarters of the way down was a landline for Exeter University. I'd already written down the name of her History professor—Robert Reardon—and, when I went to the university's website, saw that the main number for the History department was different from the one listed in Carrie's bill, suggesting this was Reardon's direct line. I dialed it, but hit a default BT answerphone message, so hung up again. The MA was interesting: Reardon was one of seven people she'd texted on the day the family disappeared, but more than that, the course was the one part of her life where she was doing something for herself. Everything else was out of some wider commitment—to the school, to friends, to Olivia—whereas the MA was solely about her. It was a small, possibly meaningless anomaly, but it stuck with me all the same. In missing persons, changes in people's lives—however small—were often where the ripple effect began.

Annabel's bill was about twice as long as her mum's and about four or five times as long as her dad's, but seventy percent of the numbers were the same nine people. Ignoring the calls to Paul and Carrie, and to the landline at the house, I checked the names and addresses Spike had got me against the names of the people she'd been e-mailing and found there was a core group of friends that she spoke to three or four times a day, seven days a week. Nothing in the e-mails she'd sent to any of her friends set off alarm bells. The rest of the calls—to recruitment agencies, to local schools—seemed to back up the picture of Annabel I'd managed to gain already.

I took a break for a moment, finishing my coffee and clearing my head, and then pushed on. Paul Ling's itemized bill made up the last three pages, and—like his wife and daughter—many of the numbers married up with the people he was sending e-mails to.

But not all.

One, made in the week before the family went missing, was to a company called Carling Reid, based in Kingsbridge. He called them just once, and only for nine seconds.

They were a travel agency.

I googled them. It was a family-run business, specializing in Far Eastern travel. *Had he been thinking about going home?* I referred back to the first PDF, which included the bank statements for the months prior to their disappearance. No money had been paid to Carling Reid, or to a travel company of any kind. The fact the call lasted for only nine seconds seemed to suggest that even if Paul had phoned with the intention of booking something, he'd changed his mind. The question was why. Had he been thinking about getting the family out of the country, or just himself? Was he running from someone?

There were four numbers in his bill that weren't Devon numbers. One was for the *Lancet*—the medical journal he'd written for—based in central London. Another was a Cambridge number, which—via one of

his e-mail chains—I knew belonged to a friend of his who now worked
in pediatrics at the CUH in Cambridge. A third entry didn't have a number *or* a physical address, just a series of question marks. It had come
through four days before the family disappeared, and Spike had made a
note next to it: *Not sure what the story is here. Think it might be a spoofing service
or some kind of re-origination call.*

A way of disguising the origin of a phone call.

Was this the reason Paul called the travel agent?

I moved on to the fourth number.

An 01822 area code.

There was no specific address attached to it, other than a road—
Long Barn Lane, Princetown. That was in the center of Dartmoor. I
brought the bill closer toward me, flipped back to the start of the records
and pinpointed the three conversations Paul had had with whoever had
called him from the 01822 number. They were all in the three weeks before he disappeared: one on Tuesday, December 20, for thirty-two minutes, the number calling Paul; one on Friday, December 23, for seventeen
minutes, the number to Paul for a second time; and, finally, Paul to the
number on Monday, January 2, the conversation lasting eight minutes. A
day after that final one, he had received the re-origination call. Twenty-four
hours later, he called Carling Reid.

I headed to Google Maps and found Princetown. It flipped to a satellite shot full of green hills and a series of yellow B-roads snaking in from
different directions and meeting at the center of the village. To the north
was the famous prison, its buildings fanning out like the spokes of a
wheel. To the south, Google had dropped an "A" pin into a square mile
full of dirt tracks, forested hillsides and walled-in farmland.

Long Barn Lane.

Switching to Street View, I landed myself at the end of it. The sun
was low in the sky, a prism of color distorting the view, but, as I edged
around, things became clearer. It was a short stretch of road, lasting for
no more than a quarter of a mile, fields on either side. I moved along it.
Initially, there were no houses at all, anywhere, but as I got toward the
road's end, I spotted a turn-off into a thin, gravel driveway. I moved forward. The driveway wasn't mapped in Street View, so I couldn't go any
further.

But I didn't have to.

It looped in, past a knot of fir trees, and then came back on itself, stopping at the front door of a dilapidated house sitting forty feet back from the road. It hadn't been lived in for months. Maybe years. Which meant the phone calls hadn't been made from the house itself. But, in the distance, my eyes had already seen something else.

It was perched on a bank, about fifty feet further on, along the main road.

A red phone booth.

23

Two miles further on from the pub, the coastal road climbed to an apex, drifting closer to the edge than at any point during my journey home. Four yards to the left of my car, the world dropped away three hundred feet, down to the shingle beach that would go on to trace the rifts and hollows of the cliffs, all the way back to the village. Beyond the brow of the hill, as the road began its descent back to sea level, I glimpsed the Ley—a sprawling gray mass, utterly still from this distance, like a sheet of polished concrete—and, briefly, spotted Mum and Dad's cottage, nestled in the hills beyond, half disguised by old trees.

But, before all that, there was another village.

Miln Cross.

It was barely visible to passersby unless you knew where to look, the ghosts of its fourteen houses perched in the shadows of the cliffs and sitting on a platform of rock that had, over forty-four years, begun falling away to the sea. As the coastal road snaked right, taking me away from the edge, it disappeared from view, apart from the spire of its church, the tattered remnants of some kind of flag rippling in the breeze at its summit.

Signs for the village appeared a quarter of a mile further on, blistered and rusting, high grass disguising the *N* in Miln and the *R* and *O* in Cross. There were no tourist trips out to it, no reason to be there other than morbid curiosity, so when I pulled off the main road, the narrow lane almost seemed to close in on me, high hedges and overgrown grass whipping against the car all the way down to the bottom, where it suddenly opened out on to a crumbling square of concrete and a rickety wooden jetty. There were no boats.

I'd been here only once before—as a child—when my dad had brought me down, eight or nine years after the village had washed away. I didn't remember much about it, but I remembered the view: Miln Cross was elevated, built on a plateau of rock about thirty feet up from where I was standing, so all you could see were the first couple of houses and, across their rooftops, the spire of the church. Forty-five years ago there had still been a bridge connecting the village to the rest of civilization, but now there was nothing left: the middle of the bridge had fallen away to the sea, leaving two disconnected walkways.

I walked right to the edge of the concrete square, sea lapping at its edges, and then up on to what remained of the bridge on my side of the water. The gap was about one hundred and twenty feet. Too big to attempt a jump. I glimpsed more of the village: a gently curving main street, full of broken cobbles, and more buildings—mostly houses— looking like they were folding from the inside. Whole roofs were missing from some, the windows empty and dark like open mouths, and walls were perforated with holes where the sea had punctured them as the storm raged. There wasn't much evidence of the landslide externally, the mud and debris washed out to sea over the course of four and a half decades, but inside the houses hardened silt spilled out of the gaps, frozen like some kind of sculpture. On countless walls throughout the village, DANGER—KEEP OUT! signs had been pinned.

As I stood there, watching the rain drift through the walls of the village, I thought about the anonymous call police had received: *I'm calling about that family that went missing—the Lings. I saw the husband and wife at Miln Cross today. You should go down and take a look.* Nothing about that made sense. In order to even be in the position to see Paul and Carrie in the first place, the eyewitness would have had to make a specific journey down here—and why would anyone do that? Perhaps to take some photographs, as a tourist. I couldn't think of any other reason. And that didn't answer the real question: if Paul and Carrie *were* in Miln Cross, for whatever reason, how did they get across? The bridge was a memory, and the village's harbor—the place where the fishermen, who'd once lived and worked here, had moored their boats—was built into the rocks on the other side of the village, out of sight. You could launch a boat from the jetty I was standing next to, but if that had been the case, if the boat had been midpoint across the water between here and the village, and the Lings were on board, why not mention it?

I lingered there for a moment, trying to understand why or how the Lings might have been taken to Miln Cross, then I returned to the car and headed back up the hill.

After a quarter of a mile the coastal road opened out and there was a turnout, cut into the cliff, a high five-foot wall tracing its circumference to stop people falling off the side. I pulled in, got out of the car and went to the wall, trying to get a better view of the village.

Three hundred feet below, Miln Cross was like a child's play set, the

remains of fourteen homes, a pub, a shop and a chapel crammed together on a shelf of land no bigger than a football pitch. The main street
ran from the broken bridge, in a gentle C-shape, all the way to the harbor on the other side, where a jetty had half collapsed into the sea, leaving the steps down, carved out of the rock itself, and some lonely planks
of wood. It was possible the man who'd called the police had seen the
Lings from here, but somehow I doubted it: you'd certainly be able to
make people out below if they were moving through the center of the
village, but it would be hard to identify them. *Unless you had a pair of binoc-
ulars.* That was a possibility, especially when there were such stunning
views out across the water. *Or you knew who they were already.* I studied the
village, turning that last thought over. *Maybe that was the reason he kept the
call anonymous. He knew Paul and Carrie, knew what they looked like, even from
three hundred feet away.* So if you were a friend or even if you only knew
them in passing, why would you be reluctant to give your name?

I looked at my watch.

Three-forty-five. An hour until sunset.

I drove on five minutes to Strete, a village halfway between Dartmouth and home, where I remembered there being a general store.
There was nowhere to park, so I bumped the car on to the pavement
outside, stuck the hazard lights on and headed in. A woman was standing at the back of the shop, pricing up kids' bucket-and-spade sets.

"Can I help you, love?" she asked, turning to me.

I nodded. "What's the biggest dinghy you've got?"

24

Forty-five minutes later, I reached Miln Cross. The sea was rough, especially this close to the cliffs, and rowing my way between the two broken pieces of the bridge in a six-foot dinghy with a couple of forty-inch oars was hard. I'd bought an electric pump from the general store, just to quicken the process, but it took me almost half an hour to get back to the place I'd been earlier, inflate the dinghy and get it ready. I still managed a wry smile as I got to the other side, though, able to appreciate how I must have looked: a 42-year-old man setting sail in a kid's dinghy.

Beneath the bridge on the Miln Cross side was a natural platform, smoothed and carved out from the rock by the sea. I rowed close to it, reached out and dragged myself in, clambering out of the boat and on to the rocks. In the car I'd had a length of tow rope, which I'd brought across. Once I was out of the boat, I pulled the dinghy up, on to the platform, and looped the rope through the rowlocks, securing the raft and both oars to a gnarled arm of rock six feet from the water's edge. Then I climbed the rest of the way up to street level, and stood and looked down the main street.

On the left-hand side there were six stone houses, all in a line, tracing the gentle curve of the road at their front. Behind them, though, the rock fell away sharply, ragged and brittle, their foundations exposed, like the bones of a body, iron pillars breaking out of the earth and reaching up to the floors of the buildings. As I moved forward, the street uneven and fragmented beneath my feet, I could see the chapel on the same side, and then another house right at the end, set back from the others, next to where the harbor was. On the right, under the looming edifice of the cliff, was the rest of Miln Cross: seven houses, consigned to oblivion, a tiny inn, its white walls blanched by four decades of sea salt, and what once had been a shop. There was hardly anything left. The cliffs weren't gray, they were black, blanketed in a wall of hardened mud. This was the epicenter of the landslide: it had moved right through the middle of the village, right to left, and into the sea, taking the shop with it. The only memory of the shop now was three half-broken external walls, and a floor of mud and concrete.

As I got to the first of the houses, the whine of the wind seemed to fade away into a gentle whisper, a strange, disconcerting sound like voices—deep within the roots of the buildings—talking to one another. There was a sudden stillness to the village, its street protected from the breeze coming in off the water, even from the sound of the sea itself: there was no roar from the waves anymore, just a soft slosh as they grabbed and shoved at the plateau the village rose out from. When I paused for a moment at the open window of the first building, it hit home: Miln Cross was a graveyard, its hushed silence the same as every place I'd ever been to where people had been taken before they were ready. In those places there was always a residue, a feeling that echoed through it.

Inside the first house was the decaying reflection of a living room, the fireplace still visible at the back, the wall to its left gone completely. At one time there might have been a picture hanging on that wall. Now there was just a view of the sea. The wall that had once divided this room from the kitchen was a memory, reduced to nothing but a pile of bricks, the interior walls of the kitchen rotten through to the support beams, criss-crossing in sodden, blackened struts. There was no second floor and no roof.

I moved on, past other houses.

In some, just like the first, daylight poured through big holes in the roofs, through gaps in the outside walls, illuminating interiors in a weak kind of half-light. In others, where the roof and the walls were still, somehow, intact, there was nothing but darkness, windows like the eyes of a skull, doorways like widening jaws, black and hermetic.

I stopped at the inn and looked through its big front windows into a building with no roof and no walls on three sides. It was like something from a film set, a facade, and beyond its only vertical surface was a mass of ossified mud, clawing its way across the remains of the floorboards. On the other side of the street the chapel was the same: one side of its high vaulted roof had fallen into what remained of the building, its two stained-glass windows had blown out, and its door had been carried out to sea at some point long forgotten.

I checked the time. Four-forty.

There was about thirty minutes before it was completely dark.

I quickened my pace across the cobbles, heading past the chapel and the inn, and down the gentle curve of the street to the harbor. It was a harbor really only in name: a set of steps was carved out of the rock, leading down to a small, L-shaped concrete jetty, which, of all the structures in Miln Cross, had probably survived the best. Huge nails fixed the jetty to the plateau itself, rust leaking out of them and running down the rocks to the water. On this side of the village the cliff face folded around on itself, creating a natural cove, which was probably why they'd built the harbor here. In years past there would have been space for three or four trawlers, maybe some smaller boats too; once they'd got this side of the village, the cove would have calmed the water for them and they'd have drifted in year after year, unhindered and impervious, until the night the storm came.

The furthest house down was right next to the jetty, angled so that it looked over it. Famously, Miln Cross had had a harbor mistress: this must have been her home. It wasn't lined up next to the others; instead it was set away, built on a separate plateau of rock about six feet below the level of the main street. Out front was a small square of lawn, reduced to a patch of sea-soaked mud, and, behind it, some kind of extension that seemed to be teetering on the very edges of the rocks. The main part of the house was like all the others in the village, the interior filled with rubble, dwindling light stabbing through the tears in the roof, the upstairs gone completely, the living room divided from the kitchen by a tiny sliver of a wall. However, at the back of the kitchen were three walls, all relatively intact, one with a doorway through to the extension.

I moved inside the house.

The smell of damp was overwhelming, an earthy stench eating its way through the house. There were countless punctures in the wall, whole slabs ripped clean away, and, from the roof, water fell in a constant *drip, drip, drip,* soaking its way through patches of what remained of the ceiling. At my feet was a layer of debris: plaster, brick, glass, sand, a twisted, gnarled fire grill fused to the floor in the center of the living room by mud as hard as concrete. When I passed through to the kitchen there were still the skeletons of a counter and a stove in place, doors ripped from it. Apart from that, it was empty. I could vaguely make out old, floral wallpaper, and through the only window—now just a square opening in the wall, dusted with glass—was a view of the jetty.

Halfway across the kitchen, I suddenly felt a gentle suck beneath the soles of my boots, and when I looked down saw that the layer of dust and debris had been replaced by half an inch of water. The floorboards were soft, like sponge, bending under my weight, and as I moved further across the room toward the door, I could feel the boards bending even more and see water running into the house from outside.

I stopped at the open doorway.

The extension might once have been some kind of storage room, but it was hard to gauge exactly how big. Thirty feet from where I was standing, it basically ceased to exist. Beyond that point, the floor and what was left of the walls and the ceiling had been ripped away completely, destroyed by the ferocity of the storm. I stepped into the room and felt it shift slightly, left to right to left again, and when I looked back, I saw that, gradually, over time, the extension had begun to lever away from the house, popping free of the bolts that had once bound it to the main building. The sea was about six feet further down, immediately beneath the point at which the extension ended. In the moments when it was still, it was far enough out of reach; when it got rougher, when the wind started to pick up, the waves sloshed up into the open mouth of the extension and ran all the way through it, into the kitchen. There was the smell of fish, of sea salt, and of dust and age, but mostly there was the smell of damp, picking at the house like a vulture.

Dum. Dum.

A noise from somewhere.

I stood there, right at the end of the extension, feeling it shift and move around me as the sea spilled in, but the sound didn't come again. To my right, out through a hole in the wall, I could see a small back garden, a similar sort of size to the front, awash in mud and rock and water, and beyond that the harbor area. Suddenly, I realized how little light there was left in the day, the sky stained gray, the sun dying somewhere out of sight.

Dum. Dum.

The same noise again. It sounded like it was coming from inside the main house. I moved through the extension, back into what had been the kitchen, and stood there in the advancing darkness, listening. A breeze picked up for a moment, passing through the cracks and fissures of the house, and it made an immense creak, like it was about to fall in on me. More water ran in, under skirting boards, through the holes in the wall, creating a pool of stagnant water, and a DANGER—KEEP OUT! sign, nailed loosely to one of the walls, flapped in the wind as it died away again. Yet even as it faded, something of it remained: a gentle whisper, almost like a chant, and off the back of it, more distant now, I could hear the same unnerving rhythm: *dum dum dum dum dum.*

I moved out on to the main street.

In the twilight, definition was starting to wash out, the interiors of the buildings fading to black, their white walls becoming ashen and indistinct. I waited for the sound again. Ten seconds. Thirty. After a minute I started to move slowly along the road, back toward the place I'd left the dinghy, but then—as the wind picked up again, funneled through the broken chasms of the village—a strange, unsettling sensation passed through me.

I stopped.

I wasn't cold, but I could feel goosebumps forming, scattering down my arms and along the ridge of my spine. For no reason I felt compelled to turn around, as if part of me sensed I was being followed. But when I looked back down the street, toward where the harbor mistress's house was, there was nothing but stillness and silence. High up on my right, on what remained of the chapel's spire, I spotted a crow, sitting alone, the tattered remnants of the flag shuddering in the breeze. It looked at me, unmoved, frozen.

Then, finally, it took off, into the night sky.

25

By the time I got home, it was pitch black. The house was quiet and cold, and as I closed the kitchen door and put the kettle on, I thought of Healy. He would have been back in London by now, staying wherever it was he'd decided he was going to stay, for whatever reason he figured it was best to be back there. He hadn't said anything before he left and I hadn't expected him to, but I knew I was right: not being a cop anymore, not being treated like one, not having the power of the badge, or a single person at the Met he could call in a favor from, had all got to him. He would have felt it keenly over the past couple of days too, first when the body washed up on the beach and he had to watch from the outside looking in; and then when I'd told him he was doing things my way on the Ling case—or not at all. London wouldn't offer him any of those things back, but he would at least be closer to his boys, and from there he could think about starting to move his life on.

I headed upstairs, showered, and then prepared myself some dinner. I ate sitting in front of Paul Ling's computer, looking at the Google Maps shot of the red phone booth in Princetown. Five days after the last of the calls were made to Paul Ling by whoever had been using the pay-phone, the family was gone. That was too much of a coincidence, especially given the remoteness of the phone booth and what had followed: a disguised call from a mystery number, then Paul's aborted attempts to get in touch with a travel agent.

And that didn't even take into account the second anonymous call to police about Miln Cross made in the days after the family was gone. I'd forgotten to ask Ewan Tasker whether that call had been traced, but I'd find out as soon as the file arrived.

I tried to make the natural leaps in logic. The only reason you'd try to disguise the origin of *any* call was to protect your identity—and there was really only one rationale for doing that with the Lings: in the days before they vanished, someone had threatened them and knew the number might lead somewhere; and then, in the days after, they'd called the police in order to force investigators away from whatever they were protecting.

Grabbing my pad, I went to a fresh page and started to make some notes—and then my phone started buzzing on the sofa next to me. Automatically, I reached down, picked it up and hit Answer, before I realized whose name was on the display: Liz.

It was too late to kill it.

"Liz," I said softly.

Silence. I imagined she was shocked I'd even picked up.

"David."

"How are you?"

"I didn't expect you to answer."

There was so much in those six words: accusation, anger, grief, insinuation. "I'm sorry about . . ." I paused. "I'm sorry I haven't called. This isn't how I wanted it to be."

"Healy said . . ." Her voice sounded uneven, as if she hadn't been ready for me to answer either, as if all the things she'd planned on saying to me—all the conversations that had played out in her head—were gone. "Healy made it sound like we'd never speak again."

"Healy loves to be dramatic."

"He was good to me."

"I know. I know he was."

A short silence, then she said, "So, how have you been?"

"Fine. I'm getting there slowly."

"Physically?"

"Physically, I feel fine." The first of the lies: I wasn't grounded by the injury, but I could feel it most days. A dull ache. A sharp pain. If I told her exactly how I was feeling, it returned us to the point at which we'd parted: my job, its risks, the people I tried to find, and how she failed to understand the reasons why. From her side there was no failure to understand anything. After all, what was there *to* understand about a job that ended up with me on an operating table? To her, to most people, it was insane: a job full of uncalculated risk. To me, it was everything that mattered.

"Are you coming back?" she asked finally.

"I don't know, Liz."

Silence. "I miss you."

"I know."

"Do you miss me?"

"Yes," I said, and I did. That wasn't a lie. "I miss what we had. I miss London and my home. I miss being close to you. I liked being able to come next door to chat with you. I liked having someone to share my life with again." I stopped, glancing at the photo on Paul Ling's desktop. *She needs to hear it. You owe her that much.* "But this is my job."

She didn't respond.

"The job is always going to come between us."

"Why?"

"Why what?"

"Why do you have to do it?" she said. There was less emotion in her voice now, and more resolve. "Why would you *want* to do a job that leads you to such dark places?"

"I have a responsibility."

"To who?"

"To the people I'm finding."

"A responsibility?"

"They don't have anyone else."

More silence, and this time I imagined she was returning to the conversation we'd had almost a year before, in the aftermath of another case. We'd been sitting in a police interview room—solicitor and client—as I told her everything that had happened in the case and why I needed her to insulate me. And then she'd said something that had stuck with me ever since: *You're trying to plug holes in the world because you know what it's like to lose someone, and you think it's your job to stop anyone else suffering the same way.* I'd denied it in the weeks after, to myself and to her face, and the relationship had begun and blossomed, and Liz had probably forgotten all about it. But somewhere, right at the back of my mind, I knew I could never get away from what she'd said.

Because she was right.

And now I had to tell her.

"I can't see you again," I said to her, and all I got back was the static on the line. "I care deeply for you, Liz, but this job has already come between us—and it always will."

I waited for a response.

A couple of seconds later, she hung up.

The Six

Destiny was on her second Martini and thinking about leaving the MGM and going somewhere else when the man sat down on the stool next to her. She'd always been bad at guessing ages, but she'd have put him in his forties. He was clean shaven and well groomed; a little thin for her tastes—but it was never about her tastes.

That was the last thing that mattered.

She turned away for a moment, trying not to get his attention—not yet, anyway—then stole a second look. Tailored black suit jacket: tick. Black shirt, Armani stitched into the breast pocket: tick. Gucci jeans: tick. Silver Rolex peeking out from under the shirt sleeves, and a gold wedding band: tick, tick. Men were weak, married men even more so, and that just meant less work for her: if they were here for the conferences and weren't getting much back home, she could have them eating out of the palm of her hand inside thirty minutes. If they'd come just for the sex, it could take less than ten.

As he ordered a beer and picked at a bowl of nuts on the counter, she started to adjust herself in the mirror on the back wall of the bar. Most people would have pegged her for older than thirty-nine if they'd bothered looking at her properly, but as the way to a man's heart was through his dick, it never really mattered that the drugs and the jail time had started to catch up with her. She took off her coat, laid it on the counter, straightened her skirt and undid the top buttons of her blouse. She had to be careful about what she came dressed in. Too slutty or even too classy and the managers would zero in on her, and the really officious ones would call the cops. Prostitution inside the city limits meant facing another misdemeanor, and that meant more time behind bars. So the choice of clothes was important, which was why she stuck to the same routine: knee-length skirt, pumps, white blouse, plenty of cleavage. Men generally didn't need much more than the last one.

When she was ready, Destiny drained the rest of her Martini and then gestured for the woman behind the bar to come over. Out of the corner of his eye, the man next to her must have seen the movement and looked around. Destiny glanced at him, back to the woman behind the bar, then at the man for a second time—it was a fabricated double take, as if she hadn't noticed him take a seat at the bar, but now she had she liked what she was seeing. The man smiled. Destiny smiled back. And then he said hello.

Gotcha, she thought.

The guy's name was Hank; he was from Texas and was in town for a conference at the MGM. After about thirty minutes he'd given Destiny his entire life story. Married. Two kids. Dentist. Liked golf, fishing and football. Big blackjack fan, which was why he was so excited to be in Vegas. "This is my first time here," he told her after buying the fifth round of drinks, not noticing she'd switched to soda, "and I kinda expected the people to be . . . I don't know . . . unfriendly, I guess. I mean, I come from a small town and when you hear about the big city, you hear about crime and drugs and all that kinda stuff. But, honestly, everyone's been really great. Even the kids serving in McDonald's are nice!"

Destiny nodded, then thought, Wait an hour, honey, then we'll see how you feel.

"Anyway, sorry. You must be bored."

"Not at all," she said, gazing into his eyes.

He colored a little as she looked at him, and if she needed anymore persuading that this was already a done deal, he shivered with excitement as she touched his leg.

"Listen, hun, why don't we get out of here?"

He swallowed.

"My car's parked just around the corner. We can go back to mine. It's a twenty-minute drive." She paused deliberately. "In the morning, I can drop you back here."

In the morning. She could see the effect that had.

Five minutes later, she was leading him out.

He was pretty drunk, which would make it even easier. They turned left out of the casino and headed north along the Boulevard. Her car, a crappy Honda Civic, was in the parking lot of a Chinese restaurant on East Flamingo. It had been closed for almost a year. Vegas had gone down the toilet since the recession—businesses going to the wall, houses being foreclosed, highest unemployment rate in the country—so there were empty spaces everywhere. She used the parking lot all the time. Close to the lights of Flamingo it was safe enough for Hank the dentist, but the further across the lot they got, the thicker the shadows became, and right at the back, hidden from view, was her Civic.

And somewhere near it was Carl.

"Wheressshh your car?" Hank slurred.

She smiled at him, but he could barely even focus on her and that suited her fine: she could drop the act. "Just down here," she said, not even bothering to look at him this time, eyes fixed on the sidewalk, scanning her surroundings for potential witnesses or, worse, cops. They were about a block from the Chinese restaurant, its sign still standing at the furthermost edge of the lot. There were fifteen thousand miles of lights in Vegas, but none of them burned here. She grabbed Hank by the arm and yanked him along, half listening to him as he began talking about blackjack again. "Fucking blackjack," Destiny muttered, "Who gives a shit?"

Finally, they got to the parking lot.

"Here we are, hun," she said, talking over him as she started marching him away from Flamingo and toward the shadows. Slowly, out of the darkness, came her Civic, its battered fender, its smashed front headlight, and after a couple of seconds she spotted Carl in his usual place, in a doorway that had once been a rear entrance for the restaurant. He nodded at her, a movement that said she'd done good. She nodded back and pulled Hank the rest of the way toward the Civic. When they got there, swathed in night, she propped him against the passenger door so that he was facing in the opposite direction from Carl. "You stay there a second while I unlock it, okay?"

But Hank was still mumbling about blackjack.

This is going to be simple, she thought, coming around the car to the driver's side and then stepping back from the Civic as Carl made his approach. She glanced at him, at the gun in his hand—a Glock 22 he'd bought for a hundred bucks in North Las Vegas—and then back at Hank. "You doe ever wanna ssssix," he was saying to himself, words slurred, head lolling from side to side, "thas the worss card you can ged. You know why a six is the worss possible card you can ged? Cos there's way more chans of bustin out."

"Is that a fact?" Destiny said, eyes on Carl.

Carl emerged to her left and paused for a moment, sizing Hank up from the other side of the Civic. He was twelve years older than Destiny, graying and overweight, but he was strong and wasn't scared of anyone. That's what she liked about him: she felt safe around him, and he always looked out for her. They'd met at a bar on East Sahara five years before, when she was fresh out of a nine-month stretch for soliciting an undercover cop and he'd just moved down from LA after doing four years for assault. Most of the men she'd been with had used her. Carl used her too—but she got to use him back.

"The sigs ish a bad cart," Hank was mumbling.

Carl moved around the Civic. "Shut the fuck up and give me your wallet."

Carl emerged from the shadows to Hank's right. Hank looked up at him, at the gun being pointed at his head. A split-second delay, massaged by the alcohol—and then he fell apart. "Oh shit, oh shit," he said, backing away automatically, one hand trying to find the trunk of the Civic behind him, the other up in front of his face. "Don't hurt me."

"Gimme your wallet, your watch and your hotel keycard."

"Please don't hurt me."

"Gimme your wallet!"

"Okay," Hank slurred. "Okay. Okay."

He began feeling around in his pocket for his wallet, but—in the panic—his hand slipped from the car and he stumbled back and landed hard on the ground.

Carl stepped forward, jabbing the gun at him. "Gimme your fuckin' wallet!"

Destiny looked out, back on to Flamingo. A few people were walking past, but no one had looked in their direction. "Hurry up, Carl," she said, unlocking the Civic. As soon as they had the wallet, the watch and the keycard, and Hank was out cold, they could go.

"You fly in or drive?" Carl said, leaning over Hank.

"Drive," came the feeble reply.

"Where d'ya leave it?"

"It's a rental."

"I don't give a fuck what it is! Where is it?"

"In the parking"—he waved his arms around desperately in front of him as if he'd forgotten the words—"parking garage! The parking garage at the MGM." He held up his wallet, Carl snatched it from him and Hank started to take off his watch.

"Gimme that fuckin' watch."

"I've got a family. I've got kids."

"I don't give a shit what you got."

Destiny flicked a look at Flamingo and then back across to the other side of the Civic. Hank seemed more sober now. That's what a gun in the face does, she thought.

"Have you got a valet ticket for the car?"

"Yes," Hank said, his voice breaking up. "In my wallet."

"Is your room card in here too?"

"Yes."

Carl flipped open the wallet and checked.

Destiny opened up the Civic, got in and started up the car, keeping all the lights off. No head lamps. No internal light. Nothing to draw attention. In the hotel bar she'd got a glimpse of Hank's wallet. He'd had about eight hundred bucks in it. He probably had more in the safe in his room. Maybe some other stuff in the car. Maybe not. It didn't matter. As Carl opened up the passenger door and got in, she knew he'd be thinking the same as her: even if they didn't get anything else, they were still eight hundred dollars better off.

"Ready to go, baby?" she asked.

Except when she looked around, it wasn't Carl sitting next to her.

It was Hank.

"What the fu—"

He moved so fast, it was like being hit by a train. In a split second he'd clamped a hand over her mouth and pulled her across the car toward him. She tried to fight back, tried to kick out her legs, but they were caught beneath the steering column. He second-guessed her next move, using his other arm to lock hers to the sides of her body and pull her in even closer. She couldn't bite. Couldn't scratch. Her screams came to nothing. The only noise inside the car was her desperate breathing, jetting out of her nostrils.

Her eyes swiveled out through the passenger door. In the darkness she could see Carl, face down on the floor, the gun on the ground about six inches away. There was a single puncture wound to his neck: a dark spot, slowly expanding, running off on to the concrete of the parking lot. "Your boyfriend is dead," Hank said to her quietly. He was totally different now: his demeanor, his physicality, even his accent. He'd spoken in a flawless Southern drawl before. Now she realized that was just a lie: he was English.

"You stole something that doesn't belong to you."

She shook her head. No. No, I didn't. No, I didn't.

"Yes, you did." Quickly, efficiently, he shifted his arm from her face to her throat and started choking her out. "And you know what that means, Destiny?"

Her vision started to blur.

"It means you just got dealt a six."

26

When I woke up, the rain had stopped and the wind had died away. In its place was the gentle warmth of autumn sun coming through the gaps in the curtains and falling across the bed. I lay there for a while thinking about how things had been left with Liz the night before, wondering if that really *was* it. Then, finally, I got up and headed downstairs.

The kitchen was like a greenhouse, sun streaming in through the rear window as it rose above the hills on the far side of the cove. I looked out. The beach was deserted, the sea calm, the sky pale but markless. I flicked on an old portable TV—the only one in the house—and then made a coffee and sat at the window, thinking about Liz and the Lings.

". . . body dumped on the beach . . ."

I tuned back in.

On the TV a reporter was standing on the edge of a winding coastal road, a block of gray-blue sea bleeding into the sky behind her. On her left was a metal barrier, tracing the turn in the road; on her right, a length of blue and white police tape snapping gently in the wind. She had a stern expression on her face: ". . . yet to confirm anything about the victim, other than to say it's a white male. However, a source we spoke to suggested that identification of the victim could still take weeks owing to the fact that—and I quote—'There are some unusual aspects to the case.' Currently, it's unclear what that means."

It means they haven't got a clue who he is.

If police really *were* saying identification of the body could take weeks—and not just feeding the media a line to keep them occupied— then that almost certainly meant the victim's prints hadn't led anywhere. There were two possible reasons for that: one was that they'd lifted prints but couldn't find a match because the victim wasn't on file; the other was that they'd failed to lift prints due to decomposition. It was more likely to be the first. Healy reckoned the body had been frozen, which would have helped preserve it, and when Rocastle had come to see me at the house, he'd inadvertently said that police believed the body had been dumped the day before, on Monday. That wouldn't give it enough time to decompose. Separation of the skin from the digits generally didn't start until the second week, and even then a good forensic tech would still have been able to lift prints from the skin, whether it was detached or not. The race of the victim was interesting, though.

A white male.

That, at least, discounted any of the Ling family. In the back of my mind, I hadn't been able to let the possibility go that the body on the beach and the disappearance of the family were linked. It seemed a compelling reason for Rocastle to have been involved in both cases and to have come to the house to talk to me himself. Now, though, I could forget about that—and I could forget about the body on the beach.

Thirty minutes later, a package arrived. It was printouts of the police file on the Lings. Ewan Tasker hadn't left his name anywhere near it, no details, no indication of who had sent it or where it had come from—but in the right-hand corner of the opening page, he'd scribbled a note: *Hope this helps. E-mailed audio file of anonymous call to you.*

Sitting at the kitchen table, I spread everything out and started going through it. A lot was a repetition of what Task had told me over the phone two days earlier, and the police interviews with Emily echoed exactly the account she'd given to me. I was pleased about the second part: too often in cases the families of the missing would neglect to tell me things, sometimes by mistake, more often because they were trying to paint a picture-perfect portrait of their loved one, believing that lifestyle or relationship choices might impact negatively on how hard I worked the case. It didn't necessarily mean Emily had told me everything: I remembered a fleeting look, inside Paul and Carrie's house, when I'd asked her why they'd waited so long to try for a second child, a look that suggested she hadn't been completely honest with me. But until I saw a direct connection to the disappearance of the family, I was prepared to let it go. Sometimes, when so much of a life was laid bare, you felt you had to cling on to small secrets in order to retain something of the person you loved. They weren't Emily's secrets, but she was their keeper now.

I skimmed the file from start to finish, then turned back to the beginning and started going through it more methodically, writing down key events in chronological order:

January 7
—*Family goes missing.*

January 8
—*Emily files missing persons report.*
—*Ray Muire thinks he sees Paul and Carrie at Farnmoor.*

January 9
—*Ray Muire calls police to report sighting.*
—*DCI Colin Rocastle and DC Stuart McInnes, plus forensics, go to Lings'*
   house. Take DNA samples, fingerprint lifts, etc.
—*Anonymous call made to police re: Miln Cross.*
—*Story gets released to the media.*

January 10
—*Barry Rew calls police to tell them he thinks he's seen Annabel and Olivia close*
   to ExCeL. (HOW DID REW KNOW ABOUT THEM/KNOW
   WHAT THEY LOOK LIKE? NATIONAL MEDIA
   COVERAGE WAS THIN ON THE GROUND, EVEN AT
   THE START . . .?)

January 11
—*McInnes takes over as lead and calls in Missing Persons Bureau (BECAUSE*
   THEY'VE ALREADY HIT A DEAD END AT THIS POINT
   IN THE INVESTIGATION?).
—*Rocastle ends interest in the case (WHY?).*

January 17
—*Police interview Carter Graham about sighting at Farnmoor.*

I found the answers to my initial questions quickly enough. Despite there not being a lot of national media coverage of the case—at that point, police hadn't released any information about the way the house had been left, which would have been the angle that got news editors interested—I soon found out how Barry Rew had recognized the girls. In two separate interviews, first over the phone with McInnes, then—thanks to the cooperation of the Met—with McInnes a second time at a station in west London, Rew talked about how his family had come from south Devon, and he still tried to keep up to date with local news. He'd read about the Lings on the internet.

It was difficult to get a sense of him from the interview. His record was attached, and it didn't make for pretty reading, yet he spoke lucidly throughout, recalling the same details and articulating them in roughly the same way both times McInnes talked to him.

One section in the second transcript particularly stood out:

MCINNES: How did you know it was Annabel and Olivia?

REW: It looked like them.

MCINNES: How can you be sure?

REW: I guess I can't be, not one hundred percent.

MCINNES: But?

REW: But I'd only been reading about them on the internet that morning. My sister used to live down in Kingsbridge, so I know the village they lived in. What happened to them, all of them just disappearing like that, it stuck with me. You don't hear much about whole families going missing like that. Like . . . not together, and definitely not down in south Devon. That place is so safe. It's like a theme park. So when I saw them, I just knew.

MCINNES: You knew it was them?

REW: I was pretty certain, yeah.

MCINNES: So who was with them?

REW: Some guy. A white guy.

MCINNES: Age?

REW: I don't know. I didn't get a good look at him.

MCINNES: Anyone else?

REW: No. Just the guy. He was driving. From my angle, I could mostly see the girls. The little one had a Mickey Mouse doll.

In both interviews, McInnes subtly pushed a parallel line of questioning, where he tried to figure out what Rew's play might be, and why he might lie about seeing the girls. But both times it went nowhere. Nothing in Rew's record, as checkered as it was, pointed toward any kind of relationship with the Lings, or with anyone else connected to the case. So that only really left one option: he genuinely believed he'd seen them.

Ultimately, though, it was a dead end. The car had never been traced, because Rew had never been able to get the police even a partial plate. The temporary roadworks had been set up close to Connaught roundabout, at the eastern end of Victoria Dock Road, where there was no street-based CCTV. There were no other eyewitnesses. And then, as I searched the file for any other interviews with Rew, any other contact the police might have had with him in the months after, I found something else. In some paperwork immediately after the transcripts, McInnes had included copies of some daily reports on the status of the investigation, which he'd e-mailed across to Rocastle. One, dated Tuesday, March 20, stood out:

No new leads. Figured it might be worth going back to the eyewitnesses, so I called Ray Muire, left a message on voice-mail, and am still waiting for him to call back. Barry Rew's a bit of a shocker, though: couldn't get him on the phone, and no one answered when I drove down to his house. He doesn't have any family, so I put his name through the computer—turns out he died on Feb 17 from a drug overdose.

That stopped me.

So, Rew and Muire were *both* dead.

Ewan Tasker had failed to mention that over the phone, probably because he'd been looking to give me the headlines rather than the detail. But clearly there was a pattern: Rew ODs on February 17; Muire falls into a river eight days later. As I read over McInnes's e-mail again, a hint of unease took flight in me. And yet investigators—and an autopsy—didn't find anything suspicious about either of the deaths.

Included in the file were contact details for Ray Muire's wife, Martha.

I noted them down and moved on.

Next were the transcripts of the interviews with Muire and Carter Graham. Task had been right about Muire's: he came across as well intentioned, but while both interviews he'd done started out well enough, building a very clear, very precise picture of his day at Farnmoor up to the point at which he'd apparently seen Paul and Carrie, his answers soon became long and difficult to follow. There were inconsistencies too. First, he claimed to have seen Paul and Carrie in front of the barn in the fields outside Farnmoor, but then in the second interview he said they'd been on the other side of it; in one interview he said the person who'd been with them looked like a man, in the second he said he wasn't sure anymore. Rocastle had done both interviews with Muire before he'd passed the case on to McInnes, and from his line of questioning it was obvious that, midway through both, he'd dismissed Muire as a witness they could rely on. Even so, it was easy to see why police hadn't dismissed him completely. I'd rarely seen such a disconnect in an interview: in one half of it, Muire was as articulate and resolved as you could hope a witness to be; in the other, it was like he was a completely different person.

Carter Graham was different. He'd talked to McInnes from New York, via video conference, having been in the States since Monday, January 2, after spending Christmas at Farnmoor. Graham spoke eloquently, answered all of McInnes's questions without hesitation and became more concerned when he heard Ray Muire was the eyewitness:

GRAHAM: *Ray* said he saw them?

MCINNES: Yes, sir. Do you know Ray Muire?

GRAHAM: He's a very old friend of mine. A dear friend.

MCINNES: So you believe him?

GRAHAM: I trust Ray implicitly.

MCINNES: He's saying he saw that family on your land.

GRAHAM: That's what I understand you to mean, yes.

MCINNES: Why would that family have been on your land?

GRAHAM: I don't know. I mean, some of it's a public right of way, so it's hard for us to police everyone who comes and goes, but I don't know . . . I've no idea why they would be there.

MCINNES: So you're saying they could have been there?

GRAHAM: I'm saying it's perfectly possible, yes. Look, I'm not home for long periods of time, and I wasn't at home at the time of the sighting, but if you speak to my PA—her name's Katie Francis—she'll know the comings and goings there. If you find any of her answers unsatisfactory, I'd be happy to get involved.

I was impressed by Graham's statement. When you had as much money as he did, things tended to lose their value quickly—including friends and family—but there was no sense of that with him. He seemed genuine, was courteous to McInnes and frequently repeated the same offer of help. Despite that, there was nothing of any real substance in the interview. It was getting easier to see why the investigation had hit a wall so quickly.

The evidence inventory listed everything—computers, paperwork, even clothes—that forensics had taken from the Lings' house in the days after they went missing. None of it led anywhere, just as Ewan Tasker had said the day before. Trace evidence, fibers, prints, were a similar dead end. I went down the list again, seeing if anything leaped out.

Halfway down, I found something: Paul's wallet.

I flipped back through my notes and found the conversation I'd had with Emily a couple of days before. *Paul's wallet—last thing to be returned in July/August.* I'd asked myself at the time why police had held on to it for so long. Most of the rest of the Lings' possessions were returned to them inside the first couple of months.

The wallet took seven.

According to the entry, something had been found inside the wallet alongside the usual array of cards, money and receipts: a list—or, at least, the beginnings of one—on a page torn from an A6 notebook. Forensics had quickly matched it to Paul's handwriting.

The list had just three words.

Parker. Cathedral. Dicloflex.

I grabbed my phone. "Parker" got me eighty-five million search results in Google, and nothing I found on the first three pages seemed to connect with the family. "Cathedral" gave me twenty-five million results, and just as little to go on. When I flicked forward to the investigating team's findings, I discovered they'd been back through every aspect of the Lings' lives on discovering the list, trying to find some kind of connection: companies called Parker the Lings had used, worked alongside or been in contact with; then anything in their life that vaguely connected them to a cathedral of any kind. They found nothing. Trying to narrow it down would have been long, arduous and futile work, and eventually the line of inquiry dried up completely.

The third word, however, was different.

Dicloflex was a prescription painkiller.

To treat what, though?

I turned the question over in my head as I moved through to the living room and switched on my Mac. Emily hadn't mentioned any illnesses in the family—but then I'd never specifically asked, and maybe she hadn't thought to say. I made a note to call her.

Now the only thing I had left was the audio file.

I dragged it out of my e-mail and on to the desktop.

Then I hit Play.

It started with a jet of static before settling down into silence. One ring. Two. Three. Then a 999 operator picked up. The person on the line asked for the police. I paused the audio, dragged it back a couple of seconds and played his voice again. "Police."

That was it. One word only.

Six seconds later, a police operator answered. "I'm calling about that family that went missing—the Lings. I saw the husband and wife at Miln Cross today. You should go down and take a look." And then he hung up. I dragged the slider back to the start of the call and listened again. The person's voice was muffled, as if they were pressing the handset too close to their face. In the background there was virtually no sound. Maybe a faint buzz that was probably the line. Only that. I went back through to the kitchen and grabbed the case file to see what forensics had made of the call. They'd been into it and ripped it apart looking for low-level sounds, and came back with a short list: the ticking of a clock, the buzz of a TV. But as I read further down, something else caught my eye.

Police had been unable to trace the location of the call, even retrospectively, and by way of explanation a forensic tech had written: *Substituted CLI.* Caller line identity. By substituting the CLI during the call's journey, you disguised its origin.

Six days earlier, Paul Ling had received the same type of call.

Maybe even from the same person.

27

There were no medical records for any of the family in the case file, but it was safe to assume that, on finding mention of Dicloflex in Paul Ling's wallet, police would have secured a warrant for them. Again, the lack of progress on the case since the discovery of the list suggested that, even if they'd matched the drug to an illness one of the family may have had, it hadn't led them to anything worthwhile. The other two names on the list were probably the reason police had held on to the wallet for so long: they'd been trying to find out if there was a connection between whatever or whoever Parker and Cathedral were and the mention of the painkiller. When I tried to second-guess the police, I kept coming back to the only theory that made sense: one was the name of a doctor, and the other was a medical insurer, or perhaps a clinic. There was no way of knowing for sure, though. I'd found no indication of a private medical scheme in any of the Lings' financials.

I grabbed my phone and scrolled through the address book until I found Emily's landline. It was Saturday, so there was a good chance she'd be at home. Once she answered, we chatted for a couple of minutes about how things were going, but I danced around much of what I'd learned so far. I wanted her as clearheaded as possible. She hadn't mentioned any of the family as having been seriously ill, probably because— if they had—she'd never seen the relevance, or none of them had been sick in the recent past.

"Let me ask you something," I said to her eventually. "Have any of the family suffered any kind of serious illness over the past two to three years?"

"Why do you ask?"

"Something came up."

A pause.

"Emily?"

"Yes." She sounded in pain. "Annabel."

"What happened to her?"

"Almost two years back . . ." A pause. "She was involved in this car accident. It was awful. Some idiot was going too fast, lost control of his car and drove right into the side of her. We were all just . . ." Another pause, longer this time. "We were all just stunned. I remember feeling . . . it's hard to put it into words. Just numb. The worst bit was having to watch her in the days after. The fear in her face. She thought she was going to lose her leg. I mean, that's what they told her. It was all I could do not to constantly cry."

"I guess Paul and Carrie took it even harder than you."

She didn't seem to hear me.

"Emily?"

"They were upset as well. I mean, obviously. It was their daughter. Paul was the stronger of the two, I suppose—he was a medical man, he dealt with this sort of thing all day. I don't mean he was unfeeling— definitely not. But I think he decided he was going to try and remain strong, because Carrie and I, well . . . we were just a mess."

"So what happened?"

She didn't respond, as if her mind were elsewhere, and then a memory came to me: standing in Paul Ling's study with her, asking her about why the Lings had waited so long to have Olivia. "Emily?"

"Sorry?"

"What happened after that?"

"I don't know. Things kept changing all the time. Some days doctors would seem more positive—though, to be honest, most days they weren't. They pinned her leg, reset it, restructured it somehow, but after a couple of weeks they were still telling her it was a fifty-fifty chance whether surgery would take properly or not." She sighed. "The idiot driving that car had basically flattened her entire leg. It was horrendous."

I recalled seeing pictures of the family that had been taken in the last six months before they disappeared, and both of Annabel's legs were intact then. "But the surgery took eventually?"

"Yes. Eventually."

"That's good. So this was when?"

"The accident was at the start of December 2010."

Almost two years ago. It was why she thought it hadn't been relevant.

"And how long was her rehab?"

"A year. But things were instantly much better once she got back."

I frowned. "Back from where?"

"Oh, they went to the States for more surgery in February 2011. Paul and Olivia stayed out there for a month and then came back. Paul had his job; Olivia had missed a month of school and couldn't afford to miss any more. But Carrie stayed behind with Belle, for the surgery, the re-covery, everything else. They came back at the beginning of May."

"Why did they go to the U.S.?"

"They were offered a second opinion: consultation, tests, surgery, the works—all inside a week. Here, they couldn't get in to see the specialist for a month and a half. She was in so much pain, she could hardly even walk." Emily stopped. She sounded on the verge of tears. "We all just wanted it sorted."

I was about to ask her who had offered them a second opinion when that last bit struck a chord with me: *We all just wanted it sorted*. I'd thought originally that it was the tone in her voice that kept registering with me. I'd become so used to people lying to me, I'd been searching her quieter, more uncertain moments for whatever it was she was keeping back. But maybe it wasn't that at all. Maybe there was no deception. Maybe it was as simple as the way she spoke about the Lings: as if she were a part of their family unit, involved intimately in their decisions, their doubts, their fears.

"Who was it who offered them a second opinion?"

"A doctor they found via one of Paul's friends."

"What was the name of the friend?"

"Do you remember Lee Wilkins?"

The name made me pause.

I remembered him well. We'd grown up in the village, gone to the same school, and then Lee and I left home and never spoke for nineteen years. In an odd footnote, I'd bumped into him in a casino in Las Vegas at the end of 2007. I'd been on what turned out to be my last foreign assignment. He'd already been living in America for seven years, trying to make the break as an actor. I remembered our conversation that night, though not with absolute clarity. We'd been getting on well, enjoying reminiscing—then he'd gone to the toilet and never returned. There was some other guy with him too.

What was it the guy had said to me?

"David?"

"Sorry. Yeah, I remember Lee. I ran into him a couple of years ago, actually. Do you still keep in touch with him?"

"No. But he and Paul became very good friends. This was before Lee moved to the States in 2000. His sister got pregnant with her second child and there were all sorts of complications while she was carrying, and then even more after the baby came along. The baby ended up becoming Paul's patient, and he was just amazing with Lee's sister and the little girl. Lee was down here all the time from London when this was going on, because his sister's husband just upped and left and never came back when he found out she was pregnant. Lee's mum was struggling to cope with the stress of watching her daughter go through all that, so Lee really stepped up to the plate. He and Paul hit it off, first at the hospital when Paul was treating the little girl, then afterward. Lee asked Paul out for a thank-you drink, and from there they developed this really close bond."

"So, what, Lee acted as a liaison between Annabel and the U.S. doctor?"

"I only know what Carrie told me."

"Which was what?"

"That Paul was talking on Skype with Lee—this was after Annabel had been told she'd have to wait six weeks here to even see the specialist, let alone get it sorted out—and he was telling Lee how desperate they were. I think Paul was trying to keep it together but at the end of the day, well . . . it *was* his daughter." She stopped for a moment. "Anyway, Lee mentioned to Paul that he knew this brilliant orthopedic guy through his job."

"So Paul made the decision to fly the family out?"

"Not exactly."

"What do you mean?"

"Lee offered to pay."

"For the flights?"

"For all of it."

"The surgery too?"

"Yes. By that stage he was earning a lot of money. Carrie said he was some kind of entertainment director at a bunch of casinos in Vegas—he was responsible for booking all the acts. I think he had his own show, I don't know. I guess he could afford it."

"Even so, that's a pretty big gesture."

"Huge."

"And they obviously accepted?"

"Paul took a little more persuading, but I remember Carrie telling me about it the next day, and it was the first time I'd seen her smiling in a month. They had to take up the offer. Not to do it would have been insane. So, a couple of days later, they flew out."

"Where did they fly into?"

"Los Angeles."

"Is that where the doctor was?"

"I don't know. It all happened so fast."

"They didn't tell you when they got back?"

"They kept quiet on a lot of the details."

"Why?"

"Carrie just said Lee was keen to keep things on the QT, that he wasn't one for big gestures and that he'd asked them just to accept the gift and not worry about the details. To be honest, that was good enough for me. All that mattered was Belle."

I looked down at the list on the table in front of me. *Parker. Cathedral. Dicloflex.* "So they never told you what the doctor's name was?"

"No, they didn't."

"That didn't bother you?"

"Why would it? Belle got better. That's all I cared about."

"Ever heard the name Parker?"

"No. No, I haven't."

"What about Cathedral—maybe the name of a clinic?"

"No."

"Do you know if they took any pictures while they were out there?"

"I don't think so," she said. "I didn't see any, anyway."

I hadn't found any in the house either; nothing relevant on any of the computers. I was hoping there might be some evidence of where they'd gone—the clinic, the doctor, anything. But it was a long shot. The trip out hadn't been any kind of a holiday, and Lee Wilkins had, for some reason, asked for discretion. I made a note to go through their phones again to see if there were any pictures I'd missed.

"A couple of final things: what were the actual dates of their trip?"

"I can find out. Hold on."

I heard her put the phone down and walk away. While she was looking, I retraced my steps, back through the conversation. The list must have been one Paul made prior to the trip. I wondered if it was part of a conversation he'd had with Lee Wilkins, or maybe even with the specialist himself. I walked through to the living room, woke my Mac from its sleep and googled Parker, adding "orthopedics" and "Los Angeles." There were four possible options, all with the surname Parker. When I did the same search, replacing Los Angeles with Lee's hometown of Las

Vegas, I got three more. I did the same with the search term "Cathedral," adding "Los Angeles clinic." Zero hits. The same in Las Vegas.

A couple of seconds later, Emily returned.

"Sorry about that. I had to dig out last year's diary. Luckily, I'm a hoarder, so I always keep these things." She paused. I heard pages being turned. "Right. So. They flew out February 3, and Carrie and Belle came back . . ." More pages being turned. "May 6."

I wrote down the dates. With a flight there was a paper trail, at least as far as LA. If they'd taken an internal connection from there—possibly to Las Vegas, where Lee was based—that would be an added bonus. Finding out where they'd gone once they landed would be harder without an idea of which doctor they were seeing, or even where he was based. I could, in principle, get Spike to hunt through hotel records in LA or Vegas for the time they were out there, but it would be a forlorn task. If Paul had noted down the painkillers Annabel was going to be taking in recovery, it was just as likely that the other two names were connected to her operation too—which meant my best hope of picking up a trail was to find out which Parker had done the operation, and what Cathedral was.

"How did they seem when they got back?"

"From the States? Ecstatic."

"They all seemed exactly the same as always? You didn't notice any changes in them in the eight months between them getting back and going missing?"

"No. Why?"

"I don't know. I'm trying to look for reasons they might have left."

"No, they were fine," she said. "Better than fine, in fact, because everyone was firing on all cylinders. Belle was healthy, so everyone was happy."

"Did the police speak to you about this?"

"About the trip to the States? Yes."

"What did they ask?"

"Pretty much the same questions you did."

Which meant they'd failed to find the doctor. Or if they'd found him, he'd been able to provide a full account of the Lings' trip out to see him. If I had to take a guess, I'd say it was more likely to be the second: Annabel went out with a serious leg injury and came back healthy, suggesting the specialist had lived up to his reputation. The best way to find him, and to close off that line of inquiry, was going to be through Lee Wilkins. I'd have to try to get in touch with him in the U.S. somehow.

"Okay, last question," I said to her, and thought about the Dartmoor phone booth that Paul had received three calls from in the weeks and days leading up to the disappearance. "Did you ever hear Paul—or maybe Carrie—talking about having a connection to anyone on Dartmoor? Specifically, Princetown. Maybe they had a friend there, or some sort of business associate? Maybe they were getting calls more regularly in those final months?"

"Dartmoor?" She sounded confused, which was all the answer I needed. "The police also asked me that. Do you think that's where they all went—Dartmoor?"

"Not necessarily."

"Then what's the relevance?"

I paused, readying the lie. "It's just a loose end."

A loose end that could be the key to finding them.

"No," she said. "They never mentioned anything."

It didn't change much: I was still going to head up there.

As I thanked her and hung up, something suddenly came to me: I'd been trying to recall the man who'd been with Lee; the man who'd come up to me at the bar in the Mandalay Bay, five years ago. And I'd been trying to remember what he'd said.

Let me give you a piece of advice. He'd been in his forties, thin and wiry, with a smooth, hairless face. *Someone will always have the edge over you, David.* He'd known my name. *You're just flesh and bones like everyone else.* He'd known who Derryn was too. *Do both of you a favor and stay out of our business.*

I'd tried to tell him that I didn't even know him. But then I remembered his response as clearly as if no time had passed at all.

No, he'd said. *But you know Lee Wilkins.*

28

Martha Muire lived in a village on the eastern fringes of Torquay, in the other direction from Dartmoor, so, as I traced the circumference of the national park, I decided against doorstepping her. It wasn't just that it was miles out of my way, or that I needed to be up and back as soon as possible in case Katie Francis called to say Carter Graham would see me. It was that she was an old woman—at seventy-two, almost five years older than Ray Muire would have been—and generally people of that generation thrived on routine. If I turned up, out of the blue, it would either confuse her or antagonize her. But if I called her first, it gave me the chance to lay the groundwork for a visit—if it even came to that.

As soon as she answered the phone, I knew it was the right decision. She sounded older than seventy-two, reading her phone number out, then stumbling halfway through, then repeating it all over again. When she'd finished, I said to her, "Mrs. Muire, my name is David Raker—I'm an investigator looking into the disappearance of the Ling family, here in Devon, back in January. I'm not sure if you remember that case from the news?"

"No." She had a gentle Devonian twang to her accent. "No, I don't."

"Well, one of the people who claimed to have seen that family in the days after they went missing was your husband."

A pause. "Ray?"

"Yes. He said he saw them at Farnmoor House."

"What did you say your name was?"

"David Raker."

Another pause. "Have we talked before?"

"Before?"

"Have you called me before?"

"No, I haven't."

A strange question. I filed it away and moved on.

"Mrs. Muire?"

"Yes?"

"Would it be okay for me to ask you a couple of questions?"

At first she seemed reluctant, perhaps a little suspicious, as if she'd answered all the questions about her husband she ever wanted to, and couldn't think who might want to know more. But, slowly, as I gently started to steer her in the right direction, she began to warm up. We spent ten minutes talking about Ray and how much she missed him, and I didn't interrupt, letting her answers build a picture for me: most of the time she was lucid and self-deprecating, playing on the fact that she was getting old, but occasionally she didn't have to play on it. She'd lose the tail of the conversation, allowing it to wander off into other areas, and every time it happened I gently steered her back toward Ray.

"So, what about Paul and Carrie Ling?"

"What do you mean?"

"He was convinced he saw them?"

"There was no doubt in his mind."

"Do you remember what he said to you?"

She'd struggled throughout to recall precise details, so I wasn't holding out for any revelations—and I wasn't disappointed. "No," she said. "I'm sorry."

"But you believed him?"

"Oh, definitely. He was my husband, of course, so I suppose your first instinct is to always support your partner. But even if that hadn't been the case, it would have been hard to dispute him. I don't remember the details, but I remember he was sure about what he'd seen." She stopped. "I mean, why would he lie about something like that?"

"Maybe he wasn't lying. Maybe he was just mistaken."

"He knew what he saw. I'm sure of it."

I didn't bother fighting her on it. She'd fallen in line behind her husband and she remained true to him, a stance that would only have hardened in the months after his death. The facts seemed less romantic, though: Muire's eyesight was declining rapidly, and he liked a drink. At best, those two things clouded the picture; at worst, they discredited Ray Muire as a witness altogether. Certainly, his interview with Rocastle didn't paint him in the kind of posthumous glow his wife was clinging to.

"He saw Paul and Carrie on a Sunday—is that right?"

"I don't really remember, I'm afraid."

"Did he often work Sundays?"

A long pause. "I think it used to depend on what was going on at the house." She paused again. "Carter, well, he would hold a lot of parties and, you know, social . . ."

She'd lost her train of thought. "Social events?"

"Yes, that's right."

"Did you and Ray ever attend any?"

"A few."

"That must have been fun."

"Oh, it was. Back when I didn't have the turning circle of the *Titanic*, I used to like a little dance." She chuckled to herself. "But about ten years ago, I became unwell and I had to, you know . . ." She stopped. "Scale back. It was a shame, but it didn't bother me as much as it bothered Ray. He was a very social animal; loved being out and about."

I saw my chance: "So did he then start going out on his own?"

"Yes."

"Where was his local?"

"We have a pub just down the road here, but mostly he used to like going back to Totnes. That's where he spent a lot of his twenties, so he still had lots of friends there."

"How often did he go out?"

"Oh, I don't know. Two or three times a week."

"Did it ever bother you?"

"Not really. He'd only ever go for a couple of pints."

"But he obviously had more than that the night he died?"

She didn't respond, but her silence spoke volumes: he liked more than just a pint or two, and it was clearly something she'd never fully managed to get a handle on, maybe at any stage of their marriage. "He never got out of control, though," she added quickly, as if assuming I'd think the worst. "He was a lovely, kind man. His father had been a drinker, and he'd just grown up in that kind of environment. When he went out, he *really* went out if you know what I mean. But he always got soppy when he was drunk. He definitely wasn't the aggressive type. I think, if he'd been like that, I wouldn't have let him do it."

If you'd ever even had a choice.

"Did you ever worry about him before then?"

"Worry about him?"

"That the combination of the drink and his eyesight might be a problem?"

"We're old, David, but not *that* old."

It seemed another weird answer, but before I had the chance to follow up on it, she said, "I'm sorry to be rude, but I'm meeting a friend in twenty minutes."

"Of course."

"If you want to know anything else, you can call me again."

"I appreciate that, Mrs. Muire. Thank you."

"It's been a pretty terrible year what with one thing and another."

"I can imagine."

"Ray going like that, then the house . . ."

"House?"

"Oh," she said, "I was burgled a month after Ray died."

"I'm sorry to hear that." But my mind was already ticking over. "What was taken?"

"That was just the thing. Nothing, really. They smashed the front door in, left the house in an awful mess, but the only thing they took was a photograph from a frame."

"A photograph of what?"

"A photograph of Ray."

29

Once I got on to Dartmoor, the weather changed. Clouds rolled in, coming fast over the hills, as I followed a lonely B-road into the heart of the park. After about ten minutes it started to spit with rain. After twenty, the roads were awash with rivers of water as big, gnarled storm-clouds opened in the skies above. Through the heavy rain it was hard to see the phone booth initially, but—as the rooftops of Princetown came into view in the distance—it emerged from behind a bank of trees that had already been stripped of their leaves for winter.

Beyond it was the farmhouse, empty in the pictures I'd seen of it on Google. As there was nowhere to park on the road, I turned off and headed up the dirt track toward the house. The road up was like the building: broken, pockmarked, and in desperate need of repair. Out front there was the space for three cars, but there were no vehicles—save the rusting skeleton of a tractor in an adjacent barn—and no sign of life. If anything, the house looked in an even worse state than it had online. A door. Two windows. Two more on the first floor, one of which was missing a small pane of glass and part of its shutter. A cluster of roof tiles were ripped off too. Everything around the house was overgrown.

I killed the engine and looked back across my shoulder, to the B-road I'd come in on, then down to the phone booth. I wasn't exactly sure what I'd been expecting. Maybe, in my more hopeful moments, some kind of marker; an idea of why someone would choose this phone in particular. But, in reality, I hadn't been expecting a revelation, and I knew why the caller had chosen this place: it was a public pay phone on the edge of a village in the most remote part of the county. No CCTV. No onlookers. No chance of being caught.

A couple of seconds later, my phone started buzzing.

Number withheld.

I pushed Answer. "David Raker."

"Raker, it's Healy."

I hadn't been expecting to hear from him, and as I tried to imagine why he might be calling I knew, instinctively, it wouldn't be a social call. That wasn't how Healy was programmed. I couldn't remember a single time in the year we'd known each other when he'd picked up the phone to see how I was. So that really left only one possibility.

He needed something.

"Healy. How are you?"

"Fine."

He didn't say anything else.

"What's it like being back in the big, bad city?"

"Same as it ever was."

"Where are you staying?"

A pause. "Just a place I know."

Terse, guarded answers. This was a conversation we'd had countless times—and usually in the days before I had to dig him out of the mire. "What's going on, Healy?"

"What do you mean?"

"You know what I mean."

A long silence on the line. In the background, I could hear the faint sounds of the city: endless cars, buses wheezing into action, distant police sirens. "I've got a question."

"Which is?"

A moment of hesitation. "You heard anything about that body?"

Here we go. "Why?"

"I'm just interested."

"Why?"

"I told you, I'm just interested."

"Come on, Healy. We both know that's not true."

Silence.

"That body doesn't matter anymore," I said to him.

"What, a murder victim doesn't matter to you?"

"You know I didn't mean that."

"Then what *did* you mean?"

I felt my hackles rise, but this time didn't bother reining myself in: "I haven't got time for another argument, okay?" I stopped, letting that hit home—but not long enough for him to cut in. "It's irrelevant, Healy. I told you that. You aren't a cop anymore. The whole point of moving back to London was to make a fresh start."

"Was it?"

"You said it yourself."

"No, I didn't."

"You *did*."

"Don't tell me what I said, you patronizing prick."

"I'm not *patronizing* you, Healy. Don't you get that? I'm trying to save you from yourself. Have you ever stopped to think about what would happen if Rocastle, or one of the others on that team, found you snooping around an active case?"

No response.

"Healy?"

"You think I'm cooked, is that it?"

And then it all fell into place.

I remembered he'd said the exact same thing to me before he'd left: *You think I haven't got anything left in the tank. Everyone thinks I'm done.* Suddenly, I could read between the lines: while he was still in Devon he'd tried to prove me wrong, tried to get back in touch with his old colleagues at the Met to show me his sources were as good as mine. But they'd turned him down flat. Now the embarrassment and anger burned in him.

"Just let it go, Healy."

"What are you talking about?"

"Forget the body. Forget everything. Start over."

Nothing.

Then, finally, he said, "I'll see you around."

And the line went dead.

30

Getting out of the car, rain drifting in toward me, I headed to the front door of the house. It was locked. So were the windows. Shutters, not clipped to the walls, swung in the wind, moaning gently as they moved. I walked around to the sides of the house to see whether I could get through to the back. On the right, it was overrun: knee-high grass crawled out of the broken concrete path, while a waterfall of brambles and ferns cascaded down from a patch of raised vegetation above. When the house had been lived in and cared for, the fact that it was carved into the slope of the hill would have made it attractive. But, after years of neglect, the moors had started to claim it back: bleak and lifeless, it had no heartbeat anymore—and, gradually, it was being returned to the earth.

On the left, I managed to find a narrow path through more vegetation, helped by the fact that the barn was directly adjacent to the property on this side, acting as a barrier between the moors and the house. I took a look through both downstairs windows before heading around. The first, to the left of the front door, was smeared with grease. It was difficult to see anything other than two vertical blobs, which I assumed were patio doors at the other end. The second window looked into a room with nothing in it. No carpet, just floorboards. No furniture. No light fittings. The only hint the room had even been occupied at one time were square marks on the faded wallpaper—like echoes from another time—where pictures had once hung. I headed around to the back garden.

Except there was no garden, just a small paved area, broken slabs sitting awkwardly in their beds, grass and weeds coming through between them. A stone wall, gently curving from one side of the house to the other, rose up twelve feet, enclosing the patio. Ferns and grass spilled over it, clawing their way down from the slope of the hill.

On the ground floor there was a back door—originally painted blue, but bleached by age and weather—a long window, and the patio doors I'd seen from the front; on the first floor, two windows, both boarded up. Cupping my hands to the glass of the patio doors, I looked inside. It was a living room, running all the way along to the window I'd been looking through minutes before. No carpets, nothing on the walls, no furniture.

Through the rear door, I could see a poky kitchen. Old-fashioned cabinets. A sink with nothing in it. No appliances of any kind. In the space where the washing machine should have been, the outlet hose snaked off across the room; where a fridge had once stood I could see four impressions—carved into stained, beige-colored linoleum—where its feet had dug in. I tried the door, expecting it to be closed.

Instead, it swung away from the frame.

I stood there for a moment, fingers still around the handle, paused in the open doorway. Then, finally, I stepped into the house and pushed the door shut. The sound of the rain dropped away instantly, reduced to a gentle background chant. Inside it was silent. Even in empty homes there was usually noise: the hum of the refrigerator, the soft tick of a clock, but here there was nothing.

The kitchen had been completely stripped back. Anything not nailed down was gone. I pulled out drawers, slowly, quietly, looking over my shoulder the whole time, into the hallway that led off this room. I expected to find some forgotten utensils, old cans of food, reminders that this place had once been lived in, but everything had been removed. Perhaps whoever had once lived here could see what was happening. The walls were decaying, blackened by damp, moisture running in trails from the coving; the cabinets were uneven, sinking in on themselves, rotting from the inside out. The whole house was dying, slowly and painfully, as if it were a real, living thing.

When I was done, I walked to the hallway door and stopped. The living room was off to the right. Stairs to the left. The empty, smaller room at the front of the building was beyond the stairs. More walls infected with damp. No furniture. No carpets. I carried on along the hall to the bottom of the stairs and looked up. I could see only two doors, but I knew there were four rooms. Two at the front. Two at the back.

I made my way up. At the top, the house suddenly got darker. The two rooms at the front—empty and stripped of furniture—both had windows, but the two at the back were boarded up. There was no light anywhere inside them. Chips of glass lay on the floor beneath the windowsill in the first, and an old dark-wood fireplace, gradually losing its color, was cut into the wall. As I took another step in, I felt floorboards bend beneath my feet, and the gentle suck of moisture. More rot. More decay.

Then a noise.

I listened for a moment. It sounded like it was coming from outside, although it was hard to tell for sure. Upstairs, the rain was louder, drumming hard against the roof and coming through to the ceiling itself where the tiles had fallen away. I backed out and edged along the hallway to the second, darker room.

This one wasn't empty.

Pushed up against the far wall was a bed: it had an old metal frame, flecked with rust, its springs on the point of collapse. On top of it was a thin, blow-up mattress.

On top of that was a sleeping bag.

I stayed in the doorway but leaned further in, just in case I'd missed someone in the shadows. But there was no one waiting. When I edged further forward, my eyes started to adjust and I made out a wooden storage box—about five feet long by three feet wide—next to the bed. I dropped to my haunches in front of it and flipped the lid.

There were three separate sections. In the first was tinned food: processed meat, vegetables, fruit, rice pudding, stacked up three tins deep. In the second was a box of teabags, packets of biscuits, crisps, some fresh fruit, a tin of powdered milk and some cereal. In the third was a portable gas stove, with a green aluminum kettle sitting on top. Basically, nothing that required refrigeration or electricity.

Then the same noise again.

Closing the box, I moved out to the landing, then down the stairs to the ground floor. At the bottom I paused, trying to pinpoint the noise. For a moment, all I could hear was the rain, sweeping in against the house. But then, briefly, I heard the same sound again; a split second of it. Shrill. Mechanical.

Is it a car engine?

Quickly, I made my way back through to the kitchen. The rain was heavier than ever, drumming against the windows. I stepped out, into the storm, closing the door behind me, and moved to the corner of the building. Peered around. Tried to see if anything had changed. There was no one approaching and my car was still where I'd left it. *But if someone's staying here, they'll be back.*

I was already soaked—clothes plastered to me, water running down my face, hair matted to my scalp—and the weather was only getting worse. Clouds were darkening. Wind was picking up. Inside five minutes the roofs and spires of Princetown—only half a mile away—would disappear behind a wall of rain. Inside ten, I'd be struggling to see the road. That meant I wouldn't see anyone approach—but, with the car still in front of the farmhouse, they'd be able to see me. It was time to get the BMW somewhere else.

I hurried across to it, mind ticking over, trying to remember any places on the way in that I could leave it. A turnout. A side road. Somewhere I could walk in from. I looked in at the empty barn, past the rusting machinery, mud and hay caked to the floor.

And then I stopped again.

Suddenly, I could hear the noise more clearly than ever. Beyond the rain, beyond the sound of it beating against the corrugated iron of the barn. I swiveled and looked back at the house. It lay dormant, dark, the undergrowth either side of it swaying in the wind, massaged by it; a sea of ferns, grass and thorns, rising and falling like waves.

But it wasn't coming from the house.

It was coming from the main road.

Someone was calling the phone booth.

31

It took me half a minute to get back down to the main road. The phone never stopped ringing the whole time. At the bottom of the drive, I paused, looking both ways. No cars. No people. The phone booth was about fifty feet further along, its glass panels steaming up, condensation breaking in thin lines out of the dome-shaped roof. Inside, it was empty.

I headed toward it as water sloshed in the gully to my side and puddles formed in the uneven tarmac. Trees swayed as I passed under them, leaves snapping and twisting. I was starting to feel cold now. The wind was icy, funneled along the road by the walls on either side of me. As I got to the phone booth and pulled the door open, there seemed to be a momentary lull, the rain easing off, the wind dying down. Then, as I stepped inside, the storm stirred and came again, great sheets of water smashing against the glass. I pulled the door shut and placed my fingers around the handset. And then I picked it up.

Silence on the line. Then some distortion.

"What do you want?" A man.

I looked out of the phone booth again, in both directions along the road, and across into the fields opposite the house. "I just want to talk," I said.

"About what?"

"About the Ling family."

No response. I looked for a third time, trying to spot him through the rain. If he could see me, I should have been able to see him.

"You need to leave," he said.

"Why?"

"It's safer that way."

"For you or for me?"

More distortion. "You think this is a game?"

He said it matter-of-factly; calmly, evenly. I turned to the house, damp and dark and being taken back by the fields around it. "No," I said. "I don't think this is a game."

"Are you sure? Because you look like you're enjoying this."

There was no one on the road. No one in any of the fields I had a view of. No one at the house. *Because you look like you're enjoying this.* Was it just a figure of speech or did he really have a clear sight of me? I removed my cell phone and placed it on top of the dial box. The line crackled and shifted, as if the caller was moving around.

"Seriously, why are you here?" He sounded more impatient now. When I didn't respond, I could sense his agitation rise again. "Huh? Why are you *here*?"

"I want to find that family."

"Forget them."

"Why would I do that?"

"Just forget them."

"Why?"

"Because they don't *matter*." His breath crackled down the line. "Nothing matters anymore. It's all fucked. Forget that family. Drop the search for them. Walk away."

"I can't do that."

He sighed. "Do you want to get killed? Is that what you want? Because they'll do it. They'll bury you so far under the earth, even the worms won't find you."

"Who will?"

"Are you listening?"

"I'm listening. Who are we talking about?"

"We're not talking about anyone. This is me *telling* you what's going to happen." He stopped, sighed, and then said very calmly, "Do yourself a favor. Walk away."

"I told you: I can't."

"Why not?"

"I want to find the family."

"Forget them."

"I can't."

"Forget them!"

I turned back to my cell phone. I'd placed it there for a reason. Moving it right to left, I pretended to scroll through the address book, and for a second time the line glitched and shifted, like the signal was drifting. There was something else, too: the very gentle sound of footsteps. *He's moving around again.* I stepped in even closer, hunching over the phone, and the same sounds came again. *He's trying to get a better view of me.*

Which means he can see me.

I dropped the cell back into my pocket, and—very casually—turned and faced out along the road. My eyes shifted left to right: from the fields, across the road, through every tangle of undergrowth and thick covering of trees, and then finally to the house.

"You think you're so clever," the voice said. Again, I didn't respond to him. "You think you're some kind of hero, riding in to save them. But you ever thought that the reason no one's found them yet is because no one's *meant* to find them?"

My eyes stayed on the house at the end of the driveway, dark and abandoned. The door. The windows. The empty barn.

"Do you think you're unkillable—is that it?"

It was the only place that made sense. If he was on the road, I'd have seen him. In the fields there was no cover. The village itself was too far away now, hidden behind a wall of rain and mist. So he had to be in or around the house. But where?

"Huh? Is that it?"

"Is what it?"

"You think no one can get to you?"

"It depends who we're talking about."

A snort of laughter. "You're an idiot—you know that? A fucking idiot. And when he gets to you, and he *will* get to you . . . don't say I didn't warn you."

The line went dead.

I continued watching the house.

And then I saw it.

A fractional movement—there and then gone again. Not in the windows, or at the door, or in the barn. In the roof. Through the space where the tiles had fallen away.

He was in the ceiling.

32

I jammed the handset into the cradle and then hurried back along the road, trying to keep my pace even and my eyes away from the roof; trying not to let him know I'd seen him. At the top of the driveway, as I turned to face the house, I stole a glance at the space in the roof—a five-tile gap where all the rain and moisture came in, where all the decay and damp stemmed from—and saw movement in the darkness. A flash of white—maybe a shirt, or a face. He was shifting position, following my movements.

My car was twenty feet away.

As soon as I'd passed it and headed to the house, he'd either know I hadn't taken his advice or he'd know I was coming for him.

So I took my phone out again, pretending to take a call.

When I got to the BMW, I started shouting into the phone, "I can't hear you!" I stepped around the car, closer to the house. "It's absolutely hammering it down."

Another step closer.

"Can you repeat that?"

Then I was right up against the front of the house. He wouldn't have been able to see me now. The angle from where he was in the roof was too sharp. I continued talking for a couple of seconds, and then, at the side of the building, dropped the phone into my pocket and headed around to the back. At the entrance to the kitchen, I eased the door away from the frame and stepped inside. Paused. Listened.

A creak from upstairs. Nothing more.

I padded through to the hallway, glancing in at the living room and front bedroom in case he'd moved, but they were both still empty. At the bottom of the stairs, I paused and looked up into the semi-darkness of the landing, wondering which of the rooms he was accessing the loft from. I hadn't been looking for it the first time.

Another creak.

I took the stairs slowly, one at a time, angling myself so that my back was to the wall and I could come on to the landing without having to worry about what was behind me. Then I worked my way forward, stopped at the door to the first bedroom—the one facing out to the front—and peered in. No loft space. I stepped sideways to the one opposite—facing out back—its interior much darker. It was the same.

Edging along the hallway, I stopped short of the next two doors. The second front-facing bedroom was smaller and easier to see into, and I discounted it immediately.

Which left the other rear-facing room.

The one he'd been sleeping in.

One step. A second. With a third, I was at the entrance to the room, and my eyes had to adjust momentarily to the shadows. I could see the frame of the bed, the mattress, the sleeping bag. I could see the box of supplies.

And then I could see a loft hatch, hidden in the corner.

It was open.

Suddenly, he came at me from my left, from the corner of the room where the darkness was thickest. I shifted forward and down, trying to duck, but he caught me hard: a fist to the ribs, the flat of his palm to the side of my head. I stumbled sideways into the room. In my peripheral vision I saw him coming again, beanie pulled down over his head, over the arch of his eyebrows, over his ears and the side of his face. He was all in black, disguised against the shadows; part of the room itself.

But this time I was ready for him.

When he tried to swing another punch, I blocked it and then drove back into him, lifting him up off his feet. As he hit the ground, the whole house seemed to shudder. Floorboards rippled. Flutes of dust erupted out of the walls. Plaster rained down from the ceiling. He rolled over on to his front and tried to scramble to his feet, but I was too fast for him: I grabbed the collar of his top and pulled him toward me. Before he had a chance to react, I had him in a headlock.

With the point of my elbow against the middle of his chest, I could feel his heart hammering against the inside of his ribs. "Are we done?"

I tried to angle my head, tried to see his face.

"Are we *done*?"

He nodded.

Shifting my body away from his, I let him out of the headlock and pushed him across the room. He stumbled forward on his hands and knees, and then—slowly, gingerly—got to his feet. Back still toward me, he removed his beanie and threw it off, on to the sleeping bag. He was five-nine, five-ten, probably thirteen stone, with blond hair.

"Turn around," I said.

He sighed. And then he did as I asked.

It was Lee Wilkins.

Firmament

Saturday, August 27, 2011 | Fifteen Months Ago

Destiny stirred in the passenger seat of the Civic and opened her eyes. Immediately in front of her were the jagged peaks of a mountain range, scorched brown, its folds dotted with pale green cholla and the graying skeletons of old trees. When she turned her head to the right, rolling it against the seat, she could see the car was about a thousand feet above Las Vegas, parked on the side of an old, dusty mining road. Wind whistled through the rusted doors of the Civic, through the windows that wouldn't close properly anymore, and she rolled her head back the other way. Outside, about twenty feet to the left of the car, a man was standing in front of a wire-mesh gate; beyond, the mining road continued, dropping down through a thin gap in the ridge before disappearing from sight. He was unlocking the gate, removing the padlock. After it came loose, he paused, the padlock in his hand, as if sensing he was being watched. And then he turned and looked at her.

It was Hank.

Or the man she thought had been called Hank.

The way he was looking at her, unblinking, hands clasped at his front, sent a cold finger of fear down her spine. As her heart started to quicken, she tried to move—but her wrists were bound together, and so were her ankles. She glanced back toward Vegas, to the lights still winking on the desert floor, even as the sun began to rise in the sky above, and wished for her time back, wished she'd never tried to take Hank for a ride. And then she remembered Carl, and how he'd been left on the ground at the parking lot, bleeding out, and an involuntary whimper passed her lips. "Oh shit, oh shit," she mumbled. "What's he going to do to me?" Slowly, reluctantly, she turned back to face the man who'd called himself Hank.

But now he was right outside the car.

Her heart hit her throat, and she made another noise: louder, more desperate, like a frightened child. She shuffled back across the passenger seat, pushing herself up against the door, as far away from him as possible. Yet he made no move: he just stood there, three feet from the car, far enough away so that he didn't need to bend to see her.

She looked down at the binds on her wrists and then back out through the window at him. He seemed faintly amused now, like he was watching an animal in a cage. "Let me go!" she screamed. He didn't move; his expression, his body, his gait, all remained perfectly still. You gotta stand up for yourself, she thought. You gotta show him you're not some helpless girl. "Let me go, you son of a bitch! I will fucking kill you!"

The smile dropped from his face.

Another stab of fear cut across her chest. It had been the wrong move. The man reached down to the driver's door and pulled it open. It squeaked on its hinges. Wind rushed into the vehicle, drawn through the door and the holes in the rusting shell. Then, finally, he bent over and slid in at the wheel, pulling the door shut behind him.

Silence.

"I'm sorry," she said, tears in her eyes. "I didn't mean it."

She remembered more about him now: the English accent, the tan, the great teeth, the way he looked at her. When she'd been trying to grift him, when he'd been Hank the dentist, she'd seen some kind of humility in him, an innocence even.

Now there was none of that.

"Please," she said, her voice breaking up. She tried to lean away from him, to get even more distance between the two of them, but her back was already against the door. She was as far away as she could get. "Look, Hank—"

"My name's not Hank."

"Okay," she said. "Okay. I'm sorry."

"Why are you sorry? I never told you my real name. There was no way you could know." He looked out, across to the unlocked gate. "You see that over there?"

She swallowed.

He turned back to her. "It's okay, Destiny. Relax."

Her eyes flicked to the gate, then back to him. She was confused now: his voice had softened, but the hardness in his face remained. He was playing games with her.

"You see that gate?" he said again.

She nodded.

"That's where we're going. There's a place down there that means a lot to me. It's kind of important in my life. I thought you might like to see it."

She glanced at him. "Okay."

"Is there something in your life that's important to you?" His eyes were still on the gate, but when he didn't get an answer, he turned and looked at her. "Is there, Destiny?"

"There was—"

He jabbed her in the throat.

The move was so sudden, so unexpected, it took a second before her brain even made the connection between what she was seeing and what she was feeling. Then her body went into lockdown. Her windpipe closed up. Her vision smeared. All the air was drawn from her lungs, and as she tried desperately to force out her next breath, all that came back was a gentle wheeze; like the last breaths from her deathbed.

"I don't give a fuck about your life," he whispered, eyes widening, face burning

with rage. And then, as she shrank away from him, pushing so hard against the door she thought she might go through it, he came at her again: one jab to the stomach— and then one to the side of the head.

And then only darkness.

She woke slumped in a chair, at a table, in an all-white room. White floor tiles, two bright strip lights on the white ceiling above. A flight of steps up to one door. A second door at the other end of the room. It looked like some kind of basement. The walls looked to be painted white too, although it was difficult to tell.

Because there were photographs everywhere.

They covered every inch of all four walls, and they all looked to be of the same man. When she tried to shift the chair away from the table, to look at the ones nearest to her more closely, she couldn't—and then realized why. The chair was bolted to the floor. One of her wrists had been handcuffed to a welded metal loop on the edge of the table. Then she noticed what she was wearing. Panties. A bra. No heels. No blouse. No skirt.

"Help me!" she screamed. But, within seconds, something tripped in her throat, and the scream turned into a painful cough, and all she was doing was hacking up saliva and blood. She spat some of it out, across the surface of the table, and then tried again. "Help me!" she yelled, raging against the silence of the room. "Somebody help me!"

The door clunked.

She turned to face it, her heart shifting in her chest. It slowly moved away from the frame and then—beyond it—she could see two men. One was Hank: he was the taller of the two, broader, dressed in the same clothes as he'd been wearing when they'd first met. The other she'd never seen before: he was smaller, stooped, walking with the aid of a cane. He looked old. Really old. Maybe ninety. He was completely bald with liver spots all over him. He paused behind Hank, hunting around in his jacket for something, and then removed a pair of glasses. He slid them on to the end of his nose.

The two men came down the steps into the room, Hank helping the older man. When the old man negotiated the final step, Hank pulled a chair out from the wall and guided him into it. Destiny looked between them. The old man sat there, hands out in front of him, resting on the cane. He was smartly dressed in a brown three-piece suit.

"Hello, my dear," he said.

He had a slight accent that she couldn't pin down.

Hank came over to the table, perched himself on the edge of it and smiled briefly at Destiny. "You should respond to people when they say hello."

Destiny glanced at the old man. "Hi."

The old man blinked, but said nothing.

Don't show them you're scared, she thought.

"Okay, Destiny, I'm going to ask you some questions." Hank removed a pen from the breast pocket of his suit jacket, and then paper. At first she thought he was getting ready to write something down, then she realized the pieces of paper were printouts. "Can you remember being in the Bellagio two weeks ago—that'll be August 13?"

She looked at him. "What's going on?"

"Do you remember being at the Bellagio?"

"What the fuck is going on?"

"You and—" He checked his printouts. "Carl Molsson."

Destiny rattled the handcuffs against the welded arch. "Why are you doing this to me?" She looked between the men. "Why the fuck are you doing this to me!"

Hank moved quickly: he grabbed a handful of her hair and yanked it back, forcing her to arch her spine and look up at him. "Answer the question, you stupid bitch."

She looked at him: his teeth clenched, his eyes glassy like marbles. "No," she said, trying not to let him see he was hurting her.

"'No,' you don't remember being at the Bellagio?" he responded. "Or 'no,' you're not going to answer the question?"

"No, I don't remember."

She looked away from Hank, not able to meet his eyes anymore, and as she did, he released her head. In front of her, the only movement the old man had made was in his eyes: they'd narrowed slightly, tightening to milky discs.

Hank placed a piece of paper down.

It was a black-and-white shot of her and Carl, taken from a security camera. They were walking along a hotel corridor, circled in red pen. In the bottom right was a digital readout: 32-CAM4A / 11:12 /08/13/11.

"Does this jog your memory?"

A second later, she remembered the evening of August 13. There had been this guy in the bar. Eric. He'd been some sort of retired doctor, up in Vegas for a few days of gambling. She'd tried to grift him at the Petrossian Bar in the Bellagio, tried to persuade him to take her to his room, but he'd turned her down. So she'd stolen his keycard. He hadn't had much worth taking, but they'd still found something.

Hank leaned in. "You remember the night of the thirteenth now, Destiny?"

"Yes," she said.

"Good," Hank said. "That's good. You're doing really well, Destiny." He tapped

a finger to the printout. "Okay, so: can you see what your friend Carl is carrying there?"

"It's a duffel bag," she said.

"Correct. And do you remember what was in it?"

"I, uh . . ."

"Save the act."

She cleared her throat; could taste blood. "A laptop."

"I need to know who you sold it to."

"I don't—"

"Think really carefully."

She looked between them. "Why are you keeping me here?"

"Who did you sell the laptop to?"

"I want to know what's going on."

"Tell us who you sold the laptop to."

"Why are you keeping me here!"

Hank made a sudden movement toward her, his eyes fixed on her, like an animal tracking its prey. She shrank automatically.

"I can't remember," she said, quietly.

"Well, you'd better start remembering."

Her brain felt fuzzy, panicked, even though she was pretty sure she knew who they would have sold it to. The same person they always took their stuff to: Leonardo. He ran a pawn shop down on Spring Mountain Road. Everything looked legit from the outside, but Leo had a nice little under-the-counter business on the side: Carl would push things his way, Leo would keep them until the heat died down, then sell them on.

"Leo," she said quietly.

Hank leaned in, his attention fixed on her. "Who's Leo?"

"Leonardo Ferrini. He runs a pawn shop."

And then she told him the rest.

"Good. That's really good, Destiny."

Behind Hank, the old man finally moved, hauling himself out of the chair, almost in slow motion. Hank glanced at him, then back to Destiny. There was nothing in his face now: just a blank, his eyes suddenly dark, his skin tanned and hairless.

"Have you got any family, Destiny?" Hank asked her. "Anyone who will be missing you?" He asked quietly, almost tenderly. It confused her for a moment, because there was no tenderness in his face, no sense that he cared either way, but then, when she'd cleared her head, the answer to his question hit home: she had no one but

Carl. She thought of her parents back in Sacramento. She hadn't thought of them in years, sitting on the front porch of their house in The Pocket, if they were even still there, Mom in her rocking chair, Dad getting his hands dirty painting panels, or working on his Ford Bronco. The thought of them, of being back home now, in this moment, even for just a second, brought tears to her eyes. She blinked, trying to disguise them, trying not to let the men see her like this. But then she swallowed, pain registering in her throat, and she was back in the room, Hank staring at her—and tears were running down her cheeks.

"No," she said. "No one will be missing me."

A short pause.

Then Hank punched her in the side of the head.

She rocked off the seat and fell away from the chair. Her legs hit the floor, her hand jarred as the handcuffs locked at her wrists, and her head smashed against the table. Her skull exploded in a firework of white static, then her vision gradually began to fade to black. She heard the two men start talking again as darkness washed in.

"You need to find it," the old man said.

"I know what I need to do."

"No loose ends."

"I know what I need to do, okay?"

Silence. "I hope you do, Jeremy. I really hope you do."

Behind an unmarked door in the basement of the Bellagio, Carlos Soto sat alone in the security room. The men and women under his supervision, the ones still working the night shift, were out in the casino; he could see them on a bank of monitors on the other side of the office, on the casino floor, at the entrance, on the edges of the bars and communal areas. He swiveled slowly in his seat, eyes drifting from the screens to the certificates on the wall behind him, every framed piece of paper a map of his progress through Las Vegas Metro. He'd been heading up Robbery-Homicide when he'd left the force and taken the job at the Bellagio—but he'd done it for a reason.

Not because he couldn't do his job anymore. His star had still been on the rise after fifteen years—the sheriff himself had said as much when he'd begged Carlos to stay. Not even because of the bodies he'd had to look at, the blood he'd had to walk through, the faces of the families he'd had to break life-changing news to. Not the tragedy, or the darkness, or the hopelessness of some of the crime. Not even for his family—because he didn't have one. His mom and dad were long gone, and there was no wife or kids to come home to, although he'd always desperately wanted both.

No, the reason he'd left wasn't any of those things.

He leaned forward in his seat to where a black-and-white printout of two people—a man and a woman—was sitting on the desk in front of him. The picture was frozen as the couple emerged from a hotel room on the thirty-second floor. The woman was in her late thirties, the guy probably around ten years older. The man was holding a duffel bag. In the corner of the shot was a digital readout. *32-CAM4A / 11:12 /08/13/11.*

This was the reason he'd left. Things like this. Things that didn't feel right, didn't make sense, didn't fit together. Things that chipped away at him constantly because he knew some secret was being buried in the ground while he stood on the periphery looking for answers. He'd left the police because he had an obsessive, almost damaging need for the truth.

And because, basically, he could never let things go.

33

Lee Wilkins looked at me: thinner than I remembered, out of condition. Sweat beaded against his hairline and his skin was a mess. If he ever got outside, it could only have been for snatched moments. He had the look of a man on the run; one frightened enough not to venture too far from the only place he felt safe.

"What the hell are you doing here, Lee?"

He didn't reply.

"Lee?"

He looked from me to the door, and I saw what he was contemplating: making a break for it. But he quickly realized the plan would fail, and as he did so he seemed to shrink in his skin. "You shouldn't be here, David."

"Why not?"

"You don't know what you're getting yourself into."

"Why aren't you in the States?" I waited for a response that didn't come. "Are you on the run from something? From someone?"

He just eyed me.

"Does it have to do with the Lings?"

He became very still, his face a mix of resistance—born out of his time alone; of a fear of whatever he was running from—and relief that he could finally talk about it. "A month after they all went missing, the cops turned up here. I thought maybe Paul had written down the address of this place and left it lying around at home somewhere."

"He didn't need to write it down."

"Because they traced my calls."

I nodded. "Why were you calling him?"

"I was lucky with the cops," he replied, as if he hadn't even heard me. "I was on the way back from the shops and saw them snooping around the house, so I just walked on past. The house was locked, and I knew they'd have to get a warrant to get inside. When they came back, a day later, I'd cleared everything out. All this shit." He paused, looked at me, then at what surrounded him. "I wasn't as lucky with you. You caught me with my pants down. I guess I've got sloppier the longer I've been here."

I looked around the room. He'd been living in a decaying shack and eating out of tin cans for months, so he'd already hit rock bottom. The effect was obvious: he had a fearful, almost frenzied expression, as if the loneliness was getting to him. Really, there were only two places to go from here: to get to this point, he'd probably already seen his fair share of violence, so I could threaten him with more until I got what I wanted; or I could try to talk him around and guide him to where I needed him.

"Lee, listen to me." I dropped to a whisper, the change in tone immediately pulling him from his thoughts. He looked across at me. "I need you to explain to me what happened to the family. Don't assume I know anything. Don't leave anything out."

Before, he'd seemed dazed, punch-drunk, but for the first time his expression cleared, like a fog being carried off. "I don't know all the details," he said quietly.

"Just tell me what you *do* know."

He sniffed; rubbed an eye. "I know that, this time last year, things went wrong in the States for me." He shifted position, dropping fully on to his backside, arm resting on the corner of the box full of supplies. "You remember you and me bumped into each other in the Mandalay Bay that time? When was that—November, December 2007?"

"December."

"Right. What are the chances of that, huh? Two guys from a tiny village in south Devon running into each other in a city on the other side of the world?"

"It was weird."

He frowned. "Weird?"

"Luck. Chance. A quirk of fate." I shrugged. "What do you think it was?"

He smiled, but there was no humor in it. "I think it was some kind of sign, one I should have taken more notice of."

"What are you talking about?"

"After I saw you, that's when it hit home." A breeze stirred inside the house, and the loft hatch began to swing. Lee eyed it, probably wondering what would have happened if he'd stayed up there, hidden properly, never called the pay phone. He'd got desperate trying to ward me off— and instead all he'd done was draw me to him. "When I first moved to Vegas, it was for a job as a compere at a comedy club just off the Strip. You know that. I told you when we met five years ago. Things got bigger and better fast. People found me funny, I was being asked to perform for longer, the pay was improving."

I gave him a look that said I didn't get the relevance.

"Anyway, sometime in 2007—this was probably, I don't know, May or June—this guy knocked on the door of my dressing room and asked me if I ever did private gigs. I said I hadn't done them before, but if the money was right I'd think about it. I mean, I didn't have a routine, really. I just filled the gaps between acts; riffed on what was in the news, on being an Englishman abroad, on the people in the audience. I improvised."

"Who was the guy?"

"His name was Cornell. He never offered me his first name, and . . . I don't know, he just wasn't the sort of guy you asked. He said he headed up this group; looked after this bunch of high rollers that flew in to the Strip four times a year to gamble, drink and screw a few whores." He stopped briefly, his voice becoming softer. "So I said yes. To have said no would have been insane. I was earning good money, but Cornell offered me more for one night than I made in a year. He made it impossible for me to turn down."

"What does this have to do with the Lings?"

He held up a hand, telling me to wait. "I did the gig. It was in the most expensive villa at the Bellagio. This place was, like, four thousand square feet. I'd never seen anything like it. I got introduced to these guys by Cornell, these CEOs, oil tycoons, industrial magnates, surgeons, Silicon Valley billionaires, and I thought to myself, 'What the hell is going on here? How did I even get to this point?' By the time the introductions were done, I was absolutely shitting myself. Most of them were so pumped up on booze and pussy they didn't even notice . . . except for this one guy. He came over to me, put his arm around my shoulder and asked me what the matter was. I said to him, 'I stand up in front of eight hundred people a night—I never get nervous about crowds, but I'm nervous in front of this one.' I told him, 'If I screw up, I leave and you instantly forget me. If I get it right, these are men that could make things happen for me. Big things. *That's* what I'm nervous about.' But this guy just patted me on the back and said, 'Everyone will love you, Lee.'" Very briefly, Lee's eyes lit up. "And he was right. They did. By the end of the evening, I had them eating out of the palm of my hand. I felt untouchable."

I pushed again. "What's this got to do with the Lings?"

"Afterward, it was like I was one of these men," he said, another hint of a smile. "One of the high rollers. We gambled and drank, and they paid for everything—casino chips, booze, call girls, everything. When

the sun came up and they began to drift away, they gave me their numbers and told me to call them if I was ever in their city. I mean, these
were men so far out of my league their cars were worth more than my
apartment." The smile became fully formed. "And then there was just
this one guy left, the one who had come up to me. Cornell had introduced me to everyone, told me what they did, and I just lost track of the
names and job titles. I couldn't remember the guy's name, and yet he was
treating me like his long-lost son. He said he was going to try and get me
a better gig—across *all* the MGM hotels. He said he knew the group
CEO. This guy was *amazing.*" He shook his head. "Inside a couple of
months, he'd organized it: I was working across the entire group, earning a ton of money, and living out at The Lakes."

I studied him. "Why you?"

"You mean why'd he take such a shine to me?" Lee shrugged. "We
went for breakfast. I didn't ask him 'Why me?' to start with because I
didn't want to look a gift horse in the mouth. But eventually it all seemed
too good to be true—so I just came out with it."

"And what did he say?"

"He started telling me this story about my stepdad."

I looked at him, confused. "What?"

"He said they were friends, that they'd grown up together."

"Where—in *Devon?*"

"Yeah. My stepdad ended up working for him."

That stopped me. "Wait, what was the name of your stepdad?"

"His name? Ray Muire."

They'd grown up together.

Suddenly I understood. "Which meant the other guy was . . ."

"Carter," Lee said. "Carter Graham."

34

Just for a moment there seemed to be no sound in the farmhouse. Lee looked across at me and must have seen something in my face. "You sound like you know them both already."

My mind turned back to the conversation I'd had with Martha Muire earlier. *Have we talked before?* She recognized my name, from when Lee and I had been at school, but twenty-five years and ill health had dimmed her memory. I hadn't made the connection between her and Lee because of her surname. But now, finally, it started to make sense.

"David?"

I looked up at him.

"Do you know them?" he said.

"I know *of* Graham. I spoke to your mum about Ray this morning."

He shifted against the bed, shivered almost, as if he were reawakening from some terrible dream. *"Really?* How is she?"

There was a flash of expectation in his face, and I realized that I was his only remaining connection to her. He wouldn't want to hear the truth. "She was fine."

"That's good." He nodded. "That's really good. I e-mail her occasionally. I rarely use my phone—it's too risky—but I sometimes catch the bus into Yelverton; there's this place with the internet." A small, sad smile. "I have to lie to her, though. I wish I could see her but . . . I just tell her I'm touring the MGM hotels in Dubai and Abu Dhabi."

"Why lie to her?"

"I don't have a choice."

"Why?"

He looked at me but didn't say anything.

"If you're in some sort of trouble, why the hell come back here? You're only an hour from where you used to live. Why not disappear to the other side of the world?"

"I know this village. We used to come to Dartmoor all the time with Mum when we were growing up. This house has been derelict for years. I can protect myself here."

"Protect yourself from who?"

Again he didn't answer; cautious, frightened.

I backtracked. "So Graham and your stepdad were old friends?"

"Oh yeah. They went *way* back. I'd never met Carter before. Not face to face. I'd seen photos of him, old photos that Ray had, but I didn't recognize him when I met him in Vegas." He gazed off into the emptiness of the room. "That morning I had breakfast with him, he just kept on and on about Ray, spinning these endless stories about them growing up, about the things they did together. Don't get me wrong, Ray had his faults, but he was special. He wasn't my dad, but I loved him like one. I never had to worry about Mum because he treated her so well. But by the end of that conversation I was sick of hearing his name. That's how ridiculous it got. To Carter . . . well, he was a brother."

In the silence that followed, the wind picked up, whistling through the gaps in the house. "So Graham promised Ray that he'd look out for you?"

The idea seemed to distress him. "Yes."

"What was the problem with that?"

"It meant I became tethered to Carter Graham, to the high-rollers group—and, worse than all that, I became tethered to Cornell."

I sensed a change in him now. "You didn't like Cornell?"

"He called me a week after Carter got me that new job, and said to me, 'Don't ever talk about the high-rollers group, any of the men who attend it or anything you hear.' I got the impression early on that Cornell didn't like me being there. He'd invited me as entertainment, a one-time-only thing, and then, thanks to Carter, I ended up with this amazing new job and became part of the group—permanently."

"You said the group was just a bunch of rich men letting off steam. That's what that entire city is built on. Why did Cornell even care whether you talked about it or not?"

"I don't know." He shrugged. "But it didn't really matter to me either way. Not talking about that group while I was house-hunting for million-dollar properties seemed a pretty good trade-off."

Somehow that sentiment didn't sit right, and we both knew it. Lee shuffled again, straightening his back against the bed frame, and turned to face me. Money could only hide so much curiosity. Being told you couldn't talk about something, without a proper reason, just made you more inclined to find out why. It was basic human psychology.

"So you just went along with it?"

"Yes." But he looked down at the floor to avoid my gaze. "Every three months, when the high rollers returned to Vegas, Carter would phone me up and invite me along, and in the days afterward I'd always get the same call from Cornell, and he'd always tell me the same thing: don't talk about anything you heard at the high-rollers group. Weird thing was, I generally didn't hear *anything*. Most of those men spent the night whacked out on booze, disappearing into side rooms to screw anything that moved."

"So who does this Cornell guy work for?"

"As far as I can tell, himself. He brings all these powerful men together every February, May, August and November, and probably gets a kickback from the casino for it. A cut of whatever gets spent. But I never figured out if that was the only job he had, what his profession was or how he knew those men. You don't ask him things like that." A sudden despondency seemed to wash over him, quickly and overtly: in his eyes, in his physicality, like something—some memory—had left the room and taken a part of him with it. "One time, I'd been seeing this woman for a couple of weeks and we'd been getting on great. I'd booked us a table at this amazing French restaurant and gone to her house to pick her up. When I got out of my car, this black SUV pulled slowly into the road and started coming toward me. It was him."

"Cornell?"

He nodded. "He stopped next to my car, slowly looked from me to this woman's house—and then he just sat there and stared at me. Literally, just stared at me. I'll never forget that. When I try and put that moment into words, it sounds like nothing, but I *swear* to you, the way he looked at me . . ." He stopped. Swallowed. "My knees nearly went. I had to lean against the car for support. I thought I was going to puke."

"He was insinuating you shouldn't be seeing her?"

"Yes."

"Why?"

"Later, I found out that she worked for a tech firm that was in direct competition with one of the guys in the high-rollers group."

"So he's mopping up for them?"

"That's what Cornell's job is: he uncovers things, and he shuts things down."

As I tried to figure out how to loop the conversation back round to the Lings, I remembered something he'd said to me earlier: *After I saw you, that's when it hit home.* He meant that night in the Mandalay Bay, when we'd run into each other. *I think bumping into you was some kind of sign, one I should have taken more notice of.*

"What happened that night at the Mandalay Bay?"

A long pause. "Meeting you there was the first time I realized what I'd got myself into. I went to the toilet, I was washing my hands, I looked up . . ." He glanced at me, the color draining from his face. "And Cornell was standing there. It wasn't one of the high-roller get-togethers, so I never expected to see him. I hadn't seen him at the casino that night. I never even heard him follow me into the bathroom."

"What did he say?"

"That's the thing. He didn't say anything. All he did was stand there. When I tried to talk to him, he refused to even speak. He just stared me down, that same look on his face. Everything about him . . ." He glanced at me again, unable to articulate what he felt. But he didn't need to. I understood. Men like Cornell rarely had to say a word, because everything they were was already written in their eyes. "Eventually, when I got nothing from him, I went to leave the bathroom—and that was when he asked me who you were."

"You told him?"

"I told him you were a journalist. I had to."

"And then?"

"And then he said there was a cab waiting for me out front." His face filled with a mix of dread and fear. "It wasn't a negotiation, believe me."

He didn't need to fill in the blanks. As a hush settled in the room, I recalled that night at the Mandalay Bay—and then the man who had come up to me at the bar after Lee had failed to return. *You're just flesh and bones like everyone else.*

Cornell.

"Tell me how all this connects to the Lings."

He eyed me, teetering on the brink of committing, but it felt like he was most of the way there already. The knowledge of what had happened to the family was starting to weigh heavy, and with secrets, most often, came guilt. The high-rollers group, its protector Cornell, the deaths of Ray Muire and Barry Rew, they were all orbiting the family; I could sense it even if I didn't have a clear sight of the links. And I could see it in Lee's face too: a subtle recognition that this confession had to come. Innocence soon turned into collusion when you found yourself chained to men you were scared of.

"After Annabel had her accident in 2010," he started, almost in a whisper, "the pain Paul was in, it was just there in his face the whole

time. So, in February 2011, I offered to pay for them. I didn't think anything of it. All I'd be doing is helping Annabel." As the wind picked up
again, the loft hatch started swinging in the shadows. He glanced at it
and then back to me. "Even so, I was careful. *So* careful. There was this
orthopedic surgeon I'd met through the group. He'd come up from Palm
Springs and gambled a ton of money. I'd heard from a couple of the high
rollers how brilliant this guy was, but Carter especially sang his praises.
He told me they were old, old friends, that he, Ray and this guy had
known each other since they were kids. He said he trusted this guy like
he trusted Ray, and that was good enough for me. That was the kind of
doctor Annabel needed. So I called this guy up and asked him if he'd see
her. He told me it would be his pleasure. All I had to do was get Annabel
out to Schiltz."

"The doctor's name was Schiltz?"

"Yeah. Eric Schiltz."

"Schiltz was English?"

"Yes. But he'd spent most of his life in the States. He moved there to
study when he was in his early twenties, and just stayed. He helped Carter set up his first international office in LA—put him in touch with
builders, planners, all that kind of thing. Then, later on, he moved from
LA to Palm Springs, to work at a hospital in Cathedral City."

Parker. Cathedral. Dicloflex. I had two out of three now.

"Schiltz became this massively celebrated surgeon," Lee continued.
"Did all the sports stars and celebrities, and then retired early with a
mountain of money. Like, *really* early, at fifty-three or fifty-four. He'd
been on the golf course for ten years at that point. He did some consultation, lectured a little, but he didn't run his own practice. He agreed to
see Annabel, though. It probably helped he knew me through the group.
If Cornell did one good thing, it was introducing me to Eric."

"What happened next?"

I could see a memory form in his eyes. "I flew the Lings into LAX,
organized for them to be picked up at the airport and driven down to
Palm Springs, and then met them down there. I put them up in this
amazing two-bedroom villa at the Parker."

And now I had all three names.

Paul must have written the list while speaking to Lee over the phone
or on Skype—Lee passing on the message about Dicloflex from
Schiltz—and I suspected the police would have come to the same

conclusion. But without Lee and the connection to the high-rollers group, it would have been hard for the cops to piece it all together: the Parker was a hotel one hundred and thirty miles away from LAX, Cathedral City was another four miles away, and the whole family had returned safely in May 2011 and remained that way until their disappearance. It must have been the reason police kept hold of Paul's wallet for so long—because they were never able to narrow down the names he'd left inside. Most likely, eventually, they wrote the U.S. trip off as an irrelevant side-note.

"Okay," I said to him. "Go on."

Lee shrugged. "Carter and Eric were both members of that group, and I knew Cornell wouldn't approve of me using them, of bringing a bunch of outsiders into contact with them like that. So I told Paul not to mention anything to anyone. I wanted the whole trip contained. Paul and Carrie probably thought I was losing it. Sometimes I thought I might be losing it myself. I was paranoid, I knew that. But I didn't want to have Cornell turn up on my doorstep, and I didn't want the Lings involved with him. All I cared about was getting Annabel there, getting her fixed and then getting them back home again."

I recalled how Emily had known nothing about the trip: no details, nothing of the clinic, nothing of the doctor that had operated on Annabel. It made sense now.

"Paul agreed to keep things quiet?"

"He was happy to oblige me—I was paying for everything, after all. Even so, I was cautious: I booked the Parker under my name, gave them cash and pre-paid mobiles."

"But it didn't work?"

"No," he said, and his voice tremored. "Everything was going fine: Annabel went in for two consultations, she had the operation, she was doing brilliant things in recovery and the four of them were having an amazing time in Palm Springs. After a month in the States, Paul and Olivia had to get back to the UK, so I stuck them on a plane and after they were gone there was no blowback. No contact from Cornell. I gave Schiltz a call and asked him how long he needed Carrie and Annabel to remain in Palm Springs, and he was relaxed about it too. A few weeks, he told me, so I extended their stay at the Parker, and a week before they were due to go home, Schiltz invites them both to his home. He lived in this suburb where all the Hollywood stars used to stay. This beautiful old place. It was a two-birds-with-one-stone thing for him, I guess: Annabel was due a final consultation and needed sign-off from Schiltz to travel back home, and Schiltz had really grown to like them and wanted to have them both around to dinner—see his home, get to know them away from the hospital. Eric . . . he was always a nice guy."

He stopped, his eyes just briefly straying to the doorway, as if recalling the life he'd led before this; before this room. But then reality seemed to hit, and he was back in a decaying farmhouse in the middle of winter and there was nowhere else to go.

"When Carrie and Annabel turned up at Schiltz's place, he must have taken them to his study." He looked at me. "And that was when it all went wrong."

"What went wrong?"

"That's why I had to leave the States."

"What are you talking about?"

His head dropped and he stared into his hands—and when he raised his eyes to me again, they shimmered in the subdued light. "Carrie . . ."

"What about her?"

"She saw something she shouldn't have."

35

The rain stopped and a pregnant lull settled around the house: dark, swollen clouds yet to tear themselves apart above us; silence inside; Lee small and frightened and half covered by darkness. He shifted against the bed, then just looked down at the floor.

Carrie saw something she shouldn't have.

"What did she see?"

"A photograph."

"Of what?"

He eyed me. "A man."

"Who?"

"I don't know." He shook his head. "But he's someone bad. If I had to guess, I'd say someone bad enough to bring down Cornell and whatever he's involved in."

"How'd you figure that?"

"We had a get-together at the Bellagio in August, three months after the Lings went home. The next morning, a few of the guys said they were staying in town, so we all went for breakfast. One of the guys was Eric Schiltz. Me and him sat at one end of the table, and he started telling me about how his room had been broken into the night before; some woman had stolen his room key and then taken his laptop."

"The photograph was on the laptop?"

"Yes. Schiltz had scanned a load of old pictures in."

"And what happened when Cornell found out?"

"You can assume he got the laptop back."

"Why can you assume that?"

"Because he's Cornell. That's what he does."

I watched Lee. He was scared of Cornell. "So," I said softly, and he stirred, like he was climbing out of a deep, dark hole, "Cornell got the laptop back—but what about the original photograph?"

"That was at Schiltz's house in Palm Springs. Cornell told him to burn it."

"And did he?"

"Yes," Lee said. "As soon as he got back. But it was too late. Because what Cornell didn't realize was that, three months before, Carrie had been in Schiltz's study."

Then it hit home. "She saw the original."

Lee nodded.

"And, what, Carrie recognized the guy in the photo?"

"Yes."

"From where?"

"From her MA."

I paused, momentarily confused—and then I realized Lee was talking about the History course Carrie was taking at Exeter University. "Her *History MA*?"

"Yes."

"What's the guy in the picture got to do with her MA?"

"I don't know."

I remembered the folder on Paul Ling's PC, the one with her notes in. It had been all about the Soviet Union in the years after the Second World War. "She didn't tell you?"

"I never spoke to her about it."

"What do you mean?"

"I only spoke to Paul."

"But Carrie must have told Paul who this guy was. They were married. If she recognized this guy, they would have had that conversation at some point, surely?"

"No. Carrie instantly recognized the guy in the picture, but she never mentioned anything to Paul. Six *months* passed before Paul found out, and that was by chance."

"Why didn't she tell him before that?"

Lee shrugged. "He always thought her MA was a waste of time. He would have preferred that, if she'd wanted to study again, she'd done something more useful, to her, to him, to the girls. I don't know. This was what he kept saying—that it was a pointless qualification. The type of person Carrie was, that would have just made her all the more determined to see it through. Don't get me wrong, they were happily married, they got on and agreed about most things—but that MA, that created some conflict."

"Which is why she never bothered bringing it up with him."

"Right."

"So how *did* he find out about the photo?"

"He'd got home and she'd left her notebook open with this picture in it. It was a photograph of a photograph; she'd taken a picture of the original in Schiltz's office with her camera phone. Got really close in, so she made sure the guy came out clearly. Paul saw the notebook, was curious, and they started discussing her MA over dinner. She ended up telling him about how she'd taken it at Schiltz's place."

"Did he ask *why* she'd taken it?"

"She lied to him and said Schiltz was helping with research into the history of orthopedics."

"But Schiltz didn't know anything about it?"

"No."

"And Paul? Didn't he realize she was lying?"

"No."

"So, if he didn't know it was a lie, why did he mention it to you?"

Lee took a long, deep breath. "Like I said to you earlier, before I flew them out for Annabel's operation, I'd told them to keep the trip on the quiet, keep a low profile. I'd asked for that one favor. Carrie was a good person—I doubt she would have deliberately gone against my wishes—but I think maybe she'd decided I was being overly cautious. Maybe paranoid. Maybe weird. That's why she didn't think for a moment that taking that photo could hurt. Paul, though, he could see I meant it. He didn't know why, he didn't know about Cornell, but he could see I was serious. I think that's why he chose to tell me about what he saw in the notebook."

"So did he scan it in and send it to you?"

He nodded. "And in the middle of November, when we had our next get-together at the Bellagio, I got talking to Schiltz and tried to persuade him to tell me what was so damaging about the photo—but he refused. He kept telling me that he was done talking about it, that I should keep my voice down in case Cornell heard. But by that time it was already too late. I looked across the room, and Cornell was just standing there, watching us." Then he stopped. He gave me a sideways glance, fear in his eyes. "He just stood there. Staring. I swear to you, it was like he could hear everything we were saying. I know it sounds crazy, but it was like he was reading my mind. I just knew. I just knew from that moment I was in deep, deep shit."

"So what happened after that?"

"I spent the whole night trying to keep out of his way, and the next morning, when everyone started to leave, I found a back entrance and headed out to my car. He was waiting for me outside. He didn't say anything, just stood there, and I basically fell apart on the spot." A pause. A smile. But there was nothing in it, just remorse. "You don't know what Cornell is like, David. The second he looks at you, you see what he is capable of. He's like . . . I don't know, like a vessel or something, carrying around all this violence and misery. When he looked at me, I just started talking and the next minute I was showing him the scan I had of Carrie's notebook, and trying to cut some sort of deal."

"Deal?"

"The Lings for Schiltz." He eyed me like I'd accused him of something. But it wasn't me attacking, it was him. He was hanging himself with his own culpability. "I told Cornell that Schiltz was the reason this had all gone to hell. I tried to play on Eric's carelessness, on the fact that he should never have had that photograph just lying around."

"But you didn't even know who the guy in the photograph was."

"No," he said. "I just tried to sound convincing. I said to Cornell, 'Do whatever you want to Schiltz, but don't do anything to the family. They're my responsibility. I'll take care of Carrie's copy.' I tried to play on their innocence: they didn't know what they were doing, it wasn't their fault, don't blame them. The reality was, I never even knew what was so important about that picture. Still don't. I just knew it could hurt Cornell."

"So did Cornell take the deal?"

"No." A tremble passed through him. "All I ended up doing was committing us both to the ground—Schiltz *and* me. Cornell said the original copy of the photograph was gone, and everything would have been okay if Schiltz and I hadn't brought the Lings into this. If Carrie had never been in that study, she never would have seen the picture."

"You're still alive. What happened to Schiltz?"

Lee looked at me and said nothing, but it was written all over his face; as tears blurred in his eyes he was remembering how Schiltz had saved the life of someone he had cared deeply about—and in return Lee had sent him to his death.

"I just ran," he said. "I booked the first flight home, I came straight here and I lay low for a couple of weeks. But it was playing on my mind the whole time. Twenty-four hours a day. What if Cornell gets to the Lings? What if he sends people after them? So I called Paul, trying to persuade him to take Carrie and the girls somewhere; book a flight, do anything, just get them all out of the country. I spoke to him three times.

Eventually I got so frustrated, I even told him to come here—I compromised my safety so I could plead with him face to face."

"Why didn't he listen to you?"

"Something changed. He drove up here on, I don't know, I think it was January 3, and I swear he left believing everything I was telling him. He could see in my face I wasn't messing around. But by the time he got home, something had changed."

"Like what?"

"I don't know. But he'd changed his mind."

And then a thought came to me: the spoof call.

It was made on the night of January 3. I'd always assumed it must have been a phone call threatening the Lings because the next day Paul had called the travel agent, albeit for only nine seconds. But maybe it was the exact opposite: maybe it was a call to set Paul's mind at rest somehow, to tell him everything was going to be fine. That would explain the short call to the travel agency. A call of that duration spoke of a man battling with uncertainty: Lee, his best friend, on the one side, telling him he needed to make a break for it; the anonymous caller, assured, convincing, telling him everything was fine. I wondered briefly how the anonymous call the police received fitted in: it had come two days after the Lings went missing, directing the cops to Miln Cross. Was it the same person? Were they just trying to throw the case team off the scent . . . or was the caller trying to help in some way? Were *both* calls trying to help the Lings in some way? My head was buzzing with static, so I let it go and moved on: "So, you think Cornell took the family?"

"I know it," Lee said, a hint of steel returning to his voice.

"Why, though? Who's the guy in the photograph?"

"I don't know."

But there was a flicker in his face.

"You said Carrie had taken a small part of a bigger photograph?"

"Yes," he said. "She'd focused in on the man."

"So what was in the rest of the picture?"

He hesitated. It didn't feel like he was lying because he was deliberately trying to keep something back. It felt like he was lying because he wanted it to all go away. But it was too late for that now. He'd told me too much, and now there was no going back.

"Come on, Lee."

"You can see Ray, Eric and Carter in the photo."

I studied him. "Muire, Schiltz and Graham are with this guy?"

"No. He's way off, in the background. They don't even know he's there."

"But do you think they knew him?"

"I think it might have been someone from their early years. Maybe they came into contact with him and didn't even realize. I think Cornell was looking for a reason to take Schiltz out. Silence him. Stop him from ever talking about what that photograph meant."

"And then there was Ray."

His head dropped.

"Do you think he *really* fell into the river by himself?" I asked him.

"Maybe I just want to believe he did."

Suddenly, the conversation I'd had with Martha Muire echoed back to me. *I was burgled a month after Ray died,* she'd told me over the phone. *The only thing they took was a photograph.* "It wasn't an accident," I said, and Lee looked up at me. "Cornell killed Schiltz. Then, whoever does Cornell's dirty work here killed Ray too."

He nodded; a lonely, mournful movement.

I told him about the photograph that was stolen from his mum's place, and then made the natural leap in logic. "Schiltz scanned in a load of old photos, right? So what's the betting he e-mailed a version of that photo to Ray—and also to Carter Graham?"

Lee instantly understood. "You think Carter's next?"

"I don't know. Do you?"

His hands were linked together like he was in silent prayer. "Yes," he said. "I think Cornell will come for Carter just like he came for everyone else." He looked at me. "Because Carter's the only one left who knows who D.K. is."

I frowned. "D.K.?"

"That's what was written in Carrie's notebook."

D.K.

At first, Eric Schiltz thought it was a sound in his head, part of a dream he was having about being back in the village he'd grown up in. But then the dream fell away and so did his sleep, and he realized he was on top of the sheets, naked, and the door-bell was buzzing. He sat up and looked at the clock. Six-forty. Who the hell was calling so early?

Shrugging his gown on, he walked to the windows of the bedroom, all of which looked out across the Mesa. Once, Clark Gable had lived in this area of Palm Springs, among its low-rise buildings and coral-colored roofs. Back then, its tight net-work of homes, nestled in the foothills of the San Jacinto Mountains, was a big gated community. Now, though, as Schiltz noted the blue Pontiac G8 parked at the bottom of the drive, his gate ajar, he was reminded that those days were definitely over.

Heading downstairs, into the center of a sweeping, marble-floored entrance hall with four rooms coming off it—a kitchen, a downstairs bedroom, his study and a sprawling living room—he stopped to check himself in the mirror and ran a hand through his hair.

Then he opened the door.

Standing on the front step was Cornell. He was dressed in a pair of denims, a black suit jacket and black brogues polished to a shine. The early sunlight, arcing in across the porch, cast his hairless skin a golden-brown. He didn't say anything to Schiltz, didn't even look at him, his eyes shifting over Schiltz's shoulder and into the house.

"What are you doing down here?"

Cornell's eyes pinged back to him. "How are you, Eric?"

Schiltz just looked at him. "Do you know what time it is?"

"Six-forty."

Cornell's eyes started moving again, darting around the entrance hall, up the stairs, into the doorways, listening to the sounds of the house. He was seeing whether anyone else was home. Schiltz briefly considered telling him there was, his brain decid-ing in that second, like a survival instinct kicking in, that the best way to head this off was to lie.

But then, as he went to speak, Cornell said, "I'm sorry it's so early."

Except he wasn't sorry. There was no contrition in his voice.

His eyes finally settled on Schiltz. They were small and dark, like an inverted photograph of the rest of him: his smooth skin; his perfect teeth; his hair, exactly parted at the side, unruffled, immaculate. He was dressed in designer clothes, the tailored jacket tracing the lines of his body. But his eyes weren't the same as the rest of him. The rest of him spoke of normality and reason; his eyes spoke of deception and violence.

"May I come in?"

Schiltz shrugged, as if it made no difference to him. But, in reality, he didn't want Cornell inside his house. Ever since Schiltz's laptop had been stolen from his room at the Bellagio, he'd noticed a change in Cornell. He'd always been a little odd: quiet, guarded, often to the point of being rude—but Schiltz had accepted those flaws. He'd known Cornell a long time, knew his background—it was just who he was. But something had changed after the laptop had gone missing: Cornell had called Schiltz obsessively for a week afterward, telling him to burn the original copy of the photograph he'd had on the laptop; the one of Schiltz, Carter Graham and Ray Muire. When Schiltz had tried to reason with him, to tell him it was just an innocent photograph, Cornell had begun to get more aggressive. Eventually, Schiltz did it, just to get him off his back. But even once the picture was gone, Cornell had called him about it, asking questions about Carrie Ling. This time Schiltz had put up more of a fight, saying Carrie knew nothing about the picture.

"Then why was she asking about it?" Cornell had said in response.

"When?"

"On the phone, that night you had your laptop stolen."

"She wasn't asking about that," Schiltz had told him. "Do you think the whole world revolves around that picture, Jeremy? We'd got talking about my big project— scanning in all the photographs—and she'd been interested in that. She's creative. She enjoys stuff like that." Schiltz had paused, letting the lie settle. He wasn't exactly sure why he was deceiving Cornell on Carrie Ling's behalf, he just knew that he didn't want her, or the Lings, on Cornell's radar. He just wanted Cornell to stop calling him.

"Who is she?" Cornell had asked.

"Just a friend."

"Where's she from?"

"Here," Schiltz lied. "In Palm Springs."

And that had been the end of the calls. From the middle of September, Cornell had stopped phoning. No more questions. No more phone calls. No more mentions of the photo or Carrie. Until, at six-forty this morning, he had emerged from the dawn light.

"Let me ask you something, Eric."

Schiltz went to push the front door shut—then stopped. Outside, he could see people walking past with their dogs, others in their running gear. Once he shut the door, he shut them all out and the world disappeared—and then it was just him and Cornell.

"You remember that woman you talked about?"

"Woman?"

"Carrie Ling."

Schiltz's heart sank. "Uh, vaguely."

"Vaguely?" A smile perforated Cornell's starched face. "But when we talked on the phone a few months back, you said she was a friend, that she lived in Palm Springs."

"She does."

"But you only vaguely know her?"

"What difference does it make?" Schiltz said, trying to add some steel to his voice. But he knew what difference it made: with one comment, he'd exposed himself as a liar.

"When did you come out of retirement?"

"What?"

"Earlier this year. I understand you did an operation."

Shit, he thought, Cornell knows all about them. Schiltz nodded, unsure where to go next. "Yes, I did. Her daughter had some complicated injuries, and her family asked if I could help."

"Her family asked?"

Schiltz nodded.

"You mean Carrie asked?"

Schiltz nodded again, not wanting to lead himself anywhere.

"But Lee Wilkins says he asked you on their behalf."

Schiltz realized Cornell had cornered him, and Wilkins had dropped him in the shit. If he admitted that Wilkins had asked on their behalf, he admitted that the request for help hadn't come directly from Carrie, and Cornell would make the last leap himself: that Schiltz hadn't known Carrie before he'd operated on her daughter. It was all a lie.

Before Schiltz could answer, Cornell started to move away from the front door toward the study. Schiltz just watched him, unsure of what to do. Did he let Cornell wander around freely, and risk being drawn deeper into the house where no one outside could see him anymore? He hated the thought of Cornell going through his things and invading the sanctity of his home. But he didn't want to be alone with him. Not now.

"What's going on?" he called after him.

Cornell didn't even acknowledge him. He just stepped into the study, out of sight.

Then a noise: Cornell was going through the drawers of the desk. Anger rising in his chest, Schiltz stepped away from the door, leaving it open, and headed for the study.

Cornell was sitting at his desk, opening up the drawers.

"What the hell do you think you're doing?"

He looked up. Not at Schiltz—it was like Schiltz wasn't even in the same room as him—but around the study, his eyes checking every surface, every space.

"I said, what the—"

"I heard what you said."

Cornell shot a look at him, and the normality fell away. A snake shedding its skin. The slick hair, the teeth, the designer clothes, they were all exposed for the trick they were. This was someone else. Another man. The one Schiltz never wanted to see again.

"Look," Schiltz said, holding up a hand and stepping back. "I don't know what it is you want, but . . ."

And then he couldn't think of anything else to say. Cornell remained still. Eyes not moving. Nostrils flared. Hands flat to the desk and perfectly parallel to one another.

Schiltz swallowed. "Look, what I said about Carr—"

"Did you burn the original?"

"The photograph? Yes, just like you asked me to."

Cornell got up and came around the desk. He took a big step forward, moving in so close that Schiltz immediately felt trapped. His heart juddered in his chest. When he tried to shift sideways, he realized there was no space for him to go because of the angle Cornell was standing at, so he tried to come back, to stand up to Cornell. But Cornell just stood there. Monolithic. Motionless.

"Look, I—"

"Let me show you something," Cornell said, and reached into his jacket. He took out a piece of paper. It was folded, quarter-size. Cornell opened it with one hand and then held it up in front of Schiltz's face. It was a scan of a notebook.

At the top of the page was the picture he'd had on his laptop, the picture he'd set fire to as soon as he'd got back from Vegas. Except it was a photograph of a photograph. Ever so slightly blurred, it had been taken quickly with something like a camera phone. Schiltz, Carter Graham and Ray Muire were all still in the picture, arms around each other, smiling, but everything that had been to the right of Ray in the original was gone. Instead, whoever had used their camera phone had zoomed in and deliberately cropped it so that the central focus wasn't the men, but the space over Schiltz's right shoulder.

"What's this?" Schiltz said.

*In the notebook, beneath the picture, were two yellow Post-it notes, each with handwriting on them. The first said, "D.K., far left"; on the other, "*Photograph taken circa 1971. California (?) USA. Other three men: Eric Schiltz, Carter Graham, Ray Muire.*"*

"It belongs to Carrie Ling," Cornell said.

Schiltz frowned, trying to put the loose ends together. "Carrie?"

Cornell didn't reply.

"Where did she get this picture?"

"Where do you think?"

He looked up at Cornell; Cornell just stared at him.

"She took a photograph of it while she was in here? She must have taken it while I'd been off making them a drink or something. Why would she take a picture of this?"

"She's interested in history."

"History?"

Schiltz looked at the photocopy again. At the edge of the picture, bleeding off, were two men. One was in a hat, flared jeans and a long-collared tan shirt. He was pointing, talking to someone out of shot.

Then there was a second man behind him, lower half obscured by the first guy, head half-turned in the camera's direction, watching the three men being photographed in the foreground. "Wait," Schiltz said quietly. "Wait, that's—"

"I know who it is," Cornell replied.

"I never even knew he was in this picture."

"You should have looked harder."

Schiltz studied the old man. He was still lean and strong at the time, silver hair swept back from a tanned face, and the picture was just about clear enough—even with the blurred resolution—to make out the thin, worm-like scar that ran from his hairline, down the left-hand side of his forehead to the ridge of his eyebrow.

"I can't remember the last time I looked at this picture . . ." Schiltz stopped. He must have seen the old man at the edges of the shot at one stage; it must have registered with him at some point. But he hadn't looked at it for years. Not until Carrie picked it out.

"You've brought trouble to our door, Eric."

"I just forgot he was ever—"

"Now I've got to clean up the mess."

Schiltz ripped his gaze away from the picture and looked up at Cornell. Silently, he'd backed away, put more space between them. Except this wasn't a retreat. Cornell was sizing him up, a cold, clinical expression on his face, like a mortician at a slab.

Schiltz cleared his throat. "Look, we can—"

"It's too late for that."

"We can make this right."

Cornell said nothing.

"Whatever Carrie's done, I can speak to her myself."

Again, nothing. But then movement: Cornell reached down, into the pockets of his jacket, and took something out. Latex gloves.

"Wait a second," Schiltz said. "This is insane."

Cornell wriggled his fingers, balled one into a fist and reached inside his jacket again. A second later, he had a bowie knife: six-inch blade, brown leather grip. "We gave you a version of the truth, because we trusted you as a friend. I've known you a long time, Eric. I thought, whatever happened, you'd never let me down."

"Listen to me: he's hardly in the picture."

"But he's still in it."

"I didn't realize! I'd forgotten."

"You were a friend." Cornell took a step toward Schiltz, fingers rolling along the knife, reasserting his grip. "But how can we trust a friend who lies to us, a friend who is so reckless he doesn't even see the destruction he's causing?"

"That picture means nothing."

"She knows who he is."

"She might not—"

"She knows who he is!"

Schiltz felt his heels hit the wall. He had nowhere else to go.

Cornell stopped, and raised the knife. "I'm sorry, Eric," he said quietly, a flicker of honesty in him for the first time. "But we can't protect you anymore. Not after this."

Five hours later, as Cornell reached the Las Vegas city limits, his phone started buzzing on the passenger seat. He reached across, picked it up and looked at the display. LVMPD/DR. Ridgeway. One of the cops he'd paid off inside Las Vegas Metro.

He answered. "What is it?"

"I thought you might want to know there's been a guy snooping around, asking some questions about that whore you got me looking into back in August. Destiny."

"I know her name. What questions?"

"Trying to find out who she is, her address, what car she drives—trying to ID her. He knows she was associated with Carl Molsson, and he knows Molsson was found dead in the parking lot on East Flamingo on 27 August. It all gets extra fishy when

you realize your friend Eric never reported the crime." Ridgeway waited for a response, but got nothing. "Look, all I'm saying is, you put two and two together, like this guy probably has, and you start to think that Eric, the whore and Molsson's murder might be tied up somehow. And, believe me, I know this guy from way back. I used to work for him in Robbery-Homicide. He's good. He'll be a real pain in the ass if you're not careful."

"What's his name?"

"Carlos Soto," Ridgeway replied. "He runs security at the Bellagio."

36

Six miles out of Princetown, we started to climb Dartmeet Hill, a twisting B-road that carved up across moorland, bisecting fields of brown fern and moss-covered grass. Rain drifted in the whole time, spattering against the windscreen. As we hit the highest point, four hundred feet above the valley, Lee turned to me, eyes distant, expression solemn.

"I shouldn't have agreed to come with you."

"What else were you going to do?"

"Stay at the house."

"It's not safe."

"It's been safe for a year."

"I found you." I looked at him. "Cornell would find you too."

By the time we got back to the village, the rain had stopped. Seagulls— just charcoal-colored swipes against the sky—squawked as they patrolled the shoreline, breaking the soft stillness of the bay; without the birds, there was only the crackle of waves breaking on shingle, and the gentle chime of boat masts, their hulls moored on the beach.

Once we were inside the cottage, I gestured for Lee to sit at the kitchen table, filled the percolator and then made a call to Robert Reardon, the professor taking Carrie's History MA. I'd got his cell number from Carrie's phone bill, but after twenty seconds it went to voice mail. I left a message, asking him to call me back urgently. When I was done, I headed through to the living room and booted up Paul's PC. Carrie's MA notes were still on there. I'd looked at them briefly once before, but this time I was hoping they might give me a clue as to who the guy in the photograph was, now I knew a little more. But it was just a chronology of postwar Russia and vague, indecipherable thought processes.

Back in the kitchen, Lee was staring off out of the window, his eyes fixed on the village below, on the houses and the hills he'd left behind for a life on the other side of the world. After about half a minute, he turned to me. "Do you think they're dead?"

The question took me by surprise. "The family?"

He nodded a second time.

"I don't know," I said, and he seemed to cling to the ambiguity of my reply. But as much as I wanted to deny it, the situation was looking increasingly forlorn. Schiltz had been shown no mercy. Muire, however much his death looked like an accident, had to have been eliminated for the same reasons. Lee would have just been bones and earth if he'd failed to escape Vegas and find a hiding place. The fact that Barry Rew overdosed after being clean for three years seemed like tacit confirmation that his sighting of them was accurate too. And everything, all the death, all the suspicion, was tethered to one man.

Cornell.

Suddenly, the silence was shattered by my phone, buzzing across the counter. It wasn't a number I recognized, but I was hoping it was Reardon. "David Raker."

"Mr. Raker, it's Katie Francis—Carter Graham's PA."

I gestured to Lee that everything was fine and then took the phone through to the living room and pushed the door closed behind me. "Ms. Francis. Good to hear from you."

"Well, I worked my magic," she said.

"Mr. Graham can see me?"

"He's got a four o'clock slot this afternoon, here at the house. He can only spare you forty-five minutes, I'm afraid—I'm sure you remember that we've got a big charity gala this evening—but he says, if that suits you, then you're very welcome to come over."

It was three-thirty.

I looked back at Lee. "Tell him I'll be there."

"Great. I'll let Mr. Graham know."

I hung up and went back through to the kitchen. Lee had helped himself to coffee and was seated at the kitchen table again, cross-legged, staring out across the bay. "Lee," I said, and he started slightly, turning in his seat. "We need to go out for an hour."

"Where?"

"I've got a meeting with Carter Graham."

"Carter?" His face lit up. "He's home?"

"He's at Farnmoor for a couple of days."

"Okay," he said, getting to his feet, "let's go."

"Don't take this the wrong way, but I don't think you should be there. I don't want him distracted. I've got forty-five minutes with him, and I can't afford for it to be a trip down memory lane. I know you'll be desperate to give him your theory too—about him, and Ray, and Eric

Schiltz—but I want that to come from me." I let that soak in, the smile sliding from his face. "I want you to come with me, because I think you should stick close given everything you've told me, but I need you to stay in the car—at least until I've got all the answers I need. Then you can go in, say hello, whatever you want."

Lee sat down again by the window.

"Lee?"

"What's the point?"

"In what?"

"In coming with you?"

"Because I promised to keep you safe."

"I'm not a kid."

"I never said you were."

He looked at me. "Kids stay in the car while their parents go in and chat with the big people. You're treating me like I'm ten years old. Why the hell am I even here?"

"I didn't say—"

"I survived for a *year*. You're not telling me what I can and can't do."

"I can't have you in there—"

"Then I stay here."

"Listen to what I'm trying to tell you: I can't have you in there *at the start*. I need forty-five minutes with him, the *whole* forty-five minutes, then you can sit on his knee and make him tell you a story for all I care. But I'm having that forty-five minutes."

"Do whatever you have to do," he said quietly.

"What does that mean?"

"It means I'm staying here."

I took a few moments. "You're coming with me."

"No, I'm not."

"Don't be ridiculous."

"You're wasting time," he said, looking at the clock on the wall.

He was right.

It was a twenty-minute drive on a clear run to Farnmoor, which meant I had to leave now if I didn't want to eat into the time I had with Graham. This might be the only shot I had at him, face to face, until Christmas—if he was even coming back then.

I looked around the kitchen and out into the living room.

The reality was, no one even knew Lee was back in the country, let alone here. No one had seen us approach, no one could see us from the road. Lee had no car and nothing to his name. Taking him with me would have lessened any risk, but the risk remained pretty small, even if he stayed. I wanted him close, because that was just how I worked, but he would only be twenty minutes down the road. And, ultimately, short of physically dragging him to the car—which *would* draw attention—I couldn't force him to come.

"Lock the doors and stay in the house, okay?"

He didn't reply, turning back to the window as clouds gathered over the beach and some of the light fizzled out. "Why did you even bring me back here, David?"

"Why do you think?"

"Because you're trying to save people."

I scooped up my car keys. "We're all trying to save someone."

37

The gates were already open at Farnmoor so I nosed the BMW up the drive and followed a series of signs around to the back of the house. A temporary parking lot had been set up for the gala. I quickly called Lee, to check everything was okay, and he sounded like he was still pissed off with me. That suited me fine as long as he remained where he was. Once I'd got back around to the front of the house, I saw there were three men, all dressed in black shirts, just inside the door, sheltering from the rain. Security. They looked like they'd come off a production line: shaved hair, wide torsos, pinch-faced.

"Can I help you, sir?" one of them said.

"My name's David Raker. I'm here to see Mr. Graham."

He didn't seem surprised, which meant Katie Francis had probably prepped him. He beckoned me toward him, briefly patted me down and then pointed along the hallway, toward the stairs. "Ms. Francis is on the first floor. She says you know the way."

Following the hallway around to the left, at the end beyond the stairs I could see two more security men at the back entrance. I wondered if they were Graham's personal security or just grunts hired to police the gala.

Upstairs, Katie Francis wasn't around.

I backed out. "Ms. Francis?" No response. "Katie, it's David Raker." Again, no response. The first floor was a mirror image of the ground floor. A couple of the doors were closed—I guessed Graham's bedroom, or his bathroom—but the rest were open: attractively decorated function rooms, a games room, then, right at the end, a library.

The library was the type of room you only ever saw in Hollywood movies: wall-to-ceiling shelving, except for a bay window immediately opposite; leather-bound books filling every space; a desk in the center, with a globe and a cigar box on it; studded, tan leather chairs, one behind the desk, two on the other side, and two matching sofas parallel to them. Finally, in the only concession to modern living, a new iMac. It was off.

As I circled the room, I saw the books were a mix of classic literature, reference material and brick-sized encyclopedias. Graham also had a section of the library dedicated to modern fiction, each of the books recovered in red, yellow or green leather to match the rest of the collection. The only other space, apart from the window, that wasn't dedicated to the written word was a narrow piece of paneling behind the door itself where twelve photographs—all black and white—ran in a vertical line.

I moved in for a closer look.

They were all of the same building, but at various stages of its construction. The first picture was of a dry patch of land, all dirt and crumbled masonry, the background just a thick copse of trees and a huge, cloudless sky. The next photo showed the trees being cut down and the ground being prepared, and from there—over the course of the next ten pictures—a generic-looking structure rose from the earth. There was nothing written on the photos, no inscription or idea of when the shots were taken, and the building itself had no signage on it, even when completed. Something Lee had said came back to me: *Schiltz moved to the States to study when he was in his early twenties, and just stayed. He helped Carter set up his first international office—put him in touch with builders, planners, all that kind of thing.* The photograph had a bleached kind of Californian feel, and dotted around in the background were other people: contractors, laborers, men in suits and hard hats.

Then, outside, I heard a noise.

I stepped back and peered through the gap between the door and the frame. Katie Francis came up the stairs, carrying a red Manila folder, and headed into her office. I waited thirty seconds, and then quickly left the library and headed her way.

She looked up as I entered. "Ah, Mr. Raker." She was standing at her desk, side on to me, dressed in a smart, calf-length black skirt, a red blouse and matching heels. "I saw your car outside. I thought you might have got lost."

"Thank you for organizing this," I said, sidestepping the question.

"No problem." She checked her watch. "Mr. Graham will be up in a couple of minutes. He'll probably want to chat with you in the library—that's where he normally sees people—but, please, take a seat for now."

I sat and we chatted politely about the gala.

About five minutes later, I clocked movement in the doorway and turned to find a man in his late sixties, slender and well groomed, leaning against the door frame.

Carter Graham.

He rolled his eyes and came all the way in. "I'm so sorry about the delay," he said, mid-Atlantic accent, arm outstretched. I got up and shook his hand. "This gala seemed like a good idea at the time."

"Thank you for seeing me, Mr. Graham."

"Carter's fine."

He had thick silver hair and tanned skin dotted with gray stubble, and he carried himself without a hint of age. When he smiled, which was often, his face was like a pencil drawing, detailed and textured, lines and creases carved into the edges of his eyes and mouth. He had a presence about him, a weight, a heft, that had probably carried him through countless boardrooms and out the other side, richer and more influential. It wasn't hard to understand, even from his appearance, why he was so successful.

"It's David, right?"

"Right."

"Follow me. We'll talk in the library." He turned to his PA. "Katie, can you bring us something to drink? Is tea okay, David? I'm afraid I gave up coffee in my thirties."

"Tea would be fine."

"Great. Come this way."

He led me out and along the hallway, back toward the library.

"You've got a beautiful place here," I said.

"Oh, thank you. When you spend as much time as I do in the air, it's nice to return to somewhere like this. I'm originally from Devon—did you know that?"

"I read that, yes."

"Are you from around here?"

"I grew up just along the coast."

"Really?" We entered the library and he gestured for me to sit on one of the sofas. He sat down on the other one. "I'm afraid I don't know very much about you. Katie mentioned you were a private investigator."

"Kind of. I find missing people."

"Oh," he said, his interest sparked. "Is there much call for that kind of thing?"

"Two hundred and fifty thousand people go missing in the UK every year. It's not about the numbers, really, it's about whether their families want them found."

"And whether they can afford you."

I smiled. "I try to make sure they can."

He returned the smile. "And you're working for the families of the Lings?"

"Family. Singular. Carrie's sister, yes. The rest of the family, his side of it, are out in Hong Kong."

"Okay." He slid back into the sofa and crossed his legs again. "Anything I can do to help, I will. To be perfectly frank, I didn't take things too seriously until I found out an old friend of mine claimed to have seen them here."

"Ray Muire?"

He nodded. "Did you know Ray?"

"No. He's obviously a name that's come up, though."

He nodded again. "Look, don't get me wrong, if the family was seen out here, I would have wanted to know what the hell was going on, regardless. But when Ray said he saw them . . ." He paused, rocking his head from side to side. For a moment something flashed in his eyes—a sadness—and I remembered how Lee had described Graham and Ray Muire's relationship: like brothers. "Ray was an old, old friend of mine. One of two I would consider to be my oldest and best, actually. I trusted him. When he died . . ." He swallowed, nodded, but didn't finish.

A couple of seconds later, Katie Francis brought in two mugs of tea, on two separate trays, with milk and sugar in white china bowls. She laid one down next to me, then one next to Graham. I thanked her, and so did he. Once she'd left he held up a hand in an apologetic gesture. "Anyway," he said, "I've talked for long enough. It's your turn. Ask me whatever you like, and let's get this family found."

38

I started by asking him about the day Ray Muire claimed to have seen the Lings. "The first I heard of it was when Katie called me and told me the police wanted to talk to me."

"What was your reaction?"

He shrugged. "I can't remember. As I said to you before, honestly, at that stage, I probably wasn't taking it too seriously. We get a lot of people crossing our land, plus I didn't know the family at all. Of course, I was willing to cooperate with police, but it wasn't until the detective . . . uh . . ."

"McInnes."

"McInnes, right. It wasn't until McInnes mentioned Ray's name that I guess my ears pricked up." That tallied with the interview transcript I'd read: Graham seemed genuinely taken aback when McInnes named Muire as the eyewitness. "Like I said, I'd known Ray a long time and I trusted him. I told the police the same thing."

"What did you make of Ray's death?"

"'Make of it?'" He frowned, sitting forward in his seat, a smooth, mottled hand wrapped around the mug. "What do you mean?"

I paused for a moment, studying him. He looked like I'd just danced on the grave of his friend. Maybe he could see the subtext in my question, and maybe he didn't like the idea of dredging up old memories that were better left buried. I didn't believe Ray Muire ended up in the river because he was drunk, not after talking to Lee, but Graham did—and he didn't want to be reminded that one of his two best friends was an old soak.

Conscious that Graham might back away from the conversation if he felt I was being disrespectful, I opted for bland: "It must have been hard for you."

He nodded. "Very hard."

"Katie said you made it back for the funeral."

"Yes," he replied, a sad, flat smile etched across his face. "I was in the middle of a tough negotiation in Tokyo, but I wasn't going to miss out on paying my last respects."

"Did the police come to the house?"

"After the sighting? Yes, I think so. I was in New York but Katie said they came to the house—as I would expect them to. If that family was here, or out in the grounds, for whatever reason, I wanted to know why as much as they did. I made it clear to her that she was to assist DCI Rocastle in any way she could."

"But you said McInnes conducted the interview with you?"

"He did. Rocastle seemed to be in charge, and he was the one that initially got in touch with me—via Katie—to arrange the interview by video conference. I spoke to him briefly a couple of times over the phone, and he explained about the family being seen just outside here. He didn't mention Ray, which was why I never realized he was the eyewitness until we conducted the VC. By then, McInnes was running the show."

Again, that tallied up. Rocastle had lasted three days on the Ling disappearance so it made sense that he would have been the one to call Graham initially. "I wonder why DCI Rocastle didn't mention that Ray was the eyewitness when he called initially?"

Graham shrugged. "You'd have to ask him, I suppose. If I was to take a guess, I'd say he either didn't have all the facts at that stage, or he was trying to avoid coloring my view of what happened. Maybe he thought I'd be mad at Ray or something."

My mind rolled back to the first conversation I'd had with Katie Francis at the house. *Do you think he might have been embarrassed about saying something to you? As if, by doing so, he was accusing you—and, indirectly, Mr. Graham—of being involved in something you shouldn't have?* She'd seemed confused by the question, as if she'd never thought of it that way. *I don't know*, she'd said. *Maybe.*

"Were you disappointed Ray didn't come to you directly?"

Graham pursed his lips, as though trying to be diplomatic. "It hurt a little. I guess he must have had his reasons. I was out of the country at the time, but if I'd been here, at the house, maybe it would have been different. He liked Katie, and she liked him, but she hadn't known him for fifty-odd years like I had. That makes a difference."

I flipped to a fresh page in the pad. "Did you know that Annabel and Olivia Ling were spotted near ExCeL in London a couple of days after they disappeared?"

"That's what DC McInnes said, yes. That obviously didn't lead anywhere?"

"No. You ever heard of a guy called Barry Rew?"

"R-E-W?"

"Yes."

"No. I haven't. Sorry."

I pushed on. "What can you tell me about a man called Jeremy Cornell?"

It took a couple of seconds for the name to register with him and it was the first time I'd glimpsed a man in his late sixties: the slight delay as he searched for the memory; the brief confusion as the conversation moved from one side of the world to the other. But, quickly, the cool, sparky brightness returned. "Cornell," he said, nodding his head, and it was immediately obvious how he felt. "How do you know about *that* guy?"

I had a duty to protect Lee, even if Graham wasn't the threat, but there was no way to lie my way through this without admitting that Lee was the thread that knitted the Lings and Cornell together. "Paul and Carrie Ling were good friends with a guy called Lee Wilkins. I think you know him."

His face lit up again, a mirror image of earlier, when I'd mentioned Ray Muire. "*Lee?* Yes, I know Lee very well. How is he? I haven't seen him for months."

"I don't know," I lied. "I don't know him. I'm just getting all this secondhand from Emily, Carrie Ling's sister. She said Lee and the Lings were close."

"I didn't know that."

"She said Lee had told them a lot about you."

"Me?"

"She said Lee really liked you."

Graham smiled; he seemed genuinely touched. "Well, that's very nice of Lee. I liked *him* very much. Ray may only have been his stepdad, but Lee had a lot of Ray's qualities and he was a damn talented entertainer too. I helped get him some work in Las Vegas." Then, gradually, the smile turned into a frown. "It was going so well for him, then he just upped and left. I don't know where he went, or why he left town, but I called Martha a few months back to find out where he'd gone, and she said he was out in Dubai. He just upped and left the job I got him. I mean, that's fine—he's a grown man, he can do what he wants—but I think Martha was a bit worried about him because she was only hearing from him once a month. You can understand. Does this Emily girl know any more?"

"No. She hasn't spoken to him for months."

He shook his head. "I really don't understand it."

"Did you see much of him there?"

"In Vegas? Yes, we had a kind . . . I guess, a kind of club going."

"Club?"

But I knew he was talking about the high-rollers group.

"We'd get together once every quarter, this big collection of us, and we'd gamble and have a few drinks. It was part social, part business. I used it as an opportunity to network, to talk to CEOs and chairmen and see if I could drive some business, but I made some good friends there at the same time."

"How did Lee get involved?"

"Ray told me Lee was out in Vegas, so the next time I flew out, I went to see him and thought he was fantastic. I suggested to Cornell that it might be fun to get him in for the evening, not expecting him to agree. But the next time I was in town, Lee turned up, did his routine and all the guys loved him so much, he ended up staying." He shrugged. "Most of us brought in a few trusted outside friends as time wore on, so it wasn't like it was unprecedented for Lee to stay. But it probably helped that everyone liked him."

"You brought in friends too?"

"Yes. Lee, of course, and an old doctor friend of mine."

He was talking about Eric Schiltz. Lee had survived by the skin of his teeth, but Schiltz hadn't been so lucky. I had to find a way to get Graham talking about him.

"So who is Cornell?"

Graham took a deep breath, like it was a question he'd wanted to know the answer to for a long time. "Honestly? I don't know for sure. He's English but he's been out in the States a long time. He told us he used to work for the Bellagio, in their security team, but now he has his own company. He's done pretty well off it, I think."

"How did he get to be the one that organized your get-togethers?"

"Through the contacts he made at the Bellagio, I guess."

I made a note to call the casino. "Go on."

"Anyway, he phoned up a bunch of us, told us the Bellagio would cover the cost of travel and accommodation, and that we could use one of the villas as a base. I think we all saw it the same way: a chance to network, to talk to other business people, to have a little fun. There were ten of us to start with, then it got bigger and bigger. Nowadays, we're doing it every three months and there are maybe thirty, thirty-two. I suppose, even though he works for himself, he probably gets a nice little kickback for bringing us in. I dread to think how much money the casino is making off us."

"What do you make of him?"

"Of Cornell?" A snort. "A creepy asshole would probably sum it up."

"You don't like him?"

"No one really likes him."

"What does he do when you all get together?"

"Do? Nothing. Mostly he just watches. I mean, you can have a conversation with him, but it won't exactly be one for the ages. Occasionally he joins in, but mostly he prefers just watching from the sidelines. It's all a bit weird—certainly for my tastes."

"Do you ever get the sense he's hiding something?"

Graham frowned. "Like what?"

"I don't know. Doesn't it strike you as odd that Lee just upped and left?"

He was about to reply, then stopped, his eyes fixed on a space over my shoulder. I sat back and hoped I'd played it right, hoped I'd managed to predict his train of thought. He blinked, once, twice, a distance to him now. I wanted him thinking about Lee's sudden departure, and then—like pins being knocked down by the same ball, one after the other—the fact that Schiltz had also been absent from the group for a year. He definitely would have noted Schiltz's absence but maybe something had taken place that meant he hadn't looked any deeper. I could really only see two reasons for that: either, somehow, he'd been convinced that Schiltz was fine, or he'd been scared into silence. Men like Graham didn't scare easily, especially this late on in life, but everyone was frightened of something.

Maybe the thing he feared was Cornell.

After about ten seconds he blinked again and it was like switching channels: the static cleared and he was back in the conversation. He looked at me. "Are you suggesting that Cornell might be the reason Lee suddenly left Vegas?"

Bingo. "I don't know. Do you?"

It was like reading a road sign now: I could almost see him making the connection between Lee and Schiltz. "My other friend, the doctor, he also stopped coming."

"Stopped coming when?"

"About the same time."

"What was your friend's name?"

"Eric. Eric Schiltz. I mentioned him earlier when we were talking about Ray. The three of us—me, Ray and him—grew up here. Ray stayed here in Devon, but Eric fell in love with the idea of the American dream. I guess I was somewhere in between: my roots are very important to me, but I always wanted to go to the States, from early on."

I paused, letting him gather his thoughts again.

"Did you ever ask Eric why he stopped coming to the group?"

"No. We had a get-together a year ago, last November time, and about two weeks later he sent me an e-mail to tell me he probably wasn't going to come along anymore."

"Did he say why?"

"He just said he didn't enjoy it very much anymore."

"Did that surprise you?"

"Yes." He nodded. "Eric loved the get-togethers. After his wife—Nancy—died, he was always out and about being social. He kept very active. I'd never met a man who hated being alone as much as him. So, yes, it did surprise me."

"You, Eric and Ray were close?"

"Oh yes." He shifted forward in the sofa and got to his feet, then walked past me toward the door. At first I thought he was about to leave, then he pulled the door open to reveal the series of twelve photographs behind it. "Come and have a look at these." I got up and walked across to the pictures, pretending to study them for the first time. "I'd been living out in California for almost a year," he continued, "desperately trying to get investors interested in Empyrean. But I was just getting nowhere. So Eric took me down to Wilshire Country Club while he was studying at UCLA, and introduced me to all these movers and shakers, all these people he'd met at the golf club, at the hospital, just in the short time he'd been out in LA. They were the difference. It's him I've got to thank."

"So this is your first international office?"

"Yes. I remember Eric and I were down there a lot, just watching it all take shape. We clubbed together and flew Ray out a couple of times too. They were good days."

I let him feed on the memories for a moment.

"Have you tried phoning him at all?"

"Eric? Do you mean recently?"

"Since you received that e-mail from him."

"I tried a couple of times, but he never returns my calls. I wanted to arrange to go down and see him when I was last in the States, but I never managed to get hold of him."

"You didn't think that was strange?" I asked. "A man you've known for all that time, one of your best friends, suddenly stops returning your calls?"

"His calls stopped, but his e-mails didn't."

"You kept getting e-mails from him?"

"Every so often, apologizing for not getting in touch."

Except they wouldn't have come from Schiltz. Lee seemed to think he was already dead by then, so whoever was sending Graham e-mails, it wasn't Eric Schiltz.

Cornell.

"Has anyone ever expressed concern over a photograph you might have, maybe of the three of you—your friend Eric, Ray Muire, you—from some point in your past?"

"I'm not sure I understand."

This already felt like a wild, unfocused stab in the dark. I knew there was a photo of the three of them, possibly—if Carrie's notebook entry was correct—taken in 1971, and Lee had seen a reference to a D.K., presumably the man in the background. But, apart from the likelihood that they each owned a copy, and the fact that Graham was the only one left now, it was about as much as I had. "Maybe you've got a photograph of the three of you somewhere at the house here that you keep hidden away for some reason."

He looked confused.

"Or maybe you've been *asked* to keep a photograph hidden?"

The same expression. "I'm not sure I follow."

"Okay. Do the initials D.K. mean anything to you?"

"D.K.?"

"Yeah. Maybe someone you knew in the early seventies?"

He seemed totally lost now.

"What about Eric? Did he maybe mention one that he had in his possession that he wished he didn't, or one that he thought might land him in some kind of trouble?"

He studied me as if he was trying to work out where this had come from—and where it was about to go. I didn't offer to help, just waited him out.

Eventually, he shrugged. "If he did, I don't remember."

I nodded. "What about Cornell?"

"Cornell?"

"Did he ever mention a photograph?"

"No," Graham said, and I caught a flash of fear in his eyes.

"Are you okay, Carter?"

"You've got me thinking."

"About what?"

He swallowed. "About whether Cornell is the reason Eric and Lee stopped coming to the get-togethers."

"When are you next due to see him?"

"Cornell?"

I nodded.

He paused, his eyes back on the pictures. At his side, both hands had formed fists, like some sort of defense mechanism. "I'm supposed to be flying out next weekend. The middle of November is when we have our autumn meeting at the Bellagio."

"Can I suggest you don't make the trip out?"

He turned to me. "Do you think it's that serious?"

"I think Cornell's interest in you might not be a consequence of your success in the business world. I think he might have invited you to the high-rollers group so he could get the measure of you. Was it your idea to bring Schiltz to the group, or Cornell's?"

Graham thought about it. "Well, he said to me . . ." And then he stopped, the truth dawning on him. "Cornell asked me if I had a friend I'd like to invite along."

"Because he already knew about Eric."

Graham seemed in shock.

"I need you to think: was there anything, growing up, anything the three of you—Eric, Ray and you—did, or were photographed doing, that might interest Cornell?"

He was just shaking his head now, dazed.

"Anyone you might have met?"

"I don't know. I don't think so."

I thought back to what Lee had said about the photograph Carrie Ling saw. There had been a man in it, someone Lee didn't know. *He's someone bad. If I had to guess, I'd say someone bad enough to bring down Cornell and whatever he's involved in.*

"I need you to do something for me."

He still looked shell-shocked. "Yes, of course."

"I need you to go through your belongings, wherever it is you keep things that are important to you, and I need you to see if you have a photograph of the three of you."

"I'm sure there must be lots of them."

"Okay. Well, if that's the case, grab any you've got. I also want you to check your e-mail inbox for any messages, or attachments, Eric might have sent you."

"Okay." He nodded. "Okay." But it was clear something else was playing on his mind. "Do . . ." He stopped, ruffled, alarmed. "Do you think Cornell's coming for me?"

"I don't think he'll make the journey over." But then my mind spooled forward: *Ray Muire had fallen into a river only a few miles from here.* "Have you got security?"

"Yes. They're all downstairs."

"I haven't got any reason to think you're in any immediate danger." I looked at him, unsure if I believed what I was saying. "But now might be a good time to call your people and get some extra men sent down here. I'd make sure that happens today. I'll also take your number, if you don't mind, just in case I need to ask you anything more."

"Yes. That's fine." He shook his head. "I can't believe this."

"It's just a precaution."

"All of this because of—what?—a photograph?" For the first time, his confidence and professionalism had disappeared. "What the hell's so important about a photograph?"

"I don't know," I said. "But I'm going to find out."

39

As I got back to the village, I passed a marked police car coming the other way, heading out into the darkness, where the road bisected the Ley and the beach. There was no sign of any other cars, no police presence anymore, not even the remnants of any police tape in and around the beach, which suggested the uniforms were either on their way through or they'd been doing follow-up interviews with some of the locals. Canvassing the whole village would take days, which meant return visits to clarify statements and check details.

Winding the car up into the hills overlooking the beach, I thought of Rocastle, of the interview he'd done with me the day after the body washed up. *I don't care if you're looking into that family's disappearance. I really don't. What I care about is closing my case, and if you're getting in my way . . . that's when we have a problem.* I understood why he'd been given the body: that required a senior cop, one with experience of working murders, and a knowledge of the local area. He ticked the boxes. But the Lings' disappearance was much less of a fit, and it was like—by passing it off on to McInnes after only three days—he knew it. *You're a clever guy,* he'd said, obviously aware I was trying to lead him down that road, *that's probably why everyone at the Met hates you.* He would never front up and tell me why he took the Ling case, even if there was nothing worth telling. It wasn't how he worked. From a single, sixty-minute conversation, I'd seen as much as I'd needed to: he was a man who gave as little as possible in order to gain as much as he could.

When I pulled into the driveway, all the lights in the house were off. That didn't surprise me: if the past year had taught Lee anything, it was how to keep his head above water. No one knew he was here, no one even knew he was back in the country, but that wouldn't stop twelve months of instinct kicking in: locking doors, pulling the curtains, using the darkness and the silence. Everything focused on survival.

Turning off the engine, I grabbed my phone and my notebook and opened the door of the BMW. Then stopped. *That's probably why everyone at the Met hates you.* Rocastle had been talking about the enemies I'd made at the Met: cops I'd had to cross in order to get to the missing, the laws I'd had to bend so I could do what I felt was right.

But how did he know they hated me?

None of the cops I'd dealt with would have put their personal feelings about me into a file. So he was either making a claim based on an assumption or he'd put in a call to them before he'd come to the house to speak to me. Or there was another reason.

He hasn't always been based in Devon.

I pulled the car door shut again and went to my phone's address book. A couple of seconds later, I found the name I wanted: Terry Dooley.

Dooley was a name from my old life, a cop I'd snared as a source after a tip-off about him and three of his detectives landed on my desk. In a moment of madness, they'd visited a south London brothel, got wasted on cheap booze and then one of them had started throwing punches. I'd called Dooley with an offer the next day: I kept him out of the papers if he got me information when I needed it. He was married with two young boys and didn't fancy the idea of only seeing them on weekends, so he took the deal. I didn't use him as much as Ewan Tasker, because he wasn't as discreet or reliable, but while Task was already in semiretirement, Dooley was still there at the coalface, working murders and making other people's business his own. He was difficult, snide and arrogant, but that was exactly why he was so useful. He went out of his way to know things about other cops at the Met, in case he ever had to use those things against them.

As I waited for him to pick up, my eyes drifted over the house and I noticed a flash of color at the top window. Lee was watching from the spare room. He waved once, I waved back, then he retreated into the darkness.

Finally, Dooley answered. "Oh joy."

"I thought you were ignoring me."

"If only it was that easy."

"How you doing, Dools?"

"Probably better than you." He didn't say anything else, but I understood. He always liked to give the impression he was dictating terms, that he had some kind of control over the way our working relationship moved. If he started pandering to me, in his head it would be a sign of submission. So he didn't ask about my recovery, except in the most evasive way. "To what do I owe this pleasure?"

"I wanted to ask you about someone."

"There's a surprise."

"You ever heard of a Colin Rocastle?"

"Doesn't ring any bells. Can I go now?"

"Just think about it for a minute."

A grunt of contempt. "*Think* about it? Yeah, sure. Why don't I put my feet up on the desk and crack out the cigars, because working murders is like a Buddhist retreat."

I got his frustration. Every time I called it was like a reminder of what he'd done: a drunken night out, a bad mistake, the thin line between a secret staying buried and his wife getting an anonymous call. The truth was, I would never make that call, even if he refused to help me, because I wasn't in the business of breaking up families. But Dooley didn't have to know that.

"I think he might have worked at the Met."

A moment of silence, as if he was taking it in.

"Dooley?"

"So what? A lot of people work at the Met."

"If I had to take a guess, I'd say he knew about me through people like Phillips and Craw." Phillips was the lead on the case that had first brought me into contact with Healy; Craw was the SIO on the case that had almost killed me. "Maybe he was involved in those cases, maybe he wasn't, but he knows who I am. Now I want to know who *he* is."

"Congratulations."

"Specifically, you're going to tell me."

He sighed. "I'm sick of this garbage you bring me."

"Yeah, well, lap it up, Dools."

No response. Then: "What did you say his name was?"

"Rocastle. Colin Rocastle."

"Gimme a sec."

He put me on hold. I guessed he was probably checking the computers or asking around. About half a minute later, he came back on. Another long silence on the line. Dooley didn't give any indication as to whether he knew Rocastle or not, but the silence didn't worry me. This was all a part of his game. "What's he got to do with anything?"

"So you've heard of him?"

Another pause. His brain was probably skipping ahead about now, trying to figure out what I wanted with Rocastle. "Yeah, I remember him now. You were right."

"He used to work at the Met?"

"Yeah."

I knew it. I pulled my notebook across to me, opened it up and wedged the phone between my shoulder and my ear. "When was he up in London?"

"Seven or eight years ago. Maybe more."

"Doing what?"

"He started out as a rubber heeler."

"He worked for the DPS?"

"It was the plain old CIB back then. CIB3 would have been the one Rocastle was in. They were the extra-special arseholes who worked out of Scotland Yard investigating Scotland Yard officers. Bunch of half-cops and circus freaks, but the Met poured a shit-ton of money into it after some bent coppers dropped their guard and got weeded out by the tabloids. When it was set up in '98, it had fifty officers working for it. *Fifty.* We wouldn't get that now, even if Jack the Ripper crawled out the fucking ground."

I wrote down the gist of what he'd said. The Complaints Investigation Bureau was the precursor to the Directorate of Professional Standards, the UK equivalent of internal affairs. The term "rubber heeler" was old-school cop slang: when, in 1971, the deputy commissioner Robert Mark set up A10, an anti-corruption branch, cops took to calling the officers that worked for it "rubber heelers"—because you could never hear them creeping up behind you.

"Did Rocastle make himself unpopular?"

"He was eyeballing his own people—what do you think?"

"Yeah, but did he do anything to stand out from the crowd?"

"I don't know," Dooley said. "Never knew him personally. I just remember a few guys saying he was an arsehole. Stiff, humorless, took a bit too much pleasure in nailing cops to the wall. He probably pretended he really loved exposing all the Met secrets."

"Maybe he wasn't pretending."

"What, are you a fan of his?"

"Maybe he just didn't like dirty cops."

Laughter on the line. "You're a naïve prick, Raker, you know that? We're talking about a guy who took down good investigators here. You think you walk in off the street with a talent for catching bad guys? You don't. It takes years. I'm not defending corrupt cops, but there's a difference between a guy who's tampering with evidence and someone who gets a bit too aggressive in an interview because some lying piece of shit won't admit to what we all know he's done. You ask me, cops like Rocastle are pond life."

"So, what did he do after he left the CIB?"

"Spent a couple of years working for Sapphire." That was the Rape and Serious Sexual Assault command. "Career went a whole lot of nowhere."

"Why?"

"Why do you think? No one liked him. No one wanted him on their team. You can't trust a guy who stabs his own people in the back."

"What if he was just doing his job?"

A snort. "Unbelievable. Aren't you listening to *anything* I'm telling you? Who gives two shits about Rocastle? He's a weasel. The way the guys tell it, the best thing that ever happened to him was when he had his existential 'What the fuck am I doing here?' moment and realized everyone hated his guts. Now he gets to spend his days down in Trumpton chasing his tail because the local corner shop ran out of toothpaste."

I saw Lee come to the top window again and look down at me. In the moonlight, he looked pale and alien, half covered by the shadows of the house.

"All right, Dools. Thanks for that."

"No problem. Don't call again."

I hung up, got out and headed into the house.

40

The kitchen was dark, only the pale readout from a luminescent wall clock casting a glow inside the room. Outside, the moon drifted in and out of cover, but when I kicked the door shut and put my notepad and phone down on the counter, a thick blanket of shadow settled around me.

Automatically, I reached for the lights inside the door.

They didn't come on.

I tried them again, once, twice. Nothing. Moving across the kitchen, I glanced out of the window, down toward the beach, and could see small dots of color everywhere: lamp posts standing sentry along the sea wall, cars passing through the village, buildings casting out watery yellow light from their windows and doorways. Up here, in the hills, there were no street lamps and the nearest house was four hundred feet down the slope.

Everyone in the village had light.

Everyone except me.

On the other side of the kitchen was a larder that I kept some old missing persons files in, with two switches on the wall next to it. One for the kitchen, one for the larder.

I tried them both.

They were dead too.

"Lee?"

My voice carried off into the house, the stillness and silence amplifying it, like I was shouting into the mouth of a cave. Lee didn't reply. I looked through to the living room. The DVD and stereo were off—no display, no faint buzz of electricity—my laptop had no light on, even though I'd left it charging, and Annabel's MacBook lay dormant. Next to it, Paul's PC was off, even though it had been on when I'd headed out.

"Lee?"

Silence for a second time.

I glanced back across the kitchen, in the direction of the microwave and the oven. Both of those were off too. Slowly, as I stood there in the dark, a sense of unease crawled its way through my system, cool in my veins, blooming beneath my ribs, my heart getting faster, as if, somehow, my body was confirming what I already knew.

The electricity had been cut.

Lee was upstairs but not responding.

Something's wrong.

Just inside the door of the larder was Dad's old cricket bat, leaning against the wall. It had been in the same place when I'd returned to the cottage months back, and I'd never moved it. I reached into the shadows and lifted it out. The rubber grip had long since unraveled, but while the willow had gone soft at the edges, the meat of the blade remained hard.

Gripping it, I edged forward, into the living room.

The cottage was a century old, so the layout didn't conform to modern design. It ran in a kind of spiral: kitchen through to a dining room, past a pair of blistered French windows, and then on to a single, narrow staircase that took you up. I moved across the living room, eyes everywhere, trying to see if anything had moved.

At the stairs, I paused.

Listened.

There was no noise.

"Lee?"

Briefly, a floorboard creaked.

I looked up the steps, into the darkness. The house was an antique, weary and old, and every footstep through it would be mapped by a succession of groans. At the top, I could make out vague shapes I'd come to know well: a long, cylindrical window on the right, cut into the outside wall; then the first of three bedrooms—the one at the top of the stairs being mine—the tiniest fragments of light coming in through its window and spilling out on to the landing.

Nothing else.

I reestablished my grip on the bat. Even in the dark, I could make out my hands: blanched white, like sticks of chalk, veins slithering through from wrists to knuckles. As I paused there, I heard faint, indistinct noises and I became uncertain as to whether it was coming from inside or outside the house. The wind could easily have been a whisper. The gentle fall of rain on the roof could have been someone softly padding around.

Raising the bat, I slowly started the ascent.

Even as I tried to rein in the impact of my full weight on the stairs, they groaned and shifted. I kept to the right, my back against the outside wall, and as I got halfway I paused and looked through the railing, along the landing, into the bathroom and the other two bedrooms. The bathroom was small: a bath, a toilet, a basin, white enamel and tiles that reflected back whatever dull glow was seeping in through a thin slice of window.

Then there were the two bedrooms.

One had remained empty from the time I'd moved in, just built-in wardrobes and old carpets. The other was the spare bedroom that looked out over the front driveway. The one I'd seen Lee in.

I edged up the rest of the stairs and stopped again at the top. There was another set of switches about a foot to my right. One was for the landing, the other for the stairs.

I reached out and pushed them both. *Click. Click.*

Nothing.

As I took a couple of steps further, a floorboard shifted beneath me and I paused, waiting for any kind of reaction from any of the rooms. But all that echoed back was more silence. Quickly, I took a sidestep, into my bedroom. It was packed with my stuff: suitcases and holdalls stacked in the corner, toiletries on top of a chest of drawers, more missing-persons files in a pile on my bedside cabinet, clothes laid across the bed.

Then: a noise.

I backed out and looked across to the spare room; the same one Healy had stayed in for four months. *That's where it came from.* Inside—not visible from where I was—I knew there was a spare bed, two standalone pine wardrobes and, next to the window, an old, discolored swivel chair, brown leather on a chrome base.

The sound was the chair turning on its base.

Someone was sitting in it.

My heart started pumping faster. I took two big steps and I was at the entrance, firming up my grip on the bat, peering through the gap between door and frame. For a moment there was nothing but shadows. But then things began to emerge: the edges of furniture, the wardrobes, the lights of the village—like the tiniest specks of paint—beyond the glass. And then the swivel chair.

Lee was slumped in it.

Eyes closed. Arms either side of him.

Quickly, I moved past the door and into the bedroom and by the time I did, his eyes were open and he was staring at me. There was something different about him now. His face was stiff and unmoving, but even in the darkness I could see the expression in his eyes. He looked at me like he was hurt or wounded—or full of remorse.

"Lee?"

"I'm sorry, David," he said quietly.

There was a creak behind me.

And then my head felt like it exploded.

A second later, everything went black.

There was sound before anything else. Voices. Two men—one I recognized as Lee; the other I recognized but couldn't place—talking in strained, irritated tones. On the dazed edges of unconsciousness I struggled to make out what they were saying, but with sound came sensation and, as my nerve endings fired into life, the voices shifted into focus, like a tuner finding its station. "You knew what you were doing by calling us," said the other voice. "I knew," Lee responded. "I just don't want to have to be here when it's done."

My head pounded, the gathering clouds of a migraine, and I could feel wet blood all over my face: around my ear, under my chin, in my mouth. I wanted to spit it out. But I didn't. I didn't move an inch.

I sat there, chin against my chest, eyes closed.

Immediately, I knew I was in the living room. There was the smell of ash from the fireplace and, softly in the background, the whine of wind as it crept through the gaps in the French windows. They were old, no longer sitting flush to their frames, and I knew the sound well now. I couldn't tell in which direction I faced—off to the doors, or the other way to the kitchen—but I knew what I was sitting on: a wooden chair, once belonging to my grandparents, that always stayed in the corner of the room. Its legs, to which my ankles were tied, were rickety, wobbling even as I sat motionless; my wrists were bound together behind me, where the back of the chair curved slightly and was much stronger.

"Who are you calling?"

It was Lee. The other man didn't reply.

"Who are you calling?" Lee said again, desperation in his voice now. *Desperation and fear.* I wondered, briefly, whether he'd been leading me on the whole time, whether this was all some elaborate ruse to get me to this point—but then immediately dismissed it. When I'd looked into his eyes in the decaying ruins of the old farmhouse, I hadn't seen a liar. I'd seen a man haunted by ghosts: the Lings, whose lives he'd probably cost; the doctor, Schiltz, who he'd been willing to sacrifice for them; then the shadow, Cornell.

But if Lee wasn't the one that had led them here, how had they found him? No one knew I'd brought him to the house. No one even knew he was back in the country.

I'm sorry, David.

His words from earlier emerged from the back of my mind—*You don't know what Cornell is like . . . The second he looks at you, you see what he's capable of. He's like a vessel carrying around all this violence and misery*—and then, on the back of that, what I'd overheard when I woke moments ago: *You knew what you were doing by calling us.*

Instantly, I understood: he'd tried to cut a deal with Cornell's people. He'd got scared while I was out, quickly working himself up into a frenzy. He'd started to believe I couldn't protect him. I'd seen it as we'd driven back from Dartmoor; not the decision he was going to make, but the slow realization. If he was returning to the open, he had to come down on the side of the fence that would keep him alive. He was petrified of Cornell, not me. He knew Cornell was a killer and I wasn't. So he reestablished contact because he thought it was the best way to save himself. He begged for their forgiveness.

And then he painted a target on my back.

"Yeah, it's me," the other man said. Whoever he was calling had picked up. "He's here." A pause. "I've tied him up. Do you want me to wait?" Another pause, much longer this time. Somewhere off to my left, I heard Lee moving, heard the wheeze of the sofa as he sat down, and I realized I was facing back across the living room, toward the French windows. "Are you sure?" He waited for the answer. "Okay." Then he hung up.

"What's happening?" Lee said.

"Shut up."

"I want to know what's happening."

"Shut your fuckin' maw."

The other man was local: he had a strong south Devon accent and sounded in his forties or fifties. His voice had a gristly, coarse kind of twist to it. I listened to him come around to my right and drop down, below my shoulder line. The next moment I felt rope tightening at my ankles, and then at my wrists, as he made sure the knots were strong.

I waited for him to get to his feet again and come back round in front of me, and then gradually I lifted my head and opened my eyes. Neither of them noticed at first.

Lee was still on my left, slumped on the sofa, staring down at the floor. He looked distant and broken, and I noticed two fresh bruises and a deep cut on one side of his face, where he'd been hit with something. His second chance was already going south.

On the far side of him were three big candles set in a line, their light casting out into the center of the room. Shadows danced on the walls.

I turned to the other man. He was removing his coat.

A dark blue oilskin.

I knew then why I recognized his voice.

It was Prouse, the fisherman.

42

A second later, they both noticed I was awake. Lee swallowed and said nothing, but came forward to the edge of the sofa. Prouse let his coat fall away from his body, like he was shedding his skin, and it dropped to the floor behind him. I tried to draw the link between Prouse and Lee, between Prouse and *anything*, but I couldn't see the connection.

He found the body on the beach.

What did that have to do with Lee?

With the Lings?

Briefly, as he came across the living room toward me, I thought of Healy, of the two of us sitting in The Seven Seas, Healy's eyes fixed on a man at the bar behind me.

Prouse.

"Finally," he said, a smile parting the untidy tangle of his beard. The smile was small and menacing, and faded as quickly as it formed. He stopped in front of me, and we stared at each other for a moment.

Then he punched me in the jaw.

It came quick and fast, before I'd even had a chance to brace myself, and as the chair rocked from side to side, one leg to another, pain rippled through my skull. His jab was like concrete: rigid and fibrous, his knuckles as hard as rocks. Once the chair settled again, I could feel the imprint on my chin: the grit from his bunched fingers, and the smell—fish and oil and sweat—from his skin.

I rolled my jaw and looked at him.

"How you feeling, boy?"

"I've been better."

Prouse smiled. "I bet you have."

I glanced at Lee. He couldn't even meet my eyes. Prouse looked from Lee back to me and mockingly puckered his lips. "Aw, are the two of you having a lovers' tiff?"

I fixed my gaze on Prouse. "What do you want?"

"I want a photograph."

The photograph. I decided to play it dumb. "What kind of a photograph?"

"You trying to trap me, boy?" he said, wagging a finger at me.

"I don't know what you're talking about."

Out of nowhere, he punched me again.

He was fast and strong, and this time the chair toppled all the way over. I hit the carpet hard, head first, and the impact reverberated through my body like a wave. Lee got up from the sofa. "Is this really necessary?" His voice was doughy and weak, and Prouse just had to look at him before he backed down. As the two of them faced off, I tried to loosen my binds from the floor. But Prouse was a fisherman. If there was one thing he knew how to do, it was to tie a good knot. Yet, while there was no give in the rope, I could feel the chair wheezing with age beneath me.

"Where's the photograph?" he said, standing over me.

"If you told me what it was of, I might know."

"Don't play smart with me, boy," he said. "That little bastard over there has been whistling like a canary, so you don't need to know what the picture is *of* to know what I'm talking about." He paused, and dropped to his haunches. "Where'd she put it?"

"Who?"

"That bitch you're trying to find."

"Carrie?"

"Where'd she put it?"

"Put it?" I looked at Lee. He'd have told Prouse about the notebook, assuming Prouse didn't know already. I turned to the fisherman. "The picture's in her notebook."

He didn't seem surprised. "No shit."

"You knew that already?"

He didn't answer and instead reached down, one hand gripping the back of the chair, one gripping the leg, and hoisted me up. I could feel fresh blood on my lips, and bruising forming along the lines of my jaw. He headed across to the other side of the living room, to where he'd left his jacket, and for the first time I noticed there was a holdall next to it.

He unzipped it and started going through it.

I glanced at Lee. He was a mess. Eyes downcast, face pale and sickly. He looked small and damaged, a shadow even of the man I'd found hiding in the farmhouse. I tried wordlessly to force him to look at me as Prouse went through his holdall, but he refused to meet my eye. Then Prouse got to his feet and turned around.

He was holding a gun.

My heart stirred.

Muscles tensed.

He walked up to me and stopped a foot short of my knees, arm at his side, huge hand deliberately covering the weapon. It looked like a Glock, but it was difficult to tell.

"What are you doing?" Lee said from behind him.

Prouse didn't answer. He eyed me, brow furrowed, as if he'd never taken the time to look before. Then he turned the gun in his palm, pushing it forward to the front of his hand, and raised it to my eyeline. He held it there. Steady. Certain. It was so close to my face I couldn't focus properly, but I didn't shrink away, even as fear bled through every pore. I just sat there, staring down the barrel, trying to keep my head clear.

Form a plan. Any plan.

"Lee says he told you what was in that picture," Prouse said.

"That's not true."

He moved the gun forward. "You saying he's lying?"

"I'm saying, he didn't know either."

I switched my gaze, up above the ridge of the barrel, to Prouse's eyes. They were small and dark, even against the black of his beard, but they had no shine to them. There was no light in them at all. *Healy was right about you. You aren't just a fisherman.* I was angry that I hadn't seen the same things as Healy. I just thought he was being paranoid.

"You know what?" he said, finger wriggling at the trigger. "I don't know which one of you bastards to believe anymore. So I'm just gonna have to beat it out of you."

"Look, I don't know who's in the photogr—"

Prouse swatted the gun across my face, opening his hand so as much of the weapon was exposed as possible. The metal hit like a hammer. The chair rocked, teetered, then finally fell back into place.

"Just tell him what you know, David!"

I tried to focus on Lee, to my left, somewhere on the edge of the sofa, but I suddenly felt nauseated. A second later, as my head rolled forward, I completely blacked out. Briefly, in the darkness, I saw a frozen moment in time: Healy and me in The Seven Seas, my face a picture of disbelief. *What, you think the fisherman's involved?* And then I was awake again, my head a fluid, swelling mass of pain, thumping like rolls of thunder.

"I got other questions for you," Prouse said, leaning in. I could feel his breath on my cheek, smell the tobacco on his teeth. "You're gonna answer them. *All* of them."

I looked at him. "I got some questions for you too."

He smiled. "You a joker, boy?"

"How about we trade? You answer mine, I'll answer yours."

The smile didn't fade from his face as quickly this time, but there was no humor in it. He had a far-off look in his eyes, like a thought had come to him, and while he was mulling it over, everything else had frozen in time. But then the smile finally did go and he turned to Lee. "Come here, Lee," he said, almost a softness to his voice now. "Come."

Lee got up, warily.

"Lee, don't trust—"

"*Shut up!*" Prouse screamed into my face. He turned back to Lee. "Son, come here. It's okay. I want to show you something." Lee edged toward him. "Don't be frightened."

Lee stopped just behind Prouse.

"I want to show you what happens when someone doesn't play by the rules." The fisherman looked from me to Lee and then back again, and I steeled myself for whatever was coming next. But then Prouse turned to Lee. And he shot him in the leg.

The noise was immense, ripping through the house before being swallowed by the groans of the wind. For a split second, Lee didn't seem to react, even though the bullet had propelled him back across the living room and into Paul Ling's computer. But then blood erupted out of the top of his thigh, the computer monitor fell to the floor, and Lee collapsed on to the sofa, face white, words lost in the agony.

Prouse looked at me. "Is that what you wanted?"

There was blood all over the sofa now.

"Is that what you *wanted*?" he shouted.

"*Listen* to me," I replied, keeping my eyes on him and my voice steady. The pain in my head was starting to make me feel dizzy, but I pushed back a fresh wave of nausea. "Whatever you want to know, I will tell you. But if you hurt him again, you get nothing."

Prouse laughed. "You got balls, boy, I'll give you that."

"Are we clear?"

"You know what that little bastard did, right?" Prouse studied me. "*Right*? He *betrayed* you. He called us up and begged for his life." Prouse started talking like a whining child: "'I'm really sorry. I'm really sorry for what I've done, please can we start again. Don't hurt me, don't hurt me, don't hurt me.' I didn't hear him begging for *your* life."

"It doesn't matter."

The fisherman snorted.

Lee was sobbing now. Prouse glanced at him, contempt in his face. "You want me to put another one in your balls?" he said, taking a step closer to Lee. Lee shook his head, desperately trying to rein in his sobs, and his whole body seemed to fold in on itself.

"What do you want to know?" I asked.

He turned back to me. "Lee told you some things."

I nodded.

"So I want to know where the photograph is."

"It's in the notebook."

"I know it's in the fuckin' notebook! "

My head was on fire, but at the same time I was trying to work out what the hell Prouse was doing here, where he fitted in and what he was talking about. He already knew about the photograph, and he knew it was in her notebook. So why was he asking where the picture was? "Listen to me," I said. "The photograph is in Carrie's notebook."

"We've got the notebook. Where's the photograph?"

I frowned. "It wasn't in the notebook?"

He leaned in to me. "Where's the other one?"

"Other one what?"

He smirked, didn't say anything.

"Look, I only know about Carrie Ling's notebook and that there's some kind of a photograph, and it's important to you and your . . ."

"My what?"

I made the leap. "Your boss. Cornell."

For the first time, something moved in the black of his eyes; a predator remembering there was an animal even worse than him. "That about the sum total of it?"

"That's all I know."

He fumbled around in the pocket of his trousers and brought out his phone again. I glanced at Lee: he was doubled over, a hand on his wound, blood leaking out over his fingers. Prouse's eyes stayed on me as he auto-dialed a number. "It's me," he said, when the person on the other end picked up. "He doesn't know where it is." Prouse shook his head. "No. But he's clever. He'll find out. If we let him, he'll find out about everything."

I flicked another look at Lee. His eyes were closed, and he'd quietened.

His hand had slipped away from the wound and was flat to the sofa. There was blood everywhere.

"You want me to wait?"

Prouse's voice brought me back. I looked at him. He was studying his watch, gun still clutched in the same hand, listening to whatever was being said.

Then he hung up.

Pocketing the phone again, he raised the gun and moved toward me. There was a purpose about him now. "This is where you and me say good-bye, boy."

He pressed the gun against my forehead.

"Wait a sec—"

"Sorry it won't be an open casket."

Then, in my peripheral vision, I saw Lee move.

"Where are the Lings?" As I asked, I could see Lee pause on the edge of the sofa, a grimace on his face. I kept my eyes on Prouse. "I just want to know where they are."

The corners of the fisherman's mouth turned up.

"Please," I said. "Give me that, at least."

"What difference does it make?"

Lee hobbled off the sofa and looked around him hazily, as if he didn't know where he was or what he was doing. *Help me, Lee.* There was an iron poker lying across the hearth that I willed him to grab. But he didn't. He didn't even seem to see the poker. He didn't seem to be focusing on anything. He looked bewildered, punch-drunk, blood all over him. He limped across to the middle of the room and fell in behind Prouse.

Prouse noticed him, turned. "What the fuck are you doing?"

Then, instinctively, I moved.

With every last atom of strength, I rocked the chair back, and then— as it shifted forward again—launched myself at him, wrists tied behind me, ankles locked in place, chair glued to my back. It was clumsy, but I managed to turn enough in the air so the weight of the legs clattered into Prouse first. All three of us hit the floor, Lee spinning off toward the fireplace. I landed on top of Prouse, something on the chair snapping, and heard his gun fall away somewhere else, hitting the carpet with a metallic rasp. My head started swimming, I felt myself drift, then I was back in the moment and Prouse was heaving me off him. I made a half-turn, the chair halting my movement.

Prouse scrambled away, looking for the gun, eyes scanning the room. Lee was on the floor beyond, moaning gently. *He's losing too much blood. He'll be dead inside ten minutes.* I took in as much of the room as I could see, trying to get a location on the gun.

Then, beneath me, the chair collapsed completely.

I rolled further away from Prouse, my arms still tied behind me, and used the wall to shuffle to my feet. He was already up, eyes desperately searching the floor for the gun.

I charged him.

He absorbed the impact, coming as hard at me as I came at him, and we stumbled sideways, toward the French windows, unable to stop our momentum—and crashed right through them. Glass shattered. Wood splintered. And then we were on the grass outside.

Rain sheeted down.

The only light was from the candles, still flickering, inside the living room. It spilled out on to the lawn like a pale puddle of water. Off to my left, in the direction of the beach, were the fence panels. Off to the right, Prouse was sprawled in a clutch of knee-length grass and nettles. I rolled over on to my front, trying to wriggle free of the binds.

Prouse sat up, looked around.

I rolled again, closer to the fence, trying to give myself some room. But now Prouse had spotted me, and he was on his feet, a violent twist to his face.

"You fuckin' little *prick!*"

Pushing my back against a fence panel, I scrambled to my feet. Looked around. Tried to find anything I could use. And then there, hidden in the dark, I spotted it.

The nailgun.

I'd been using it to put up fence panels two days earlier.

I took a step to my left and scooped it up. Prouse was six feet away. I gripped it, fed the fingers of my right hand around its body—and then stopped. *Shit. Where's the trigger?* I couldn't feel my way around it properly, not with my wrists so close together.

Then I realized.

I had it the wrong way up.

I glanced at Prouse. He was four feet away, teeth gritted, great big sinewy arms in front of him, black eyes and beard like splashes of mud against the white of his face.

I turned the nailgun.

Don't drop it. Don't drop it.

Then the head of the gun caught on the binds. Three feet. *Come free, you bastard.* I jerked at it. Again. Again. *Please come free.* Two feet. I hooked at it again. *Come on!*

Finally, it came loose.

I arced my body to the left in a C-shape. Prouse was only a foot away, the tips of his fingers brushing the fabric of my jacket. So I leaned in toward him—and I fired.

Dmph. Dmph. Dmph.

Three six-inch nails hit him in the stomach.

He stumbled back, mouth open. I fired again, not caring where the nails landed on him, just as long as they did. One passed through his hand. The others I couldn't tell.

He made a gurgling sound, then, as the rain continued pelting down, hit a bump in the lawn, slipped and fell on to his back. He hit the ground with a *whup*, and it was like a ripple passed across the garden. He just lay there, the grass parting for him and then reaching in again as he became still, closing like an emerald coffin lid.

I wasn't sure whether he was dead or alive.

Dropping the nailgun on to the grass, I headed back through the shattered remains of the glass and into the living room. Lee was on his side on the floor, a pool of blood surrounding him. "Lee?" No response. I dropped to my knees, my wrists still tied behind me, and used the top of my thigh to roll him on to his back. His eyes were closed. "Lee?"

Again, no reaction.

Come on, Lee.

I put my ear to his mouth, but I couldn't feel his breath. When I came back up again, I had a brief moment of dizziness, rolling from side to side like I was adrift in an ocean. Once things settled, I shifted left on my knees and dropped to his chest.

Please be alive.

But there was nothing.

No breath.

No heartbeat.

PART FOUR

43

Three hours later, I watched as a forensic team continued to move through the house. They were done in the kitchen; now they were in the living room. There were three of them, all dressed in the same white paper boiler suits: one at the rear doors dusting down the frames; one on his hands and knees at the sofa taking scrapings from the blood; and one out in the garden, on his haunches, placing a marker by a stray nail. The electricity had been restored, but they'd also set up two big stand-alone lamps.

After forensics had bagged my clothes I'd had my statement taken, and now I was watching the scene-of-crime officer ripping a uniform apart for not sticking to the prescribed route in and out of the house. "It's there for a bloody reason!" she shouted at him. The SOCO was a woman in her forties, with a soft expression that was at odds with the sort of things she must have found at crime scenes. She emerged from the living room, passed me at the kitchen table and then headed outside, into the night.

That was when I saw Rocastle.

He was out on the driveway, holding an umbrella above him, talking to a couple of uniforms, one of whom was an inspector. The inspector had come in as I was giving my initial statement, and listened to what I had to say. He looked officious and naturally inclined to disbelieve anything anyone had to say, which was good preparation for what was coming next. After Rocastle nodded a couple of times, he made a bee-line for me.

Inside the door he stopped, flicked the rainwater off his umbrella and leaned it against the wall. Then he unbuttoned his coat and came across the kitchen.

Outside, the weather was getting worse, storms swelling in the sky out to sea. He sat down. "Weather could be better," he said.

"A lot of things could be better."

"True." He reached inside his jacket pocket and took out the same notebook and pen he'd had the first time he'd been to the house. He placed them down on the table, set them parallel to one another and took a long, deep breath. "Sorry about your friend."

I nodded.

He looked out of the window. "You remember when I came up here the first time? I think my exact words to you were, 'If you're getting in my way, that's when we have a problem.' You recall how I asked you not to get involved in my case?"

"I didn't realize I *was*."

He smiled. "That's cute."

"I mean it."

He turned back to me, running a hand through his beard. "I don't know what kind of village idiot you're used to dealing with down here, David, but the fisherman that just happened to turn up at your house earlier on was a fairly significant part of the case I was trying to build. You do remember that case, right? The one where a body washed up *on the fucking beach*?" He spoke softly, but he was angry. His words were clipped and sharp, the muscles in his face set like concrete. "Another case that has absolutely nothing to do with you *somehow* ends up with you front and center of it. I'm wondering, do you have problems understanding basic English, or are you just willfully ignorant?"

"Prouse tried to kill me."

"So you say."

"What, you think I'm lying?" I leaned forward, pointing to the bruises streaked across my face like ink spills. "Why don't you take a closer look at these?"

He didn't respond.

"What am I supposed to do when someone comes to my house, puts a gun against my head and tells me he's going to blow my brains out?"

He shrugged. "You'd know better than me."

"What's that supposed to mean?"

"Well, you're the one with all the experience of catching bad guys. Maybe we should be wheeling you out at police training days. Hell, maybe you should be in charge."

I shook my head. "This is pointless."

"Well, you're right about that, at least." We sat in silence for a moment, staring at each other, then Rocastle flipped the cover on his notebook and picked up his pen. "Your statement says you don't know why Prouse turned up here and attacked you. That right?"

"Yes."

"He didn't say?"

"No."

"So he was just completely silent the whole time?"

I looked at him. "When you came to the house, I asked you whether there was any kind of connection between that body on the beach and the disappearance of the Lings."

He put his pen down again. "So?"

"So, is there?"

"I thought I already answered this."

"You sidestepped the question."

His eyes narrowed. "Where's this going, David?"

"You told me to keep my nose out of your case and that's exactly what I've done." I looked at him with a blank, unreadable expression and let that settle. It wasn't totally true, but I didn't care. "Prouse was your witness, not mine. Prouse had nothing to do with me. Up until tonight, he had nothing to do with the Lings—I haven't found a single link between him and the family. So why the hell was he trying to kill me?"

"I don't know."

I smiled ruefully. "Of *course* you don't."

"What do you want me to say?"

"Stop being so obtuse."

"Ob*tuse*?"

"You're just making this harder."

"How exactly am I making this harder, *David* ?"

"Prouse links the cases."

"Not anymore he doesn't."

"It doesn't matter if he's dead or alive, he links them."

"He's useless to me now."

"He's not usel—"

"He was my best fucking lead!"

In the living room, the forensic team all looked up. Rocastle glanced at them and then slumped back in his chair, arms crossed, and turned and looked out of the window.

"Look," I said, keeping my voice even, "I don't expect you to like me. I accept that the police will view me with suspicion, wherever I go and whatever I do. There's nothing I can do about that. If I cared about what people thought, I'd never find a single person. You, as much as anyone, must know that." A brief smile formed on his face, as if there was some resonance to what I was saying. "I just want to find out where the Lings are. That's what I've been asked to do. That's what I *want* to do. That family, they deserve to be found."

The forefinger of his right hand, flat to the notepad, started tapping out a soft rhythm. A seagull squawked and passed the house. Finally, he shifted in his seat and fixed his gaze on me. "So what are you proposing?"

"How about comparing notes?"

A snort. "Is that a joke?"

"No," I said, "it's definitely not a joke."

He could see the rest written in my face: *Or you can refuse—and I'll just keep on digging, and keep getting in your way, until I find out where the family have gone.*

Rocastle turned to the window again and looked out into the night, his eyes tracing the shoreline, the sea wall and, finally, the cove. "The body on the beach," he said quietly, distantly, a far-off look in his eyes, "it's a waste of time. The case is going nowhere. No dental records, no prints, nothing in the database." He smiled, just a parting of the lips, but this one was more mournful. "All we know about him is that someone stuck him in a fridge."

"How did he end up on the beach?"

A shrug. "To start with, we worked from the assumption someone had thrown his body from the top, over the side of the cliff. But we've been studying the tidal patterns."

"You think he washed in?"

"I think he was dumped out to sea."

Out to sea.

He glanced at me and saw I'd made the connection. A subtle nod of confirmation. "You can see why I was so interested in Mr. Prouse. He had his own boat, no one in the village seems to know that much about him—at least not what he does in his personal life—and something your friend Healy said to me also stuck. He said, when Prouse took him to the body, the fisherman showed no emotion at all. Zero. He wasn't surprised or horrified by the sight of what was there on the beach. In my experience, even an old sea dog like Prouse would balk if he'd found a corpse, however many times he'd seen it."

"You didn't have anything to tie him to it?"

Rocastle shook his head. "No."

"What about the Lings?"

"What about them?"

"Is there anything that might connect Prouse to them?"

He held his hands out in a *you tell me* gesture. "I was only on their disappearance for a few days. You probably know all this already. McInnes was running the show, but he'd just got a promotion, was new to this part of the world, and the super said I should ride along for a few days, make sure everything was all right. So I helped set things up."

"What did you make of it?"

"Them disappearing? Probably the same as you. It was weird." He became distant again for a moment as he cast his mind back. "It was all weird. That was another reason the super asked me to help out. The way the house was left—the dog wandering around, the food on the stove—nothing at Farnmoor, nothing at Miln Cross, and yet we had two unreliable eyewitnesses spinning two pretty convincing stories; and then there were a whole bunch of leads that went precisely nowhere." He seemed almost to shudder out of the memories. "Did you find your way to that old farmhouse up on Dartmoor?"

I nodded.

"What was that all about?"

"You didn't find anything there?"

"McInnes said it was empty."

"It wasn't empty." I looked through to the living room. Lee's body had long since gone, but his blood remained, dried and hard on the carpet and the sofa. In the light from the lamps, it looked pink and streaky, like a floor of frayed ribbon. "Lee was living there."

"In the house?"

"In the roof. He said he saw McInnes snooping around, and by the time he came back the next day with a warrant, Lee had cleared the place out. McInnes was just unlucky."

"And you weren't?"

I shrugged. "I had the advantage of knowing Lee. He wasn't worried about me in the same way he was worried about the cops. That made him sloppy." I remembered what else he'd said to me when he'd called the phone booth. *Do you want to get killed? Is that what you want? Because they'll do it. They'll bury you so far under the earth even the worms won't find you.* I looked at Rocastle. "Lee was running from something. A group of some kind. I think they might have been the same people who kidnapped the Lings."

"Based on what evidence?"

"Based on what Lee told me."

If I wanted to get something back, I knew I'd have to give him something in return. So I met him halfway. I told him about what had happened to Annabel, her accident, her recovery in the States, how Lee had paid for and organized everything, and how Schiltz had been their doctor. And then, finally, I told him why it had all gone wrong. "Carrie saw some sort of photograph at Schiltz's place."

"Photograph?"

"A photograph she shouldn't have seen."

"Of what?"

"I don't know. But, whatever it was, I think that's why the family was kidnapped. Trouble was, Carrie made a copy of the photograph and she hid it somewhere, and now no one can find it. And whoever these people are, and whoever they work for, they're trying to get to it, whatever the cost—because it's big enough to bring them all down."

"So she didn't tell them where the copy was?"

I looked at him silently, and we both understood. *She didn't tell them, and it cost her.* A sadness settled around us, heavy and funereal.

"Nothing about the Ling disappearance felt right," Rocastle said. "That guy in London—Rew—getting back on the drugs after three years of being clean. Him and Muire ending up six feet under the ground inside eight days of one another." He shrugged. "Even for a man who believes in coincidence, that takes a lot of swallowing."

"Why didn't you ask around about Rew yourself?"

"What are you talking about?"

"You must have had contacts at the Met?"

He didn't reply for a long time, eyeing me, trying to figure out how I knew about his time in London. "I was CIB, David. A rubber heeler. Do you know what that means? It means no one trusts you. No one wants to help you. In all my time up there I only met about three people who ever treated me like a cop and not some sneering backstabber." He sighed. "When Muire died, the Ling case got flushed. It was over. In February, we had no leads, no idea where they'd gone, all we had were two eyewitnesses—and, by March, we didn't even have that. We just had a drunk floating in the Dart, and a dead junkie. We had no trail to the Lings, not at the start and not at the end. And now my latest case is going down the shitter as well." He looked into the living room, where the forensic team were finishing up. "So, how is Prouse connected to the

Lings?" He said it quietly, remotely, not even really a question. "I don't know. You tell me."

He continued staring at the forensic team.

The conversation was over.

"Well," Rocastle said, flipping his notebook shut and tuning back in. "I'm sure I don't have to remind you everything I just told you, I told you in complete confidence."

"You don't."

He looked at me momentarily, as if he wasn't sure he believed me, then pocketed his notebook and stood. "I'd better see how the search for our old friend Prouse is going."

I nodded.

"You said he headed up into the hills?"

"Yes. After I managed to get the better of him, I came back inside and checked on Lee, and . . ." I paused, a moment of clarity hitting me like a wrecking ball: *two hours ago, he died on your living-room floor.* "I went back out to the garden and he was gone."

"We'll find him," Rocastle said.

"I hope you do."

"He can't have gone far."

I watched Rocastle go, then looked down toward the sea wall, to where my car had been parked for the past three and a half hours.

No, I thought. *Prouse hasn't gone far at all.*

44

At the Ley, a mile out of the village, I killed the car engine and listened to the rain on the roof. The darkness was absolute. There were no more street lights until a small knot of houses another mile further on. Here, out on the edges of the lake, there were only sounds: water gently lapping on the shore; animals, out in the black, cawing and crying out; the constant, unceasing whine of the wind, and the gentle chatter of rain.

I grabbed a flashlight from the passenger seat and headed around to the trunk. Very softly, its noise deadened by high banks of shingle between the Ley and the beach, the sea crackled, its noise metronomic like a record stuck in a loop. I popped the trunk, lifted it up and a pair of eyes caught the light from the flashlight. Prouse—gagged, arms tied, ankles bound—looked up at me. There was blood all over his front: his stomach, his arm, on his cheek, matted like treacle in his beard. In his hand one of the nails remained, piercing the triangle of skin between his thumb and forefinger. I'd tied his hands together so that one set of knuckles was pressed to the other, making it impossible for him to remove the nail.

His eyes flicked past me, trying to get a sense of where we were. He'd know soon enough. He knew this area better than me. But for now, I enjoyed the sense of confusion in his face. His eyes moved left, right, over my shoulder and down past my hip, trying to understand where he was and how he'd got here. But then he had to start blinking away the drizzle as it drifted in at him, and I filled in the gaps in his memory: "You killed Lee Wilkins and you tried to kill me." He eyes fell on me. "Now I'm going to find out why."

I clamped two hands on his arm and heaved him out of the trunk.

He came halfway and then his clothes caught on something, the breath jetting out of his nose making him sound almost feral, like a muzzled dog. I pulled at him a second time, hauled him all the way out and dumped him on to the dirt track. He cried out again, the noise instantly washed away by the melody of the lake. I shone the flashlight back up the dirt track I'd come in on. It was a quarter of a mile long, overgrown and silent. On the edges of the water, this far in, all anyone would see from the road was a wall of reeds.

I'd be fine here for as long as I needed to be.

Bending down, I ripped the duct tape away from his mouth and stuck it to the car in case I needed it again. His breathing began to regulate. I didn't let on that my own head was still pounding: I'd hit the side of my skull before anything else when the chair had tipped over, and the paramedics who'd attended to me after I'd called the police, and lied to them about Prouse, told me I had mild concussion and gave me a dose of aspirin. I'd waited five hours after the police left, to make sure they weren't coming back and to try and clear my head, but it had made no difference at all.

"You're in some deep shit here, boy," Prouse said.

He was hoarse from the gag, from trying to scream through it, from the lack of air in the trunk. I changed the settings on the flashlight so it switched to a muted yellow glow, and then set it down on the back bumper of the BMW, angled toward him.

"Where is the family?"

His lips peeled back in a smile. He tried to shift position on the mud, but with his hands and legs tied together he just slithered around like an eel caught on dry land.

"Where are the Lings?" I said again, in exactly the same tone.

"Why the fuck should I tell you?"

I reached around to the back of my trousers and removed the Glock 19 he'd been pressing to my head only hours before. His eyes narrowed when he saw it, as if he didn't think I'd have the balls to fire it. "Let me ask you something," I said, placing the gun on the bumper, next to the flashlight. "Does it even bother you that you killed a man tonight?"

Prouse shrugged.

"That's all Lee gets? A shrug?"

He shifted against the ground, trying to find a more comfortable position. "He had a big mouth on him. You talk as much as he did, you gotta expect it to come back at you."

"Who else have you killed?"

"What does it matter?"

"Did you kill the Lings?"

He looked around him, as if he'd figured out where he was. A bird squawked out on the water. "You brought me to the Ley. That's clever. Where did the police go?"

"The other way."

A quick look toward the gun. "So now what? You gonna shoot me?"

"I don't know," I said.

He tried to find some subtle giveaway in my face, a hint of weakness, but I kept my gaze fixed on him and I could see the first flicker of doubt pass across his eyes. I could use a gun. I'd grown up firing them in woodland only two miles from where we were, and I'd been forced to fire them since; not because I wanted to, but because if I hadn't I'd already be buried in an unmarked grave.

But I wasn't going to kill him.

If I did that, there would be nothing to separate the two of us.

"Where are the Lings?" I asked again.

"They're dead."

I stepped away from him—a reflex action, as if some mechanical part of me was repelled by the idea of it—and as my legs hit the car, the flashlight rocked off the bumper and hit the dirt track. Darkness. I dropped to my haunches and felt around for it. When I had it in my hands again, I turned it in Prouse's direction and found him in the same place: on his back, looking along the water's edge at me, skin pale, eyes like lumps of coal.

"All of them?"

"The husband and wife I did myself." There was nothing in his voice, just a cold efficiency. He sniffed and rubbed his chin against his shoulder. "I took them to the barn."

"The barn?" And then I realized what he meant. "At Farnmoor?"

"Walked them out to the fields and shot them in the head. *Pop, pop.*"

He looked at me, his face like a mask: no attachment to the words, no feeling for what he'd described, just an abstract void. *Keep it together*, I said to myself, *keep it together*. But I could feel myself losing focus. *He murdered them both in cold blood.*

"You were the one Ray Muire saw Paul and Carrie with."

"Muire," he replied, almost spitting the name out. "Arsehole wasn't even supposed to be in that day. *No one* was supposed to be in that day. It was a *Sunday*. I planned it specifically because it *was* a Sunday. Then, next minute, he's singing to the coppers."

"How did he even see you?"

"*Oh*," he said, almost sneering, "because he was blind?"

"Are you saying he wasn't?"

"I'm saying he could see just fine."

I frowned. "What?" He didn't reply. "What are you talking about?"

Suddenly, the rain started getting heavier. He slithered around on the ground, hands still behind his back, ankles looped together, trying to ease himself clear of the puddles.

"Prouse?"

"Muire dug his own grave," he said. "He was a dead man the moment he started chirping to the coppers. The fact that he was a part-time drunk just made it easier."

"You killed him too?"

"I gave him a little shove." He was unaffected by anything he was saying. He wasn't even trying to get a reaction from me. This was just a cool, detached listing of the facts. "Followed him, watched him get pissed, put him in the river on the way home."

"As easy as that."

He shrugged. "I just do what I'm told—then I take the money."

"From who?"

"From whoever's paying."

"Who paid you to kill Paul and Carrie?"

He just stared at me. "Katie Francis."

There was something blacker and more menacing about him now, as if he could see his answers were unbalancing me. Francis had looked me in the eyes when she'd talked about the Lings, about Ray Muire too, and I'd never glimpsed a hint of deception. Now Prouse was trying to feed off the uncertainty he could see in me.

"Why did she want them dead?"

He shrugged. "She was following orders too."

"From who?"

"Shit runs downhill."

"From *who*?"

Somewhere, out on the main road, a car passed. Automatically, I turned toward it to make sure it wasn't coming down the track, and then, when I turned back, Prouse was looking up at me, his eyes unlit, hostile. "I feel sorry for you, boy," he said quietly. I didn't reply, my mind racing. "There you are, running around trying to find a family that no one gives a shit about, and all the time you ain't got one fuckin' idea who you're up against here. How can I make this clear to you? Your precious Ling family—they're dead."

He said it so quickly, without a single flicker of emotion, that it felt like I'd been knocked off balance again. Then the anger started to build.

"Now you can stop running around like an arsehole," he said, flatly.

Without thinking, the rage burning a hole in my chest, I bent down, grabbed his collar and hit him with everything I had. I broke his nose instantly, could feel it turn and buckle, and just as I drew back again, his body already limp and unresponsive, blood all over his beard, I managed to stop myself. I took a woozy step back toward the car, clenched fist ringing with pain, Prouse lying unconscious on the dark of the track.

"Shit."

I checked the time on the phone. 5:57 a.m.

The sun was going to be up in an hour.

Kneeling down at Prouse's side, I shook him awake. He was struggling to breathe, his nose a twisted mess of bone and blood. I waited for him to come round and look up at me, then dropped him to the ground, grabbed the gun and pressed it against his eye.

"Who was giving the orders to Katie Francis?"

He moaned gently.

"You've got three seconds."

His other eye widened, as if he was trying to focus.

"One."

He moaned again, blood bubbling at his nose.

"Two."

He hacked up a glob of saliva.

"Thr—"

"Okay, okay," he said, slurring his words.

"Who was giving the orders to her?"

"There's someone in the States."

I pulled the gun away. "Cornell?"

He nodded.

Lee had talked about him having local help. Prouse was that help; Katie Francis was. He looked up at me, eyes glazed and empty. "They just tell me what I need to know. Cornell told Francis to split the family up: I'd take care of the husband and wife here, Cornell would take care of the girls."

"The girls are dead too?"

He just looked at me, distant, drifting.

I grabbed him by the throat. *"The girls are dead too?"*

He nodded—and then blacked out.

I shoved him back against the dirt and walked away, huge,

thunderous swells of anger tremoring through my chest. *They're all dead. You failed them.* But then, against the sounds of the Ley, Prouse was talking again, mumbling something else. "What?" I turned and moved back toward him. "What did you say?"

". . . a marked man."

"What did you say?"

He rolled his head against the dirt track and looked at me. "The photograph."

"What about it?"

"Carter Graham's a marked man."

"Graham's next?"

He didn't respond.

"Is Cornell coming for Graham?"

"He's coming for everyone."

"*When* is he coming for Graham?"

"Run, boy." His eyes widened. "Just . . . run."

"What's Cornell protecting? What's in the photograph?"

"I took him out in that box," he said, words bleeding into one another. I tried to figure out what he was talking about. He looked disorientated and couldn't focus. I'd hit him hard. Maybe too hard. I hadn't cared at the time, but I cared now.

"What are you talking about, Prouse?"

"They said to put him in Haven."

"Haven?"

"They said, put him in Haven, the same place I'd put the husband and wife. So I took the boat out . . ." His eyes rolled up into his skull, like he was about to pass out.

Husband and wife. He meant Paul and Carrie.

"Prouse," I said, slowly, evenly, "where's Haven?"

He came back, blinking, trying to focus on me, even though I was only a matter of feet away from him. "I wedged that box in tight . . . but I didn't lock it properly."

For a second time I heard a car approaching on the main road. I looked up, unable to see it from behind the reeds, then turned back to Prouse, trying to figure out what the hell he was talking about. *He'd put someone's body in the same place he'd put Paul and Carrie.* "Where's Haven?" I asked again, trying to temper my irritation.

"Where I was supposed to put him."

"Who?"

"The beach."

"The beach?"

"The body."

That stopped me. "The man you found on the beach?"

"Cornell told me to put his body where I put the others," he continued, like he hadn't even heard me, and then he started to drift.

"*Listen* to me." I shook him awake. "Where's Haven?"

"The water," he said softly.

"*What* water?"

"I hit a wave, and the freezer box toppled over, and everything went overboard." His eyes rolled. It was like he couldn't even hear me now. "Everything went overboard."

"Are Paul and Carrie buried in Haven?"

He just looked at me.

"Prouse?"

"I couldn't do anything about the body," he said, eyes blunt and impassive. "The tide took it too quickly. But the coppers wouldn't be able to identify him. I knew that. That's why, when that boy found the body, washed up there on the beach, I thought, 'If I report it, if I go and speak to that ex-copper, your mate Healy, on the lad's behalf, the other coppers won't think I was the one that done it.'"

I grabbed him by the collar and yanked him toward me. "Tell me where Haven is!" But then I noticed something: blood was dripping from the back of his head. *Shit.* I turned him. In the light from the flashlight I could see the damage: there was a black wound on the dome of his skull. My eyes traced the ground. Directly beneath his head was a rock.

When I'd punched him, I'd punched him back into the rock.

And now he was bleeding out of the back of his head.

I laid him back down gently.

"Prouse, listen to me." He blinked a couple of times, his eyes eventually finding my face. "I'm going to call you an ambulance, okay? But first I need to know something."

No reaction from him.

"Where's Haven?"

"Where I buried them all."

"Yes, but *where* is it?"

"In with all the water."

This was going nowhere. "Paul and Carrie are there, right?"

"Yes."

"What about the girls?"

He shook his head.

"So where are Annabel and Olivia buried?"

"I don't know."

"Where are they, Prouse?"

"I don't know."

I studied him, searching for a lie, but he wouldn't have been capable of spinning a lie. Not now. Fresh blood leaked from his nose. "*Think*. Tell me where the girls are."

"Cornell."

"Cornell killed them?"

He nodded.

My heart sank. "Where did he put them?"

He stared up at me.

"Prouse?"

Nothing from him now. His eyelids fluttered.

"Haven," he said softly.

Haven. He'd talked about putting them in with all the water.

Had he dumped them out to sea?

I'd have to figure it out later. Now, I had to get him an ambulance. He was dying in front of me. I grabbed my phone—once I'd called it in, I'd get the hell out.

He muttered something incoherently.

The line connected.

All of them are dead.

"Kalb."

I looked at him. "What?"

"Kalb."

"What's Kalb?"

No response. His eyes were closed now.

"Prouse?" I said to him. "What's Kalb?"

"The man on the beach."

"The one you were supposed to put in Haven?"

He nodded, then mumbled, "He's the man in the photograph."

Instantly, I killed the call.

"Wait, the man in the photograph is the body on the beach?"

He didn't reply.

"Prouse?"

No answer again.

He's the man in the photograph.

D.K.

Or *D. Kalb.*

Then, from somewhere behind me, footsteps.

45

I grabbed the duct tape I'd pinned to the car and placed it against the fisherman's mouth. Then I killed the light. The footsteps stopped as soon as it was dark. For a while—maybe ten seconds—the night was like standing in front of a black wall: there was no definition to anything, no hint of any object in any direction. About six feet away, somewhere on my right, Prouse was moaning gently. I ignored him, ignored the sound of the water stirring on the lake, something gliding across its glassy surface. The rain had eased off again, but there was the whistle of a soft breeze, like air traveling through the neck of a bottle. And behind it all was the sea, its noise smothered by the whispering movement of the reeds, by the banks of the Ley, but still impossible to stop, there in the background.

I ducked my head, closed my eyes and willed myself to listen.

No footsteps anymore.

No sound of movement at all.

I looked up again. Slowly, I started to be able to make out the curves of my car, six feet away, parked between the dirt track and the lake. Off the other way, Prouse's face emerged from the night, like a swish of gray paint, looking in my direction. I couldn't see it clearly, couldn't tell if he was conscious or not anymore, but the jet black of his beard gave him a sinister, otherworldly look; like a man with only half a head. Briefly I thought of the man in the photograph, of the girls, and then of Paul and Carrie Ling, buried in a place called Haven I might never even find. But I instantly pushed it away.

I couldn't afford for my concentration to stray.

My hand out in front of me, I inched back toward the car. As my fingers brushed the bodywork, I dropped down again and listened. The noise of the Ley seemed to deaden. For a moment, all I could hear was the rhythmic rise and fall of the sea, but then the breeze rolled in across the lake and the reeds started rocking from side to side, the movement creating a soft chant, like a monastic choir. Swapping the gun from my left to my right, I traced the circumference of the car, keeping out of view of the track, until I found cover at the front of the BMW, next to the headlights, and could see any approach.

Except I wouldn't see any approach.

It was too dark.

Which meant it was also too dark for whoever was here.

I came out from behind the car, keeping low, and moved silently across the track to the other side. From memory, I knew the track zig-zagged back up to the main road, first through a maze of reeds right down here on the lake, then through the high banks of trees and bush that smothered the sound of the sea, then finally across a sprawling swath of flat grassland. I'd heard vehicles out on the main road, but not in close, which meant, if someone had got this far down the track without me hearing, they'd come in on foot.

Pausing, I looked out to my left. On this side there was no lake, just an ocean of shoulder-high yellow grass, vaguely drawn against the dark of the night, growing out of wet, mulchy ground. I used it as a guide, moving alongside it and quietly up the track, into an enclosed area, tall reeds on both sides. Suddenly it became difficult to see anything, thick knots of reed obscuring whatever vague definition I'd managed to gain before. I stopped, trying to force my eyes to see more. Twenty feet ahead—maybe more, maybe less—an animal scurried across the track, one side to the other.

I took another step forward, eyes trying to pick out any movement, any sign there was another person here, but after ten paces I stopped again. There was no light now, not even a hint of it: nothing coming through the reeds, no break in the clouds, just a black mass. Feeling around in my pocket, I removed my phone, and then stood there, trying to pick out sounds coming down the track at me. If I switched the phone on, I immediately put myself on the map; if I didn't, I stood here in darkness, cast adrift and walking blind.

Then a noise behind me.

Footsteps.

Twenty feet away.

I turned slowly, feet soft on the ground, gun up in front of my face. The blackness was total, like standing with your nose against a wall. There were no edges, no shapes or definition—just the night. Nothing else. As I squeezed my fingers harder against the grip of the gun, a stone scattered along the path, toward me, settling somewhere to my left.

Despite how cold it was, I could feel sweat all down my back, tracing the length of my spine; feel my heart pounding in my chest, its echo in my ears. I swallowed, and in the silence it felt like the noise was immense. I tensed, expecting some kind of reaction.

All I got was silence.

But then, a couple of seconds later, there was a gentle squeak; one tiny moment of sound that seemed to carry along the track like a gunshot. Blind in the dark already, I closed my eyes, trying to focus my other senses, trying to understand what it could be.

Then it came to me.

The soles of someone's shoes.

Six feet away. Maybe less.

We're right next to one another.

I opened my eyes and pushed against the resistance of the trigger, squeezing it to its halfway point, ready to fire into the dark if I had to— but then there was another noise.

From the Ley this time.

A gurgle.

Suddenly, I heard the scratch of boots against the track—much less than six feet away—and someone took off, back in the direction of Prouse. The Ley was so silent now, the movement seemed to rip across it, one side to the other. Birds scattered somewhere in the darkness, the *whup, whup, whup* of flapping wings, and as the footsteps died out, the wind picked up again, passing through the reeds either side of me. In the quiet of the aftermath, they made a disconcerting noise, almost human, as if warning me to stay where I was. But I didn't. I followed, moving fast and quiet, and headed back to the lake.

Gripping the Glock, I got there as quickly as I could, jogging along the track toward the car. I stumbled a couple of times, hitting uneven patches beneath my feet, but when I emerged from the tunnel of reeds there seemed to be a subtle switch in the light: the total blackness of the night had given way to a soft charcoal hue; still dark, but not totally.

I lifted the gun to my eyeline.

No sign of movement.

Prouse was on his back, arms out either side of him, half in, half out of the water. I didn't approach him from directly across the track. Instead I edged around the BMW, making sure no one was using it for cover. Once I could see him again, I stood with my back to the lake and scanned the area. The field of yellow grass was still swaying, its gentle ballet of movement massaged by the wind, but now I could see it had been bent, a path trampled through it. *An escape route.* I crossed the track, keeping my head low, and paused on the edge of the grass. I could only see for about forty feet, even in the changing light. But I saw the path carved into it—snaking across the belly of the field—until the darkness finally claimed it back.

I returned to Prouse.

His blood was washing out into the lake by the time I got there, both eyes looking up to the heavens like chunks of polished black marble. He was making a gentle gurgling sound, a single, controlled puncture wound visible at the bottom of his throat. It was the work of a pro. Someone who knew exactly what they were doing. In a matter of minutes, Prouse would be dead—but not before he'd suffered. I looked back across my shoulder, to the grassland. *Whoever it is, they're here.*

I realized how lucky I'd been: in the darkness, between the reeds, I'd been blind—but whoever had come for me had been blind as well. My car would have told them I was here, but not where—and their one noise, right at the start as they approached, had been what saved my life. If I hadn't heard it, I'd have been here with Prouse—and the killer would have come up behind me and put a knife in me too.

I wiped down the Glock and left it on the shore of the Ley, next to Prouse. As I did, his fingers brushed my jacket.

I looked down.

He started coughing, and as blood spilled out on to his beard, I wondered if he'd ever imagined, even in his darkest moments, whether the end might come like this, out here on the edges of the Ley, alone and cold, with no one to claim him.

Maybe violent men never thought about the end.

Maybe they never feared it.

But, as I looked across the track to the route his assailant had used, back through the grass, I knew the end came for men like Prouse, just the same as anybody else.

Just the same as the end had come for the Lings.

46

As I got to the main road, I looked down at the clock. Just after six-thirty. Dawn would be breaking in about fifteen minutes, sunrise about thirty minutes after that. I quickly went to my phone and put in a search for "D. Kalb." Eleven million hits, but nothing immediately useful: the website and Wikipedia entry for a musician; a university lecturer in Canada; LinkedIn profiles for professionals with the same surname; Facebook profiles, Twitter accounts, Tumblrs. I looked again at the clock and knew I'd have to come back to it later. I needed to call Carter Graham, to warn him he might be in danger. Jamming the phone into the hands-free cradle, I scrolled through until I found his number and hit Dial.

Finally, a groggy, barely awake voice said hello.

"Carter, it's David Raker."

It took him a couple of seconds to place the name. "David?"

"You need to listen to me."

He cleared his throat and I heard a squeak, like mattress springs, and the sound of him shifting around in bed. I remembered then that he'd had the gala the night before.

"Hold on," he said. "I need to find my glasses."

"Did you organize extra security yesterday, like I told you to?"

"Wow." He coughed a couple of times. "It *is* early."

"Did you organize extra security?" I repeated.

"Yes. Just as you suggested."

"Are they at the house with you?"

"Yes. They're here now."

I breathed a sigh of relief. "Okay. Good."

"Why, is there a problem?"

"There might be."

"What kind of a problem?"

There was no way to break the news gently. "You're in danger."

"What?"

"You remember I talked to you about Cornell yesterday?"

"Yes."

"That you have something he wants?"

"Yes."

"I think one of his people is coming for it."

"*What?* When?"

"Now." I gave him a couple of seconds to process that. "You need to prep your security team. Put them on high alert and lock down the house. Don't let anyone inside. Is that clear?"

Now he was awake. "Yes," he said, his voice already shredded with fear.

"How many people do you have there?"

"Seven."

"Good. Prep them all, put them at the entrances. After you've done that, I want you to call the police. Just dial 999 and tell them to come to the house. Then, after that, phone direct into Totnes and ask for DCI Colin Rocastle. Tell him I sent you and that it's to do with Prouse. He'll understand that. Are you getting this?"

"What's Prouse?"

"It doesn't matter. Just do as I say, all right?"

He sounded panicked. "What the hell does Cornell want?"

He wants to kill you.

"Look, I know you're in shock here, but there are some questions I need to ask you—so try to clear your head. Do you remember I asked about a photograph yesterday?"

"Yes."

"Ever remember having your picture taken with a guy called Kalb?"

"Kalb?"

"I think it might begin with a K. K-A-L-B."

"No. Should I?"

I changed tack. "Did you find a picture of the three of you?"

"I found a few."

I paused. Carrie had put a date on the photograph of about 1971. That would have placed the men in their midtwenties. "Okay, listen. Do you have a picture there of the three of you—Ray, Eric and you—perhaps taken when you were all out in the States at the same time. Maybe Ray was on holiday, or maybe he'd come out to see your LA office."

"Uh, I can go and grab them, I suppose."

He sounded reluctant to go anywhere now.

I told him to go ahead and do it. As he put the phone down, I looked both ways along the empty road, looking for any sign of life—of cars watching me, of people hiding out of sight—and a sudden realization hit: Cornell was trying to close the circle. He was killing off anyone even remotely connected to the photograph. They'd failed to get me at the Ley, but they'd come for me again—after they'd done for Carter Graham. I felt sure of that. Like Muire and Schiltz, he was tethered to Kalb somehow, even if he didn't know how, and once he was out of the way, I was a minor bump in the road. Just a loose end. I glanced right, out along the road, to the village. In the hills above it was my home.

I couldn't go back now.

It was too risky.

"Okay."

Graham was back on the line.

"What have you got there?" I asked him, still scanning the road, left to right.

"I've got four photos of the three of us."

"Describe them to me."

"This first one was taken at our thirty-year school reunion back in 1991—"

"What about the next one?"

"Uh. This was a golfing holiday we took to Palm Springs. We stayed with Eric for a week, and then had a week up to Napa, wine tasting. It was a surprise for Ray's fortieth."

"So that would have been 1985?"

"Correct, yeah."

"That's not it. Next one?"

"This one was when we all met up in London in 1996."

"That won't be it either. What about the last one?"

A pause. Then: "Oh, I remember this. This was taken when the office was being built in LA—so it would have been February 1971. *Ish.* Eric and I clubbed together and flew Ray out for a holiday. I think he'd just split up from his girlfriend."

This could be the photograph of Kalb.

"Describe the picture."

"Uh, well, there's Ray and me in the center of the picture. I can see one of the city's mountain ranges in the background. I'm not sure which one. Eric took the picture—"

"Wait. The picture doesn't have all three of you in it?"

"No. Just Ray and me."

"Are there any other people in the background?"

"In the background of the shot?"

"Yes."

"No. It's just Ray and me."

Damn it.

"Is there another picture from the same trip, with all three of you in it?"

A pause on the line.

"Carter?"

"It's weird," he said, distantly, as if caught in a memory. "Eric e-mailed a picture, I don't know, maybe a year ago, maybe eighteen months. Something like that. He was scanning in all his old photographs. I remember it because it was taken around the same time as this one—except his one had all three of us in."

"Did you print off a copy of it?"

"Yes."

"So where is it?"

"I don't know. I keep all my pictures in the same place."

"Which is where?"

"In a shoebox in the library."

I realized what that meant. "Does anyone else know about the shoebox?"

"The shoebox? Katie might know."

She'd taken the photo for Cornell. Just like the copy Ray Muire had.

"What about your e-mail? Would a copy still be in there?"

"No," he said. "I get such a vast amount of e-mails, as you can probably imagine. I only keep the last six months' worth. That's why I printed off a copy of it."

I tried not to let my frustration show: "Okay, put all the photos back."

"Why?"

"I'll explain when I get there."

"You're coming over?"

"Yes. Now. There are some things you need to know."

He sensed something ominous in my voice. "Things?"

"I'll be there in twenty minutes. Just make sure your security are doing their job, and call Rocastle as soon as you put the phone down. It's fine. He knows you already."

"He looked into that family's disappearance."

"Right. Do me another favor: don't speak to anyone about what we just talked about, okay? That includes Katie."

He seemed confused by the request. "Wha—why?"

"Just trust me."

"You're . . ." He stopped, a tremor in his voice. "You're worrying me here, David." He meant he was scared. This was probably as close as he'd come to the unknown, of not being in control of a situation, for a long time. "David?" It sounded like a plea now.

"Prep your security, call the police, call Rocastle—got it?"

"Okay."

"I'll be there in twenty minutes. Everything will be fine."

But I wasn't sure if I really believed that or not.

47

I accelerated away, heading east and joining the coastal road, and left the Ley and the village behind. Farnmoor was three miles away. The best time I could hope for, if there were no traffic, no jams anywhere along the narrow lanes, was fifteen minutes. Driving any faster, I risked hitting another car—or falling into the sea.

After a mile, my phone started ringing.

I glanced at the display. Number withheld. Thinking it might be Graham, or even Robert Reardon, Carrie's university lecturer, I reached over and answered.

But it wasn't either of them.

It was Healy.

A ripple of anger hit me immediately. His timing was terrible, as always—and if there was ever a moment when I didn't need to play passenger as he slid slowly into self-pity, it was now. "Healy, don't take this the wrong way, but you'll have to call me back."

"You'll want to hear this," he said.

I glanced at the clock. I'd already become caught in a conga line of slow-moving cars, and I'd promised Graham I'd only be twenty minutes.

Calm down.

He's got his security team.

He's called the police.

And then, as Graham lingered in my thoughts, I remembered something he'd said to me about Cornell: *He told us he used to work for the Bellagio, in their security team.*

I filed that away and turned my attention back to Healy. "What is it?"

"You remember what you said to me?"

"About what?"

"You wrote me off."

Another spear of anger. This time I couldn't keep a lid on it. "I haven't got time for this shit. I never wrote you off—I said you were a good cop. Don't twist my words."

Silence.

"Fine," I said. "I'm done."

I reached over, ready to end the call, when he spoke again. "You want to know what they've got?"

"Who have got?"

"The police."

"What are you talking about?"

"The body on the beach."

I paused. "Healy—"

"Those arseholes I used to work with," he said quietly, "they thought I had nothing left to give. Well, fuck them. Fuck everyone. I'm a better cop than they'll ever be."

"What have you done, Healy?"

"What have I *done*?" A snort. "I've *done* what I did for twenty-six years: I got the answers I needed from wherever was necessary. I proved a point."

"Who did you speak to?"

"Does it matter?"

"Have you put yourself at risk?"

Another snort. I started to wonder whether, for him, this was the morning after the night before. There was a soft lilt to his words, as if he was still drunk. "Do you mean have I put *you* at risk? Is that what you mean, Raker?"

"Believe it or not, I've spent the last year trying to *stop* you from landing yourself in shit. You might want to cast your mind back—once you've sobered up."

No reply.

"If you want to share what you've got, then great." I glanced at the clock. Seven-twenty. "If not, we'll have to save this fight for another day."

"Officially, police are saying the body belongs to a white male between seventy and ninety," Healy said, a sudden determination in his voice. "Unofficially, it's the higher end of the scale. We're talking eighty-five to ninety. No dental records. No matching prints. No medical records. The guy's a ghost. I was right: the body was kept on ice before it ended up on the beach. Maybe a week, maybe more—the coroner's trying to narrow down TOD. One thing that might interest you: the guy has scarring under his left arm."

"Scarring?"

"The skin was flayed."

"Does it match up with anything on file?"

"No. They've been through the databases. If there was any match, they wouldn't be hunting around for a name. The only thing they've got is the size of the scar. It's a small surface area. Like, *really* small. Only about a centimeter squared. But whether he did it himself, or someone else did it to him, the knife went in deep. Like he was cutting something out. Forensic tests are ongoing. Results expected in the next couple of days." He paused for a moment. "Oh, and something else: they found sand in his lungs."

"Sand?"

"Tiny traces of it."

"From being washed up on the beach?"

"No. It's not local."

"So where's it from?"

"Same story as the skin. Results not yet in."

In front of me, the line of cars ground to a complete halt. *Shit.* I turned back to the phone. "Where'd you get all this information from?"

"What do you care?"

"Stop *fighting* me all the time, Healy."

"I'll see you around."

He hung up.

Ahead of me, a motor home was maneuvering through a narrow lane, everything static behind it. As I watched it, a residual anger remained, burning a hole in the center of my chest—but I cleared my head, took what he had told me, and moved on. I couldn't afford to get hung up on Healy, on the point he was trying to make, on all the misguided, aimless punches he was trying to throw. In the moments when he was introspective, almost delicate, it was easy to get drawn in by the promise of a different man; but this side of him you just had to cast off into the wind.

I shifted my mind back to before he'd called, to what Carter Graham had said about Cornell working for the Bellagio security team, and then to what Prouse had said at the Ley: he'd killed Paul and Carrie, and Cornell had taken care of the girls. If Cornell had worked for the Bellagio, they must have had his personal details there, which meant he'd left something of his life, of his background, of his whereabouts, on file. The people who'd hired him would have done all sorts of background checks, because you didn't just walk into a security job without being checked out. And, in turn, without having to give something of yourself away.

Grabbing my phone, I went to the browser and straight to the Bellagio site. There was no number listed for the security team on the contact page, just a general information line. I noted it down, backed out, and headed to Google, putting in a search for "Bellagio Director of Security." There was no picture—but there was a name: Carlos Soto.

I punched in the general inquiries line just as traffic started moving again.

"Good evening. This is the Bellagio. How can I help?"

Through the cell, and across five thousand miles, it sounded like I was talking to someone on the moon. "I was hoping to speak to Carlos Soto in security, please."

"Thank you, sir."

The line went silent. A couple of clicks.

Then it started ringing again.

I glanced at the clock. Seven-fifty. That meant it was just before midnight there. Security staff worked all sorts of hours, so there was a good chance Soto was there.

I just hoped I'd get lucky.

But I didn't.

Click. "Hi, this is Carlos Soto, director of security at the Bellagio. I'm afraid I can't take your call at the moment, but if you leave your name and number, I will get back to you as soon as I can. Alternatively, one of my colleagues will be happy to help." He went on to list a few names and their direct lines, but the signal began to wane as I moved closer to the coastline's black spot. If the high-rollers group was bringing in the sort of money Lee had suggested, the hotel wasn't going to palm Cornell off on to a glorified mall cop—they were going to give him their top man.

That meant it was Soto or no one.

I listened to the rest of his message, then left one of my own, hoping the signal would hold up. "Hi, Mr. Soto, my name's David Raker. I'm an investigator based in the UK. I was hoping I could talk to you about a man named Cornell."

I figured that would be enough—so I left my number and ended the call. Almost immediately my phone started ringing again.

Carter Graham.

I picked up. "Carter—is everything all right?"

"David," he said. He was whispering. Immediately I could sense the alarm in his voice. "He's here. I think he's shot one of my security guards. I'm so scared."

"Okay, calm down. Who are you talking about?"

"Katie says she saw a man with a gun coming from the barn." He sniffed. It sounded like he was crying. "Help me. Please."

Katie says . . .

"Listen, Carter. You can't trust Katie."

He was crying.

"Carter. Are you listening to me?"

"What?"

"I said you can't trust—"

Suddenly, there was a massive noise in the background.

"Oh *fuck!*" he screamed. "Oh shit!"

"What the hell was that?"

"That's him firing a fucking gun!"

I pulled the phone from the cradle. "Okay. Listen: did you call the police?"

"Oh, *please,*" he said, words deformed by tears.

"Carter?"

"Please," he said again, "please don't kill m—"

And then a second gunshot.

The line went dead.

48

When I got to Farnmoor, the gates were wide open and I'd become lucid enough to see how fast I'd been drawn in, how unprepared I was. Whoever this man was, he was armed and he was a killer. I wasn't either of those things. I'd left Prouse's Glock back at the Ley—and now I had nothing to fight back with.

I drove past the gates, on about an eighth of a mile to where I knew there was a turnout. Leaving the car there, I backtracked along the lane until I saw a space in the hedge that traced the perimeter of the grounds. From this distance, everything seemed normal. No movement. Nothing out of place. The rain had eased off, leaving the lane awash, but this close to the coast the drizzle was massaged by a cold sea breeze that made it difficult to hear anything but the gurgle of water and the whine of the wind. I headed further down the lane, toward the gates, and then watched the house again, this time from the bottom of the driveway. No sign of the police, or of Rocastle, even though it had been the first thing I'd told Graham to do when I'd woken him up. Instead there was a stillness to the house, a pallid hush, that it had never had before.

I'm too late.

Darting in through the gates, I arced right, following the boundary hedge to where an orchard sat, perched on a gentle slope. Beyond it was the side of the house, where I could see the window into the library, its glass dark and indistinct. Further around, the swath of green that encircled Farnmoor dropped away toward the sea, running left to the cliff's edge, and right to a series of fields on which I could see the empty barn.

The one Prouse had killed Paul and Carrie in.

Hunched behind a knot of apple trees, I waited to see if there was any reaction to my movement. Any eyes on me. Any sign I'd been spotted. In the windows of the house all I could see was a reflection of the grounds and the growing blackness of the sky. As I moved further around, right to the edge of the orchard, I saw three cars at the back. One I assumed was Katie Francis's, a Lexus I'd seen parked in exactly the same place both times I'd been before. Further down were a series of five garages, four closed, one open: inside the open one was a red Porsche Cayman. It must have been part of Graham's collection. The other one was a black Audi A4 with SECURITEAM stenciled on to its side.

Graham's security detail.

He said he had seven men here.

Where the hell are the rest of their cars?

The remnants of the previous night's gala were evident: the marquee was still up at the rear of the house, ribbon was attached to the doors and windows, and behind one pane of glass I could vaguely make out a balloon. Along the gravel path, running between the orchard and the house, I could see plastic beer glasses and discarded cigarette butts, in doorways, on windowsills. Briefly, I wondered why there was no clean-up staff here.

Then I realized.

It's Sunday.

Graham must have given them the day off.

A sudden rush of wind carved in off the sea, ghosting through me, and I shivered there, alone, in the orchard. It was cold now, freezing cold, the rain getting harder, leaves falling from the branches above me, cascading past my face like fallen wings. My eyes fell on the rear door, one I assumed would lead through to the kitchen and then on into the belly of the house. It was my quickest route inside, but it was also dangerous: I'd be approaching from a different direction, entering hallways I hadn't used, passing rooms I wasn't familiar with. But going in through the front door meant going around the house.

And that was an even bigger risk.

I'd be passing windows.

I'd be exposed.

I grabbed my phone from my coat and checked it. A single bar. I dialed 999 and listened to it ring, the reception drifting in and out. Then the line died. I tried again, got as far as asking for the police, and then I lost the signal for a second time. *I'll have to call from the landline.* Pocketing the phone, I watched the house for a few minutes more.

Then I broke cover.

Sprinting across the open ground between the orchard and the house, I moved in a diagonal, across to the rear door, and—as I got closer—realized it was already ajar. I hit it hard, pushing through into the kitchen and stopping the door dead before it hit the wall.

Silence inside.

Ahead of me, the kitchen—all chrome and brushed steel—split in an L-shape: one branch led into a cove that doubled up as a pantry; the other opened out into a bigger, brighter space, with a granite-topped island sitting under a slanted roof full of skylights.

Beyond it was the door.

I headed around the counters, grabbed a knife from a rack, then padded through to the hallway. The stairs up were about a third of the way along. The other times I'd been, I'd approached from the opposite direction and there had been people working. This time there was no sound anywhere and the whole place was empty. I felt my heart shift, instinctively knowing this wasn't right, and then a sense of dread started to wash over me: ten minutes before, Graham had called me in desperation, in tears, in fear of his life.

A gunshot had drowned out his plea to be spared.

Now there was only stillness and quiet.

I passed vacant rooms, frozen in party mode: balloons and decorations, glasses on tables and mantelpieces, the smell of spilled booze and cigarette smoke. When I got to the bottom of the stairs, I looked up, saw nothing, and headed straight past, all the way to the vast front room that had been the central focus of the gala. There was no one inside, but—as I backed out—I noticed the front door was fully open. Outside, it was still raining.

Returning to the stairs, I paused and looked up.

As the steps spiraled right to meet the landing, I noticed something on the wall. A smear. *Blood.* I felt compelled to look behind me again, in both directions, the size of the house suddenly intimidating, its ceaseless, deathly silence sending a cool finger down the center of my spine. Then my eyes fell on the blood again, and I saw more beyond it: on the carpet at the top of the stairs, on the walls around it, on the door frames.

Slowly, I started the ascent.

49

About halfway up, something made a noise—a dull thud—and I paused there. Five seconds. Ten. Fifteen. After twenty, I began moving again and, at the top step, reestablished my grip on the knife. It was big and weighty, and would be fine up close. But the assailant had a gun. Unless I could surprise them, I might as well have had nothing.

I stood there and listened.

The only noise now was the rain at the windows.

Along the hallway, at the end, was the library. To my right were two function rooms, mostly empty of furniture. Further down on the opposite side were the same doors that had been closed the day before. Graham's bedroom. Maybe his study. I started down toward them, flicking a look toward the library, my mind racing. Why wasn't there any sound? *Because the killer's waiting for you, drawing you in.*

Or everyone's already dead.

I'd gone about twenty paces when I saw more blood on the walls. I could make out finger smears, as if someone had reached out for support and then toppled to the ground. There was a trail of it in the carpet, from the point the finger smears ended, all the way along the hallway, to the first closed door.

I headed for it.

And then stopped again.

Immediately to my left now was Katie Francis's office, the edge of her desk visible and part of the window behind it. There was blood on the door, around the door handle, a handprint on one of the panels. Something mechanical moved in me, a thick, desperate sense of inevitability, and then, gripping the knife, I pushed at the door with my sleeve.

It inched back.

Katie Francis sat upright in her chair, but the chair had drifted out from under the desk on its wheels. Her arms looked like they were reaching down for the floor, fingers grasping at the floorboards; her body was tilted slightly to the left, her head angled in the same direction, but resting against her shoulder. One of her shoes had spun off and away.

Her killer had put a single bullet through the center of her forehead. Her blood was all over the wall behind, her life painted there in one grotesque arc, but her eyes were the worst part. They were wide open, looking right at me, and even while the light had gone, you could still see the echoes of her last moments: all the fear, all the desperation.

I quickly backed out, immediately zeroing in on the closed door along the hall. The blood trail leading to Graham's bedroom had begun in Francis's office. My heart pounded against the inside of my ribs like a ball of rock, even though I already knew what I'd find. *Graham. Dead.* I knew as well, intuitively, that the killer was gone.

This hell was their aftermath.

At the door, I hesitated, sleeved fingers wrapped around the handle, wondering if I even had the stomach for what was on the other side. Memories flashed in my head like a strobe: the evil I'd faced down before, the devils and executioners, the innocent people they'd tried to bury and the carnage they'd left in their wake.

I stepped closer and opened the door.

Graham's bedroom was long and simple. Against the far wall was a king-sized bed, three standalone wardrobes to its right and a wall-mounted TV. Closer to me, at the other end, was a desk with a laptop on it and a lamp.

There was so much blood it was difficult to imagine what the room might once have looked like. It was on the walls, on the windows and across the laptop. On the floor, sprawled between the desk and the bed—black T-shirt, shaved hair—was one of Graham's security detail. I recognized him from being at the house the day before. He'd been shot through the back of the head. Blood washed out from under him, suggesting he'd taken one in the stomach too, but it was hard to tell for sure.

Because next to him was another corpse, awash in blood.

This one was Carter Graham.

50

His face was pressed right into the skirting board, as if he'd been smashed into it—pushed there by the power of his attacker—and there was a horrible contortion to his body, neck angled one way, body the other. He lay stomach down, knees to the floor, and a pool of blood was clawing its way out from under him, slipping into the gaps between floorboards and running across the room toward me. He'd been shot in the chest. I took an involuntary step forward, drawn to him, drawn to help him, then stopped and looked down: my feet were in his blood, in the blood of his security guard, and reality kicked in. *What had I touched with my hands since I'd been here? What had I left my prints on?*

I backed up, the pool of blood following, and then kept going all the way to the door. Walls, door frames, handles, I couldn't remember anymore. I'd been on edge—and I'd been sloppy. I hadn't been thinking. In my pocket, I felt my phone start to buzz. I didn't answer it, my attention drifting back to Graham: eyes closed, nose pressed to the wall, mouth open, body twisted horribly. *Something isn't right.* My phone continued to vibrate, a series of gentle purrs in the silence. *Something isn't right about the way he died.*

He'd said he'd had seven men in his security team.

But there was only one here.

After lingering on Graham for a moment more, I headed out into the hall and along to the other closed door. It wasn't a bathroom or a study, it was a room full of filing cabinets, stuffed with paperwork. I checked the other rooms, rooms whose open doors I'd passed in the days before—but there were no other bodies. There was no more death.

So, where the hell are the rest of the security?

For a second I stood there, frozen, my head full of noise. Then I became aware of the phone again, buzzing. I took it out and looked at the display. Caller unknown.

I answered, the signal drifting. "David Raker."

"Let me tell you how the past twenty-four hours has been for me, shall I?" *Rocastle.* He came straight out of the traps. No greeting, no introduction. The reception was terrible, but marginally better than outside. "Late last night I have to sit and listen to your bullshit about not being involved in my case. I'll give you your dues, Raker, you spin a

convincing tale, even for a suspicious old man like me. You told me
Prouse took off across the hills. Do you remember that?"

"That's where I saw hi—"

"Right. That's where you 'saw' him. So, tell me: if he headed out
across the hills, why the *fuck* was I standing next to his cold, hard corpse
at the Ley this morning?"

"I don't know," I said, keeping my voice even.

"You don't know. Right. Are you even *remotely* familiar with the geography in this part of the world? *Are* you? Because the hills you talked of
are in completely the opposite direction to the Ley." His voice had taken
on a different tone now: he'd dropped to a hushed, caged fury. "Which
must have meant he double-backed on himself. But *that* can't be right
because my search area was *two fucking miles across*! If he came back to the
village, we would have got him. Instead, some couple finds him down by
the lake!"

"I don't know what to say. I thought I saw—"

"I don't give a shit what you saw. In fact, I don't give a shit about a
single thing that comes out of your mouth." He paused. I could hear him
breathing, almost wheezing, as if he couldn't get on top of his anger. I'd
slowly moved back along the hall and paused outside the bedroom,
looking in at the bodies. It was such a mess, so much blood between
Graham and me, it was hard to tell exactly what his injuries were—not
without getting close, without turning him on to his back and leaving
myself all over the crime scene. I'd thought chest, but it could have been
gut. He'd bled a lot, and it was still coming.

"Now I've got this bullshit at Farnmoor to deal with."

That brought me back into focus. "What?"

"Carter Graham called me an hour ago."

So he *had* called Rocastle, just as I'd told him to. I looked into the
bedroom again. What did I say? That I was here, standing over Carter
Graham's body? That I'd walked all over a crime scene without even
thinking about it? I was already in deep shit with Rocastle. If I told him
what had happened, I'd be signing my own death warrant.

"What did Carter say?" I asked.

"Carter? *Carter* said he thought 'they' were coming for him."

I looked at the body. "He's right. There's—"

"Oh, I *see*. This is another one of your fantasies."

"Listen—"

"No, you listen, you lying bastard. I just had to leave a murder scene for this pile of shit because you know what my super will say if we don't drop our drawers for Carter Graham? *Do* you? 'You've got to get down there, Colin, because this guy pays fifty grand a year into our police community fund.' Sod the stiff lying on the shores of the lake with half his brain slopping out the back of his head. Who cares about him? He's just a fisherman. Much better that I go to the house and babysit millionaire Carter Graham."

My eyes lingered on Graham for a second more, on all the questions that would go unanswered, and then I headed off along the hallway. I didn't stop to look in at Katie Francis again. She'd made bad choices, and she'd sided with the wrong man, but she didn't deserve what had been visited upon her. I couldn't bear to look at her again.

I headed through to the library, eyes gliding over every surface, trying to find anything that might connect Graham, connect any of this, to Kalb; anything at all that might give me an idea of who he even *was*. Pulling my sleeve down to cover my hand, I opened and closed drawers and pulled books out of shelves. But there was nothing.

Rocastle was still swearing at me.

I cut in. "Just listen to me for two seconds, okay?"

"No."

"There's someone here in Devon. I think they've been sent by a—"

"*No*," he said again, almost screaming it down the phone. "I'm going to make this very simple for you. Wherever you are at the moment, you're going to head home. There, DC McInnes and two uniformed officers will be waiting to arrest you."

I sighed. "There's no time for this."

"You had us wasting hours yesterday searching a *barren fucking hillside*, so don't talk to me about having no time!"

Rain swirled in as I got down to the front steps of the house.

"Raker?"

"Do what you have to do," I said—and then hung up.

51

As soon as I got back on to the main coastal road, I took the first turning back off it and followed a series of ten-foot-wide lanes west, in the vague direction of the village. I wasn't sure what I was going to do, but I knew I didn't want to pass Rocastle as he came the other way, toward Farnmoor. I needed time to think, to plan out my next move.

If I thought my home was off-limits before, the likely destination for a killer looking to finish the job, then it definitely was now. If I let myself get arrested, nothing got solved: the Lings wouldn't be found and Cornell would disappear, having closed the loop. I was the only one left now, the only one with any kind of connection to the photograph, to whoever Kalb was and why he represented such a destructive risk to Cornell. And yet, basically, I knew nothing. I didn't even know Kalb's first name. We were miles apart.

Suddenly my phone started buzzing in my lap. I glanced at it, expecting it to be Rocastle. But it wasn't. It was a number that I didn't have logged. An Exeter area code.

Reardon.

Carrie's university lecturer.

I jammed it into the hands-free and pressed Answer.

"David Raker."

"I've got three messages to call you." He was so indignant, he didn't even introduce himself. I'd decided against mentioning Carrie in any of the voice mails—it was a risky strategy, but I wanted to come at him cold. Using Carrie as bait would have given him time to gather his thoughts before phoning. "What exactly is it you want?"

I felt underprepared for this phone call—my mind still turbulent— but I didn't want to lose the opportunity to speak to him.

"I want to talk about Carrie Ling."

There was a brief hesitation. "Oh. Carrie. What about her?"

"I don't have much time, Robert, so I'm going to cut to the chase: her family have asked me to find her, and I think you can help. You ever heard of a man called Kalb?"

"I don't think I—"

"He was part of her MA." I left that hanging there, rain lashing against the roof of the car, the cold, barbed winter air crawling its way inside. "Robert?"

"I can't discuss private matters—"

"Look, I haven't got time for this dance. I want to know what her MA was about and I want to know who Kalb is. And you're going to tell me."

"You can't talk to me like that."

"Are you listening to what I'm saying?"

"I heard—"

"It's the *reason* she and her family disappeared."

"I don't know . . . You can't . . ."

"Would you prefer it if I didn't find her?"

"That's ridiculous. No, of course not."

"Do you want that on your conscience?"

"I have a clear conscience, thank you."

"What about if they're dead?"

No answer.

"Robert?"

"Do you think they're dead?"

He sounded different now—his bluster gone—and I knew where the question had come from: the point, probably a few months after they went missing, when he started to realize Carrie and her family weren't coming home again, and he began to wonder why.

"Do you think they're dead?" he said again.

"I think there's a good chance of that, yes." I let that soften him up even more. Then I went at him again. "Did Carrie ever show you a photograph of a man named Kalb?"

He seemed unsettled by the change of direction.

"A photograph?"

"It would have been taken in about 1971."

A pause. "She said she had one in her possession."

"You never saw a copy of it yourself?"

"No."

"Did you request one?"

"I told her I'd like to see it. She said she'd send it to me."

"But she never did?"

"No. I don't know why."

I thought I could take a pretty good guess: Lee Wilkins would have been telling Paul that the photograph could land them in trouble; Paul would have told Carrie the same. She was wrestling with her conscience.

"Did she tell you where she found the picture?"

"No."

"She only described it to you?"

"Yes. We only ever talked about Kalb over the phone."

That had probably saved Reardon's life. Cornell and his people would have been through Carrie's e-mails and found no mention of Kalb. There was no mention of him in the dissertation notes she'd left on Paul's PC either. If she'd referenced him even once in an e-mail correspondence with Reardon, the professor would have been in the ground like everyone else. He couldn't begin to understand how lucky he was.

I moved up through the gears.

"So who's Kalb?"

A long, deep breath came down the line, sounding like a burst of static. He was still hesitant, a man brought up on traditional values, on the protection of people's privacy, their ideals, their integrity. But those values were worthless when you were already in the trough with the pigs. We weren't dealing with incorruptibility.

We were dealing with killers.

I heard a door close. "What is it you want to know about him?"

"Let's start with Kalb's first name."

"Daniel."

Daniel Kalb.

D.K.

"He was going to be the subject of Carrie's dissertation," Reardon continued. He sounded different now, forlorn. "Are you familiar with the Yalta Conference?"

"I probably need a refresher."

"Churchill, Roosevelt and Stalin met there in 1945, on the shores of the Black Sea, along with about seven hundred other diplomats, to organize the postwar makeup of Europe. They discussed a range of things, but arguably the most complex debate was over Poland's future. Churchill wanted free elections for the Soviet-liberated countries of Eastern Europe; Stalin wanted to maintain the USSR's power in that part of the world and argued that twice in the preceding thirty years Germany had used Poland as part of an, if you like, 'invasion route.' Roosevelt was somewhere in the middle, but basically needed Stalin because he needed the Soviets' military help in the war against Japan."

"And Carrie was interested in the postwar Soviet Union?"

"Yes. Especially Poland."

That tied in with the notes I'd found on Paul's PC.

"She wanted to use Yalta as a springboard for her dissertation," Reardon went on. "At that stage—the stage when she first started talking about it—she didn't have much more than that. She indicated she was interested in the seven years between the end of the Second World War and the moment the People's Republic of Poland came into being in 1952; essentially, a Soviet puppet state. I told her that it was too broad a canvas, that she needed to pare it down. She went away and I didn't hear from her for a few months."

"Did those couple of months coincide with her trip to the States?"

"Yes."

"And when she got back from the U.S., things had changed?"

The line drifted slightly. Reardon said something, but the reception dropped out. I was coming into a black spot. Rainwater washed across the narrow lanes, spraying everywhere. There were no turnouts and I couldn't stop—if I did, no one would be able to pass. Instead, I took my foot off the accelerator and slowed to a crawl, trying to prolong the signal for as long as I could.

". . . the photogra . . . entire course . . ."

"I lost you for a second. Can you repeat that? You were saying that things changed after Carrie got back from the States—they became more focused on Kalb?"

"Correct."

"Which meant what?"

"Which mean . . . changed the entire cour . . . of her MA. Her outline used Yalta as the pivot still, but she turned . . . on its head." I leaned toward the phone, trying to pick up on the words that kept dropping out. "From the end of May, maybe the start of June, her dissertation didn't become about the years *after* Yalta, it became about the years *before* it. Specifically, she beca . . . terested in the seventeen months between . . . and . . ."

"Wait, what dates?"

". . . and Carrie had done a hell . . . lot of reading: Polish history, Soviet history, the major beats of the Second World War. All of it. By . . . she was . . . and was knowledge . . ."

"Can you repeat that?"

". . . so she already knew about So—"

And then the line died.

Damn it. I reached forward and pressed Dial again. It rang three times and then stopped. I heard a snatch of Reardon's voice, the vaguest sense of a *hello,* then nothing.

I tried again and he came on a little clearer this time. I looped the conversation back round to where we'd left off, but then he started talking about something else: "Carrie sent me a very strange text on the day she disappeared."

That rang a bell. I remembered Reardon had been one of seven people—the rest, friends and family—that Carrie had texted on the day she'd disappeared.

"Strange how?"

"I don't know. It just said, 'Dissertation is in the laptop.'"

"Laptop?"

"That's . . . she . . ."

He was breaking up again.

"*Her* laptop?"

". . . don't know."

And then the call bombed out again.

Dissertation is in the laptop.

As far as I could tell, Carrie didn't *own* a laptop—certainly she hadn't left one in the house—and when I'd been through Paul's PC, I'd found only some vague, typed-up notes about life in the Soviet Union in the 1950s. I'd always assumed she'd used his PC, most likely during the day when he was at work.

Clearly, Reardon had no idea what she was talking about either and, in the police investigation, no laptop had ever been recovered and attributed to Carrie. McInnes's team hadn't interviewed Reardon in any formal capacity, but they would have seen the text sent from Carrie's phone on the day she disappeared, and he would have told them the same thing he just told me, that Carrie had sent him a weird text.

Dissertation is in the laptop.

I looked at the clock. Midday.

I needed to get a signal on my phone and spend some time finding out who Kalb was. But, more than that, I needed to stay hidden—and I needed to work fast.

52

I knew I had to get off the grid as soon as possible, but a couple of minutes after Reardon faded out, the signal kicked in on my phone again and it started buzzing in the cradle. I glanced at the display, expecting it to be Reardon; instead it was a ten-digit U.S. phone number.

"David Raker."

A short, echoey buzz. "Mr. Raker, it's Carlos Soto."

"Mr. Soto. Thanks for calling me back." Just up ahead was a small passing point in the lane. I pulled into it, trying to save the signal I had. "It must be late there."

"I've just finished my shift."

"I appreciate your time."

"What can I do for you?"

"I was hoping I could talk to you about a man you might have come into contact with at your casino. His name's Jeremy Cornell. I think he organizes a get-together—"

"I know him," Soto said. "What concern is he of yours?"

"Concern?" I stopped. Soto was polite but terse, probably because Cornell brought in a shitload of money for the casino and he didn't want to rock the boat. This was going to be hard work. "His name came up in an investigation I'm putting together over here."

"Who do you work for again, sir?"

"I work for myself."

"You're a private investigator?"

"I trace missing people."

"And who's gone missing—Mr. Cornell?"

"No. Not Cornell."

A pause. "I'm not sure I follow."

"Cornell may know some things that could help me—but unfortunately I can't get hold of him. However, as I understand it, he spends a lot of time at the Bellagio."

"So you want me to fill in the blanks?"

"Something like that."

"I can't comment on individual customers, sir."

He was playing a straight bat, as I'd expected him to. I backed out and came at him a different way. "Okay. Fair enough. Let me ask you something else: how long have you been in charge of security at the casino?"

"What's the relevance of this?"

"I mean, I'm sure I can find out, but . . ."

I didn't finish the sentence, just let it hang. He didn't answer immediately, as if he was trying to pinpoint the reason I might ask. Then, eventually, he said, "Two years."

"So you wouldn't have worked there when Cornell did?"

"Pardon me?"

"You wouldn't have worked at the casino at the same time as he did." That meant Soto was immediately redundant. "Is there anyone else who might remember him?"

"Sir, I think you may be confused."

"How's that?"

"Mr. Cornell never worked here."

That stopped me. "At all?"

"Not before I arrived, and certainly not since."

Certainly not since. There was a hint of something in Soto's voice—defiance, animosity—but I let it go for the moment and wheeled back to what he'd said before that.

Mr. Cornell never worked here.

Which meant it was all one big lie. He'd lied to Graham, lied to everyone in the high-rollers group—about his history, about who he was and about what he did.

"What do you make of him?" I asked.

"Of Mr. Cornell?" A pause; one that lasted longer than it should have. I recalled what he'd said earlier: *Not before I arrived, and certainly not since.* "I don't particularly have an opinion of him either way," Soto said eventually. "He's a valued customer."

"That's it?"

"Pardon me?"

"He's just a customer?"

A moment's hesitation. "Yes."

"There's nothing else?"

The line shifted slightly. "I'm not sure what you're suggesting."

This time, I didn't respond.

"Mr. Raker?"

I glanced in my rearview mirror, checking for cars. "Look, I'm not here to get anyone into trouble, I'm just trying to find some people that Cornell might have known."

"I don't know what that has to do with me."

"You're familiar with Cornell."

"I'm sure a lot of people are familiar with him."

"I think you have an opinion on him."

He didn't reply this time.

"And I'd like to hear that opinion."

Nothing.

"I'm right, aren't I?"

"What, are you a mind-reader?" The tone changed instantly. "I don't know what you want me to say—or why you called."

"I'm trying to find a family."

Silence on the line.

"I'm trying to find a family who went missing. They spent some time in your part of the world between February and May last year. I think Cornell knows where they are."

More silence.

I wondered whether I'd played this right. For all I knew, Soto could have been working for Cornell. But, somehow, I didn't think so. The way he'd sidestepped questions, trod carefully around them, was deliberate; a man trying to stop himself being cornered.

"I can't help you, Mr. Raker."

"Are you sure?"

"Am I *sure*?"

"Look, I just want to find out about—"

"*Listen* to me," he said, his reply suddenly loaded with venom. He'd lowered his voice too, as if it was the only way he could keep a lid on his anger. "I don't give a damn about your case. Is that clear enough for you? I don't care about the family, and I don't care about you. All I care about is staying alive—and going after Cornell is like rocking the hornets' nest. You make him angry, and everyone on your radar gets stung. Just leave it alone."

A second later, he was gone.

Ring

On the northern fringes of the Southern Highlands golf club, south of Las Vegas where the I-15 started its gentle, lonely journey into the desert, was the house belonging to Carlos Soto. Part of a small, gated community in San Sevino, it was tucked away in a triangle of land between South Highlands Parkway and Dean Martin Drive. From the Parkway you could see some of it, hidden behind a six-foot wall: a window on the side for one of the three bedrooms; a door beneath it, leading out of the kitchen and into the backyard; a covered area immediately outside the rear doors; and then a small, ten-meter swimming pool. You couldn't see the backyard or the pool from the road, only the gentle shimmer of the water reflecting off the cream-colored exterior walls.

But Cornell wasn't out on the road.

He was inside the house.

He'd been watching Soto for seven months now, ever since a cop on his payroll called Ridgeway warned him that Soto was sniffing around. Soto could have been a problem. He was just a security grunt now, but he'd been a cop before. A good one, by all accounts. That made him dangerous. So Cornell headed him off. He found out about the things Soto held dear, and he started watching the intimate rhythms of his life.

Soto left at seven every weekday morning, unless he was working weekends, when he'd usually take Thursday and Friday off. On weekends he always left later, between 10 a.m. and 12 p.m., and always came back after midnight but before 3 a.m. Cornell got to know Soto's route through the casino too—where his office was, his weekly meetings, the people he talked to most—and then, finally, he got to know his home life, invading the sanctity of his home, letting his gloved fingers touch Soto's furniture, his bed linen, his clothes. Soto had no wife, no kids, and both his parents were dead—and he was lonely. Desperately lonely. On his computer, in the history, Cornell found lots of dating sites, evidence of short, failed relationships, some sort of diary where he talked about wanting kids—a son he could play baseball with, a daughter he could watch grow up and become a mother—and then a blog full of dripping sentiment where he wrote about his father. He knew Soto went out to eat a lot, and he mostly ate by himself, usually at a hole of a Tex-Mex place near the airport where he seemed to know the manager. But Cornell knew that the manager and the food weren't the real *reasons Soto went there. The real reason was he liked to get his dick hard talking to a waitress called Ellie.*

Cornell knew about her too: thirty-six, from Seattle, divorced.

He knew everything about Carlos Soto, but Carlos Soto knew nothing of him. The best Soto had was a connection between Schiltz and the whore, and the fact that Cornell had asked for the CCTV footage and room key information from the night the laptop was taken from Schiltz's room. The rest was just a bunch of loose ends. Everything in Cornell's life—the photograph, the old man, Firmament—were buried so deep, if Soto ever had the resources to get there, Cornell would be waiting. Seven months of watching him gave Cornell all the advantage he'd ever need. He was in control of Carlos Soto.

And, somewhere down the line, he knew he would kill him.

Just like everybody else.

Cornell stopped at the rear doors. Both closed, they led out under the covered roof to the kidney-shaped swimming pool. Around it were a series of small, potted palms and a barbecue. An inflatable pool chair drifted across the surface of the water, right to left, caught in a faint desert breeze. But it was something else that got Cornell's attention.

Removing his phone, he dialed into Las Vegas Metro, and asked to be connected to Lieutenant Ridgeway, the cop who had first raised Soto as a potential problem.

"Homicide," the detective said.

"It's me."

A pause. "Uh, is there a problem?"

Cornell enjoyed the concern in Ridgeway's voice, the moment of panic as he tried to figure out what he might have done wrong. "Let me ask you something, Mr. Ridgeway."

He turned away from the swimming pool and looked back across the living room. Sixteen-inch tiles throughout, immaculately clean. Off-white walls. Maple cabinets, all of which he'd been through, each of them full of inane reminders of Soto's worthless existence. At the back of the room, a breakfast bar divided the living room from the kitchen, and then an island was beyond that. Cornell zeroed in on a set of expensive Japanese cooking knives stuck to a magnetic strip. He started back across the room toward the knife rack, keeping Ridgeway waiting.

"Hello?"

"I really hope I haven't been the victim of sloppy police work," he said, and, as he got to the island, ran his middle finger, protected by latex, down the flat of one of the knife blades. It made a gentle whine. "You haven't let me down, have you, Mr. Ridgeway?"

"It's Detective Ridgeway."

"It's whatever I want it to be."

There was a pause on the line.

Cornell prolonged the silence. He touched a santoku, ran a finger down the hardwood handle, and it shifted on the rack, the blade rocking gently against its bed.

"Did you get me everything you had on Soto?"

"Yes," Ridgeway said. "Of course. Why?"

Cornell looked out through the rear doors. "A few things still concern me."

"Like?"

"I've read over the information you sent, I've watched him for seven months, I know everything about him, every detail of his tedious life—and yet there are still things that continue to surprise me about him. Little details. Things that are . . ."

"That are what?"

Cornell shrugged. "Out of kilter."

"Out of kilter? What does that mean?"

He listened to Ridgeway, his breath making a gentle crackle on the line. "You do know that, if you've missed something, that's going to be . . . a problem."

"Is that a threat?"

"Why, does it sound like one?"

"You're damn right it does."

"Oh, well, I'm sorry about that," Cornell said. His voice was quiet, steady, but there was something in it. Something that, even along the phone line, even as Ridgeway sat on the other side of the city, would have killed his bravura. "You told me Soto didn't have any brothers or sisters."

"Yeah, that's right."

"So he's got no nieces or nephews?"

"No."

"No children he doesn't know about?"

"I think he would have mentioned if he'd had kids running around."

"Maybe he didn't like you enough to say."

"He liked me."

"What about now?" Cornell said. "Do you think he likes you now that you've fucked him over for a retirement fund?" Silence on the line. Cornell looked around the house, eyes over everything, then out through the rear doors. "Does he like kids?"

"What do you mean?"

"Does he have a taste for them?"

"What?"

"Does he?"

"Are you insane? No."

"How would you know if he did?"

"I'd know, okay? Carlos is a straight arrow, as honest as—"

"You sound like you still care for him." Cornell didn't say anything else. He left the knives and returned to the rear doors of the house. "Do you want him to succeed, Mr. Ridgeway? Is that it? Do you want him to find his way to my door? Because, I assure you, before he does that, I'll be burying you in the desert and your family will be next to you."

Ridgeway cleared his throat. He suddenly sounded nervous, penitent. "Look, I got you everything I had on Carlos, okay? That's it. That's all there is in the system."

Cornell didn't respond.

"Cornell?"

"Did you look into that other thing for me?"

"Yeah." Ridgeway dropped his voice to a whisper. "Nothing."

"No reports of any sightings?"

"No."

"You need to work a bit harder, Mr. Ridgeway."

"I'm trying—okay?"

Cornell once again chose silence.

Ridgeway carried on, filling the dead air, keeping his voice low. "Listen, I know you've got plenty of friends in this town. I know that. But just remember something, okay? Soto, he was a good cop, and the assistant sheriff, he's not . . ." He paused. "The AS, he's a straight arrow too. He hasn't got the same arrangement we've got, so he still likes Soto and still rates him. Hell, the AS actively tried to stop him leaving when he got that job at the Bellagio. So, sure, snoop around his house, follow him everywhere, do whatever you have to do to protect whatever it is you have, but if you try to do anything to Soto, you're taking a risk. If he goes missing, if you do something, I promise you they'll notice and—"

Cornell hung up.

Pocketing the phone, he stood at the glass and looked out at the pool. The breeze had died and the inflatable chair had stopped its journey across the surface of the water.

And so too, next to it, had the rubber ring.

Carlos Soto got home just after eight. He flicked the lights on immediately inside the door and then carried a grocery bag through to the kitchen, dumping it on the counter. The worst thing about coming home to an empty house was the silence. He turned the TV on, lowering the volume, and then went to the maple cabinets that housed his music system, and hit Play. He didn't care what album he'd left in there, just as long as it played loud.

After unpacking the groceries, he sat at the island in the kitchen frying some steak and checking his messages. Most of them were from the foreign-marketing director, whose job it was to get whales in from Asia, showering them with complimentaries in exchange for a night spent making six-figure bets in the baccarat lounge. They'd brought in a guy from Macau who ended up getting rushed to the ER at four in the morning after losing eight hundred grand and drowning his sorrows in a mountain of coke. Now they were having an argument about what to do: the marketing director wanted Soto to use whatever juice he still had with Las Vegas Metro to get the possession charges dropped; Soto thought the guy should take his punishment. Chances were, with the amount of green he had in the bank, he'd probably be flying home with a slapped wrist and a fine, anyway. That's what Vegas was built on: the people who had money—and then everyone else.

But halfway down his inbox, another message caught his eye.

Ellie.

She was a waitress at Texico Mexas, a restaurant on Peco that he went to a couple of times a week. The food was mediocre, but Carlos liked her, had done right from the moment he first saw her, so he kept going back. She was sweet and a little shy, and when she smiled at him he forgot—just for a minute—about how much he hated coming home. He forgot about lying alone in bed, about nights spent at his laptop trying to put into words everything he felt, about sitting in the tub and wondering if this was it for him: a single man at forty who'd never met the love of his life and would never get to see kids of his own running across his yard, never get to shoot hoops with a son out front, or sit his daughter down on his lap and squeeze her tight when she found a movie too frightening.

So he'd asked Ellie if she wanted to go on a date. At first she'd said no, probably not ready to get involved so soon after her divorce. But he'd tried again, slowly but steadily, over a couple of months, and eventually she'd laughed at how persistent he was, and had agreed to have dinner with him. Carlos smiled as he read her text: she was telling him it was fine to pick her up at 7 p.m. on Wednesday—and that she was looking forward to it.

Carlos put the phone down, slid the steak out of the frying pan on to a plate, added some creamed spinach, then grabbed a knife from the rack and took it through to the TV.

Then he stopped.

Turned back to face the knife rack.

The santoru was at an angle.

He placed the plate back down on the breakfast bar and looked around the room. Nothing else seemed out of place. Moving upstairs, he checked each of the bedrooms and then came back down again, into the kitchen. He walked to the knife rack and pushed the santoru back into place. It held true and straight, just like it always did. The magnet was strong enough for the knives never to move, and he couldn't remember the last time he'd used the santoru for any cooking. And yet it had shifted.

Carlos turned and headed for the rear doors.

He flicked on the lights in the yard.

Outside, everything was still, tiny circular globes tracing the circumference of the pool. His inflatable chair, the one he sunbathed on, was still on the surface of the water.

But then he saw he'd left the rubber ring out.

"Shit."

He rushed over to his cellphone and scrolled through his address book until he got to Ellie's number. There were two listed for her. Her cellphone and her landline.

Except, in reality, he didn't know her landline.

And this number didn't belong to Ellie.

It was the number for a motel in Henderson, about sixteen miles east, out near the 515. Listing it under Ellie was an insurance policy, in case he ever misplaced his phone.

Someone answered. "Hello?"

"It's me."

"Is everything okay?"

Carlos looked back, out through the rear doors to the rubber ring. "It's Cornell," he said. "I think he might have broken into my house."

53

Emily had given me a spare key for the Lings' place back at the very start, so I headed north to their home at Buckfastleigh. I wanted to give the house another sweep in light of the conversation I'd had with Reardon—but, also, I wanted to get away from the coast.

I used lanes instead of main roads, and it took me about three times as long, but as the house finally came into view, I pulled into a turnout half a mile further on and waited. In the silence, I thought of Kalb again and pulled my phone out of the hands-free. There was a regular signal, but no 3G. I wasn't going to be getting on the internet anytime soon.

After five minutes, not a single car had passed me and there was no sign of a tail; and as my eyes drifted back toward the house, I knew it would also be too cold and too wet for people to be walking around. That could work to my advantage. Once I was out of the car and inside the house, any voices or cars close by would act like an alarm call.

Firing up the BMW, I drove on past the house and left the car on an old, disused farm track behind a line of oak trees. They were gradually being stripped of their leaves for winter, but although the car wasn't completely hidden from view, it was better than leaving it in the open. I locked up and headed back to the house.

In the entrance hall, under the glass-domed roof, I paused and took in the emptiness of the place—the kitchen in front of me, the stairs to the left, the door into Paul's study and the living room beyond it—and tried to visualize the night the family had been taken. Cornell was careful. Even if he hadn't come himself, he would have made sure he sent men he could rely on. They might have surprised the family and wanted to get them out of the house as quickly as possible, but one of them—maybe more than one—would have stayed behind to clean everything down, to make sure there was nothing left for police.

Except maybe they still missed something.

I placed my mobile phone down on the telephone table in the hall. I'd removed the battery and the SIM card and turned it off. If Rocastle wanted to find me, if he tried to track me through my phone, he'd have to work for it. Being in this part of the world would help: there was greater distance between base stations, making any signal I gave out much more difficult to pinpoint. But, for now, I was choosing not to give any.

I focused on what I was here for.

Dissertation is in the laptop.

Paul's PC and Annabel's MacBook were still at my house, and there was no going back for them—but while it was possible that when Carrie talked about her dissertation, she meant she'd put it on to Annabel's MacBook, somehow I doubted it. I'd been through it and found nothing; just two weeks in the life of a 24-year-old.

Searching the ground floor again, I opened every cupboard and drawer, looked in every corner of every room. I opened books, flicked through them in case something, some clue, had been left inside. I took photo frames off shelves and flipped off the backs, looking for hidden messages or hints at what had happened on January 7. I worked my way through the kitchen, into the living room and back around to Paul Ling's study.

Nothing.

Upstairs, the house felt colder and emptier, like an emaciated mirror image of the ground floor. I wondered if it was because this was where they'd slept, where they spent the majority of their time; the place where—like a graveyard—they came to rest.

I moved through Paul and Carrie's room, their wardrobes, their drawers, under the bed, into the connecting bathroom. In Annabel's room, as I passed in front of her bookshelves, in front of books that spoke of her future, of a career, of a life, I had a sudden distressing sense of clarity. This wasn't a missing persons case anymore, at least not in the sense I had any hope for them. It was a search for bodies; for the final resting places of a scattered family.

Maybe not even a search.

A wake.

It became even harder to keep a lid on my emotions as I moved to Olivia's room, every surface recalling her innocence, every space a reminder of her brief eight years. I looked around, at the boy bands plastered to the walls, at the Disney Princess clock and the *High School Musical* duvet, at the cabin bed with stickers dotted along it. Underneath the bed, on a pull-out desk, were the things I remembered seeing the first time: a lineup of tiny plastic dogs, two Barbies, a 3DS, a tin full of pencils, and then a toy computer—a big chunk of red plastic—with a camera on a stalk, molded to look like a caterpillar.

A toy computer.

I took a step closer to it.

No. This is ridiculous.

But I reached down anyway and pulled it across the desk toward me, flipping the lid to reveal a yellow keyboard embedded in a white surround, and a twelve-inch screen.

I booted it up.

It made a series of chirping noises and, thirty seconds later, a functional desktop appeared. On the right were three folders: "Movies," "Games" and a painting program. Nothing else. You couldn't even create a new folder, so you certainly couldn't import anything to it. I used the trackpad and went to "Movies," knowing there was no way Carrie could have got her dissertation on to here. Inside the folder were seven videos.

I clicked on the first one. A movie of Olivia came on: she was dancing around her room, hair done up, singing into an empty tube of Pringles. It felt somehow intrusive watching her, and I thought again how desperate this move had been. When one video ended, the next one started up automatically: Olivia again, taken moments after the end of the last video, same clothes, same Pringles tube, a different song. I watched her, anguish mixed with frustration, and then got up and went to the window. As I looked out into the road, one video stopped and another began. Olivia again, a third different song.

Where next?

The road was still quiet. No cars. No people. Beyond, out on the lake, small boats—smudged and indistinct—drifted across its surface. All the time, rain continued falling.

Behind me, Olivia had stopped dancing and was talking to the camera. "When I get older, I'm going to have twenty-five dogs and they're all going to run around the garden chasing each other." Listening, I felt a deep, pervading sadness. "I'm going to call one of them Lexy, and she's going to be the mummy, and look after all the pups."

As Olivia's voice played in the background, I tried to get everything straight in my head. Things had quickly gone bad. All three men, anyone who knew who Daniel Kalb might be, were dead. The police were going to come at me for lying about Prouse. The trip up here had been wasted. There was a dissertation on a laptop that didn't exist.

Where the hell do I go next?

"What's going on?"

"Shut up. Just shut up."

I turned back to the laptop.

Olivia was gone.

"But, Mum—"

"Just *shut up.*"

The next movie was a shot from the landing, down through the slats in the bannister, in the direction of the kitchen. The quality of the footage was poor, everything blocky and pixellated. But then I realized what I was seeing: Paul Ling being filmed from upstairs, backed up against one of the kitchen counters, the fridge door open next to him. There was a four-pint bottle of milk on the floor, slowly emptying out across the lino.

Spreading around his feet.

And around the feet of the man who had come for him.

54

Next to Paul Ling was a man, dressed head-to-toe in black, a balaclava on his head with the eyes, nose and mouth cut out. He was holding a gun. For a moment, everything was still—and then, like an animal trap snapping shut, the man grabbed Paul by the arm, spun him around, clamped his other, gloved hand to Paul's mouth and put the gun to his head.

"Quiet."

"But Dad is—"

"Quiet."

Carrie and Annabel. They'd been upstairs when the man had come for them. A couple of seconds later, another voice, off camera: "Daddy!" It was Olivia. "Daddy!" She sounded distressed. The camera rocked a little, and I heard a sharp intake of breath from Carrie—the helpless cries of her eight-year-old were like a knife twisting in her guts.

"They've got Liv now," Annabel whispered, tearful. "Who are they, Mum?" Her voice was painful to listen to: she was so utterly terrified, it was like she'd regressed.

Ten years old again.

"Mum?"

"I don't know." There was a degree of control left in Carrie's voice, but slowly it was starting to slide away. Her voice wobbled briefly. "I don't know," she said again.

"Why are you filming?"

"Because someone needs to know."

"Needs to know what?"

Carrie didn't reply this time. She shifted the camera right—along the slats of the stairs—and Olivia came into shot. Both women audibly gasped, and the sound distorted in whatever feeble microphone Olivia's computer had. Standing in the doorway of the living room was Prouse, looking toward the kitchen. He also had a balaclava on but I could see the remnants of his beard and recognized the blackness of his eyes. He'd lifted Olivia right off the ground, and though her legs were kicking furiously, she made little sound. His big, gloved hand covered her mouth, reducing her cries to a soft muffled moan.

"What are we going to do?" Annabel said.

From the left of the shot came the other man, dragging Paul along the hallway. Paul was now limp, unconscious. Again, the women made soft, suppressed sounds, fear caught in their throats. "The others must be upstairs," Prouse said. Somewhere close to Carrie, I could hear Annabel starting to cry properly now, unable to stop herself.

The other man dropped Paul on to the hallway floor.

A dead weight.

"Do you want me to go and get them?" asked Prouse.

The other man didn't reply, his hands wriggling in his gloves. His eyes scanned the hallway, the living room, the study, and as they drifted up toward the camera a memory took flight in me, a flash of déjà vu: five years ago, in a bar in the Mandalay Bay.

That same look.

It was him.

Cornell.

He'd come for the Lings himself; flown over from the States to make sure it was done properly. And, immediately, I felt certain he was here again. The man who'd come for Prouse. The escape route through the grass. The massacre at Farnmoor. He'd come over, ready to finish things once and for all. Now the only one left was me.

"Come on," Carrie said to Annabel.

I heard Prouse say something else, but then his voice was gone. For ten seconds the footage descended into a blurred, pixellated mess. When it settled again, I could see where we were: in Olivia's bedroom, exactly where I was. Carrie placed the computer down on the pull-out desk. Behind her was the door, the posters of the boy bands, and—in the shadows of the room—Annabel, glancing from Carrie to the door, from Carrie to the door, over and over. For a few brief seconds I watched the living, breathing versions of them, not the ones I'd seen in photographs, not the ones Prouse had talked of. In that moment, even as the shadows of their deaths began to form, they were very much alive.

"I think this has to do with Kalb," Carrie said, leaning in to the caterpillar camera. I could hear her breath, short and frightened, Annabel wide-eyed behind her. "Paul was right. He said we were in danger. He said it had something to do with the notebook. But I didn't believe him." She paused, tears shimmering in her eyes. "I didn't believe him."

Then she got out her phone.

"What are you doing, Mum?"

Carrie didn't respond. She was making a call, concentrating on the phone, looking down at it, as she held it in her lap. Then I realized something. She wasn't making a call.

She was sending a text—to Robert Reardon.

Dissertation is in the laptop.

"Are you calling the police?" whispered Annabel.

"There's no time for that now."

"What are you doing then?"

"Leaving a trail."

"Mum!"

Carrie looked behind her, still operating the phone, and I realized then what she must have been doing: deleting any evidence she'd sent the text to Reardon. It occurred to me again how fortunate Reardon had been: whether she'd meant to or not, Carrie had left no route back to him.

Out on the landing, a floorboard creaked. She threw the phone off to the side, and I heard it hit the wall with a dull thud. Then she leaned in, all the way up to the microphone, until only her chin and her teeth were visible on camera. She stayed like that for five or six seconds. The camera shifted to the right as her chin brushed against it. "The dissertation is in the laptop," she said, a low whisper now. "Please. Somebody help us."

Then it cut to black.

For a moment, I sat there stunned.

But then my brain started to fire again.

Dissertation is in the laptop.

I looked down at it, its red plastic case, its caterpillar camera. It was the perfect hiding place. Cornell had been through their machines, phones, through anything Paul, Carrie or Annabel would have used to communicate—but who would have thought to have checked Olivia's toys? The hiding place was too good, though, *too* effective: not only had Cornell failed to find what Carrie had hidden inside it, but so had the police.

Slowly, I started going through it, checking the other movies on there: they were all of Olivia playing around in her room. There was a ninety-second limit on files, and the maximum resolution was 352 x 288 pixels. If I somehow got them off the laptop and blew them up, they'd be unwatchable. But none of them was her dissertation. There were no USB slots on the machine, no e-mail function, no way of getting anything on to it.

So I played the movie again.

There was a sickening inevitability to it the second time, like watching a death in slow motion, and the moments with the girls—Olivia screaming for her dad; Annabel's tears shining in the half-light of the bedroom—were even more affecting somehow. Both of them were so young, even Annabel, and neither had any remote understanding of why this was happening. I watched those last ten seconds again: Carrie coming in close to the camera, whispering into the microphone, her voice cleaved through with so much fear.

Then the camera shifted to the right.

Dissertation is in the laptop.

In it.

I picked it up and turned it over. On the bottom were four screws, fused to the plastic. There was no way Carrie, or anyone else, would have been able to open it up with a screwdriver. But in the middle was a slot for four D-size batteries. I flipped it off.

Inside was a memory stick.

I felt a charge of electricity pass through me, a buzz in my veins. It was about four centimeters long and a quarter of a centimeter thick, just a plain red casing with a slimline USB connector. If it was any thicker, it would never have fitted in front of the batteries. But Carrie had thought it out. *Paul was right. He said we were in danger. I didn't believe him.* Except a part of her believed him enough, even as she'd told him he was overreacting, to copy her dissertation across to the memory stick and hide it inside her daughter's laptop. And now I had what Cornell was looking for. The thing that had cost countless people their lives.

Now I had the thing that could bring him down.

55

There was a campsite a mile south of Totnes with a small room next to its shop that had a computer and internet access. I'd been past countless times on the way along the A381, seen the *"Surf at the beach—then come back and surf the web!"* sign out front, and I knew this time of year it would be empty. They were a week short of closing for the winter so the whole place was deserted. I paid for a couple of hours, then pushed the door shut.

In the silence of the room, I started to realize how tired I was. It had been twenty-four hours since I'd last slept and I was beginning to feel exhaustion dragging at me, deep down in my bones. But I pushed it away and tried to press on, slotting the memory stick in and double-clicking on its icon. Carrie had called the stick "Diss/CL." I'd expected to find Word docs full of notes, interview transcripts, perhaps some scans of history books; instead, it contained a single folder called "Pics." There were fifteen photographs inside.

I opened them up.

As I saw the first, I felt the tiredness slip away immediately. Eric Schiltz, Carter Graham and Ray Muire were all in the center, arms around each other's shoulders, all smiling at the camera. They were young, in their midtwenties, all dressed in the same early 1970s fashion. It wasn't the original—the picture was of a frame with the original photograph inside. *This is it. This is the one Carrie must have taken in Schiltz's study.*

In its background a building was taking shape, at the midway point of being constructed, and as I double-clicked on it and zoomed in, I felt something else fall into place. *It's part of a series I've already seen.* This was Carter Graham's LA office, rising up out of the Californian dust. The other stages of its assembly were documented in the twelve photographs I'd seen behind the door in the library at Farnmoor. I wondered why he'd never made this one a part of it, then recalled something he'd said: *Eric e-mailed a picture—I don't know, maybe a year ago, maybe eighteen months . . . I remember it because it was taken around the same time as these ones— except his one had all three of us in.* Even if he'd wanted to include the picture of the three friends standing next to the office, he wouldn't have been able to. Because Katie Francis had been into Graham's e-mail and deleted it.

Just like she or Prouse had done with Ray Muire.

Just like Cornell himself had done with Eric Schiltz.

I remember Eric and I were down there a lot, watching it all take shape, he'd said to me. *We clubbed together and flew Ray out a couple of times too. They were good days.*

I looked around the edges of the shot.

The backdrop was dusty, without landmarks, but I'd read that Graham had chosen Marina Del Rey, a man-made harbor south of Venice Beach, for his LA office, and I knew from my time in the city that it had only opened in 1965. Five, six, seven years later—when the picture was taken—it would still have been a development, full of pockets of space. On either side, people and machines milled around—construction workers, the right angles of heavies and cranes, big piles of concrete slabs and huge metal girders.

My eye was drawn to the far left.

There were two men.

One, in a hard hat, was pointing to something off camera; it looked like he was talking to someone else, perhaps relaying instructions. He could have been the foreman.

Then there was the second man. He was in his early fifties, almost entirely obscured behind the foreman, only his top half visible. It looked like he'd been in the process of stepping back as the picture was taken. His shape had a gentle curve to it, as if he was leaning away. He was slim and well built, smartly dressed in a pale blue flannel suit, with a waistcoat buttoned up underneath. He had a tan, silver hair swept back from his face, and a thin scar—colored a deep pink—running down the left side of his forehead, from his hairline to the ridge of his eyebrow.

I clicked through to the next photograph.

It was a second camera-phone picture taken in Schiltz's study of the photo frame. Same resolution, same light. Except this time Carrie had cropped in on the man to the left-hand side. Graham, Schiltz and Muire were all to the right, Muire barely in it at all.

This had been the one she'd had in her notebook.

This was the epicenter.

This was Daniel Kalb.

56

I sat there for a long time, just staring at Kalb, wondering who he was and why he might have been there. Why LA in the early 1970s? Why at the building site? Why did this photograph even matter to Cornell, forty-one years on? And then another thought came to me: *because this could be the last remaining evidence Daniel Kalb ever existed.*

I moved on.

The third photograph wasn't of Kalb at all. It wasn't of anyone. It was a black-and-white shot of a forest, tall trees reaching up into the sky from a vast bed of pine needles. There was a gap among the trees, probably about the size of a small barn, where nothing grew, and on the right-hand side of the picture, a path—maybe twenty feet across—cut through the forest, arrow-straight, its eventual end obscured in a bright shaft of sunlight.

The next picture was shot across a bed of grass; a meadow of some kind. On the other side, I could make out the red roof of a bungalow, a chimney, a street light outside the front window. I clicked through. The fifth photograph was another shot of the same meadow, but this time it was higher up off the ground, and I could see more of the house: a little square of front garden, another building to its right with a pale blue roof, and—at the top of the shot—telephone wires, birds perched on them, one after the other. There was something else too: among the grass, half obscured but not covered completely, were railway tracks. There were two sets, one running parallel to the other. When I tabbed through to the next picture, I got an even clearer view: this one had been taken in winter, with snow on the ground, and the hard weather had compressed the grass, so that it seemed less overgrown and the tracks were more visible. It was shot from a different angle: down the lines, instead of across them. There was something else as well: to the left of the picture, a hundred feet from the bungalow, I could see a platform.

Suddenly, a memory flared.

Did I recognize this place?

All three photographs looked like they had been taken relatively recently—probably the last five to ten years. In the third, to confirm it, I could see a silver Skoda Octavia. In the bottom corner of each was a stamp: © *Museum of Modern History*. I didn't know the location of the museum, but it was clear Carrie had taken these from its website.

I clicked through to the seventh picture, hoping to find another shot of the platform, but instead it was of something different: a group of five men sitting at a table. They were all laughing at something. The photograph was black and white, and looked older than the last ones. Much older. The men's hairstyles were short and severe, hair melded to their scalps and glistening with oil, and their fashion spoke of the 1940s or early 1950s. Behind them on the wall was a map, too fuzzy and indistinct to see in detail, that looked like Europe, from the western curve of the Norwegian coast down to the Franco-Italian border and east into Russia, as far as the Ural Mountains. In the center, hands flat to the table, was Kalb.

He looked in his early twenties.

Over two decades before he had accidentally strayed into the shot behind Carter Graham, Ray Muire and Eric Schiltz, he looked different: younger obviously, with no hint of the gray that would mark him out later on, but he seemed more intense too. He wasn't laughing like the others. Instead, his mouth was turned up in a half-smile. Nothing more. He was the only one looking directly into the camera, his eyes so dark they were like ink spots on the film. There was no scar either. The one that had run from his hairline to his eyebrow wasn't a part of him then. It must have come later on.

I moved on to the next.

It was a posed shot of Kalb, probably taken in a studio, but there was no way to tell for sure. He was about the same age as in the previous picture—twenty, twenty-one—but the definition had become fuzzy over time, and the background was just a wall of black. He was looking at the camera, the view of his face the clearest it had been in any shot I'd seen of him so far: hair parted in the middle and slicked down either side, not even a hint of a smile. Still no scar. He was clean-cut and handsome, despite his sobriety.

Then I noticed something.

On the right were a couple of small white blobs, running diagonally against the indistinguishable darkness of his clothes. I selected the area and zoomed in. Two squares.

Silver collar pips.

He's wearing a uniform.

The memory flared again, but this time more clearly: something Robert Reardon had said to me before we'd got cut off. *Her dissertation didn't become about the years after Yalta, it became about the years before it. Carrie had done a hell of a lot of reading: Soviet history, Polish history, the major beats of the Second World War . . .* I zoomed back out and looked at Kalb again. And as I did, a dreadful realization broke like a wave.

I clicked through to the next picture.

"No," I said quietly. "No, not this."

Another old black-and-white photo, but this time not of Kalb. It was the place I'd first thought to be a meadow, except there was no grass on it now. Just the railway lines.

Because it wasn't a meadow.

It had never been a meadow.

A train was at the platform, and in the background I could see the silhouette of a guard tower rising up out of the earth, looking across the tracks. Out of the train spilled hundreds of men, women and children. Uniformed officers were waiting for them as they came off, a few gesturing away from the platform, to some unspecified point off camera. I thought of the picture I'd seen moments before of the pine forest; of the empty space where nothing grew. *That's where they were being sent.* It had never been a barn there.

It had been a gas chamber.

In the middle of the shot, watching everything, was Kalb.

She already knew about So . . . Reardon hadn't had a chance to finish what he was saying before we got cut off. But he didn't need to now. *She already knew about Sobibór.*

The Nazi extermination camp.

57

I put my phone back together, sliding the battery in and powering it on. I didn't care anymore. I just dialed the number and waited. Reardon answered after a couple of rings.

"Hello?"

"It's David Raker."

"Mr. Raker. We got cut off earlier."

"Daniel Kalb worked at Sobibór."

A pause. "Yes."

"Her dissertation was going to be about Polish history post-Yalta," I said to him, letting it unfold, needing to hear it myself to get it straight in my head. "But then she saw that picture of Kalb, in the States in the early seventies, and she changed her mind. Like you said to me, she'd already done a ton of reading on Polish history, so she knew about the camps—Auschwitz, Treblinka, Belzec, all of them—and she knew about the men who had run them. She knew that Kalb had gone into hiding at the end of the Second World War. That changed everything. She turned her MA on its head and she went after him."

"Yes," Reardon said. "Yes, that's right."

Reardon had probably seen the headlines early on—one of his students finding a man who'd helped send two hundred and fifty thousand Jews to the gas chamber. The hunt for the last Nazi.

Then something Healy had said to me surfaced in my mind: the old man on the beach, the man I now knew to be Kalb, had had scarring under his left arm. *It's a small surface area. Like, really small. Only about a centimeter squared. But whether he did it himself, or someone else did it to him, the knife went in deep. Like he was cutting something out.* I didn't need the full forensic report. I knew why the scarring was there.

"Was Kalb in the Waffen-SS?"

"Yes," Reardon said. "How did you know that?"

"Because he had the SS blood-group tattoo."

Some members of the Waffen-SS—especially early in the war—had their blood group tattooed on to a space near their left armpit. It allowed doctors to quickly identify their blood type in case a transfusion was needed and their dogtags were missing. But Kalb realized, after the war, that it was like having a target painted on him.

So he cut it out.

"How the hell did he end up at Sobibór?" I asked.

"We only have third-person accounts of a lot of this, but it looks like he started out as a guard at Dachau, then he was ferried out to the Eastern Front as part of Operation Barbarossa—the invasion of the Soviet Union. That's where he got his facial injury. After that, he was sent back to Germany to recover, then—for whatever reason—landed at the Hartheim Euthanasia Center in Austria, working for a man called Franz Stangl."

Stangl. In 1942, he became commandant of Sobibór. A year later, he was running Treblinka. While Kalb was in the States in the early 1970s, swanning about a free man, Stangl was being put on trial for the murder of nine hundred thousand people. He'd been on the run until his arrest in 1967. I'd done stories on Simon Wiesenthal, the Austrian Nazi hunter; even interviewed him. He'd been the one who'd found Stangl holed up in Brazil.

"So Stangl chose Kalb as his deputy at Sobibór?"

"Yes."

"How old was Kalb at the time?"

"On May 16, 1942, when Sobibór became fully operational, he would have been twenty-four. He was young, but very highly rated from what we can tell. Stangl chose him personally."

That made Kalb ninety-four at the time of his death. He'd had a long life he hadn't deserved, but he'd gone out in a box, being sailed out to sea somewhere by Prouse. Yet, still, one thing remained unanswered: what connected him to Cornell?

"And after Stangl left for Treblinka?" I asked.

"Kalb ran Sobibór—until the uprising."

The uprising.

I'd read about it, but I let him fill in the blanks.

"On October 14, 1943, about three hundred prisoners managed to escape the camp. Most of them died—they were either shot, or killed by mines—but about fifty to seventy made it to the end of the war alive. Himmler wasn't impressed, as you might imagine, so he ordered all remaining prisoners to be killed, and then tore it down. The whole camp."

"So what happened to Kalb?"

"Afterward, a lot of the officers there, and at Treblinka, were put on anti-partisan duty in Trieste in Italy. It was basically a death sentence.

Highly dangerous work. There had been an uprising at Treblinka too, a couple of months before Sobibór, so it was a kind of punishment for the soldiers; the price they paid for letting prisoners escape the camp. It was also an insurance policy for the Nazi hierarchy: if men like Kalb and Stangl didn't make it, they couldn't report back on what had gone on in any of the death camps."

"And after the war?"

"No one knows. After he was posted to Trieste, he fell off the map. But it's probably likely he used ratlines to get himself out of Europe and across to South America. That's what a lot of the Nazi fugitives did: Eichmann, Mengele, Stangl himself. He got out and he stayed hidden." Reardon paused, a quiet, contemplative silence on the line. Then, softly: "He might never have been seen again if it hadn't have been for Carrie."

I looked at the picture on the monitor, the Jewish families being led off the train and away from the platform, the children desperately clinging to their mothers, and anger flooded my system. Then my eyes shifted to Kalb, who was standing there watching them. He disappeared in 1943 until a single photograph, taken in 1971, put him in Los Angeles. Then suddenly—forty-one years later—his body washes up on a beach in south Devon.

How the hell does all this fit together?

"When Carrie said she thought she might have found evidence that Daniel Kalb had been alive and well in America in the early seventies, well, you can imagine my . . ."

I tuned out and tabbed on to the next picture.

It was a top-down artist's impression of Sobibór. Then on to the next, a photograph I barely had the stomach to look at: bodies piled up in a heap, discarded like their lives meant nothing. Men. Women. Kids. Then the next: Kalb in another official photograph, this time in the uniform of the Obersturmführer when he'd been running the camp in 1943. He had three silver pips and a silver stripe on his collar. The background was blank, just a wall of gray, but the scar was visible on his face now.

What connects you to Cornell?

I sat there, staring at him.

And then a thought came to me.

It wasn't just the scar Healy had mentioned to me in the conversation we'd had about the body on the beach. He'd also said that Kalb had had sand in his lungs.

Tiny traces of it. It's not local.

So where's it from?

Same story as the skin. Results not yet in.

I thought of Carter Graham's Los Angeles office, rising up out of the Californian earth. I knew Kalb was in the States at that moment, possibly living there. I could put him in Marina Del Rey, in an actual location. But what if he wasn't actually based in LA?

What if he'd just been up for the weekend?

I thought of something Healy had spotted that very first day: the body had been frozen. You'd freeze a body to preserve it. You'd freeze a body if you were taking it a distance.

I took him out in that box, Prouse had said to me, and suddenly it all started to fall into place. Kalb had been packed into a freezer box as a way to hide him. Cornell, for whatever reason, had decided to take Kalb's body on a five-thousand-mile trip.

That's why Kalb had traces of sand in his lungs.

Because he and Cornell had both lived in Las Vegas.

And Las Vegas was in the desert.

58

There were three pictures left. As I moved to the next, an old color shot of a woman in her forties sitting on a wall, my phone started buzzing. I'd forgotten to turn it off again after talking to Reardon. Now Rocastle was calling. He would have been at Farnmoor for a couple of hours by now. He'd have seen what carnage Cornell's men had caused. Now he was looking for someone to blame. I watched the phone moving toward me, its purr loud in the silence of the room. Outside, the sky was darkening above the treeline.

What I should have done was turn the phone off.

But he needed to hear some things.

So I pressed Answer.

"I don't know where you are or what you're doing, but I'm going to find you," he said, immediately on the attack. "Have you even got one *clue* what I just stumbled into?"

He meant Farnmoor. I played it safe: "Is Graham all right?"

"Is he *all right*?" A snort. "I think he's pretty far from all right."

"What happened?"

"Don't feed me that shit, Raker."

He'd already made up his mind that I had something to do with what happened at the house. That's how I'd thought it might go. "You're angry. But you need to listen to me."

"I'm going to work night and day picking away at this fantasy you're building," he continued, as if I hadn't even replied. "I'm going to prove you lied to me. I'm going to find out about all the horseshit you've probably fed me on the Ling family, on Prouse, on what happened here. I'm going to get the files for every case you've ever worked and I'm going to pick them apart one by one until I've got enough to send you down."

"Are you finished?"

"Am I *finished*?"

"This has nothing to do with me."

"*Really?*"

"The man who did this is the same man who killed Prouse. He's the same man who took the Lings. His name is Jeremy Cornell. He's protecting—"

"Doesn't it ever end?"

"—a guy called Daniel Kalb who—"

"Doesn't it ever end with you?" he said again. "Huh? It's always someone else's fault; it's always someone else who told the lie. This is *your* fault. You think we had any of this down here before you arrived? This is the fucking *countryside*, not some inner-city ghetto! Everyone here was doing fine until you rocked up. *Now* look at what we've got."

"He's white, early forties, has black hair and—"

"Where are you?"

"Rocastle—"

"Where *are* you?"

"You need to find this man."

"I don't *need* to do—"

"*Listen* to me. You find this man and it ends. Understand? I can *prove* this arsehole is behind everything, and I'm willing to meet you and give you everything I have. But I'm not turning up to any meeting where all you care about is putting me in handcuffs."

"You're unbelievable, you know that?"

"Is that a no?"

"What do you think?"

"Then this conversation is over."

I ended the call, shut my phone down, and removed the battery and the SIM. Then my eyes returned to the old color shot of the woman sitting on the wall. Next to her was a garden full of flowers, beautiful roses in full bloom. Beyond that was a rock face of some kind, rising up and beyond the top of the frame. Like the pictures of modern-day Sobibór, this one had a stamp in the corner too: © *Devonshire Historical Society*.

I tabbed through to the next one.

It was an old black-and-white picture, seemingly taken about the same time as the last photograph: a big group of people gathered together in a street. Men were in the back row, women in the middle, kids knelt at the front. They were all smiling for the camera.

Same stamp in the corner.

I counted up the faces: forty-one. Twelve men, thirteen women, sixteen kids. That made forty-two if you threw in the photographer. Around them were indistinct buildings, difficult to make out. I cast my eyes along them, trying to see if any of the men were Kalb. They weren't. There was a wide age range among the adults—some looked in their early twenties, some were probably touching ninety—and by their fashion, by their hairstyles, which was all I had to go on again, I'd have put the period as late 1960s.

Then I saw the same woman from the previous picture.

She was right on the end of the line of women, smiling broadly. I would have definitely put her in her late forties now. She was plump but dressed smartly, like she'd just come from work, in a cream blouse and a matching navy blue skirt and jacket. There was something sewn to both shoulders of her jacket, some kind of embroidered patch.

I clicked through to the last picture.

It was a shot of the same woman, again dressed in the same clothes, but this time with a dark coat over the top. She was back on the wall I'd seen her on in the first photo. The roses were gone, but, judging by the coat and the trace of breath in front of her face, this was because it was winter. Off to her right was the cliff face I'd seen in the first shot of her, rising up and out of the frame; off to her left was a building, a house, with a brass nameplate on it.

I've seen the house before.

Not here. Not in these pictures. But I knew it. Around her was a vast swathe of blue.

It wasn't sky.

It was sea.

I knew who this woman was now. I didn't know her name, but I knew what the embroidered patches on her shoulders were: she was a harbor mistress. She was sitting on the wall of her garden watching boats coming in, because that was her job. That was the role she served in the village she lived in. All the others, all the people in the previous shot, were her neighbors. The pub landlord. The minister at the chapel. The manager of the general store. And all forty-two of them were dead by October 1968.

This was Miln Cross before the storm.

I wondered for a moment about the photographer. Most likely, they were someone visiting for the day. A friend. A relative. But even while I saw the logic in that, I couldn't quite dispel another thought: that the Miln Cross pictures were in with the shots of Kalb, of Sobibór, of its awful, barbaric history, because Carrie had found something else out.

That Kalb had been here at some point.

That, before he went to the States, he might even have called it home.

And the reason he wasn't in the shot, the reason he insisted on taking the picture himself, was because he never wanted to be. The villagers might not have known who he was—but, if he got photographed, if he got caught on film, someone, somewhere might.

Now, almost forty-five years later, Miln Cross was just a tomb for the people who'd died in the storm.

And, I realized, for Paul and Carrie Ling.

As I looked at the house behind the harbor mistress, I remembered going inside it. I'd been all the way through to its extension and I'd stood and looked out to sea only feet from where Prouse must have buried them. *I was supposed to put the old man in Haven, the same place I'd put the husband and wife.* My eyes drifted over the woman's shoulders.

To the name on the brass plate.

Haven.

59

As I reached the other side of the water, a shaft of moonlight pierced the clouds, arcing down out of the sky and hitting the middle of the village. I climbed up, out of the boat, on to the rocks, and paused there; one hand clinging to the raft, the other gripping what was left of the bridge on this side. Ahead of me, the main street in Miln Cross was temporarily lit, its broken cobbles, its collapsed roofs, its lonely, decaying buildings. But on the edges of the moonlight, in the places it didn't reach, there was only a thick, impenetrable dark.

I looked at my watch.

Seven-thirty.

I secured the boat in the same place I'd done the first time, then hoisted myself up on to the main street. Below the plateau the village was on, waves sloshed and gurgled, massaged by the cold wind that swept in across the bay. I was chilled already, my hands frozen from the rowing, my clothes dotted with seawater, but I pushed it from my mind.

All I was focused on was the house.

Haven.

I'd brought a rucksack with me, so I unzipped it, got out a flashlight and flicked it on. The beam arrowed ahead of me, between the buildings and into the curve of the street. Beyond the edges of the moonlight, beyond the bend, the house was hidden from view.

As I started walking, I felt cobbles move under my feet, shifting and sliding like I was on a bed of tennis balls. It didn't help that it was slick with rainwater. Off to my left, I passed the first of the houses, segregated slightly from the rest. I directed the light inside. Not all the homes had been the same design: this one had two floors, its second now fallen away, along with the roof. The only thing left was a staircase, stopping midway, as if waiting to be completed. As the wind rose and fell, drawn through the open windows, the holes in its walls, I heard a soft whine, like an echo from a different time.

Then it started to rain again.

It was soft at first, a gentle drumbeat against what was left of the houses, but as the clouds were drawn together, and the moonlight began to die away, it got harder.

All I had now was the flashlight.

Caught in the beam, rain became needles dropping out of the sky. I directed the flashlight right, to where the houses on that side, built on the edge of the sea, began to emerge from the dark. It was hard to see them as homes now, as places people might once have chosen to live in. Illuminated by the flashlight, they were gnarled and rotten, decomposing, the village a graveyard of bodies, and of memories, and of secrets. As the road dropped away, feeding into the curve, the buildings seemed to close in, their size and shape disguised by the oil-black of the night, shadows encasing them so that all I could see were the holes in their front: doors and windows open, apertures drawing you in. But nothing beyond that.

Nothing but darkness.

Midway down the street, the toe of my boot hit a dislodged cobble and I stumbled forward, dropping the flashlight and reaching out to the nearest wall. With a rhythmic clatter, the flashlight continued rolling away, hitting a ridge where a pavement had once stood, before stopping dead. When I looked back, trying to find the loose cobble, I couldn't see it; not because of how black it was, but because there wasn't a cobble. I'd tripped myself.

I was burned out.

As I stood there, hand against the wall, I could suddenly feel it everywhere, in my muscles, in my bones, thumping behind my eyes. Even adrenaline couldn't carry you after forty hours. I reclaimed the flashlight from the ground and took a moment.

I shouldn't have come here.

I should have waited until morning.

I should have slept.

When I took my hand away from the building, I felt a residue cling to my fingers; gluey, like an adhesive. It was sea salt, years of it having blasted the remains of the buildings. But in my exhaustion, among the ghosts of this place, it felt like something worse: an unpleasant, rotting corruption. A reflection of the man who might once have lived here.

Dum. Dum.

A noise.

A memory flickered in my head of standing in the harbor mistress's house and hearing the same sound the last time I was here. I lifted the light away from the cobbles, up to my eyeline, trying to see what lay beyond the curve. But it was like shining it into a wall. At a certain point, about thirty feet on, nothing came back. Edging further, I kept to the left, passing what remained of the chapel, its walls destroyed by the landslide, a wave of hardened mud forming a new floor—about six feet off the ground—inside the church. More houses. The shop and pub on the opposite side.

And then I was around the bend.

Dum. Dum.

For a moment, the wind dropped away and all that was left was the rain, tapping against the bricks and mortar, its noise like a lament from the heavens. Haven was about two hundred feet further along, on the right, the harbor obscured behind that. I swung the flashlight from side to side, trying to see what was down there. Everything suddenly seemed still: no wind, no moan as it moved through the village seeking out its injuries, its blemishes, the holes ripped from it by the storm. I took another step, an unthinking hesitation in my stride, one I didn't recognize until it arrived. Then I understood: something wasn't right.

I dropped the flashlight down to my side.

And that was when I saw him.

He came up the steps from a boat moored, out of sight, at the harbor. There was a thin flashlight clenched between his teeth, and he was wearing an army-green apron.

In his arms was the body of a woman.

Goosebumps scattered across my skin as her face, eyes still open, caught the dull glow from the light. The rest of her seemed to be wrapped in some kind of tarpaulin. The man paused briefly, a momentary glitch in his stride, as if sensing he was being watched.

I flicked the flashlight off.

And Cornell looked up the street toward me.

60

He paused there. Even submerged in the dark, in the doorway of an empty, lightless house, there was a moment where it seemed like he was looking right at me. He had a calm, measured expression on his face, despite holding a body, despite the blood down his apron, inky-black in the soft light of his flashlight. He tilted his head slightly to one side, a bird-like movement that I recalled with such clarity it seemed impossible that it was five years since I'd seen him in the flesh; then he rocked forward, readjusting the body in his arms. As he moved, the shadows reset themselves, filling his eye sockets until they were just black discs, then carving down across his tanned, hairless face in short, sharp angles. Even so, something about him registered with me; a recollection, a feeling I'd seen him before somewhere. Not just in Vegas half a decade ago.

Somewhere else.

I retreated further until my back was pressed against the wall of a house and damp was soaking through my jacket, on to my shirt. It was freezing cold. The chill air. The wind. The rain. Ahead of me, Cornell tilted his head the other way, as if trying to force himself to see further, and then he turned—flashlight still in his mouth—and headed inside.

Moving quickly, I shrugged off the rucksack and propped it against the house. I'd brought the flashlight, a penknife, my phone, some rope and a foot pump for the dinghy. I also had a wetsuit. I laid the flashlight down next to me, removed the penknife and left the rest where it was. There was no signal here, so the phone was worthless; I'd brought it for after, once I got back up to the coastal road. The rope was for the bodies—or what was left of them. Prouse had talked about them being in Haven, but also in the water. He'd been confused, but I hadn't taken any chances. That was what the wetsuit was for.

But it was a plan conceived before Cornell.

Before I knew he was here.

I flicked the blade out of the penknife. It was three inches long, about half an inch wide. It would put a delay in his step, but nothing more. There was no light around me, none close to Haven either. I looked up, to the cliff edge three hundred feet above. Dark cloud was stitched together like a quilt. I'd have to approach him slowly, and I'd have to approach blind. Using the flashlight would give him my position.

Sliding the penknife into my back pocket with my left hand, I used my right to guide me down the road, toward the harbor. I didn't move as fast as I could have done, wary of hitting an uneven spread of cobbles, of making a noise, but as I worked my fingers along the walls of the buildings, the stone seemed to fall away, like the structures were just ash.

Fifty feet from the front of the house, I stopped.

Dum. Dum.

The same noise again, even clearer.

The rain was heavier now, running under my boots in streams, between cobbles, into the pockmarks pounded out of the earth by the waves. I could hear it slopping past, but I couldn't see it. I couldn't see anything. All I had was what I could hear and what I could feel. When the wind came, it was biting, and an uncontrolled shiver passed through me. I was soaked to the bone, shirt and jacket like a second skin. I edged forward, careful where I was putting my feet, the houses on my right disappearing from my grasp, rising up on to a higher portion of the plateau. But the road down kinked to the left. I couldn't use the buildings for support anymore, so I'd have to go it alone. Unsupported. Unguided. As I got closer to the house, the wind came again, even colder than before, a gentle, childlike murmur following in its wake.

Movement.

A brief glimmer of a flashlight inside the house.

If he was still moving around in there, he hadn't seen me. I moved faster down the road, letting the soles of my boots skim across the cobbles, trying to ensure I had time to stop myself when I hit uneven patches. As I approached, the light came again and again, drifting left to right inside what had once been the living room. When I was twenty feet away, I could see the plateau drop off, and I remembered that Haven was built on a bed of rock about six feet lower than the rest of the village. As the light spilled out again, I recalled more of the house: a garden running from the front, all the way around the side to the back, penned in by a crumbling stone wall; the collapsed extension on the back, falling away to the sea; the direction of the house, different from the others, its windows facing off to where the trawlers must once have docked. Now there was only Cornell's boat, or the boat Cornell had borrowed: a mini trawler, thirty feet long, with a ten-foot deckhouse and a high-powered lamp bolted to the front of the cockpit.

Inside, the light came again: left to right, left to right. *Is he digging in there?* Moving even closer to the wall, I tried to see in through one of the empty spaces that had once been a window—but all I could see was the ridge that had once been the second floor, and huge wall punctures, some going all the way through, some only as far as rotting cavity walls.

Dum. Dum.

It was coming from somewhere at the side of the house.

Perching myself on the wall, I swung my legs over and dropped on to the lawn. It squelched beneath my feet, the soles of my shoes sinking into the mud. The other houses, six feet above, were spared this: half an inch of water that never left, soaking into the house and the garden, and then coming again, daily, as waves broke—over and over—against the rubble of the house. I stood, feet sinking further, and gripped the penknife.

He was still shifting around in there. Still working on something.

Light swinging, left to right, left to right.

At the edge of the door, I paused, my back to the wall of the house. I could smell the damp now, rolling out of the house like an ocean swell. Then, slowly, I leaned in.

Looked around the door frame and into the house.

The inside was just as I remembered: debris—dust, glass, plaster, brick—scattered across the floor; the interior partitions that had once divided the living room, kitchen and back bedroom all gone; hard mud from the landslide matted against the walls, an old fire grille half-submerged in it, like a statue rising from its plinth; the skeletons of the counter and the appliances, rusted through, in the kitchen; then the door through to the extension.

Hanging from the rafters, under a roof that was mostly a memory, was a length of rope. It hadn't been there last time, which meant Cornell had added it tonight. At the end of the rope was the flashlight he'd had in his mouth, secured with a knot. He'd set it rocking gently, its soft glow rhythmically painting the walls, so it would look like movement.

It was a trap.

61

A second later, there was the soft suck of footsteps across the garden—and then it felt like he broke my jaw. The punch was so hard, I left the ground, clipping the side of the house and landing on the wet grass like I'd fallen from the sky. All my breath, every last drop of air, seemed to burst out of me and, after that, there was only pain: it tremored across my face, taking my breath away for a second time. As my senses restarted, I could smell rust on myself and realized he was using an old anchor chain, had it wrapped around his fist to protect his hand, to increase the damage, to ensure I couldn't respond.

The flashlight cast light out of the house like a strobe, passing through its spaces in a series of blinks. He came at me: there, gone, there, gone, from light to dark on repeat. I retreated, attempting to get some distance between us, brain firing, trying to figure out how to fight back—but then my back hit the edge of the property. I turned and looked up. A six-foot vertical rock face rose out of the drowned garden to street level.

Shit.

His fist clamped on to my shoulder, trying to suppress me, to keep me in place. The light from the house blinked in our direction again, and it momentarily freeze-framed him: fist above his head—chains wound tightly, all the way up to his elbow—eyes dark and controlled, expression blank, unreadable. Then the punch came. I shifted to the side and felt metal brush the side of my face, and as his momentum carried him through, I smashed the meat of my boot into his knee. A soft crack. He made a short, sharp sound—an animalistic growl—and staggered back across the lawn, reaching down for it.

Scrambling to my feet, I charged him.

I hit him every bit as hard as he'd hit me, my shoulder smashing into his chest, my weight carrying us through the front door of the house and inside. His head clipped the flashlight on the rope and the lighting changed instantly: fast flashes, our shadows flickering on what remained of the walls. We landed on the floorboards, dust spitting up, water fanning out around us. As he tried to move, tried to come at me again, he cried out, the second time even more feral than the first, and I saw his lower leg was limp.

I'd broken his knee.

Getting to my feet, I loosened the knot on the rope, removed the flashlight, and pulled the line down from the rafters. He'd shifted across the floor on his backside, soundlessly, his pain internalized. But then, as I moved over to him, something in his face stopped me. There was a weird kind of calm to him suddenly, a light being switched off, even though his leg was damaged. A tilt of his head. Then that half-smile broke across his face again.

"What are you smiling at?"

He didn't say anything, just stared at me.

I walked around him, keeping my distance until his back was to me, then quickly grabbed him under the arms. He didn't react. Didn't struggle. Didn't put up a fight at all. Alarm fluttered in my chest. I looked over his shoulder, trying to see if he had anything hidden, anything that would still give him an edge. There was nothing in the pockets of his jeans, nothing in the front of the apron. I cast my eyes out to the rest of the room, into its dark corners, then back over my shoulders to the extension. Cornell had just given up.

Why?

What had I missed?

I began hauling him across the room, through the stagnant water, to where one of the counters still stood, its exterior eaten away by mold. Inside it, there were two lengths of rusting iron, originally there to support the counter top. I propped him against it.

When I went back for the rope, he said something.

"What did you say?"

His head was forward, against his chest. No response.

"What did you say?"

My eyes lingered on him, then I grabbed the rope and began looping it around him, securing him to the iron support and pinning his arms to his side. His head was still against his chest and he was almost silent now, like he'd gone into some kind of trance. I felt a brief moment of vulnerability, but pushed it away, concentrating on the binds. By the time I was done, there was nowhere for him to go. No way for him to escape.

And yet, somehow, I still didn't feel safe.

It was hard to tell whether he was conscious or not. I dropped to my haunches about five feet from him and leaned to the right, trying to get a clear view of his face.

His eyes were closed.

"Cornell?"

He didn't respond. Didn't even move.

Dum. Dum.

I grabbed the flashlight off the floor and shone it beyond him, to the open doorway into the extension. Flicking a look at him, silent and still, I got to my feet and inched past. As I walked, debris scattered against the toes of my boots, and water moved in a V-shaped wake, out under the counters, into the rotten skirting boards.

Dum. Dum.

When I got to the door, I directed the flashlight inside. It was exactly as I remembered it: a space—probably once a storage room—that finished about thirty feet from where I was standing, the rest of it torn away by the power of the storm. As I inched forward, waves lashed against the rocks five or six feet below and water began to slosh in. It ran past me, through my legs, and washed out into the kitchen.

Dum. Dum.

That same ceaseless pulse.

I shifted away from the edge, felt the extension sway with my weight, and slowly returned to the house. As I stepped back into the kitchen, I heard a gentle sound, like a tap running, and saw a puddle of water slowly pouring out into the room from under a skirting board. The wall panel above it had two holes at the top and bottom, and had started to bend and soften over time. After five seconds the water flow started slowing, then it stopped altogether.

I looked back at Cornell.

Head still bowed. Silent. Still.

Then I remembered the body he'd been carrying.

Heading out, I moved around to the side of the house, a biting wind rolling off the water. My wet clothes felt like sheets of ice, and my jaw was starting to ache even when I breathed. I rolled it a couple of times. It wasn't broken, but it was painful and I could feel blood and fragments of teeth rinsing around. I spat them out on to the lawn—barely even that, just a square of standing water—and cut through the darkness with the flashlight.

She was dumped, face down, against the house.

About eight feet beyond her, the garden dropped away to the sea, the boundary wall—a crumbling memory—going with it. Every time the waves boomed on to the rocks, fresh seawater fed across the lawn, seeking out the holes in the house. That explained the water coming in under the skirting board: next to where the body had been left there was a fist-sized hole, water running into it like it was being drawn into a drain.

Dum. Dum.

I moved toward the woman.

He'd left her there to come and take care of me, and I felt a swell of anger at the way she'd been cast aside. There was no life in her, her suffering over, but what remained had been afforded no respect; she'd been dumped against the house like a bag of rubbish. The closer I got to her, the more water fanned out from my feet and went back through to the house. The hole next to her made a gurgling sound, like somebody being choked.

Dum. Dum.

I stood over her, pausing for a moment. This was a crime scene. If I moved her, if I rolled her back toward me, I was interfering with it. But then I realized it was too late for that: she'd been moved from wherever she'd originally been kept. Cornell had carried her up from the boat and then discarded her when he'd seen me. So I bent down, touched her arm—as rigid as concrete now—and turned her over.

It was Katie Francis.

"You shouldn't have come here," a voice said behind me.

I turned.

Colin Rocastle was pointing a gun at my face.

62

Rocastle led me back toward the house, his gun pressed against the back of my head. "You're working for *Cornell*?" I said to him, but he didn't reply. We passed the boat again, off to my left. The narrow deckhouse door had blown open, stairs leading down into a half-lit interior, and I could see at least one other body, wrapped in the same tarpaulin, a single, blood-flecked arm escaping the covers. If they'd brought Francis here, they'd brought the security guard as well—and they'd brought Carter Graham.

As I reentered the house, Cornell looked up from the floor, that same expression on his face. He'd given in because he'd known he wasn't alone. Rocastle forced me to my knees behind Cornell, one hand on my shoulder, one pushing the gun in harder against the dome of my skull. "Untie him," he said.

I started loosening the knot.

Outside, the sea was relentless: it boomed against the rocks, emerged from the cracks and fissures of the house, before drawing all the way back out again. And then it would come again, metronomic, a dam breaking and draining, over and over.

I kept my head still and scanned the room, trying to figure out where I went next. I had a gun to my head and was cut off from the mainland. I didn't have any options. If I made a break for it, if I even got as far as doing that, I would hit a dead end, whichever direction I headed. I couldn't take Cornell's boat because I didn't have the key. I couldn't go back for the dinghy because, as soon as I got out into the water, they'd pick me off.

"Faster," Rocastle said, jabbing me with the gun.

Half an inch of water, maybe more, was remaining inside the house at all times now. It was freezing. Before long, I couldn't feel my skin anymore, only the pressure of my kneecap against the floor, spongy and rotten and bending to my weight. Next to me were the skirting board and the wall panel. As I pulled the knot away, finally freeing Cornell, water began running past me, out from under the boards, escaping into the room.

Dum. Dum.

Rocastle grabbed me by the collar and hauled me to my feet, then shoved me out into the center of the house. He went to help Cornell, help unravel the rest of the rope, but Cornell pushed him away, eyes fixed on me. He used one of the counters to pull himself up and then ran a hand through his hair, straightening it. In that moment, I saw everything he was: all the destruction and violence, all the lives he'd ruined.

"Well, well, well," he said, an empty smile opening out across his face. "This is an unexpected surprise." He looked at Rocastle, a flash of anger in his face. "Isn't it, *Detective* Rocastle?" I looked between them, unsure of what was going on. Then his anger instantly vanished, and all that was left behind was that smile.

But the smile was just a lie, a piece of tracing paper I could see right through; and as he stood there, he tilted his head and looked at me, eyes darting from one point of my body to the next, like a butcher sizing up a carcass. He wriggled his fingers, stretching the muscles, and then looked around the room. He was searching for the chains he'd had on his wrists. When I'd tied him up, I'd tossed them across the room, toward the extension.

I turned to Rocastle. "Why?"

A minor shrug.

"Was the money worth it?"

This time he gave me nothing.

"All the money in the world can't be worth this."

Behind him, Cornell put a finger to his lips. "Ssshhhhh."

Water began running into the house, under his feet, between his legs, out to where Rocastle was standing. Cornell didn't notice, his eyes on me. Rocastle glanced down at the water, watching it approach him, then looked up at me again. His face was an utter blank. No emotion, just a glazed-over stare. The gun was gripped in his hand at his side.

Dum. Dum.

The noise came every time water entered the house.

Dum. Dum.

And every time it drained back out again.

Cornell moved away from the edge of the counter, limping. He took a couple of steps, then stopped. "What, I wonder, was the point of all this?" he said. I remembered his voice now: low, sharp, an indistinct accent that was difficult to place. As I watched him take another step toward me, I felt the same sense of recognition I'd had earlier; as if I'd seen him before, somewhere else.

Not just Vegas.

He tilted his head as he looked at me. "Was the family worth it?"

I didn't answer.

"Were they worth dying for?"

"I haven't found them yet, so I couldn't say for sure."

Cornell picked up on something in my voice; a tiny tonal shift, a moment when my reply had betrayed everything I was feeling. "Why do they even matter?" he asked.

"Everyone matters."

The corners of his mouth turned up again. "I've known men like you before." He took another step toward me. "Do you think you've got some *attachment* to the family?"

I didn't respond.

"You think you understand them?"

I flicked a look at Rocastle. He just stared at me.

Cornell's lips peeled back into another smile. "That's it, isn't it? They're the replacement for . . ." He paused, ring finger rubbing against his thumb as he tried to recall her name. "*Derryn*. Are they your pretend family now she's rotting in the earth?"

I gave him nothing.

He nodded, then ran a hand through his hair, ensuring his parting was as straight as possible. "The Lings are all just bones now too—you *do* know that, right?"

"They deserve a proper burial."

"We *gave* them a burial."

"I doubt that."

"Sure we did," he said, limping toward me, stopping six inches from my face. Rocastle moved around to my left, lifted the gun and placed it against my temple. My heart shifted in my chest. "Where's the photograph?" Cornell said.

"What photograph?"

"Where's the photograph?" Cornell said again, as if he hadn't heard me.

"I don't know what photograph you mean."

I could smell him now: hair oil and lotion, and the faint trace of cigarette smoke. When he got no response from me, he leaned forward, his mouth stopping an inch from my ear. "You know," he said, hot breath against my face, "it doesn't really matter. If you tell me where it is, that's great—that saves me a problem. If you don't, I'll just go on looking for that picture after you're dead. And I'll find it. Because that's what I do."

"Why do you even care about it?"

He blinked; said nothing.

"Kalb's already dead. Everyone who might have even been vaguely connected to him is dead. What can the photograph *possibly* have in it that matters anymore?"

He seemed faintly amused, as if he were listening to the reasoning of a child, then his eyes stopped at my stomach. "Tell me, how did it feel when you were dying?"

I ignored him and glanced at Rocastle. "What about you?" Something flickered in his face. "Do you even know *why* you're killing?"

"I've always wondered what it must be like," Cornell said.

I turned back to face him.

"What it must be like when the light goes out."

"Maybe one day you'll find out."

"Maybe," he said. "But not today." There was a sudden kind of stillness to him. In any other man it would have looked like mourning for all the misery he'd wrought. But not this man. "You of all people should understand what we're doing."

I smirked. "Is that a *joke*?"

An expression formed, as if he was genuinely surprised. "Why else have you been running around for all these years, being shot at, being stabbed, trying to rescue hopeless cases like your idiot friend Healy?" I glanced at Rocastle: because of him Cornell knew everything about me. Every detail. "Why? Because, like me, you have a cause."

"Daniel Kalb isn't a cause."

"You don't know anything about him."

"Graham, Schiltz and Muire knew him—and look where it got them."

"They only knew a part of him; a version of his history. But, ultimately, that was enough." He shrugged. "The pictures they had, what they knew about him, what Ray saw at Farnmoor, we couldn't let that go. Ray had started to suspect Katie might be involved in something too, which is why he went to the police instead of her. He liked a drink or three, but he was still sharp enough. We had to do some repair work on that."

I frowned. But then it slipped into place, and I turned to Rocastle. "You doctored the interviews you did with Muire."

"He made some adjustments," Cornell said.

"You mean Muire's suspicions about Katie Francis?"

Cornell drew in a long, deep breath, hands back at his sides. "That, and Muire telling the world how *clearly* he saw your precious Paul and Carrie."

Another memory: standing over Prouse at the Ley and then, before that, speaking to Martha Muire, and her telling me about the missing photograph. *Did you ever worry the combination of the drink and his eyesight might be a problem?* I'd asked.

We're old, Mr. Raker, but not that old.

She'd meant his eyesight. News that he was half blind had come as a surprise to her. And then, a day later, Prouse was saying the same thing to me: *He could see just fine.*

I looked at Rocastle. "Muire's diagnosis was a sham." Instantly, I could see in his face that I was right. "You never went to see a doctor. You faked the diagnosis. That's why both his interviews go totally off the rails—because you altered them."

Cornell broke out into a smile. "Bravo."

I ignored him, fixing my gaze on Rocastle, replaying what Cornell had said: *Muire only knew a version of Kalb's history.* And if Muire didn't know the full story, neither did Schiltz or Graham. Neither did Rocastle. "Do you even know who Kalb is?"

A movement in his eyes.

"This is a man who killed two hundred and fifty—"

Cornell punched me in the throat.

It was so sudden, so fierce, it felt like my body had shut down. I staggered back, grasping at my windpipe, trying to force air up and out of my body. My vision blurred. And then I hit a wall, felt it bend against my weight, dust showering me from above, water running out from somewhere unseen—against my legs, my ankles, my feet.

Cornell took a couple of steps in my direction, leg dragging through the water like an anchor. Rocastle remained behind him, almost cast into darkness. My throat was on fire, acid burning at the top of my chest, and I could feel swells of nausea. I closed my eyes for a second, trying to clear my sight. When I opened them again, Cornell was closer: he'd moved again, this time in silence. The only thing that spoke of his approach was the wake fanning out from his shoes. "Where's the photo-graph?" he said.

This time it was my turn to smile.

I saw the anger in his eyes. "Where's the photograph?"

"Gone," I replied, my voice hoarse.

"Gone where?"

"Tell me where the Lings are buried."

He grabbed me by the throat again, teeth gritted, hands like the jaws of a shark. I could feel myself blacking out. *"Tell me where the fucking photo-graph is!"*

His face blinked in and out.

And then, finally, everything went dark.

When I woke again, Cornell was looking down at me. Rocastle was next to him, gun in the belt of his trousers. As I tried to tune back in, Rocastle reached down and hauled me up. I rocked back against the wall, using its sodden bones for support.

"You know," Cornell said, calmer now, "this is exactly how that little bitch tried to play me. *Carrie.* When she told me there was another copy of the photograph floating around, she tried to use it as a bargaining chip. 'I'll tell you where the photograph is, if you let me and my family go.'" He lowered his voice. "She was pretty strong. Pretty resistant. But eventually she gave in: it was in the laptop. So I thanked her, and then I had Prouse walk them both to the barn."

But she didn't tell him which laptop.

Even at the end. Even as she suffered unspeakable torment.

"So why are you still looking for it?"

No response. No emotion. "When you've got as much money as me, you can solve all sorts of problems. So I put those two girls on a jet to the States, while Mum and Dad were already feeding worms." He stopped, eyeing me. He was trying to use the girls to get a reaction out of me. "They landed at Henderson Airport, got waved through by a man I'd handed a suitcase full of money to, and their trail—*boom*—just disap-peared. You can take your time when they're off the grid, *really* get the answers you need."

"Why take them to the States?"

Cornell just shrugged. "All you need to know is after they gave me what I wanted, I drove them up into the hills, cut them both into pieces and buried them in the desert."

A tremor passed through me. "You fucking prick."

"Oooooh," he mocked. "Are you angry?"

He was three feet from me.

"Are you upset that your new family got—"

I grabbed him by the throat, clamping my hand on to his windpipe, squeezing so hard I felt cartilage pop against my fingers. An anger burned in me I'd never felt before. As he started to choke, I shoved him away. He stumbled, his leg locking up, and then I went at him again, hitting him harder than I'd ever hit anything in my life. It felt like I broke every bone in my hand—but I didn't care, didn't even react to it. This time it sent him crashing back into the counter, the whole thing reverberating, part of it coming loose and falling to the floor, into the water. He tried to sidestep away from me, his back to the wall panel, but I grabbed his hair—a handful of it, as much as I could get—and drove him head first into it. He made a soft grunt as the wall panel erupted into a puff of plaster, a shiver passing through the house.

And then it felt like my head exploded.

I lurched sideways, slumping against the ground. Out of the corner of my eye, through the fuzzy haze of semiconsciousness, I realized Rocastle had pistol-whipped me. He came around, placed a foot either side of me and pointed the gun at my head. Next to him, Cornell pulled himself free of the wall, water running out past him, over his legs. He wiped his wrist across his face and then looked at me. He was burning with rage. Blood ran from his nose, from the corners of his mouth, my hand clearly printed on his throat. He looked across at Rocastle. "Were you enjoying the show, you fucking maggot?"

"I took care of him."

"After he put me through the fucking wall!"

Cornell got to his feet, dusted himself down.

And then I saw them.

In the cavity wall behind the panel.

Two bodies, one on top of the other.

They were wrapped in black plastic bin liners, secured with brown packing tape. I couldn't see their faces, couldn't see any flesh, any indication of who was who. But it had to be them. And as water poured into the house again—from across the garden, through the spaces in the exterior, and then in through the cavity wall—the bodies moved on the waves, gently knocking against the interior wall.

Dum. Dum.

"Time for you to join them," Cornell said.

Rocastle reached further down, placing the tip of the barrel against my forehead. And in that moment, my thoughts didn't echo back to the time I'd been left to die by a killer just like Cornell; they returned to something Healy had said to me as he'd left my parents' house for the final time.

See you on the other side.

My muscles tensed. My heart accelerated.

But then, as Cornell took another step closer, eyes widening at the thought of my death, Rocastle straightened, swiveled to face him—and shot him through the head.

63

Ten seconds later, the house was silent. Cornell was on the floor, one leg buckled under him, water lapping at his body. Rocastle had collapsed against the edge of the wall panel, the bodies barely feet from his head, wind whistling quietly through the splintered building. His knees were up at his chest, his arms resting on them. He still held the gun.

"Rocastle?"

Nothing.

I clambered to my feet, heading across the room to the wall—but then his eyes pinged to me and he raised the gun up off his knee. "Where the hell are you going?"

I nodded to the bodies. "Where do you think?"

He shook his head. "Sit down."

"We need to—"

"We don't need to do *anything*," he said. He gestured to Cornell, blood floating off across the surface of the water. "That wasn't for you. It was for me. I needed to be free of him." Then his eyes darkened. "I haven't decided what to do with you yet."

"But Paul and Carrie—"

"*Sit* down."

I paused there—him sitting, me standing—letting him know that it was the wrong decision. Then I did as he asked. He followed my every movement before slowly drifting back out of the conversation, eyes becoming distant, body sinking in on itself.

"Is that Paul and Carrie in there?"

He nodded.

I took a long breath, struggling to find the words. Prouse had told me they were dead, but a part of me had hoped it was another lie. "And the bodies in the boat?"

He shrugged. "The people at Farnmoor. I don't even care anymore. In the end all the killing just washes over you." A pause. I decided not to press him again—not yet. He had a look I'd seen so many times in the faces of reluctant killers: a need to confess, even as every atom told him to keep quiet. In the brief silence, wind pierced the wall of the house and cast itself out across the water, ripples merging and forming. Then, just as I sensed it would, the confession came: "It was never supposed to be like this. I never wanted it." His voice was quiet, as if he was repeating something, a speech he'd been over in his head countless times. "I wanted a retirement fund. A good education for my kids. A house they could grow up in, open space and fresh air. I didn't want them to have what I had: parents who barely remembered we were even there, a childhood where I was making my sister dinner when I was ten years old. I wanted a *life* for my kids. But how could I ever give them that when in every promotion I went for, every interview I did, I got sandbagged by cops who hated me for who I was?"

He meant a cop who investigated other cops.

A rubber heeler.

"So you hooked up with Cornell."

"I met him at a fund-raiser." He paused. "I never liked him, but we eventually came to an arrangement. He needed someone on the inside, making sure certain things were kept off the books. I wanted the insane amount of money he was offering me to do it." His eyes drifted off into space again. "It was fine to begin with. But then it all started to unravel when Carrie saw that photograph. I never asked questions. I never even knew his real name was Kalb. They always referred to him as Thom. They said he was Swedish."

"He wasn't Swedish."

"Where was he from?"

"Germany. He ran a concentration camp."

This time he nodded, but the information didn't even seem to register. "I didn't like the direction things started going. Cornell made me get everything I could find on that family, on anyone who knew them, and when I started to have doubts about it, when I said I was going to stop taking his money and back away, he had Prouse start following me around." He glanced at me. "At first, I thought, 'He's just a fisherman.' But then I started to realize he wasn't *just* a fisherman. I'd get home and he'd be waiting in a car outside my house. I'd take my children to the park and I'd look up and see him watching. I confronted him one time, and he came right out with it: 'Do what Cornell asks, or we kill your kids.' I started to realize there was no way out when I got to school one day to pick my son up, and that ratty fuck was standing there, keeping my boy entertained."

Seawater washed into the room, out from behind him, across to where I was. My eyes moved to the hole in the wall panel; to the bodies in it. To Paul and Carrie Ling.

"So you just went along with it?"

For a moment, anger flared in his eyes. "No, I didn't just *go along* with it." But then he paused, and the anger ebbed away like the water in the room, and he returned to the soft, controlled tone I'd begun to know him for. "That call to Paul Ling on January 3, I made that. I didn't know he'd just been to see Lee Wilkins. I didn't know anything *about* Wilkins. But I knew Cornell had said he planned to take the family on the seventh."

So it had been Rocastle that had made the spoof call.

"What did you say to Paul?"

"I'd considered taking them myself, getting them out of there, putting them somewhere safe. So I called him up and told him he was in trouble but everything was going to be fine. I told him I was a friend and he needed to sit tight. Cornell never found out about the call, but it was like he could see right into my head: the next day was when I turned up at my boy's school and saw Prouse there with him . . . so I killed the plan."

It made sense now.

On January 3, Paul received Rocastle's call from an untraceable number; the next day he made a short, aborted call to a travel agency. My assumption had been that he was wrestling with uncertainty. I remembered the video on Olivia's laptop, too: *Paul was right. He said we were in danger. He said it had something to do with the notebook. But I didn't believe him.* Paul might not have mentioned he'd been to see Lee, but he had discussed the threat with Carrie, the content of the phone call, and she'd played it down. From what Emily had told me, from what I'd read, from what I'd seen of her myself, Carrie was composed and pragmatic, even in the face of something frightening. But Paul hadn't been paranoid. He wasn't overreacting. She should have listened to him.

"Were you the one who tipped police off about Miln Cross?"

He looked up from the floor. Nodded once. "No one took it seriously. Look at this place. It's a fucking memory. I phoned in the tip and then went into the office the next day, and McInnes and the rest of the boys were pissing themselves laughing about it. I had to sit there and laugh with them, knowing it was legit." He looked at the gun, tilting it slightly. "They sent a boat around with two uniforms in it—and that was the end of it."

"They didn't find anything?"

"They looked, but we'd hidden the bodies too well." He glanced at the panel. "This whole thing, it's new. It looks old—that was the whole point. It looks like it was a part of the original house. But we warped it and softened it to make it look that way. And these holes in it"—he pointed to the fist-sized punctures, top and bottom—"that's how we lifted it off the wall. All that money I was being paid and what it basically came down to was body disposal. Getting rid of the evidence. Slowing decomposition. The water, the smell of rot, that would cover up some of it. But, just to be sure, Cornell made us embalm all the bodies and then wrap them up in plastic. Airtight, so the insects wouldn't get in."

For a brief moment there was complete silence: no waves, no water running in, no wind, no rain against the walls. I studied him. "Didn't you ever worry that cops like McInnes would find out? That you'd leave a trail?"

"All the time. But I managed to keep things tight. There were no mistakes, nothing to lead back to any of us: not me, not Prouse or Francis, not to Cornell or whatever the hell he was involved in across the pond. Things were nice and clean for a long time—and then Prouse screwed things up by dropping Kalb's body in the water."

"Why was Prouse taking care of it?"

"I didn't think there was much that could go wrong. Cornell had boxed Kalb at source and put him on ice. He was packed in like a sardine. We kept him like that from the moment he landed. So I assured Cornell that Prouse could handle it. I'd had enough. I was thinking about an exit strategy and I didn't want to deal with another stiff." A grunt, eyes on the space in front of him. Then he looked across at Cornell, lying in the water. "There's my exit strategy: another dead body."

A trace of a smile on his face; a flicker of irony.

I moved again.

"Hurting people never bothered Prouse, probably because he was as thick as shit," he said, his voice even quieter and more reflective. He sounded jaded, worn out. He sounded broken. "He botched the whole thing: let the body just go. If it wasn't so desperate, it would have been funny. Except Cornell didn't find it funny. He went crazy. Batshit insane. And when Cornell went insane, people got hurt." He looked up at me, a hint of contrition in his eyes. "And then finally it ended up in that clusterfuck yesterday. Lee Wilkins called Cornell, begging for forgiveness. I think he found the guts because he thought Cornell was still in the States

and wouldn't be able to get to him. Maybe he thought Cornell would
slowly warm to the idea of him coming back into the fold. Wilkins was
that kind of idiot. The truth was, Cornell had just landed in London—
but he was still miles away—so he called me and told me to take care of
you. That's all I was to him: some chess piece he could move around.
But I wasn't down here either yesterday—at least not until much later. I
was up in Bristol on a training course, and it didn't finish until six." He
stopped, smiled to himself. "A Saturday training course. Can you believe
that? The one and only time one of those has ever come in handy. So I
had to send Prouse. The fact you were still alive, and your place was already swarming with cops when I arrived, told me Prouse had failed
again."

"So you came after me at the Ley . . ."

"Yeah. But it was pitch black and I couldn't see shit. I had to get
closer, and that was when you heard me. Cornell told me to kill you, so I
followed you, out on to that path full of reeds. But, honestly, I couldn't
see a thing."

He glanced at me, at where my feet were, but he was gone now; so far
into all the thoughts he'd ever wanted to give voice to that he hadn't seen
me move two feet closer.

"And Farnmoor?" I asked him, trying to maintain some momentum.

He rubbed an eye. "That was why Cornell had flown back in: to take
care of Graham. But that was when I knew I had to get out of this. I
watched Cornell put one in Katie Francis's head, midsentence, while she
was sitting at her desk talking to him, and I thought to myself, 'What the
fuck am I doing?' Even if Kalb's some magic bullet that brings this
whole operation down, none of this is worth it. I knew the killing would
just go on and on, because as long as the photograph was still out there,
Cornell didn't know where it was and he could never rest easy. He'd just
have to keep cutting people down."

"Did Cornell ever say what connection he had to Kalb?"

Rocastle shook his head.

And now I would never find out.

"All I knew was that he was bad news. You only had to watch Cornell
to see that. As soon as I found out Graham had called you and you were
going to Farnmoor, Cornell started panicking about . . ." He paused.
"He was panicking about certain things, worried you'd get to the house,
find out how this Kalb guy connected everything, how all this crap

knitted together. Plus, he wanted to get back to the States as quickly as possible. So I told him to go and make preparations for his return to the U.S., and that I'd take care of you. I'd make sure everything was sorted, that there would be no blowback."

"And just like that, he trusted you?"

"Cornell didn't trust anyone. But the situation at Farnmoor . . ." His eyes flicked to me and away. *He's keeping something back.* "He was just persuaded to do things a certain way, that's all. We had a discussion. I told him I could lure you in more effectively than he could. I was a cop. You and me, we might not have seen eye to eye, but whatever else you thought about me, you saw me as a cop. With me, your guard would be down." He shrugged. "I said, 'That will make him easier to kill.' Eventually, he agreed."

.   "But you didn't kill me."

"No." He shook his head. "I didn't."

I remembered the moment, earlier, when Rocastle had led me back into Haven. *Well, well, well,* Cornell had said. *This is an unexpected surprise—isn't it, Detective Rocastle?* He thought I was dead already. He'd assumed Rocastle had taken care of me.

"Why not kill me?" I asked.

"I couldn't find you, for a start. I left Cornell's handiwork untouched at Farnmoor, wanting you to find that slaughter. Then I kept up the pretense—all the bullshit, like I was mad at you, like I was going to bring you down, but the reality was, I couldn't care less. All I wanted was for you to find that scene at the house and then to find out what was going on. I knew Cornell would want to stay tonight, to help me dump the bodies here, to make sure the job was done properly this time, but then, once we were done, he'd piss off back to the States thinking everything's sorted, including you. Meanwhile, you could carry on getting to the answers. Instead, you screwed things up by arriving here."

"Why did Cornell bring Kalb back to the UK?"

Rocastle shrugged.

"And no one at the airport batted an eyelid?"

"Cornell told anyone who asked that Kalb was his uncle and that he'd died while out in the States. Kalb's body was in a custom-made, refrigerated box, and he had a fake Swedish passport, so everything looked fine. Not that there were many questions. Cornell had this nice little arrangement—a guy on the payroll at London City Airport, and a guy on the take at some airport in Las Vegas. He could come and go as he pleased. In and out like he'd never even been here."

London City Airport.

Suddenly, something else fell into place. *That's why Barry Rew saw the girls at ExCeL. They were on their way to the airport, less than two miles down the road.*

"Cornell split the family up because he found Carrie and Annabel upstairs in their house the night he came for them," Rocastle went on, "and he became convinced they'd talked to one another about Kalb. He wanted them separated, so he could go at them one after the other. He did Carrie first. It was terrible. Him and Prouse, they just . . ." He stopped for a long time. "I couldn't let him do that to the girls, or at least, I had to *try* to prevent it. So, after they'd finished with Paul and Carrie, after Prouse had taken them to the barn, I pretended to Cornell that the police had picked up his scent and that he should get the hell out. I told him to fly back to the States and leave the girls with me for a couple of days, and I'd send them on if he wanted. But he didn't trust me."

"Why?"

"I don't know. Maybe he could see it in my face. Having kids changes things in you." A flash in one of his eyes. "So he flew back to the States, thinking the cops were getting suspicious, and he left Prouse orders to put the girls on the next available flight. That's who Barry Rew saw driving them to the airport. That *fucking* fisherman. But before they left . . ." He touched a finger to his eye. "I told Annabel I'd make it right."

I looked at him. "Make it right how?"

"It doesn't matter now."

"Make it right how, Rocastle?"

"It doesn't matter anymore."

"Of course it matt—"

"I failed them!" he screamed at me, and then immediately bowed his head, looking down at the floor. "I failed them both. I couldn't make it right. Now they're both dead."

I gave him a second. "Do you know where they're buried?"

All I could see was the top of his head, his face vaguely reflected in the water. He didn't reply for a long time, then—quietly—he said, "Firmament."

"Firmament? What's that?"

"Where they're buried."

"Is it in the desert, like Cornell said?"

He nodded again.

"Is it a town outside Vegas?"

"I don't know."

"How do you know about it then?"

"I overheard them."

"Who?" I said. "Who's them?"

Then he looked up—and raised the gun.

"I'm not jeopardizing my kids' futures."

He aimed it at my chest. I stopped and held up my hands. Instinctively, I went to reason with him, knowing he was caught midway between guilt and acceptance, knowing I could use his vulnerability to turn him around. I started moving a hand toward him.

"Your kids are going to be fine, I promise."

He started shaking his head. "No one can know that I told you. I don't want to give anyone a reason to come after my kids. Do you understand? *You* have to find out."

"Find out what?"

One more step and I was on him.

"Find out what, Colin?"

"It's over for me," he said.

"It's not over."

"It's *over*!"

He moved the gun right and fired past my left shoulder. It passed so close, I felt the air shift around my head. I staggered back, my body automatically tensing for the second shot. But nothing came.

And when I looked at him, I saw tears filling his eyes.

"It's over," he repeated, all his fight gone. He wiped away the tears, even as more came, lowered the gun and then looked across the room at me. "This morning I deposited three hundred and forty-five thousand pounds into a bank account. The pin code is four-oh-four-seven. The card is in an A6 envelope. I posted the envelope through your door."

"Is that why you wanted me to go home?"

He nodded.

McInnes wasn't waiting for me. The card was.

"I know you don't owe me anything," he said, more tears starting to form in his eyes, "not after everything I've done, but my kids . . ." He tailed off, unable to speak, tears running in trails down his cheeks. I started to realize what was going on, why he'd left me the card. "My kids don't deserve to suffer because I fucked everything up."

"Colin, *listen* to me: we can sort this out."

"Give the card to my wife. Tell her I'm sorry."

"Rocastle!"

I moved quickly across the room, flashing-forward to what was about to happen. And as he looked at me, tears spilling down his face, there was a moment that moved in slow motion; a silent conversation, as clear as if he'd spoken the words aloud to me: *I'm begging you, if you do this for me, tell my kids I was everything they wanted me to be.*

And then he placed the gun in his mouth.

And he pulled the trigger.

64

Emily locked up her car and then crossed the driveway to the front door. I'd left it open so she could come straight in. I glanced out of the kitchen window, out across the beach, bathed in the watery light of a clear autumn day. In front of me, on the desk, was my pad, but I knew everything already. I'd seen their bodies with my own eyes. It was all burned into my memory: pulling the wall panel down, their corpses inside, the smell finally hitting. I'd watched flies escape into the dark and insects spill out, dying the instant they hit the standing water. I'd rolled the bodies out of the wall cavity and torn away the plastic. And when their faces looked up at me, I knelt there, next to them, as a deep sadness throbbed in my chest. It felt like I'd let them down. Even though I'd found Paul and Carrie, just as I'd promised Emily I would, all that moved through me was a sense of failure. If the search for them had already become a wake, now, finally, at the end, it was a funeral.

As I'd scrubbed down the walls, trying to erase my part in the carnage, I'd thought of Emily, of my worst nightmare coming to pass: telling her that Paul and Carrie were dead. I didn't even know about the girls; didn't really know what to tell her. There was no way I could go chasing around America trying to find the location of their bodies. But equally I couldn't tell police here in the UK what I knew without revealing that I'd been there as Rocastle and Cornell had met their end. Then, finally, when I'd moved out into the night, into the last of the wind, into rain that had gradually turned to drizzle, I had looked down into Cornell's boat and seen yet another body from Farnmoor.

Carter Graham's murder had gone unreported once when Rocastle had cleaned up Farnmoor after I'd been there. But it wouldn't go unreported again. And as I'd thought about making the anonymous call to the police, I'd realized that was exactly what I'd have to do about the girls: dial into Las Vegas Metro, try to persuade them to instigate a search for Annabel and Olivia, give them everything I had—including Firmament—without compromising my anonymity. Then hang up and hope that was enough information for the police.

That, with that, the rest of the Ling family would be found.

After a while, I didn't know what else to say to her. Emily sat there at the kitchen table, sunlight on one side of her face, and cried. When someone's world has fallen apart, there aren't the words to rebuild it, so I didn't waste her time with meaningless platitudes. I just took her hand, and I held it, and I let her grieve for the family she loved above all else.

Her tears went on for so long, she seemed to shrink in on herself, like all her air had escaped and wasn't coming back. Eventually, her hand began to slip from mine.

I got up and walked across to the sink, filling the kettle and setting it going again. On the shelf to my right, above the counter, sat a brown A6 envelope with an ATM card in it and Carrie's memory stick. I hadn't decided what to do about either of them yet. If the three hundred and forty-five thousand pounds had come from Cornell, if that's who Rocastle had taken the cash from, then it was blood money. He was financing his kids' futures with earnings that had cost people lives. But that wasn't the fault of his children.

"What about Annabel and Olivia?"

I nodded. I hadn't told her about Cornell, about anything to do with Kalb. I hadn't had the chance to even get that far before her tears had ended the conversation. But she knew the basics: they were all dead, taken by a man who had stopped at nothing to disguise the identity of a mass killer; that the family had been separated early on; and that now, ten months later, their bodies were on different sides of the world.

"I'm going to call the police in Las Vegas."

"You're . . ." She paused, wiped her eyes. "You're not going to go over?"

"I'm not sure what that would achieve," I said to her softly. It would be a journey without a map. I'd looked "Firmament" up when I'd got home, and there wasn't a town in the entire United States with that name. I had no starting point. I hadn't been to Vegas for five years, had only been to Nevada three times in my entire life. "The police might have heard that name before somewhere. They'll know the area. They'll know where to look."

She shook her head. "You've got to go."

"I can't, Emily. I'm sorry."

"You've *got to*," she said, and then a fresh wave of tears came. I didn't come back at her again, just let her anger, the sense of helplessness, slowly ebb away.

"They'll find them," I said, the words sounding hollow in my mouth. *"Please."*

I wasn't flying out to the States, no matter how many times she asked, but I didn't say anything this time, hoping my silence would act as my answer. Beside me, the kettle started whistling, steam taking flight into the spaces above our heads. She began sobbing again. I filled the percolator with fresh water and then added two spoons of powder.

"Paul and Carrie's . . ."

I turned back to face her. "Sorry?"

She looked up, cheeks strewn with tears like tire tracks on a battlefield, and I saw something familiar: the same look she'd had when I'd asked her about why Paul and Carrie had waited so long to have Olivia; the same sense she was holding something back.

"Paul and Carrie . . ." She stopped again. Sniffed. Wiped her eyes. "When you asked me why they waited so long to have Olivia, to have a second shot at IVF, I . . ." She paused again, but I knew what was coming. She'd lied to me. "I didn't know how to tell you."

"Tell me what?" I heard the change in my voice, the undercurrent of anger—but I didn't care. "If you've held something back about them, all this time . . ."

"It's not about their disappearance."

I frowned at her. "Then what's it about?"

"You wanted to know why there was such an age gap." She looked down at the table in front of her, her hand flat to it, fingers spread. *She can't make eye contact with me.* "I lied to you," she said softly. "Olivia was IVF. But Annabel wasn't."

"What are you talking about?"

"Everything I told you, about them not being able to find an Asian sperm donor, about the process not being as advanced in the eighties, I was making all that up."

"Why?"

Finally, she made eye contact again. More tears, but not born out of the loss she felt for her sister. Not this time. "At the time they were *desperate* for kids," she said, voice taut, rubbed raw by the tears, "but Paul had his problems and the IVF wouldn't take for them. It just wouldn't take. They did it, over and over—like, seven or eight times—and every time it failed. They thought they were never going to have kids."

She swallowed, the light in the room changing as cloud blew across the sky.

"And then I got pregnant."

"*What?*"

"It was a stupid mistake. *Stupid.* I was on the pill, and it became an instinctive, mechanical thing. I took it without thinking, same time every day. But then . . . I forgot."

Suddenly it fell into place: why she always referred to the family like it was her own, as if she was part of it, their day-to-day routine, their DNA; and the way she talked about Annabel's accident. *We were all just stunned. It's hard to put it into words. It was all I could do not to constantly cry.* On and on, talking like a mother about her daughter. It explained, too, why Annabel looked nothing like Paul.

It explained it all.

"I was doing my exams. It was getting on top of me—that's why I forgot to take the pill. You probably remember how I used to put myself under so much pressure when I was studying. But I knew, if I got the right grades, I was going to Cambridge."

I looked at her. "Wait, this was *before* university?"

She nodded again, and—slowly—her expression shifted, as if she was preparing the way for what was to come. Her eyes filled with tears. "I was seventeen," she said.

A sudden, powerful realization took flight in me.

"You're Annabel's father, David."

PART FIVE

65

The flight started its descent into McCarran at two o'clock, local time. I'd been in the air ten hours, sleeping fitfully, unable to clear my head. Once I landed, I needed to be lucid. I didn't know where I was going, or even where to start, but I knew I needed to be smart and reactive. And yet I felt overwhelmed. Any moment of joy I managed to draw from the shock of what Emily had told me two days before was instantly tempered. I'd look at the pictures of Annabel I was carrying, the pictures of Olivia too, and knew that, if I found them, I'd find them like I'd found Paul and Carrie. There was a biological link between Annabel and me— but that's all it had ever been. Only Emily, Paul and Carrie had ever known the truth, and only Paul and Carrie could ever claim to have been her parents. So when I thought of Annabel, of what I might find of her, I didn't feel the visceral, organic pain of a father. I'd never been that to her. I never *would* be that. But what I felt, instead, was an intense, wounded sorrow. A grief. A regret that I would never get the chance to sit down with her, even to tell her who I was and why she should care.

Because she was gone.

And she was never coming back.

The room at the Bellagio looked out across CityCenter, a seventy-six-acre, nine-billion-dollar copse of skyscrapers that hadn't even existed when I'd last been in the city. It rose out of the early evening dusk, glass and neon shimmering against the fading desert sky, and by the time I'd showered and returned to the window, Las Vegas had changed again, the huge, overblown theme park replaced by a symphony of artificial light. I raided the minibar, opened a bottle of bourbon and watched it all from the shadows of my room.

A couple of hours later, I roused myself and took the lift down to the casino floor, men hunched over craps tables, old couples sitting next to each other at slots. Off to my right were hundreds of video poker machines, none of them being played, screens blinking, speakers blaring. Off to my left was a bar, fenced in on a raised platform behind a curved mahogany bannister. I headed up there, ordered a beer, then grabbed a seat adjacent to the main corridor through the casino. I watched tourists wandering past in shorts and T-shirts, some dragging suitcases on their way out of town, some counting chips as they made their way in. When my beer arrived, I started to realize how tired I was. I hadn't slept properly for five days—and now I was jet-lagged and on my way to being drunk.

I tried to focus my mind on what I was here to do, removing a map I'd bought at the airport and opening it out across the table. If Firmament was where the girls had been buried, it wasn't the name it was officially known by. In the morning, hopefully on the back of some sleep, I'd hire a car and head up to the main Las Vegas Metro building on Sunrise Avenue, about ten miles northeast. I seriously doubted I'd get much in the way of help, but, if I could get someone to talk to me, I might be able to get some sort of steer on where to go looking. Maybe someone had heard the name before. Maybe Firmament had come up in conversation. Maybe, if I was lucky, it might be related to a crime.

Or maybe it'll lead nowhere.

I pushed the thought away and went back to my beer, looking around the casino. This was the only place to start. This was where the high rollers had come, where they'd been as recently as a couple of days ago. This was where Cornell had made his money; the very center of his universe. If there was a trail, I knew it would start in the Bellagio.

I just had to find out where.

I dreamed of sitting at the windows of a hotel I didn't recognize and looking out across a desert. There were no hotels, no buildings, no roads. It was just a vast, unending swathe of scorched land, cracks carved into it, cholla scattered like they'd fallen out of the sky. In among them, shimmering in the heat, were two crosses, planted into the earth, each constructed from lengths of whitewashed wood. Their names were on them.

Annabel.

Olivia.

As I got to my feet and went to the window, fingers pawing at the glass, trying to go through it, desperately trying to reach them, I felt a hand on my shoulder and a voice—small and comforting—at my ear. *It's okay. They're fine. They're in a better place now.*

It was Derryn.

But when I looked behind me, she was gone.

And then so were the graves.

66

The next morning I woke just before seven. I'd only slept for five hours, but I'd done it in a single stretch and immediately felt better, despite the tug of jet lag. I showered, changed and headed downstairs to the Pool Café. It was early and only fifty-five degrees, so there was no one in the water yet, and no one on the sun loungers either. But the sun was out and there was a high of seventy-three later, so it was unlikely to stay that way for long.

I ordered some steak and eggs and some extra toast, then finished my first cup of coffee while looking at a picture of Annabel. I had pictures of both the girls inside my wallet now, cut down to passport-photo size. Olivia was next to her sister, clutching the Mickey Mouse that Barry Rew had seen her with as Prouse had been driving them both to London City Airport. I'd put their photos in as a reminder of why I was here. I didn't need the motivation, but I needed the fortitude. I didn't know how long this would go on. It might be a day. It might be a month. I might leave without ever having found them.

After my breakfast arrived, my appetite began to wane, moments flashing in my head, imagined images of their final days, and when I'd ripped those away, echoes of what Cornell had said to me. *I cut them both into pieces and buried them in the desert.*

I got out the map I'd bought the day before, and opened it out. It was the greater Las Vegas metropolitan area, east as far as Lake Mead, north as far as Gass Peak, west to Red Rock Canyon state park and south to Sloan Canyon. The Mojave desert ran through to California, Utah and Arizona beyond that, but this was going to be ambitious enough for now: about seven hundred square miles of relentless, alien terrain I didn't know.

I buried them in the desert.

Something vaguely resonated with me, something in what Cornell had said, but as I tried to pull it out of the dark, it seemed to slip further away.

"How are you doing today, sir?"

I looked up.

A man was standing next to my table, nodding at my unfinished plate of steak and eggs. He was about forty, slim and well dressed in a green check shirt, denims and a pair of brown shoes. He was wearing sunglasses, but the sun was arcing in behind him—along the edge of the hotel's thirty-three-story south tower—and down through the lenses; so, even as they wrapped around his head, his eyes were visible, his gaze moving from my breakfast to the map and then, finally, to my wallet, open on the pictures of the girls.

I flipped it shut.

"I'm doing fine, thanks." I looked around, spotting waiting staff serving at other tables. He wasn't one of them. "How are you?"

Behind him, the three curved arcs of the Vdara hotel clawed at the sky, sun winking in its windows. "I'm good," he said. "Do I detect an English accent?"

I nodded.

"Cool. So, are you over for a convention?"

I started folding up the map. "Something like that."

"Sounds mysterious."

"Not really. I just have some business to take care of."

"Of course you do." But he didn't attempt to move. "You've got your map and your photos, now all you need is the location."

I shot a look at him. He'd shifted slightly and turned to his left, the sun arrowing past him at a different angle, his sunglasses dark and opaque. I couldn't see his eyes now.

"What did you say?"

He looked around him, as if he was making sure no one was close enough to hear, then pulled out a chair and sat down. "You're a long way from home, Mr. Raker."

He knows my name. "Who are you?"

"An interested party."

"Interested in what?"

"You know," he said, ignoring the question, "this isn't your backyard now. This tough-guy thing you've got going on, it won't work here. I don't know how things play out over in England, but here we don't go sticking our noses in where they're not wanted."

"It's America. Everyone sticks everything everywhere."

He smiled for the first time. "Very good."

"Do you work for Cornell?"

He didn't say anything, but he didn't seem confused by the name.

"I'll take that as a yes." I pushed the plate of steak and eggs to one side and leaned across the table toward him. "I wouldn't go expecting a call from him anytime soon."

A frown formed on his face.

"In fact, about now he's probably having his heart weighed."

As the man remained still the hotel continued its forward rhythm, like a heartbeat: women on hen weekends, couples hand-in-hand, businessmen checking their phones.

"It's over, my friend," I said to him. "Your boss isn't coming back. Your wages aren't going to get paid this month. So, why don't you tell me where the girls are buried?"

For the first time he moved, reaching up and removing his sunglasses. He looked to have regained some of his composure, his dark eyes impassive, not betraying a single thought in his head. He placed the glasses on the table and then looked off, out across the pool area, toward the southern limb of the main hotel tower. I could see he was thinking about his next move. The king was dead, now his jesters were running around in a panic.

"You're going to tell me," I said to him, and he seemed to flinch when I spoke, as if all the noise around us—the people having breakfast, the whine of planes in the sky, the drone of cars on the freeway—had all faded into nothing. "One way or another."

Finally, he looked back at me. "You're just one man."

"But I've got all the motivation I need."

"What are those girls to you?"

"Since two days ago, they're everything."

He nodded, staring at me, an acquiescence moving across his face. I thought I saw a moment of conscience play out, a flicker of self-reproach, as if he saw—in that second—all the torment he'd brought to his victims' lives, on the orders of a man out of control.

But it wasn't that.

Because he didn't work for Cornell.

"Mr. Raker," he said. "I'm Carlos Soto."

67

I followed him out of the city in a Dodge Challenger I'd hired from an Avis in the lobby. We wound north along Las Vegas Boulevard, through a canyon of monolithic casinos, until the tourist brochure fell away and all that remained were the faded wedding chapels, single-story malls, and strip clubs most people never came far enough to see.

At the junction for Charleston—a straight six-lane boulevard bisecting the entire length of Las Vegas—we headed west until the city began to fizzle out entirely, the looming specter of the Spring Mountains ahead of us, shadows forming in its tan-colored folds. Soto indicated, pulling his Ford Expedition into a diner on his right.

Inside, we found a booth at the back and he ordered breakfast and I just asked for some coffee. He hadn't said much at the Bellagio; just that, after my call, he'd been on to the internet and done a little digging on me, and that—when he'd done a sweep through the casino floor the previous night—he thought he'd seen me in the bar.

"I figured you'd probably fly out," he said.

"You don't even know me."

"I know enough."

"What do you know?"

He shrugged. "I know that you're the type."

"Type?"

"The type that doesn't let things go."

We were both quiet for a moment, the waitress placing cups down in front of us and pouring our coffee. After she was gone, I said, "Why have you brought me here?"

"You want to find the girls' graves."

"I'm not going to find them in a diner."

He looked out of the window, off toward the Spring Mountains. "I'm sure I don't need to give you my history. I'm sure you already know it. I was a cop for a long time but it started to get to me. I couldn't let things go. Most cops can handle finding a victim on the side of the road with their head smashed to paste. You're not unfeeling about it, but I guess you become capable of detaching yourself. That's the theory, anyway." He turned back to me, acceptance in his face. "But it didn't work for me. I couldn't switch it off. So I took the job at the Bellagio, and it had been fine. It paid good money. Everything had been swell. And then Cornell turned up with his high-roller friends and it all went to hell."

"How?"

"He asked me to get him some footage from the hotel. One of his group had a laptop stolen from his room." He eyed me, as if trying to see if that meant anything. I kept my face even, unmoving: he was talking about Schiltz. "I was resistant to it, but I knew it was going to be hard to turn him down. He brought in a shitload of green for the casino, plus he was . . ." He shook his head, staring off into space. I knew what kind of word he was trying to find: something to describe Cornell, the way he'd carried himself, the threat he'd given off. "So I did it. But my problem came back to haunt me: I couldn't let it go."

"So, what, you went after him?"

"No, not exactly." He paused, fingers around his coffee cup, turning it in circles. "Things didn't add up. The guy whose laptop went missing never reported it. Can you tell me why you wouldn't report that? Then there's the woman who stole it, a prostitute who served some time up in Cali. She's vanished. No trace of her anywhere. *Then* there's the guy she was working with, her boyfriend, her partner-in-crime, whatever the hell he was. We know a bit more about him because he's got plenty of ink on his rap sheet. He's found in a parking lot off East Flamingo. Stabbed in the throat. Any of that sound right to you?"

"Could you link any of it to Cornell?"

"Me?" He shook his head. "I don't have that power. I'm running a casino security team now, not a homicide department. I don't have access to that kind of information."

"What about the friends you had at Las Vegas Metro?"

A humorless smile. "What friends?"

"You burned all your bridges?"

"No. It wasn't that. I thought I had a lot of good friends left there. Picking up the phone to them was the first thing I did. But I got nowhere. Zip. People I trusted never got back to me, not even to tell me they hadn't managed to find anything out. And the next time that bunch of high rollers came to town, I looked around the room and saw Cornell watching me, this insidious expression on his face, and I realized he knew exactly what I was doing. And not because he could read it in me—because someone had told him."

He was paying off the cops.

Just like he was doing at home.

"So I stopped looking for the prostitute and stopped asking questions about the laptop going missing. Because, ultimately, I didn't want to end up out there."

He nodded in the direction of the desert. Except, as he turned back to me, something about his expression stuck. It wasn't that I didn't believe what he was saying. I did. But it felt like his conviction had waned at the last; that, when he told me he'd taken a step back, that wasn't quite true.

"So you don't know where the girls are buried?"

He looked up, as if deciding whether to commit himself or not. "I followed Cornell every day for a month. He used to come into the hotel and sit out by the pool, 12 p.m. to 3 p.m. The only time he ever deviated from the routine was when he went to the airport down in Henderson. That's where a lot of his high rollers came in. Henderson's mostly corporate aviation."

Soto's eggs Benedict arrived.

He waited for the waitress to leave us.

"He'd take the same route in and out of the city every single day," he continued, gesturing to Charleston with his fork. "*This* route. Charleston. When he got out into the desert I stopped tailing him, because when you get into the flats you don't have a lot of places to hide. It would have been easy for him to see me." He paused, knife and fork hovering above his plate, steam curling up past his face. "Except on a Wednesday, when he'd stop at a drugstore about a mile back."

Soto started eating, a frown on his face, still unsure as to what role the drugstore played in his routine. But, as I looked out into the desert, a thought formed in my head.

Kalb was an old man.

What if the drugs had been for him?

"One day," Soto said, his voice bringing me back, "I got a cab here and told the driver to wait. Then, when Cornell came past, we followed him out into the desert." He studied me, food in his mouth, and I knew this was the moment we'd been working toward. "He was using Charleston to get to one of the old mining roads, out in the foothills of the mountains. He was going somewhere elevated."

And then I remembered what it was that Cornell had said to me at

Miln Cross, what it was I was trying to pull out of the dark at breakfast:
I drove them up into the hills.

I drove them up into the hills.

Then I cut them both into pieces and buried them in the desert.

Up into the hills.

"What road is it he turned off on?"

"It hasn't got a name, but it's where Charleston straightens out. There's a one-, two-mile stretch of road where it's just up and down. There's a green gate. That's all I saw."

We both looked out of the window.

"That's where Firmament is," I said quietly.

68

Under a vast blue sky, I pulled in next to the green gate fifteen minutes later. Charleston, this far out of the city, was empty. No cars. No sound. The desert was completely silent.

I got out of the Challenger, went to the gate and slid the bolt across, then pushed it all the way open. The track beyond it snaked up into the folds of the mountains, curving around to the left and out of sight. In the middle of the day, the sun beating down out of the markless sky, everything seemed a different shade of orange; some of it a beautiful hue, like the color of a sunset; some of it, brown, burned, scorched by the endless heat.

Ascending out of the desert floor, with Las Vegas hidden on the other side of the mountain, the features of the valley soon became indistinguishable, just a series of dust-colored peaks. After about a mile, the road kinked left, into a kind of enclosed wave of red rock, like a tunnel with no roof. Singed cottonwood began appearing halfway along, looming overhead, and then I emerged into a flat, circular space, surrounded by trees and loose rubble. Across from me, sitting like it was wedged between two rocks, was a gate.

There was no view of either side of the desert floor from where I was, but when I got out of the car and walked over to the gate, about eight feet high and padlocked, I saw the road dropped down—tracing the folds on the opposite side of the mountain—until it disappeared out of sight. Another wave of rock, like a mirror image of the one I'd just been through, hid the full view of the valley, but I could see glimpses of Las Vegas and assumed, at some point further down, the road would give you a view of the entire city.

I looked around.

It was lonely and isolated, and—but for the gentle sound of birdsong—absolutely silent. It was colder too; maybe four or five degrees cooler than the desert floor. I grabbed a jacket from the car, locked up and then headed back to the gate. The padlock looked pretty new. The gate was older, but still tough enough to keep out any unwanted visitors.

I didn't have any picks.

So there was really only one way in.

I hauled myself up the front face of the gate, using its mesh for footholds. It shook against my weight, rocking slightly in its bed, but it took about ten seconds to get over.

Once I landed on the other side, I followed the old mining road around to the right and down through the second wave of rock. Five minutes later, I emerged on to the other side, and Las Vegas appeared, a couple of miles away, and three thousand feet below.

The view was breathtaking.

Ahead of me were the edges of a sandy building.

It was nestled in a flat area, surrounded by a natural ring of red rock—almost like a wall—and a scattering of cottonwood. If I'd approached it from any other direction, I'd have missed it. As I got closer, I could see more: it was a big, single-story property with a slanted coral-colored roof. Two windows on the near side, then, as I got even closer, a deck out front. The deck was made from wood, supported on a pair of stilts and looking out over the sprawling city. An ornate, hand-crafted rail traced its entire circumference.

The closer I got, the more something started to stir in me. A recognition. A sense that I'd seen this place somewhere before. The front of it came into view: more windows and a front porch, hemmed in behind a replica of the deck's railing. I walked on, past the front porch to where the road continued its trail down the side of the mountain, and on the other side of the house was some kind of adjacent building. Plain, white, no windows, no doors, its access point from inside the main house. It looked like it was sitting about five or six feet further down the slope. I returned to the house and moved up on to the porch.

Then I reached down and tried the door.

It bumped away from its frame.

Immediately inside was a long, thin room, all done out in dark wood and divided into two by a six-foot-wide brick fireplace, running from floor to ceiling. In its center was a bed of ash. I inched further in. Off to the left were steps down to what I assumed would be the adjacent building. At the bottom of the steps was a closed door. Ahead of me, the room ran all the way through to the deck, sofas and a La-Z-Boy on the other side of the fireplace, as well as shelves full of books and DVDs. There was a television too, mounted on to the wall. Off to my right, a hallway fed off, five doors visible from where I stood.

The place had the feel of an old hunting lodge, but it was more modern and better furnished. The floors were beautiful—polished oak, expensive rugs laid in patches across it—and the house had all the mod cons: a Blu-ray player, a Bose sound system, and while there was no cable this far out of the city, it was well served by a satellite decoder.

Then, a noise. Like a buzz.

It had come from the hallway.

I edged across the living room. The first door led into a big kitchen that, like the living room, connected with the deck. Three en suite bedrooms. One separate bathroom. One of the bedrooms was empty. Not even carpeted. The other two were decorated. One was full of junk: empty picture frames, tiny statuettes, candles, china, loose change, a lifetime of worthless junk.

On the wall, above the bed, was a photograph.

No frame, just fixed there with a pin.

It was Miln Cross.

I backed out and looked across the hallway to the other decorated room. It was minimalist: a bed, a wardrobe, a bedside table. Clean, no clutter. A different room. *A different person.* My mind reeled back to what Soto had said in the diner: he'd seen Cornell pick up a prescription from the drugstore, same time every week. I'd wondered if it had been for Kalb. But if I was right, Cornell wasn't just picking it up.

He was bringing it home.

They'd been living together.

I headed back along the hallway, into the living room, my eyes already fixed on the opposite side of the house, on the steps. Then I heard the buzz again, from behind me.

I turned.

Something caught my eye.

Where the wall met the ceiling, close to the fireplace, there was a security camera. It was focused right on me, a red light winking above its lens. I kept my eyes fixed on it and moved toward the center of the room. It moved with me. When I stopped, it stopped.

I looked back at the steps. To the closed door at the bottom.

It's a panic room.

And someone's inside.

Moving more quickly, I took the steps two at a time, dropping about six feet into the earth. The sun—coming into the living room in bright boxes of light—disappeared and the house darkened. There were no windows here, no sun in this part of the house.

There was no handle on this side of the door.

No way of getting in.

But when I went to touch it, the metal cold against my hands, I heard a clunk and the door slowly eased backward. Whoever was on the other side had opened it up. I felt my heartbeat quicken, my muscles tense, knowing that none of this made any sense.

Why would you open a panic room?

To start with, as the door got to the halfway point, all I could see was darkness. But as my eyes adjusted, I could make out another flight of stairs, shorter this time, down into an all-white room. There was a table with handcuff arches fixed to it, the sort you normally got in a police interview room. Two chairs, one on either side. A second door, right in the corner. And everywhere, on every wall of the room, were pictures.

I edged down the steps.

In the subdued light, it was hard to make out the details of the photos, so I reached into my pocket and took out my phone. Slowly, I moved it across the wall of faces.

Except they were all of the same face.

Daniel Kalb.

This is his life.

These were memories of him the rest of the world were never meant to see. There were hundreds of photos, taken in different places, stuck to the wall in chronological order, like an album. I saw him in Miln Cross before it was washed away; in the fields of south Devon, working on a farm; his feet in the sand with Start Point lighthouse a mark in the distance; him, looking pensive, by a window, the London skyline visible; happier as he stood by the water in Santa Monica, the pier framed behind him; a shot of him in Vegas, outside the Sands before it was demolished; more and more of him in Vegas, on the Strip, at a golf course, on the edges of the city with the mountains in the background. They went on and on, his hair getting grayer, his body losing its shape, his face sliding toward his throat. I noticed, once he got to the States, the severity of his scar had reduced, the pinkness disappearing. He'd had work done on it—so much so that, by the end of his life, as his skin creased and liver spots appeared, it was hard to see at all.

The last photograph, on the other side of the room, right next to the second door, was different: it was the only one, of the hundreds pinned up, where he wasn't alone.

It was taken out on the deck.

There were three people in it.

Kalb was in the center, an old man in his nineties, eyes milky, leaning slightly to his right, his walking stick bearing all the weight. On one side of him was Cornell. He was dressed in a black suit, black tie, his hair oiled down and perfectly parted at one side. His face was a total blank— just an emotionless stretch of skin, eyes like a fallow void.

Then there was someone else.

I looked from face to face, eyes falling back on Cornell. I understood why it felt like I knew him now, like I'd seen him before. It hadn't been in Vegas, five years ago.

It was in the face of his grandfather.

And the face of his father.

Next to me, I pushed the second door open and it swung into a small, dark space, lit by a single lamp. In the center of the room was a trapdoor, a padlock securing it in place.

Against the far wall, a man was sitting on a chair, looking at me, a half-smile like his son's marked in his face. Both hands were wrapped around the shotgun on his lap.

"Welcome to Vegas," said Carter Graham.

69

Carter Graham looked across the room at me and then tilted his head slightly. Physically, he and his son were different enough for me not to have ever made the connection. Graham was big and broad, over six feet, knots of muscle in his upper body, even as the end of his sixties approached. Cornell was smaller—five-eight, five-nine—lean, skinny, much more like his grandfather. The skill that Graham had that Cornell had never been able to harness was the ability to mask who he really was. Looking at Cornell was like gazing into the chaos: you could see everything he was once you studied him hard enough.

The only time I'd seen that chaos in Graham was now.

As my eyes got used to the change of light, I quickly scanned the room. Against the wall immediately to my left were two small black-and-white monitors, their screens showing the views across the living room to the panic-room steps, and out from the front of the house, along the trail that led back to the gate. On top of that was an empty cup and a half-eaten tin of papaya in syrup, a fork standing in it. The trapdoor in the center of the room looked like it was made from steel: heavy, reinforced, studded with screws all the way around its edge.

"Don't I even get a hello?" he said.

"What the hell's going on?"

But I already knew: I'd been so conscious of digging myself a grave at the house, of leaving more evidence, of giving Rocastle another reason to come after me, I'd never checked Graham's body. I couldn't have. If I'd crossed the room, I'd have left my footprints in his blood: it was all over him, under him, the whole place a massacre. I remembered the way his body had been left: contorted, neck twisted at what seemed like an unnatural angle, face pushed all the way into the skirting board, as if he'd been blown halfway across the room. But I realized why there had been all the blood between us, and why he had lain with his head away from me: so I wouldn't approach him and he wouldn't give himself away. All I'd see was a crime scene I knew I couldn't touch and his PA down the hall, a bullet in her head. I remembered then what I'd thought at the time: *Something isn't right. Something isn't right about the way he died.* I'd thought it was the fact there was only one security guy with him, despite him lying and telling me he had seven. But it wasn't that. It was that, deep down, somewhere unacknowledged, I knew.

"That was sloppy police work at the house, David," Graham said.

"It was a crime scene."

"Well, I think we both know that's not the case now, don't we?" He paused, eyes narrowing. "I would have thought you'd be more careful about these things now. I mean, what was it that almost led to you losing your *own* life?" We both knew what he meant. He'd read up about my last case. "*Exactly.* You are, I'm afraid, an incompetent idiot."

"And yet I found you."

"Yes," he said, nodding, a wry smile. "That *is* true."

"And I found your son."

A darkness moved across his face.

"And I found out who your father was." Everything was slowly shifting into focus. I let it all unfold, lining everything up for the first time. "All that blood, it wasn't yours. It was that security guard's. You cut him open and let him bleed out across the room."

He said nothing, but I knew I was right.

"All this—and the irony is, you could have killed me at the house."

"Rocastle," he said quietly, venom in his voice.

My mind shifted back sixty hours.

Rocastle told me what Cornell had been like on hearing that I was on my way to the house. *As soon as we found out you were going to Farnmoor, he started panicking about . . .* Then he'd stopped himself. But I knew what Cornell had been panicking about now.

Carter Graham.

About it all coming tumbling down around his father.

"Jeremy was a good boy," Graham said. "He was effective; had his grandfather's pragmatism. But he was always a little . . . *frenzied* around me and my father. Family was absolutely everything to him. I suppose you can understand it: we were the only people who ever really loved him. Basically, we were the only people he ever knew." His face had softened at the thought of his son, but then it hardened a second time as he returned to Rocastle. "So Rocastle used that weakness, that one weakness. Katie, my security detail, they were both dead. We killed Katie because she knew far too much, and we were trying to clear up the mess *you* were creating—and the security guy was just in the wrong place at the wrong time. Jeremy put them out of their misery. Rocastle, he just sat there—like he always did—judgment in his eyes, but never any words."

The plan was a mess; a reactionary, desperate mess. There had been no endgame other than to throw me off the scent. The irony was, they could have used it to discredit me, make me look paranoid and barely cognitive. If Graham had come out as alive and well after I'd shouted from the rooftops about his death, I would never have been taken seriously again. Katie Francis and the security guard would already be buried somewhere they'd never be found, and the police would be all over me for lying about Prouse. But, in truth, I doubted they'd even thought that far ahead. It was why Rocastle was able to manipulate them so effectively. Both Graham and his son only cared about their family.

"You thought you could keep everyone onside with money."

He smirked. "I didn't *think*. I *did*. Believe me, you pay people enough, they soon lose their conscience. Plus it never hurts to apply a little pressure."

I thought of Rocastle: the money Graham had paid him for his help, that was now on an ATM card in my kitchen; and Prouse threatening to kill his kids.

"Why not come after me at the start?"

"You were just another snoop asking questions about a family no one would ever find. I wasn't concerned. None of us were. We'd seen off the police, we'd slowly picked off anyone who even vaguely knew about my father. We were feeling pretty secure."

"And then the body washed up on the beach."

He nodded; a flicker of sadness. "That fucking fisherman," he said, voice quiet but seething with anger. "We'd already smoothed the fallout from the photograph. When that stupid *bitch* took her picture, Jeremy went and closed off every avenue: her, her family, Eric, Ray, that drug addict in London—there was no trail to my father. It was all sorted. But then, a month ago, Dad started getting ill . . ." He paused and then glanced at me, and for the first time I saw compassion in his face, reminiscent of the man I thought he'd been. "Dad had had a long life, a *good* life—but he had been ill for a while. Four, maybe five years. A couple of weeks back, he *really* went downhill, and we realized this was the end. So we spent the day together, the three of us, up here on the deck . . . and then a day later he was dead." He paused, and I remembered the last photo on the wall outside: the three of them, at the end, Las Vegas in the distance behind them. "He told us he wanted to be buried at Miln Cross. It was the place he loved best. He said Devon was the only time in his life he ever felt like he wasn't on the run."

"So why'd he leave?"

"The harbor mistress." He looked down at the shotgun in his lap. "She had her aunty to stay for a couple of weeks—this old Jew from Vienna, who had never traveled abroad before—and she recognized Dad straight away. She'd been in Sobibór. Dad had lived in Miln Cross since the end of the war, unnoticed. They loved him there. Thom Graham: born in Gothenburg to a Swedish mother and English father. He had it all worked out. I didn't even know his real name, who he was, until I was twelve."

"One big lie from the start."

He shrugged, like he hadn't heard me. "As it turned out, him being spotted was a good piece of timing, one of those supreme pieces of fortune that can only be fate. We both got out of there the night of the storm—but, officially, only I did. I pretended I was down in Dartmouth when it hit. That's what I told everyone, over and over. That my father was one of the forty-two. A lot of the bodies were buried under landslides, crushed under fallen masonry. But eleven other villagers were never accounted for, their bodies just washed out to sea. No one questioned whether he was one of them or not, whether I was telling the truth. They just believed me. I mean, who would lie about something like that?" A nasty, vindictive smile filled his face. "Meanwhile, we both started a new life in London. I moved my company there, and when I expanded into the States, it seemed an even better idea to move him to LA. New country, no questions, space to disappear."

"Shame you got sentimental."

He frowned, initially confused, then he understood what I meant: taking the body back to Miln Cross, even if it had been packed in and frozen for transportation, had cost them everything. It had cost him his son's life. And, as soon as the police back home began making the connections between who Cornell was and where he came from, they would come for Graham. It was why he'd so vehemently protected his father for so many years, why he'd encouraged Cornell to do the same, why they were prepared to kill to safeguard his secret—and why he'd so obsessively kept Kalb out of any and all photographs. Kalb was his father:

Graham didn't want him being put on trial, being dragged back to Europe to face justice. But he knew as well that his whole company would go down the toilet the minute shareholders and investors realized he'd been harboring a Nazi—and that Kalb was his own flesh and blood. If Carrie had been allowed to propagate the photograph, or publish her dissertation, Graham's whole business empire, everything he'd ever built and cared about, would collapse around him. It was why this house, Firmament, was the only place his father had ever existed. Once, as a man, now only as a series of photographs. The walls were a chronology of their life, pinned in a locked room in a house no one knew was here; the one place Carter Graham could return to, to remember his father.

"Where are the girls buried?" I said to him.

His eyes drifted to the trapdoor.

I took a step toward him, anger flaring in me, then—in the blink of an eye, with a quickness that defied his age—he had the shotgun up off his lap and pointing at me.

"Why don't you stay there, David?"

"I'm not leaving without them."

"They're just maggot food now."

He saw the pulse of anger travel up my throat, and broke out into a smile: "I don't know what Jeremy got up to here, but he was careful and that was all I cared about."

"Why the fuck are you even here?" I asked him.

He shrugged. "As I said, Rocastle tricked me. He told me I should get away after Farnmoor. He said it would take a few days to clear up the mess. He said he needed to get rid of you. Except he was a snake in the grass. He was busy telling me one thing, Jeremy another. We both believed him, because we thought the money was all he cared about."

"Where's Cornell's mother in all this?"

"I never wanted kids," he said. He hadn't answered the question, but I sensed it coming. "It was a mistake, outside of my first marriage, with a woman I hardly knew. By then I was well known, so the damage to my reputation could have been considerable."

I got it immediately. "You killed her."

"She had a big mouth," he said, and when I saw the look in his eyes it was like Cornell had come back from the dead. "Her surname was Cornell so, aside from giving birth to Jeremy, she made one useful contribution. After he was born, though, my stance on children changed slightly.

I liked the idea of being able to shape someone, bend them to your whim, enable them to do things you weren't capable of yourself. So when he was only a few days old, I brought him up here to live with my father, in this house I built."

Suddenly, something else clicked into place.

This house.

I knew why I recognized it.

"Yes," Graham said, seeing that I understood. "Those photos I showed you weren't my office in LA. They were the side of this house. You can see why I kept them close."

I made the natural next step. "Is this place what the high-rollers group paid for?"

"*Very* good. I started to realize I needed to keep this place entirely off the grid so we set up that group, creamed a little off the top and cooked the books. It worked beautifully. You'd have to look hard to see Firmament even existed."

"What about Schiltz and Muire?"

"What about them?"

"Did they know who Kalb was?"

"No. Only a version of his history—one that I made up." He paused, and I recalled Cornell saying exactly the same thing. "I told them, early on, in the days after we moved to London, that the British government wanted us to keep Dad's identity a secret, and that was why I was telling everyone he was dead. I said I couldn't tell them any more, but I hinted he was informing on the Soviets, and that was part of the reason we were moving out to the States. As you can imagine, that played out pretty well back in the sixties."

"And they believed that bullshit?"

"It was the Cold War, David. Anyone believed anything." He lowered the shotgun slightly, still aiming at me, but using his knee for support. "Plus they were my friends."

"Friends who you killed."

"The irony is, they would probably still have been alive if Eric hadn't started scanning in all his old pictures. They knew Dad, they knew not to take pictures of him, so I never worried about that side of things until Eric's photograph landed in my inbox."

"And Cornell—did they know he was your son?"

"Yes. I told them the truth: that it was a mistake, a one-night stand,

and that his mother abandoned him, and he was living up here in secret with his grandfather."

"That's not the truth."

"It's close enough."

"You lied to everyone."

"What about Lee?" he said. He was smiling again, a mirror image of his son. "*That* was a good turn, wasn't it? Asking him to come and entertain us. I was thinking of Ray." The smile lingered on his face—and then it dropped away. It felt like we were at the end of the road now. All the secrets were out. Now there was just me and him and a gun.

I drove them up into the hills.

Then I cut them both into pieces and buried them in the desert.

"Open the trapdoor," I said.

"I'm the one with the gun, David."

"It's over for you. In a week, everyone will know who you are. You think holing up here in the wilderness is going to stop the tide from turning? You're done, Graham."

He got out of his seat, shotgun against his hip, pointing it at my stomach.

I held up a hand. "It's over. You know it is."

"It's over after I put a hole in your chest."

Then something moved on the monitors.

70

We both flicked a look at the monitors, an automatic reaction. Someone was approaching the house. As Graham moved, the shotgun moved with him; a foot, maybe less.

But enough.

What he'd done seemed to hit him.

By then it was too late.

I smashed into him, chair toppling over, both of us crashing into it and falling to the floor. I already had hold of the barrel of the gun, wrestling it from his grip, directing it up to the ceiling. He pulled the trigger. The sound was immense: a throaty *boom* that sent a debilitating ringing through my head. It took everything I had to cling on. He pulled the trigger again, more desperate this time; and while it wasn't as loud, my hearing dampened, defective, it was painful, like he was sticking his fingers into an open wound.

But I held on.

We rolled half a turn, side to side on the floor, and then—with every last drop of strength I could pull out of the ground—I yanked it free from his grasp, the momentum carrying me across the room and into the bank of monitors. They rocked on the table and fell to the floor, coming to rest next to me. But the feed didn't cut out. Through the corner of my eye, I saw an indistinct figure was almost at the house, a gun down at their side.

I didn't try to get a better look.

Not until Graham had been properly put down.

Getting to my feet, I headed across the room and pressed the end of the gun into the center of his spine. He'd been trying to scramble across the floor, back out the door.

"Where do you think you're going?"

I glanced up, into the room full of photos, then back to the monitors. The figure was on the front porch.

It was Carlos Soto.

I didn't try to put it together, didn't think about anything else apart from the girls. "Give me the keys for the trapdoor." Graham remained still. "Give me the fucking keys!"

He slowly moved his arm, sliding it down his side to his pocket. I pressed the end of the gun harder into his back so he knew not to screw around. As he reached in and I heard a faint jangle, I glanced back at the monitor. Soto was inside the house.

What the hell is he doing here?

Graham got out the keys and held them up to me.

"No," I said. "You're unlocking it."

I reached down, grabbed the back of his shirt and hauled him into the center of the room. Then I pulled the door closed. It clanged shut. There was a lock on the inside, a wheel, like you found in bank security vaults. I spun the wheel once, hard, and it went through a series of rotations by itself. Then it made a soft sucking sound. It was locked. On the other side of the room, Graham had backed up against one of the walls. There was blood on his face.

"Unlock it."

He crawled across on all fours and started going through the keys. I glanced at the monitors. Soto was on the stairs, coming down to the panic room. When I turned back to Graham, he'd selected a key and was sliding it into the padlock. A turn. It popped open.

"Take off the padlock."

He did as I asked.

"Now open it."

He looked from the gun to the trapdoor, knowing there was no choice now. Then he slid his fingers in around the handle welded into it, and slowly pulled it up and over.

A smell instantly took flight across the room.

I tried to ignore it, tried to fight against the voice in my head. *Don't do it. Don't do it. Don't do it.* But I had to. I had to make sure it was them. I had to see my daughter.

Stopping on the edge of the trapdoor, I looked down.

A square metal chute, about four feet wide and about thirty feet long, dropped down to the side of the mountain, stopping about six feet above it. What I could see of the slope, visible beyond the end of the chute, was steep: a forty-degree gradient, maybe more. It was why the deck had been built on stilts. Below the end of the chute, a hole had been cut out of the dirt and the rock, and then filled in again. It was a rough circle, full of sand. *A burial ground.* Items were scattered in the scrub around it: a necklace, the broken heel of a stiletto, a torn shred of blouse pierced on a clump of cholla. And then, in the center, something else.

Olivia Ling's Mickey Mouse doll.

"That's where he would put the bodies," Graham said quietly, matter-of-factly, as if he were describing something routine.

It felt like everything was moving in slow motion.

I felt dizzy.

"I'm sorry, David. But they had to go."

My vision blurred.

"You must understand that."

I moved quickly.

He held up a hand. "Wait, David, it's—"

"Shut up," I said, jamming the end of the shotgun into his face, forcing it into his mouth. He started gagging on it. *"Shut the fuck up!"* I could hear the tremor in my voice but didn't care, didn't care about anything anymore. "You're going to pay for this."

He tried to speak, his voice muffled.

I jammed the stock in against my shoulder, gripped the fore-end and pumped it once. His eyes widened, his noise getting worse, an animal going crazy. Images flashed in my head: running through the woods as a boy, Dad setting up targets for me to shoot; a farm up in Scotland, an east London forest, the moment I thought I'd breathed my last, all the cases that would never leave me. And then Derryn, behind me, as I looked out through a hotel bedroom window across a vast desert, at two graves.

It's okay. They're fine.

They're in a better place now.

Annabel.

Olivia.

"No," I heard myself saying, like someone else was speaking the words. "No, I'm not the same as you." I slid the shotgun out of his mouth, hearing him take a deep breath, like he'd been underwater, drowning. "No, whatever else, I'll never be the same as you."

I flipped the gun in my hands.

Leveled the stock at him.

And then smashed the butt of the gun into his face.

He went out cold.

Getting to my feet, unsteady, emotional, I went to the door of the room, spun the wheel and stepped back. Raised the gun, ready for Soto. The door popped gently away.

A pause.

A couple of seconds later, fingers fed in around the edge, gripping it. Then, very slowly, the door started to arc back, revealing the room full of photos.

Then Carlos Soto.

"What do you want?" I screamed at him, looking down the sights. I brushed an eye with my shoulder, trying to clear my vision while keeping both hands on the gun.

But everything just blurred again.

"It's okay."

"What are you *doing here*?"

"It's okay," he repeated. He reached down, carefully placed his gun on the floor, then straightened. His eyes moved from me, to Graham, to the hole in the floor. He could smell it too. He could see the flies that had come up the chute from the sand-covered pit, escaping into the room we were in. "Everything's okay, David," he said. "I'm on your side."

71

Twenty-four hours later, I sat at the same table overlooking the same part of the pool as the day before. The morning was completely still. No breeze, just desert sun arrowing out of a clear sky. I ordered a beer and a Cobb salad, and realized how alien this place felt after five months in a tiny Devonshire fishing village. Not just the huge fake facades and the sweeping excess of it, but other, smaller things, like the weather. I couldn't remember the last time I'd ever felt a day like this, when there wasn't even a faint stirring in the air.

All the loungers were taken, men and women baking in the heat, and the pool was full. Old men swam lengths. Glamorous couples dipped their toes in. Kids screamed with laughter. I watched a brother and sister, no more than six, chasing each other around its edge, the girl laughing riotously as her brother failed to catch her. Eventually the boy started to cry, and his dad pulled him in for a hug, asking him why his sister was so cruel, before winking over the boy's shoulder at the girl. She laughed and returned to the pool.

After my lunch arrived, I picked at it while rereading the *Las Vegas Sun*, flicking all the way through to sports I'd never really understood, even when I'd lived here, then back to the front page. Carter Graham looked out at me. It was the photograph he used on his company's website. EMPYREAN CEO: BODY FOUND AT VEGAS HIDEAWAY. Beneath that was a sub-headline: MULTIMILLIONAIRE CARTER GRAHAM ACCUSED OF KILLING MISSING PROSTITUTE. SOURCES SAY MORE BODIES TO COME. They didn't realize yet that it got worse still, echoing across decades and spanning continents.

I folded up the paper and pushed it aside.

The previous day, I'd spent four hours in a police interview room telling them what I knew. It helped having Soto there. He vouched for me, and that seemed to carry a lot of weight. He'd run Robbery-Homicide for seven years before making the switch to casino security, and the assistant sheriff still seemed to rate him highly, even more the people who'd once called him captain. I told them everything I could, only holding back on details that might lead me into trouble. Back home, I'd broken the law, I'd used hackers and informants, and I didn't want that reverberating from the other side of the world. But I painted them enough of a picture: of Graham, of what he was protecting, of the son he let loose on the streets of a city the cops here cared about deeply. I didn't worry that the men and women interviewing me might have been on Graham's payroll; if they were, they were sweating it out waiting to be found, and unlikely to do anything to make themselves known. And, anyway, I sensed that Soto wanted that to be his job.

That, once I left, he'd find them and have some kind of revenge.

As the sun started to drop out of the sky, I headed back up to my room, showered, and then watched it fall the rest of the way, melting into the ridges of the Spring Mountains.

The lead on the Graham murders, a cop called Cowen, had told me to remain in the States until they'd given me the all-clear to go home. I didn't anticipate leaving anytime soon. It would be difficult enough pulling together every loose end from what had happened on their own doorstep, let alone coordinating tasks and tethering leads with a police force five thousand miles away. Cowen told me he was due to speak to McInnes over video link, and after he told me, I wondered what McInnes would make of all this. I'd only met him once, stumbling around in Rocastle's shadow, but now he was going to be investigating Carter Graham, and would eventually find his old boss at the end of the trail.

At about eight o'clock I started to fall asleep, my body finally giving in after days of irregular rest. But then my phone began buzzing across the bedside table. I reached over and looked at the display. It was a text message from Healy. *Graham is all over the news here. THANKS, Raker. I had £100 worth of shares in Empyrean, you arsehole.*

I smiled to myself.

This was his way of reestablishing contact after our last conversation had ended so abruptly; hidden deep down, as hard as it was to believe, it was probably even an apology too. It was Healy all over: not willing to concede all the ground, but cognizant enough to know that, when it came down to it, I was the only person he had left. His wife was gone, his sons barely wanted to know him. Whatever else I was to him—however much he tried to fight me, tried to plow a lone furrow—in the end, he knew that much.

You're welcome, I replied. *I'll give you a call when I get back.*

And then an image of Emily came into my head.

I'd called her the day before, briefly, to tell her what I'd found, and it had been the most difficult call I'd ever had to make in my life. Inside three days her whole family—everyone she'd ever cared about—had been committed to the ground. She may have prepared for this moment, tried to harden her resolve and accept the reality of what was coming, but a small part of her would have clung on to the idea that they were alive.

I dialed her number and waited for it to connect.

"Hello?"

"Emily, it's David."

"David," she said quietly.

I could hear she'd been crying. "How has today been?"

"Hard." She paused. "Really, really hard."

I sat up in bed, then moved across the room, back to the windows, neon blinking in the glass. Five years ago, what felt like a lifetime ago, I'd promised Derryn I'd bring her to the city. She'd always wanted to see Las Vegas—but I'd never had the chance.

She was gone before I could make it happen.

Back then I'd been a different man—yet to be marked by the death of my wife—a man who knew nothing of the missing, of the world of the lost, of the way life tethered you to people and to moments, over and over in different ways. The Lings, Annabel, they all could have lived if I'd recognized Cornell for what he was the first time I saw him. I could have cut him off at source. I could have saved them all. But I never would have known about my daughter. I never would have met Emily and found out the truth. Because if I'd been a different man, I wouldn't have been with Derryn, and she wouldn't have persuaded me to start finding missing people, and her death wouldn't have helped me find my place in the world. And all that followed—the case that almost killed me, the move to Devon—would never have taken place.

Nothing was random.

Everything was connected.

"I'm sorry, Emily," I said to her finally.

"For what?"

"For this."

I could hear her voice start to turn again, tears twisting her words: "You don't have to apologize to me. I asked you to find them. You found them. You brought me . . ."

Closure.

Except, for her, it wouldn't feel like that.

And, as I looked out at the millions of lights, I knew—for a long time—it wouldn't feel like that for me either.

72

I pulled the Challenger into Texico Mexas—a fast-food restaurant on Pecos, east of the airport—just after nine. At night, this far from the Strip, Las Vegas was like any other West Coast city: low-rise buildings; small, two-color billboards; orange sodium lights running off into the darkness. After I'd got off the phone to Emily, Soto had phoned through to my room and asked me to join him. He said his girlfriend, Ellie, worked here on weeknights, and she'd get us a thirty percent discount on our food. I never considered myself much of a food snob, but Tex-Mex wasn't really my thing. I'm not sure it would have been Soto's either if it wasn't for Ellie. Yet it wouldn't have been the right thing to have turned him down. He'd led me to the bodies of the girls, so at least I could try to process it, and he'd watched my back at the station when I'd needed it. I owed him this.

Inside, I spotted him in a booth at the back.

A waitress asked if she could seat me, but I told her I was fine, and weaved across the restaurant. "How you doing?" he said, getting up from his seat and shaking my hand.

"I'm okay."

But, even though he didn't know me, he could see that wasn't the case. One of the ways I'd been so successful in my work was through suppressing my emotions, knowing when to keep them concealed and when it was fine to let them drift. Even if I paid lip service to it, I couldn't bring myself to pretend everything was fine.

I couldn't describe how I felt.

Words had once been my gift. But not now.

We sat down and talked for a while about where the police investigation was, and Soto said he'd spent most of the day on the phone to his friends in the department. "It's just like you said," he told me, fingers around a beer bottle. "It stretches far and wide."

I nodded. "Graham was a powerful man."

A woman came over a couple of minutes later, and when I saw her name badge, I realized this was Soto's girlfriend, Ellie. She was in her late thirties, small and slim, auburn hair tied back from a porcelain face. It wasn't hard to see why he'd taken a shine to her. She seemed quiet, almost shy, but she had the kind of smile that lit an entire room.

"Are you in town for long?" she asked me.

I glanced at Soto. He obviously hadn't got to the stage where he talked about his work with her. "I'm not sure," I said, smiling. "Probably a couple of weeks. We'll see."

She asked what we wanted, and we both ordered chili.

"How long have you two been dating?"

They looked at each other, and I could see the answer immediately: not long. They had the kind of glow you only really saw in couples right at the beginning of their journey. Things started to develop after that, not for the worse, just in a different way.

"It's been four and a half months," Soto said.

"That's great."

"What about you, David?" Ellie asked.

"Me?"

"Have you got someone to go back to?"

I paused. "Not at the moment, no."

Ellie disappeared back out into the restaurant, and Soto and I started talking about the case again, then moved on to baseball, which I knew nothing about, and the recession, which I knew more of. I remembered, in 2007, I'd arrived in Vegas before everything had gone south. As I ordered a third beer, the edges slowly started to fall away. I rated alcohol alongside Tex-Mex—I could take it or leave it—but, tonight, it was going down well.

"So, I wanted to tell you something," Soto said after a while, faintly, something moving in his eyes. Then it was there in his face, plain, like it was written in neon. "It's about the girls. I don't know whether this will help or not, but you deserve to know."

I slumped back in the seat. "What?"

"I'm sorry I didn't tell you before, I just—"

"What is it?"

He hesitated. "You remember I said Cornell had a man down at Henderson Airport? That was how he was able to transport everything in and out of the U.S.?"

I nodded.

"Well, I wasn't totally honest with you." There was no hope in his face, just a starless dark. "I told you I'd followed him to the airport that one time, during the two weeks I tailed him. Well, that wasn't true. I tailed him for a lot longer than two weeks and I followed him to the airport maybe seven or eight times."

"Just get to the point," I said, hearing a hopelessness in myself now.

"One time, he chartered a plane out of the country and he didn't come back for a week. He'd gone out to organize the kidnap of that family you talked about."

"So?"

"So he came back one day ahead of them."

I didn't say anything.

He looked at me. "I watched him return the next day, waiting for those girls to come off the plane. I'd checked in with Henderson, managed to get them to tell me which planes were due in, and when I heard there was one coming in from the UK, I knew it had to be something to do with him." He swallowed, pushed his beer to one side.

"Carlos . . ."

"Listen to me," he said. "In the airport, he had to act normal. He had to be a regular passenger; a guy waiting for his two daughters to get off the plane, or whatever. It didn't matter if he knew a man who could get them through immigration. It didn't matter if this guy knew who he *really* was. Everywhere else in the terminal, he had to be normal. He couldn't make a scene. So, as soon as he saw them coming, he did things like give them a kiss and take Olivia's Mickey Mouse doll from her and play with it, because he thought that was the type of thing a father might do for his child."

He stared at me, uncertain.

"He could act normal," Soto went on, "he could put on an act. But the girls . . . they couldn't. They were shit-scared. I could see it in their eyes. Whoever had sent them out from the UK had obviously threatened them, told them not to say a word, but the little one, she was in tears, and the older one just kept telling her everything was going to be okay."

"I don't want to hear the rest," I said to him.

"You do."

"I *don't.*"

"Believe me, you do."

I just stared at him.

"Next minute, everything went to hell."

"What do you mean?"

He looked off, beyond my shoulder.

I followed his line of sight and saw he was looking at Ellie, taking a tray of food to a table just down from us. She smiled at him, he smiled back—a small, tight smile; maybe not a smile at all—and then he turned back to me and it fell from his face.

"Suddenly, security swarmed on him—like, seven or eight guys—and he ended up getting separated from the girls. Just got dragged off around the next corner."

"Why?"

"I found out later, someone had called in an anonymous tip. Someone from the UK. They'd told the airport Cornell had drugs on him."

Rocastle.

I remembered his words to me: *I told Annabel I'd make it right.*

"I didn't need to know those girls to know they were in danger."

"Why are you telling me this?"

"I guess it was just instinct," he said, ignoring me. "He didn't have any drugs on him, so he was in and out of wherever the security team took him pretty fast afterward."

Next to me, Ellie arrived at the table, carrying our food.

"But by then it was too late for him. They were gone."

She put down our plates of chili.

"I just did it, automatically, but then, after a couple of weeks, I started to realize I couldn't trust anyone. I didn't know who was working for Cornell, even in Metro, didn't know who he had on his payroll and when I was being watched by his people."

"What are you talking about?"

"So it's been my secret for ten months."

Then, out of the corner of my eye, I realized it wasn't just Ellie that had come to the table. There were others, just behind her, who had followed her across the restaurant.

I turned in the booth.

And, suddenly, they were standing there next to me, sisters holding each other's hands, the eldest one with a smile on her face that was like looking in the mirror.

I felt my heart swell up.

Felt tears blur in my eyes.

And then Soto said, "David, I want you to meet Annabel and Olivia."

Author's Note

In the interests of full disclosure, and if you hadn't noticed already, I should probably admit to altering the history and geography of Devon's Start Bay area ever so slightly. I hope I've managed to do it without causing offense, while also remaining true to a very special part of the world. For those who may be interested, the village in which Raker grew up is based closely on Torcross, while the tragic events of Miln Cross were inspired by the real-life story of Hallsands. Five thousand miles west, Las Vegas has remained (largely) untouched, with only some very minor adjustments made for pace and clarity. But, here, I must give a special mention to Peter Earley's *Super Casino: Inside the "New" Las Vegas* (2000), which is a brilliant account of modern-day Las Vegas. I was fortunate enough to visit the city in the early stages of my research; on my return, *Super Casino* answered almost every question I forgot to ask. It comes highly recommended.

Finally, the character of Daniel Kalb is completely fictional.

Acknowledgments

When I said to my editor Stefanie Bierwerth and agent Camilla Wray that I wanted to do something different in *Never Coming Back*, I'm sure they were reaching for the prayer beads the moment I put the phone down. But, if they were worried, they never showed it, and their unswerving support and editorial brilliance has made Raker's journey to Devon (and Las Vegas) smoother than I could possibly have hoped. I must also give a special mention—and thank you—to Rowland White, who stepped in while Stef was away, and who has worked so hard for me from the minute he first read the manuscript.

In truth, there are so many people at Penguin who have done such amazing things for this book, my only disappointment is that I've never had the chance to thank them all in person. I hope I can rectify this in the near future, but in the meantime a massive thank you to everyone for putting in the hours on my behalf, from sales through to marketing, from PR to editorial and beyond. I'm also indebted to the team at Darley Anderson, particularly Clare Wallace and Mary Darby in foreign rights. Most people only get to see the book when it's done, but my family get to see it (or at least its effects) when it's far from finished and things aren't going *quite* as well. So thank you to Mum and Dad for always being there, to Lucy and Rich for the same, and also to the Weaver family, the Linscotts, the Adamses and the Ryders. But, most of all, thank you to Erin, who surprises and amazes me every single day, and to Sharlé, who never complains when Raker and I head off into the hills together for months at a time, and without whom none of this would be possible.